BREAD AND SALT

ALSO BY VALERIE MINER

~

NOVELS
Traveling with Spirits
After Eden
Range of Light
A Walking Fire
Blood Sisters
All Good Women
Winter's Edge
Murder in the English Department

STORY COLLECTIONS
Abundant Light
The Night Singer
Trespassing
Movement: A Novel in Stories

NONFICTION
The Low Road: A Scottish Family Memoir
Rumors from the Cauldron: Selected Essays, Reviews and Reportage

STORIES

BREAD AND SALT

VALERIE MINER

WHITEPOINT
PRESS

San Pedro, California

Published by Whitepoint Press
A Whitepoint Press First Edition 2020
whitepointpress.com

Cover and book design by Monique Carbajal
Cover photograph by Valerie Miner

ISBN 978-1-944856-15-1

Library of Congress Control Number: 2019954651

WHITEPOINT
PRESS

FOR

Rose Pipes and Kath Davies in celebration of
decades of friendships and with gratitude for
their beneficent hospitality

Contents

BREAD AND SALT

Il Piccolo Tesoro

I'm stepping into an espresso bar, fragrant with strong coffee and sweet cornetti, when my attention is drawn uphill by a weathered pink and green sign offering a vacancy at Il Piccolo Tesoro. The small treasure. I'm not greedy. The adjective appeals as much as the noun promises.

I chose this Ligurian village in the sensible way, by spreading a map of Italy across my kitchen table in Toronto, closing my eyes, and sticking a pushpin into destiny.

Stanza in affitto: one of the phrases I know by heart.

At the door of the rambling house, I knock assertively.

"Good morning." A big man, all beardy and Scots, ushers me into the elegant marble vestibule. I peek around his shoulder at the parlor, posh with Turkish rugs, brocade armchairs and hand-painted shades atop filigreed floor lamps. The large picture window offers a grand view of the Mediterranean.

I extend my hand. "Adrienne Moreau. I've come about the room."

"Malcolm Gordon." His grip is firm. "One moment, please." He gestures to the parlor. "Make yourself at home."

I cross the parquet floor, walking through Malcolm's argument with a Bulgarian tenor who is leaving behind a trail of unpaid bills. The foyer is blocked by huge boxes and leather suitcases. For a penniless opera star—I don't even pretend not to eavesdrop—the Bulgarian is well-kitted out. I strain to catch the rest of the spirited exchange, but their accents rival each other in density.

Seated in a purple velvet wing chair by the window, I peer through palm fronds at sun light glinting on the waves. The garden is so lush that I can smell the roses, mimosa, wisteria and the resin from the stately old pines. I'd gone through months of doubting my decision—leaving

Canada, my job, my friends, abandoning everything—to pursue a dream. To live life for as long as I have. Right now I'm absolutely sure that I'd move into Il Piccolo Tesoro even if I need to wash dishes to pay rent.

~

Each day during my first months at Il Piccolo Tesoro, the sunny Mediterranean weather reminds me that I am far from Toronto. Blissfully far. I've never been happier than in my pretty room at the villa with the sea view. A few miles over the French border, this would be a pension. Back home it would be a boarding house. Ken and Susan can't believe I've traded my nifty downtown apartment with its primo view of the Toronto skyline for a room. It's difficult to explain. Our villa is hardly luxurious, yet I shudder to think of a different life. Perhaps I'm exaggerating this morning, wound up about my evening performance at the Trattoria. And I'm late for practice. No, no, I don't rehearse at Il Tesoro. Residents are careful not to disturb one another. Ken and Susan also can't believe I have a paying gig.

After twenty-five years of teaching music to lackadaisical teens— soul diminishing even to a Bodhisattva—I vowed to take my talents elsewhere. Somewhere warm. I never felt at home in my native Toronto. Susan calls me *Doña Quixote*. Maybe I'm not performing at La Scala but it's music; it's fun, and it's a living. The evening shows and the tips— I might add the tips are increasing—support me. I don't need much else with my small pension from school.

Modestly is how we live here. Arda has a poetry fellowship from the Armenian government. Professor Ismo and his wife Taina survive on his University of Helsinki retirement fund. Fabio earns small honoraria for his translations and essays. We are all quite comfortable in this spacious house, enjoying meals prepared by Lola and Sofia. I don't know how Malcolm manages on our trifling rent. Being here is a miracle every day.

Usually Harold and Lettie, my thin, sixtyish English neighbors, are already at table when I arrive. "Salt and Pepper," Ismo jokes in their absence because they are always bickering, usually about the same subject. Where will they live after Liguria? They've tried Cornwall—too cold. Andalucía—too hot. The shimmering Provencal village of Gordes—too many steps. Every day they have a new complaint about Liguria, and soon I stop listening.

"Another performance tonight, Adrienne?" Lettie asks. Her recently blond hair is cut in a snappy Michelle Williams style. Cute. Her Chanel No. 5 is subtle today.

"Yes, *'Les Feuilles Mortes, La Vie en Rose, Je T'ai Dans La Peau, Le Bel Indifferent.'*"

"So admirable, dear, the stamina. Your third month of performing those little Piaf songs." Lettie blinks incredulously. "I really don't care for other languages."

"The more I learn," I answer lightly, "the happier I feel."

She shrugs. "Spanish fluency wouldn't have made hellish Carboneras any cooler. And the language sounds so dirty to me. God, the lisping. I stood back so I wouldn't get sprayed."

I should mention that English is our lingua franca at the villa because of the multinational cast.

Harold is more simpatico. "Also, *'Padam, Padam'* and *'Bravo pour le Clown,'* I hope."

"Bien sûr!" I smile. "I love 'Padam, Padam.'"

"That's your Celtic blood," he says, "your melancholy heart."

Lettie clears her throat.

Happily, Sofia arrives at that moment with the vellutata di fagioli.

This is Fabio's cue. My round, bald neighbor always appears as food is served. In letters to Susan and Ken, I call him 'Famio' because he's ever hungry, savoring each morsel. When teased, he says enjoying food is part of a deep epicurean philosophy.

At the head of the table, Malcolm waits for everybody to sit before he speaks. "I see someone left The Guardian Weekly open in the drawing room this morning." He tugs the left side of his reddish brown beard. His thick, dark eyebrows are like swallows about to swoop in opposite directions. Not one grey hair, although he must be sixty. His sternness becomes more charming than intimidating as the months go by.

Arda tilts her head; black brown hair falls over one eye. "I am truly sorry. I was in the middle of an article when my mobile rang."

"Damn phones," he bursts out. "Excuse me, but I asked people to keep them in the bedrooms. We don't want the parlor strewn with paper like the bottom of a birdcage."

Malcolm's ban on newspapers and mobiles downstairs are among his Victorian quirks. He's curating an atmosphere of genteel decorum and mutual consideration, nineteenth century Edinburgh in twenty-first century Liguria.

Arda persists; indeed persistence seems to be an Armenian trait, judging by the compatriots who've visited her. "Family troubles. Mother was ringing from Gyumri," she sniffs. "Father is in hospital."

"Oh, dear." Taina settles her competent palm against Arda's trembling shoulders. Her English is the best of anyone here, with hardly a trace of Finnish. "What's wrong?"

I want to look like Taina when I'm seventy-five—straight hair; piercing, intelligent blue eyes; shiny skin; dancer's posture. I adore her signature cherry pink lipstick.

Arda holds back tears. "We do not know the diagnosis. A blockage. Something in the heart."

"Arteriosclerosis," Famio declares, lavishly buttering a thick slice of olive ciabatta. He inhales the yeast and brine, takes a bite, then touches the linen napkin to his lips.

See, cloth napkins, how elegant is that? And candles at dinner. But I'm getting ahead of myself.

"What does that mean?" Arda's almond eyes deepen, a doe prized in the rifle's sight.

"An illness in old men," explains Fabio. He sprinkles two spoonfuls of Parmigiano on his soup. "Does your father smoke?"

"Is my father Armenian?" Arda lifts her tiny avian shoulders up and down, up and down.

"They'll give him bypass surgery, a common procedure." Fabio pours a glass of his private wine. He never offers to share, which doesn't bother me because I don't drink before a performance. But Arda looks like she could use a sip.

I want to say something hopeful about recovery, but I rarely talk about my Stage 3 breast cancer diagnosis, chemo, surgery, radiation, and the long—please god make it longer— remission. My silence isn't denial; more superstition. Also I don't want to relive the fear I felt each time they drew blood, the doubt I still feel after five, six, ten years of good results. Moving to Italy is a statement of faith.

"Enough," Malcolm intervenes, "you're scaring the poor girl, Fabio." He turns to our stricken bird. "Arda, come see me after lunch. My cousin had blocked arteries, and he's fine now. In fact, he's become a fitness zealot, driving his wife in Dunlop crackers. Don't worry."

"Thank you, Malcolm. I apologize…the newspaper." She breaks into heaving sobs, abruptly leaving the table.

"Let's all try to keep the house tidier, shall we?" Malcolm murmurs, clearly abashed by Arda's response.

That evening everyone attends my show except Lettie, who says 10 p.m. is her bedtime, and Arda, who somehow found funds to fly to Armenia for the weekend.

The Trattoria Canzone e Cena is a small al fresco café overlooking the sea toward Camogli. Tonight the crowd is thin, so I appreciate support from Il Tesoro. Even dour Malcolm has appeared. I found the perfect dress with Taina's help, from the Vintage English Rag Shoppe where she works Saturdays in Nervi. I needed something sexy yet appropriate for a fiftyish singer. Black with slivers of cobalt to the waist and then from the knees down to the hem. I love the little sleeves fluttering against my arms. The sandals could be a better match, but I trust people won't be staring at my feet.

Taina and Ismo share a bottle of rosso with Harold. Malcolm sips his "national beverage," single malt, straight up. Fabio has ordered prosecco and a large plate of antipasti which he savors slowly.

The passing tour boat—a final horn—is my prompt to begin. I'd appreciate an introduction but Signor Ferrando dislikes formality.

For Harold, I begin with *"Padam, Padam."*

He laughs, a full, hearty, knowing laugh. Tears run down his cheeks, and at the end, he's cheering, which ignites the others. Although I must admit Malcolm seems distracted.

Next, *"La Vie en Rose"* inspires a table of women from Genoa to weep.

Then, *"Les Feuilles Mortes."*

I conclude with *"Bravo Pour Le Clown."* Harold and crew give me an ecstatic send-off. Signor Ferrando nods three times which signifies a small salary raise. The Genovese invite me for grappa. As I sit in the warm evening, sipping from the tiny glass and absorbing the compliments of strangers, I am content. It's all over—the mastectomy, the divorce, even the faculty meetings. I glimpse at the first star, tempted to wish for a bigger audience, but remembering Arda's father, pray, instead, for his good health.

~

Late one morning as I enter the parlor, I find Harold working on his stamp collection at the large mahogany table. The black leather notebook is opened in the middle, its left page filled with turquoise, puce and chartreuse stamps. He's scrutinizing a new prize with his magnifying glass, one of last week's birthday gifts from Lettie, I imagine.

Wary of intruding, I slip back into the vestibule.

"It's all right, Adrienne," he calls. "Come see the lovely bird on this old British Honduras stamp."

"Sweet." I peer over his rounded shoulder. "You and your stamps and Lettie with her embroidery—you really are quite alike."

"And the embedded question is—why do we bicker so much?"

I blush.

"We're perfectionists of different kinds." He shrugs. "Even the arguments, I guess, are a kind of intimacy."

"It's not you so much," I falter, hapless, slumping down to the couch.

He smiles ruefully. "You don't know Lettie yet. She's truly a dear, and she's weathered a lot." He regards me seriously. "As the oldest child she carried too much. That's the source of her fierce certainty. But she was 'just the girl,' and her parents sent her to work at seventeen to help pay her brothers' school fees. She's always felt ignored. I thought I could change things. That I could make her happy."

"Ah, yes," I sigh, remembering how I hid Ken's vodka bottles, dragged him to funny movies, planned trips to Montreal and New York, anything to dispel the shadows. It took Susan and eventually AA to do that. No more rescues for me. And it all worked out: my best friend and my ex-husband are happily wed and still in my life.

"More fool me." He shrugs.

"I'm sure you've enriched her life immensely."

"She is life itself to me. I don't know what I'd do without her."

"You're both lucky, then," I answer inanely. Suddenly I understand Lettie's affection for Princess Margaret, another overlooked daughter with a stolid air of pretension. And I have a new appreciation for Harold's public joviality.

~

At dinner, Fabio critiques my latest performance. "Delightful, Adrienne. But you must learn some Italian songs, *'Straini Amori, Sapore di Sale, Anema e Core, La Solitudine.'"*

"I thought she did a super job myself," declares Ismo.

"I agree." Malcolm nods. "Quite fine. Splendid high notes."

Lettie takes a sip of the budget Pinot Grigio she buys at Ekom. I remind myself that she's offered to share it several times, although no one accepted. Why do I only see her cranky side?

Lettie speaks up, "You all came traipsing in late enough again last night."

"We tried to be quiet," Taina winces.

Lettie waves away the apology. "I know it's silly, but I worry about Harold driving at night."

I turn to Fabio. "Italian songs, I agree. But it's hard to find the sheet music."

"Now if we had Wi-Fi here as the other villas do," Ismo launches into his favorite campaign.

"It's true," says Harold. "Our friends Nigel and Lizzie have excellent reception at the Villa dei Palmas. They get BBC telly and all sorts of useful things."

Malcolm reddens, then clears his throat. "Do you know where BBC reception is perfect? In England. You might be happier back in Birmingham. Or, for the time being, at the Villa dei Palmas. Signore Folle told me she has an opening."

Harold shrugs and shakes his head.

Lettie takes a long sip of wine, stares into the middle distance.

Dinner conversation has stalled. Everyone is tired. Most of us are finished, waiting for Sofia to serve the sorbet. But Famio is relishing his last morsel of rare lamb, cutting it into smaller and smaller pieces. Chewing slower and slower. He once confided he finds food superior to sex—less complicated, more satisfying, usually there when you want it.

I notice everyone is fascinated now, as Fabio pops the final scrap into his mouth.

~

At breakfast one morning, Arda looks relaxed. "Father is feeling better now. Fabio was right—about the illness and the cause. My *hayrik* has promised to stop smoking. We shall see."

"I'm so glad he's better," says Lettie. "You know the English have cut down on smoking. Only about twenty percent of Britons smoke now."

Arda is impassive. "Do you know Armenia has a Stonehenge that predates your British site by over 3,000 years?"

Here we go again.

Malcom laughs into his beard.

"Please pass the cornetti," Fabio says.

~

In September, I discover a different side of Fabio as he hands a bouquet of red roses to Taina. "Buon Compleanno!" He sings "Happy Birthday" in English with a strong baritone.

Taina's eyes widen. "How did you know?" She turns to Ismo, who shakes his head.

Sofia enters carrying a small white cake, a single candle glowing on top.

Taina takes a deep breath and blows out the flame.

Malcolm nods approval. "It was all Fabio. Apparently, he is our cortegiano."

As the months pass, Fabio treats each woman to a birthday bouquet. Year after year.

~

I'm touched that most of my neighbors come to the Trattoria once or twice a month to cheer me on. Malcolm, as ever, is paterfamilias, kind and sympathetic, while holding himself at one remove.

Altogether Malcolm cultivates an air of mystery, skillfully dodging personal questions. He'd have you think he has no past, no career, no family. He says he arrived in Italy as a young man and fell in love with wintery waves crashing on the jagged grey rocks and with the fireflies winking in fragrant summer gardens. He worked hard enough—at something—to open Il Piccolo Tesoro. We do know he's a small time philanthropist, administering educational projects in Eastern Europe and West Africa.

One day curiosity gets the better of me, although after all his kindness, I shouldn't trespass into Malcolm's privacy. But it's only a twenty-five minute ride to Genoa, a good library and a search engine. E qui! The internet reveals that Malcolm Gordon, only child of Scots aristocrats, had a storied career as young photographer, selling his work to the Tate Modern, MOMA, AGO, the Guggenheim at Bilbao, many world-class museums. Then one afternoon in his forties, Malcolm's car was rammed by a drunk driver. His wife and two children died. After a year of surgeries and physical therapy, Malcolm permitted one last exhibition—ten years of family photos. Then he dropped out of sight.

All at once, I'm weeping with sadness and shame.

~

Suddenly, it's the fifth anniversary of the day I met Malcolm and the Bulgarian tenor. We all seem to enjoy one another more as time passes, perhaps conscious of the rarity of our domestic troupe. Sometimes I wonder if we—collectively—comprise Malcolm's latest work of art. I've never revealed my library discovery. If others want to search, they can. Malcolm has a right to his private grief, just as I keep my blood counts to myself. Now, even though I don't quite understand him, I feel a deeper fondness.

Malcolm helps us see the best in each other, praising Fabio's translations as they appear in literary magazines, asking Harold about his philately and passing on unusual African stamps. He has framed one of Lettie's less fussy embroideries and hung it over the sideboard. He's fascinated by Taina and Ismo's youth in northern Finland and draws out their childhood stories. Whenever Arda publishes a poem, she's asked to recite it at dinner in Armenian and English.

Not much changes outwardly. Arda has a new Dutch boyfriend. Then a Romanian. The last fellow was a professor from Ghana. After each break-up, Fabio waits for a discreet period before asserting himself, always to be gently turned away. In recent months, Arda has stayed up late sipping chamomile tea with Malcolm. I imagine him offering avuncular advice about persistence and courage. She's still looking for a book contract.

Fabio has gained a little weight, but his daily passeggiata keeps him fit and his appetite strong. Now that he's resigned to Arda's platonic friendship, he is translating three of her poems for a literary journals.

Ismo and Taina, at eighty, don't look the slightest bit diminished and still swim daily at the municipal pool where they have a dozen friends. Taina worries about her husband's diabetes—yes, he does have some numbness in his fingers—and reminds him a little too often to test his blood sugar.

My latest lab work is free of cancer markers.

"Stage three," the doctora puzzles.

"Yes." I smile. "I have a happy and fulfilling life."

"You're doing something right." She fingers the crucifix hanging on a silver chain on her grey scrubs. "He is watching over you."

Whatever, whoever it takes. I nod.

Meanwhile Lettie and Harold never manage to find a new home, so they remain in the adjacent room, arguing into the night, forestalling mortality by postponing their future.

Harold keeps his voice down, but the walls are thin. "Greece is a beautiful country. The Aegean and the Mediterranean. The Parthenon. The Acropolis. What history."

"History!" Lettie protests. "We'd be there in the present. They speak an impossible language. Haven't you heard that expression, 'It's Greek to me?'"

I pop in my earbuds and Mozart, Bach, Britten, Copeland distract me from their global itinerary. Deep at night, earbuds guard my serenity. I never hear anything from upstairs, from Arda's "garret" as she calls it or next door in Malcolm's master bedroom. For a large man, he's light on his feet. Likewise Fabio and the Finns are quiet on the floor below mine.

My career at Trattoria Canzone e Cena remains steady, the audience increasing gradually. Now I sing four nights a week, tending to draw an expatriate crowd, mostly Canadians or others seeking romantic memories to take home. I'm no star, just someone who loves to share good music. An attractive enough woman with skillfully highlighted brown hair and—if I do say so myself—a dazzling smile. During the day, I read about Liguria, study Italian and write—in longhand, Malcolm would approve of my penmanship—slightly exaggerated stories about my Ligurian adventures to Ken and Susan and other old friends. Perhaps in my next life, I'll meet Mr. or Ms. Perfect and have a couple of kids. But compared to my parents (Mom gone to cancer at forty and Dad spending the next thirty years looking for love), I have landed beyond fortune.

One July evening in my sixth year, when the relentless heat takes an edge off paradise, Fabio raises a question to distract us from the weather. "What do you admire in men and in women?"

"That's easy," Harold bites. "Beauty in women. Conviction in men."

"I see it differently," asserts Lettie. "Power in men. Elegance in women."

Taina shakes her head. Her hair has grown from white to shimmering silver. "Kindness. In a person. Regardless of gender."

"Yes," I agree. "Plus good cheer and loyalty to friends."

"Come, come," Fabio frowns. "Do play along. I say courage in a man. And grace. Yes, grace in the fairer sex."

Malcolm is shaking his head, the indulgent father tolerating a harmless diversion.

Fabio nods to Arda.

"Ok," she whispers. "I admire intelligence in a woman. And in a man, tenderness." She blushes, inspecting her cerulean fingernails.

~

I should have sensed something. Seen the hint in Arda's blush. Should have wondered why they both left town for a long weekend. But all of us are completely flabbergasted one Sunday evening when Sofia emerges with two bottles of champagne and a classy little wedding cake.

Malcolm raises a glass "To my bride." And Arda stands in response, clinking her glass with his. "My husband."

Lettie gasps.

Fabio clutches his heart.

Taina claps. The rest of us join in.

Gobsmacked, that wonderful English expression, is the only word for our response.

As she serves the cake, Arda apologizes. "We eloped because my family would not approve such differences in age and religion. We wanted to invite you, would have invited you, but worried you would have gone to troubles."

"Gone to a lot of trouble?" Lettie corrects gently, perhaps unconsciously.

"Yes, yes. But we wished to celebrate with you. So the champagne. The cake."

Malcolm waits impassively for his slice.

"Lovely," Harold proclaims. "Congratulations to both of you!"

"*Kyllä!*" declares Ismo. "May your marriage be as blessed as mine."

Taina squeezes his hand.

That night, in my second floor bed, I can't help but listen for sounds from above. Lettie and Harold are quiet for once. Perhaps they, too, are listening. But the bride and groom are as discreet as ever. When I awake the next morning, I realize they've probably been lovers for months.

~

Each year people take short vacations or trips home, and I miss my Tesoro neighbors. Taina and Ismo go to Oulu each Christmas. Fabio spends August on the beaches of Sicily. Every May, Malcolm visits his cousin in Dunlop, at the same time Arda goes to Armenia. I've returned to Toronto twice; Ken, Susan and I have visited Paris, Prague and Budapest. I'm always happy to return home to Il Piccolo Tesoro.

~

Normally, I sleep long and peacefully. Especially if no one is traveling. One windy winter morning, I awake to a terrible racket at 1 a.m. The gates have blown open and clatter raucously. Early for the garbage collectors. Too lazy to pull on my coat and go outside, I lie in bed and try to meditate. When I finally fall back to sleep, I dream about an old man crawling around the garden. Dressing for breakfast, I have a moment of panic. Ismo. He looked so drawn and weary yesterday. A cold has kept him from the pool all week.

I race downstairs, the first to arrive at the table, which is set, as usual, with delicate blue Vietri china, fresh bread, jam, sliced meats and perfectly ripe cheeses.

Fabio shuffles in. "What a terrible night." He yawns.

"Did you hear the gate?"

"No, no. That maddening motorcyclist next door kept sputtering up and down beneath my window."

I grow frantic about Ismo. Usually, he's early for breakfast.

Harold follows Lettie, each of them uncharacteristically quiet.

Arda slips in and nods to Sofia for her tea.

"Good morning." Two voices. Ah, those lovely Finnish accents.

"Great to see you," I burst out.

Ismo regards me quizzically.

"It's always nice to see you, dear." Taina looks puzzled.

We sip coffee and tea, waiting for Malcolm.

The few attempts at conversation are subdued. It seems everyone has had a hard night.

Fifteen minutes pass.

"How is your father, Arda?" asks Taina.

"Fine. He is fine. Smoking again, of course."

"How regrettable," responds Lettie. "In Birmingham his friends would…."

Arda looks through her. "Maybe he smokes because he doesn't live in your enlightened country. Maybe he smokes because he lives in a cold, crowded flat in Armenia."

"It would be rude to start without Malcolm," Fabio says, eyeing the Fontina.

"He was awake when I left," Arda murmurs.

"Perhaps he pressed snooze for once," Harold chirps, trying to raise our spirits. "Even the Scots eventually have to relax."

Lola screams from the top floor. "Oh, no, *¡Oh, no, Dios mío, no!*"

Arda takes two steps at a time. Fabio follows. I'm next to arrive, just in time to see our cortegiano faint at Malcolm's door.

Arda kneels next to the bed, crying, whispering to Malcolm, squeezing his hand.

I've never seen our ruddy Pict so pale and wan. He whispers to Arda.

Ismo rings for an ambulance.

Fabio recovers, then disappears.

Everyone else peers in anxiously.

Ismo scoots us away. "Give the man air. Taina, love, would you take the others downstairs?"

Helpless, we return to the table.

Sofia trembles carrying the quiche.

Lola serves the rest of the meal alone.

I nibble on a cornetto, managing to swallow half.

Sirens flay the cold morning air, then an emergency team blows through the door, and pounds up the stairs—three sturdy volunteers from the commune. Soon the men reappear, warily balancing Malcolm on a stretcher to the ambulance.

Ismo kisses Taina's cheek. "Arda and I will follow in a taxi. I'll call when we have news."

"What can we do?" Lettie sobs, clutching Harold's elbow.

"Hush, dear; he's in good hands."

Her jaw tightens. "Surely whoever takes over will raise the rent."

"Don't be crass," It slips out, after years of restraint. "He's not dead. Most likely, he's had a heart attack. He told us his cousin survived and is fine."

"Now, now," murmurs Fabio. Color returning to his cheeks, he takes a second helping of quiche. "This is a stressful time. Let's all try to get along."

"I'm sure he's all right," I say.

"Actually, we can't be sure of anything," says Harold, taking Lettie's hand.

One by one, we excuse ourselves from the table. From my bedroom window, I see the gates are securely locked, the garbage bins still full.

~

The house is eerily quiet as we gather for dinner.

Lola appears, pale and sniffling, struggling with a huge platter of roasted lamb leg. "For Signor Fabio's birthday. Signor Malcolm ordered it last week."

Fabio's embarrassment almost conceals his delight.

"Malcolm, always so thoughtful." Taina purses her lips.

She looks pallid without lipstick, a sure sign that earth has slipped from its axis.

"Happy birthday, Fabio," Harold says.

"Many happy returns," I declare a little too gaily.

We nibble, pursuing a conversation about world affairs, as if to gain Malcolm's approval.

Outside, a car slides to a stop on the rainy street. Our heavy front door opens to admit Ismo, looking exhausted, and a shattered Arda.

My stomach turns; I hold back the tears.

Arda numbly takes a place at the table, hands folded on her lap.

Ismo continues standing as we read the dreadful news in his face. He looks ancient this evening.

Taina rises to kiss his cheek.

Fabio offers Ismo and Arda, then the rest of us, a glass of his special rosso.

Ismo takes a deliberate sip before speaking. "Malcolm," his voice falters and he starts again, "our great friend Malcolm wasn't as lucky as his cousin."

"Oh, oh, oh," Arda is sobbing.

Fabio reaches for my hand, and I'm grateful for the touch.

Ashen Sofia puts a sturdy arm around Lola's quaking shoulders.

Ismo clears his throat, and continues. "Our great friend Malcolm died at 5 p.m. Arda and I were both with him as he passed peacefully. We stayed afterward to arrange for the funeral home. And the lawyer."

"Lawyer?" Lettie looks terrified. "Of course he would have a lawyer. Probably knew he was ill. Probably...." Arda shuts her eyes and bows her head.

"Lettie, love, do give it a rest," whispers Harold. "I know you're anxious darling, but this isn't the time...we're all in shock."

She rushes upstairs.

"The lawyer will arrive at 10 a.m. next Thursday," Ismo explains. "Apparently Malcolm wants, wanted us all to be together. I suggested he arrive after breakfast. Does that suit?"

Everyone nods.

Arda's eyes remain closed.

I doubt anyone gets much sleep. My heart is heavy; I wish I could have said good-bye to Malcolm. I worry what will become of this house. The people. My job. My new life. One night as I sit in the kitchen, trying to read, Harold appears at 4 a.m. to prepare tea for Lettie. Fabio wanders in with a bottle of cognac but wisely opts for a cup of Harold's brew.

~

Thursday morning is stormy. Pine trees rustle noisily. After breakfast, we drift into the drawing room and wait for the avvocato. The air is redolent with coffee and Lettie's new perfume.

A diminutive, grey-haired Signor Natale arrives appears in the doorway. He is nattily attired in a pin-striped suit and a red bow tie, dapper as any representative of Malcolm would be.

I notice that, actually, all of us are in our Sunday best. Taina is wearing a new, pinker lipstick and crystal earrings. Sofia and Lola have changed from their uniforms into smart skirts and blouses. All this out of respect for Malcolm.

"I'm happy everyone could attend," Signor Natale says in musical English.

"Of course," Lettie's voice is brittle, nervous. "We are all friends of Malcolm."

"You are," Signor Natale peeks over his reading glasses, "Mrs. Batchley?"

"Yes," she frowns suspiciously. "How did you know?"

"Malcolm and I were *vecchi amici*. He talked about everyone here, so I felt I knew each of you as I entered the room."

"Odd, that…." Lettie's voice trails off.

Signor Natale's eyes widen, with disbelief or irritation. "Shall I begin reading the will?"

"The will!" exclaims Fabio, reddening. "I assumed you were here to inform us about the sale of Il Piccolo Tesoro."

I glance at the faces registering surprise, alarm and anticipation. Arda studies her nails.

"Yes, yes," says Harold. "I would assume the will, itself, would be read to the family."

"Really!" Ismo interjects, uncharacteristically brusque. "You really don't get it? Why do you think he was supporting us all these years?"

"Supporting us?" bristles Lettie. "I certainly don't know about your private arrangements, but Harold and I scrupulously paid rent on the first of each month."

"Rent!" exclaims Arda. "You imagine the pittance we paid actually maintained this fine place, provided such food, covered the salaries of Sofia and Lola?"

The two maids blink at each other.

I take a deep breath. Of course I knew—even Lettie must have known—on some level.

Tears well in Taina's bright blue eyes.

Fabio is weeping and blowing his nose.

"Shall I begin?" Signor Natale is not a man for public emotion.

"Yes, please," sighs Ismo.

"I, Malcolm Gordon, being of sound mind and whole body, bequeath all assets, including photographic royalties, bank accounts and my dear Piccolo Tesoro to my beloved wife, Arda Gordon."

I join the collective intake of breath. Arda sits back in the big armchair.

"My first provision is that Mrs. Gordon maintains our education programs in Eastern Europe and West Africa."

Ismo nods solemnly.

Restlessly, Harold stretches his neck from side to side until Lettie signals him to sit still.

"I also ask her to maintain the present financial arrangements with the current residents in perpetuity."

Fabio jumps up and bursts into applause.

Arda smiles faintly, then purses her lips.

The rest of us sit stunned.

"Individual bequests include the following: For Fabio Bisio, a case of his favorite Barolo each month as long as he lives at Il Piccolo Tesoro. For Sofia Ramirez and Lola Castro, a trip home to marry and celebrate a happy honeymoon."

Lettie coughs.

Taina, Ismo, Fabio and I all say in unison, "*¡Felicidades!*"

"For Harold and Lettie Batchley, a round trip to Birmingham to jog their memories. Then, to commemorate their return to Il Piccolo, a case of *Bisol Prosecco Valdobbiadene Superiore di Cartizze*. For Taina and Ismo Kuoppala, my music library and lifetime season opera tickets to Il Teatro Carlo Felice. For Adrienne Moreau, the deed to La trattoria Canzone e Cena, where she can share her beautiful voice as long as she likes."

I am shaking and crying and suddenly wondering if the Bulgarian tenor whose room I took ever found an audience and a home.

~

Over the next few years, days pass slowly and quickly, and each of us evolves, some in surprising ways. Arda's debut book receives international acclaim, but, as she says, success in poetry rewards the ego more than the purse. This spring, Fabio's essays are honored with a *Premio Napoli*. I have a brief health scare at Christmas. Nothing since. Harold and Lettie are enjoying their conversational Italian classes more than they expected. Sofia and Lola laugh easily.

There's sad news, too. You would expect that.

Ismo's funeral is simple and very moving. So many tributes and stories. At eighty-five, despite those years of swimming, he had grown frail and simply couldn't beat the flu which turned into pneumonia.

After the service, our dining room is laden with pastas and roasts and salads and cakes brought by neighbors. Ismo had become a kind of Nordic *anziano del villaggio*.

Fabio takes the first plate; the rest of us follow.

The small dark girl scoots behind Fabio, who lifts her on his shoulders. "Should you like to start with sweet or savory?"

"Cake, cake!" the child declares. "Chocolate. Lemon."

Unusually fluent for her age, she speaks English, Italian and Spanish.

"Malina! Malina, how often have we told you not to bother Uncle Fabio?" Sofia escorts her daughter to a chair. "Really, Fabio, you spoil her so."

"Manners!" Her other mother appears. "How will she learn if you're always spoiling her?" chides Lola.

"Manners! Do I hear Malcolm's voice?" I laugh.

Taina kisses the girl's forehead, leaving a spot of cerise lipstick.

Malina grins.

"I often hear Malcolm's voice." Arda stands, arms akimbo, and declares, "You don't think he'd leave us to handle this place by ourselves, do you?"

The Whole Story

Ropes of blood and earth. The grape vines are carmine, ruby, scarlet, gold and brown. Brilliant blue sky. It's cooling down after a blissfully warm Thanksgiving holiday in our hilly California haven.

As we drive Highway 128 south to SFO, I still smell the sharp, tangy sage near our front deck and the glowing Meyer lemon tree. Those tiny pink roses are blooming again—as they do every California season when the hills metamorphose: green to gold to grey.

How high will the snow reach when we return to Madison to finish the frigid fall semester? Will our car start at the arctic airport? Have the apartment pipes frozen?

On either side of this highway, the grass has gone winter dun. So far an hour on the road. Two more to the airport. We should have set off earlier, but it's hard to leave the cabin. We'll make the flight if we drive intelligently, focus, if people don't slow down to gape at the pumpkin patch on 101 South. Surely last week's gawkers have gone Christmas shopping.

"We'll make it fine," I hear myself say.

Jane nods.

November light evaporates by the minute. Late fall. Winter really. I will look forward to December 22 when the earth tips toward daylight, and we return to the cabin for Christmas break. Our refuge. We do have lucky lives, especially lucky to have our small respite in the tranquil Coastal Range.

Jane sighs.

"What's up?"

"I don't know." She keeps her eyes on the road.

Jane is great with rental cars, a natural driver. "Sad about going?" I ask.

"Yeah, and stressed about missing the plane. I mean, I know we won't. Still, I'd rather enjoy the landscape than ride the accelerator and chug adrenalin."

"Chug adrenalin?"

"Ugh," she exhales sharply. "I want to be here as long as I really am here. Instead of worrying about the airport, I'd like to savor these gorgeous hills."

I sigh because we both travel too much for lectures and conferences. I'm beginning to understand that there's nothing as fine as being at the cabin, witnessing the vivid floral debuts, the acrobatic murmuration of birds, the shifting night sky.

As we round a familiar curve—near Gibson's Ranch— vans and RVs screech to a halt before us.

Jane coolly taps the brake. See what I mean? A natural driver.

Plumes of noxious black and grey smoke twist above the two lane road. Are we trapped? Behind us cars are skidding. I hear a thump. Then another.

Jane pulls nimbly onto the graveled shoulder.

"Isn't that Carolyn Gorman?"

"Yes!" I wave at our neighbor, then notice the fire.

Giant flames blaze one hundred yards down the road. From that hillside a blue Mini Cooper stares down, its hood pried open like the jaws of a starving crocodile.

I close my eyes, remind myself it's been 25 years since the accident. Pay attention. Stay in the present.

The car could explode. We need to get out of here. All of us.

People climb from their big and little fuel efficient and gas guzzling vehicles. A regiment of stranded spectators, arms akimbo, waiting.

Waiting for us.

"Let's turn around and take the Ukiah Pass," I suggest, perhaps a little too urgently. "We'll still make the flight if we take the longer route."

Jane shrugs, watches.

I pumped and pumped the brakes on Dad's old Buick.

I follow her gaze to the car on the hill and the station wagon upside down on the highway. We're not like the pumpkin gawkers. We all feel some complicity, some bond here. There but for the grace of....

Carolyn Gorman waves four flares. I'm not surprised that Carolyn is prepared for emergencies. An expert gardener and prize-winning baker, she's like a senior citizen girl scout.

The perfect neighbor.

"Anyone have a match?" Carolyn calls.

No smokers in this healthy home-from-the-country caravan.

A woman wearing a comfortably baggy beige sweater is telling everyone—anyone who will listen—that there were no casualties.

"I called 911," she reassures us, "even though everyone got out."

"Alive," I sigh.

If only the kid had been wearing a seat belt. If only the road hadn't been slick. Damn Wisconsin winters.

"There were two couples," the beige woman sounds like she's addressing a class. "Side-swiped by a truck. Both are OK."

Relieved, I momentarily forget about returning the rental car, our check-in time, the red-eye, my morning classes. And about the fire danger ahead.

"Might as well take a look," says Jane, grabbing her backpack. "I mean we can't go forward and can't reverse."

Take a look! I want to scream. Instead, hot tears rim my lids.

Of course we can turn around. But she wants to know more. She and a dozen others who cautiously walk down the highway, moving warily, as if on another planet.

Jane may be a fool, but she's my fool, and I catch up with her, silently taking her hand.

She squeezes tight.

As we approach the crash site, a middle-aged man warns, "You don't want to go any further."

I feel younger—rather than the same age as he—because of some authority in his voice which I'm about to defy. Curiosity, alarm and unappeasable grief drive me forward.

They all forgave me. The police. The insurance company. My parents. Even—

eventually—the mother who was driving the other car. An accident they all said.
Defective brakes. Nothing to forgive. So they said.

A brown shoe on the highway shoulder. A man's loafer. Just one shoe.

Nothing you could do, the therapist kept reminding me. Nothing. Make the most of your life. That's your charge.

Smoke up the hill. Dark plumes from the grotesque blue car. For some reason, the flames have receded a bit.

People wait. White vacationers in their thirties to fifties mostly. Four Latino workers in a truck. And a few kids. More than a few dogs.

"I saw him." It's the woman in the beige sweater. I saw the guy in the beat-up brown truck who did this. Sideswiped the Mazda station wagon which slammed into the MiniCooper. Then just sped away."

I shake my head, sorry for all of us, the victims, the delayed bystanders, the trucker.

"See the tire tracks there?"

Mean, grey rubber snakes melted into the road.

"At least one person died," announces the middle-aged man.

I lose a breath.

The woman in the beige sweater starts to protest, then realizes, perhaps, she doesn't know the whole story. "It was a big collision."

From two cars behind, I hear a man repeat to his friend, "One of them died." The flames are smaller, red and yellow. Why don't we get the hell out of here?

Beige woman continues, "I saw the truck guy driving earlier, really erratic, and I pulled over."

"They say she died on impact," reports the male authority. "A consolation. Very sad consolation."

Who are these people? How do they know all this?

"Her husband or partner or hell, how do I know, her brother is still in the Mazda. Door is jammed."

"He can talk."

I stare at the smashed grill of the green station wagon wondering if the driver can hear us all talking about him.

"I told him EMT is on the way."

"Yes, I called them," the beige woman repeats. "I did see the second couple leave. They jumped from the station wagon and walked down the highway. Safe." Her eyes fill. "I thought everyone survived. I really did."

His name was Andy Rafferty. The newspaper showed a cute, blond five year old poised with a baseball bat. I bet the cap was red, but that was before color photos in newspapers.

"Wonder the entire place isn't burning up," reasons the middle-aged man.

Sirens. Suddenly, finally sirens.

Late and pathetic. An old red fire truck. One. Why aren't there more? Where is the ambulance? The cops?

Reading my mind, Jane says, "Volunteers. We're lucky they arrived so fast."

Our refuge, our home away from work and Midwestern winters and city noises feels as frail as it has always been.

I compel myself to look around. Yes, we're just outside the Valley. Still close to home. Carmine, ruby, scarlet, gold and brown leaves ruffle the vines. The ranches over the hill will be growing pink roses and Meyer lemons.

"Remember the firehouse gala opening in July?" Jane smiles.

Of course. Flags, chicken and tri-tip on the grill, foil wrapped potatoes. The fashion show of new green fire retardant suits that camouflage our friendly, ordinary neighbors as exotic astronauts.

One of the space walkers rushes past now. Clara from the store? Doctor Stan?

Yes! The EMTs are taking the driver on a stretcher to their ambulance. He's answering their questions about the day and the month and President of the United States.

Our vigil is over.

Spectators begin to retreat. Aid has arrived. Shock and spectacle are subsiding. Daily pressures return.

Waiting and watching is the woman in the beige sweater. I imagine she'll testify when the sheriff finally comes. I imagine her in court. If they catch the truck driver.

I touch the woman's arm. "Good-bye for now. Take care. We're driving an alternate route."

She smiles courteously, thinly, as if she's never seen me before.

I haven't told Jane the story. She knows depression kept me out of high school for a year. I need to tell her; somehow I've been waiting for the end of the story, the whole story, whatever that is.

All the way to the airport, I think about the burning car. I wonder about the driver of the battered brown truck. I hope he turns around.

Safe. That's how I felt on our warm deck, under the blue sky on those brief fall afternoons so far from the thin rime of distant winter.

Escape Artist

You glance out the window at the tranquil spring evening. Three stories down to the glorious almond blossoms and purple magnolias dazzling the campus after long dreary rains. Northern California heaven.

It's been a productive, but long, day of teaching, running meetings. You're tired, hungry for supper and a little cranky. Damn fluorescent light buzzes above your desk. Skkst. Skkst. Shots of toxin straight into the cortex. How long before you get brain cancer? Cheer up; low blood sugar brings out your gloomy. Come on. Only two more midterms to read and you can leave the office before dark.

A knock on the open door.

Your heart sinks and inadvertently you check your watch.

The handsome blond student shifts from one purple Nike to the other. His flushed face tells you he's run here. Sweat drips along his left cheek. His right hand is fisted: tension hardens his blue eyes.

"Hello there," you say.

Throat clearing and then, "Are you Marcia Dunway?"

"Yes." They never address women as professor. At least he didn't call you by your first name as so many students do. "How may I help you?"

Shuffling into the office, he perches on the grey folding chair, watchfully, as if training for the FBI.

Some kids automatically pull their seats right up to the desk, lean over, elbows on your papers. Others stretch back, expectant customers. The shy ones usually alight on the edge like this.

"How may I help you?" He blinks, snaps his gum.

Running with gum in his mouth, you're suddenly worried for him. He studies you.

Pay attention. You were up late last night obsessing about Mom's accelerated Alzheimer's. You may be tired, but your office door is open. You are a professor. He is a student. This is your job.

Closely he inspects the walls. It's almost comical, as if he's casing the joint. A fairly straight kid, he looks more Ivy than Berkeley.

"You don't recognize me," he says, deadpan, bold.

You troll through a mental album of former students. There is something familiar about the kid, but you can't place him.

Another knock.

Your favorite colleague Milt pops his head in the office.

"Finished at the salt mine for the day. Don't stay too late. Again."

"Yes, Uncle Milt," you laugh.

He looks over the student (who is staring at you) and slits a thumb across his throat, subtly advising you to send the kid away.

You shake your head. "Have a good evening, Milt."

"Seriously, Marcia, at the department party, Dana made me promise to kick you out of the office before dark."

"Duly warned," you note, hoping the student will pick up on the lateness of the hour.

"And Dana's right; it's not safe."

"Good night, Professor Weinstein. Say hi to Eva for me."

You turn your back to the visitor. "Sorry, I can't remember. Please tell me your name."

He glares, exhales through pursed lips, almost whistling.

An image from the morning paper: that young sniper in Cincinnati, from a wiccan cult. Weird. You thought witches these days were good folk—pagan environmentalists, right?— something benign.

He continues to watch you, eyes full of—yes—longing.

"I know we've met," you try.

His jaw stiffens.

Your patience is dwindling.

"It's been a while," he offers, as if playing a creepy game.

That's it. You're exhausted. You flip through a file on your chaotic desk, hoping he'll get the hint. Dana will have dinner ready soon. And Milt's right about the dangers of cycling along College Avenue after dark.

Suddenly he mumbles. "You used to be my...."

"Sorry?"

"You used to be my aunt," a harder edge to his voice now.

Puzzled, you study his petulant face. And then—"Artie! Artie, Roberta's son. How are you?" He was an affectionate little boy, very attached to Brad. Adored his uncle. Yes, he looks exactly like your ex-husband's sister. You count the years— twelve, thirteen—since you've seen little Artie, who, through the miracle of life, is now a young man.

"Arthur," he corrects you solemnly.

"Arthur," you nod to the once delightful child who was a demon at checkers.

"I'm fine," he looks you coldly in the eye. "How are you?"

"Fine, thank you." You're still smiling despite his curtness. The dutiful aunt, you ask, "So you're a student here at Berkeley?"

"Yes."

So like his uncle in the passive aggression. And the monosyllables. You had to pry conversation out of Brad, too, especially after he became a total pothead. For years you begged him to agree to couples' counseling. Every night he came home from work and went upstairs with his stash to watch TV and eat junk food and giggle. You think about the shock on his face when you finally told him you needed a separation.

"It's not working for whom?" he'd demanded.

"What year are you, Artie?" You hear that old reasonable tone you used with Brad in the last years. "Junior?"

"Sophomore, of course." His voice is almost inaudible again. "As you remember, I'm 19 now."

Outside the sky is greying. Nearby buildings are losing shape. This is not a student consultation, more like a family stealth attack. As you know, as if you'd remember his birthday. As if Roberta hadn't cut you off when you tried to maintain contact, even sending back Christmas cards. In those days, you still cared about Brad, worried about him, and still thought Roberta was your friend. Well, after years of therapy, you're a little more realistic about people.

"How do you like college so far?" you ask. You are not obliged to keep chatting. But you're surprised to find you feel a tie to Brad and his nephew, nostalgic for what might have been.

"Fine," he's reading a student exam upside down.

Shoving the tests into a briefcase, you check your watch again. You can't help asking one more question, "What's your major, Artie?"

"Arthur," he corrects you. "Chemistry."

"Just like your Uncle Brad and his uncle before him." Of course he'd follow his hero to Berkeley, to chemistry.

"Glad you actually remember the family," he smirks.

That's it. The filling station is closed. "Nice to see you again, Arthur. I really do need to close up shop now."

"You cut your hair."

Reflexively you touch a short, tight coil at the nape of your neck.

"We used to call you Aunt Rapunzel."

You laugh. Brad always loved your long curls, claimed he rescued you from your crazy family. In a way, he was right. Brad's love and support allowed you to become an escape artist, disappearing through the haze of smoke and alcohol and out the door of your family's tiny tenth floor apartment in the projects. Yes, you've always been grateful to him, even if he didn't turn out to be such a prince. You weren't a total princess.

Of course you returned to your family after finding your footing. These last two years, your sister Anna has been good about sharing in the caretaking of Mom. Sometimes you and Anna even laugh about growing up in that chaotic, scary apartment.

"Do you still live with that Dana person?"

What is the story? Did Brad send him? The times you tried to reconnect with Brad—you were still worried about his doping—he ignored your calls and emails.

"Your partner," he persists.

Clearly he didn't register the banter with Milt. Enough. "My personal life isn't an appropriate topic for a student. I wish you well here at...."

"Are you still a feminist?"

"Yes, of course."

"Mom knew it. She spotted it early."

Knew what? This kid is full of weird energy. You are tired and hungry; it's ridiculous to feel threatened. Brad is too proud to have sent him. Arthur has come of his own accord. Imagine the whole family still being angry with you. But is it your fault that Brad has become a recluse, that for years he's smoked too much dope to hold down a job? Obviously divorce was a good move for several reasons.

"And I see from your posters, you're still into radical politics. That hasn't changed."

Clara usually comes to empty the waste cans by now. Why is she delayed tonight? The sky is already plum colored. If you worked in a bank, you'd have a discreet button to push.

"Look, Arthur, it's late. Is there some way I can help you?"

The little towhead ate all the wedding cake left on people's plates. He stared at Brad with giant, admiring eyes. His uncle, the handsome, gallant groom. Since Artie's dad died, Brad had become both father and uncle.

You think about racing Artie to the hospital two years after the wedding when he got anaphylactic shock from a bee sting.

"No," he says in that flat voice. "I just came to see the person who used to be my aunt. Out of curiosity."

Let it go, Dana would tell you. Breathe.

But the cordial aunt intervenes, "Drop by again if I can be of help."

He looks at you vacantly.

You stand.

Slowly, he rises, then leans back against the Faith Ringgold print, hands in his pockets, sweaty head on the last syllable of her name.

Of course it's preposterous to think he'd pack a gun. Still, he could have a knife. You're losing your grip. Stop it. You tried with Brad, you really did. Where the hell is Clara?

His eyes lower. "Good-bye, then." He sounds downcast.

"Good-bye, Arthur."

"Thanks."

"Pardon?"

"For saying good-bye. I always did wonder where you went."

He turns, walks toward the door, then swivels, waving once.

You see the six-year-old kid clapping when you and Brad picked him up at the hospital. He hugged Brad as if he would never let go. As Brad drove to Roberta's, you cuddled Artie in the front seat, inhaling the antiseptic and sweat, grateful he was safe.

You wave back, wistful for the people you and Brad and Arthur used to be.

Standing at the door now, you watch him walk away. It never occurred to you that Artie remembered you. After Roberta cut you off, and Brad ignored the calls and emails, you tried to detach. And now you feel both guilt and sadness. For one more loss. In Artie's life and yours.

He's strolling down the corridor in a deliberately schlumpy gait that reminds you of his uncle who used to be your husband.

What a relief to have the current version of your life restored. Soon you'll be telling everything to Dana over supper in your sweet rented bungalow, far from the horrible high rise of your childhood and petulant men posing as princes.

You stand in the hall until you hear the reassuring sounds from around the corner—the elevator door yawning open and then, finally, shut.

Imagine, waiting thirteen years to say good-bye.

Returning to the office, you close the door behind you and press the lock before sitting down.

As you gather your papers, you feel lucky. Lucky for ten years and still going strong with Dana. Lucky to have a job you love. Lucky for California's no-fault divorce laws.

No fault.

A tap on the door.

You hold your breath.

Banging now. You feel the vibrations; watch the wooden door shake. Persistent, heavy thumping.

You look out the window into the darkness, three stories down to the dimly lit sidewalk.

Breathe. You try to concentrate, run your hands through your hair. OK, grab the phone; get under the desk.

First you call hopefully, "Clara?"

But of course, Clara has a key.

Quiet as the Moon

"I'd like to send this priority, please." A young woman's voice.

Margaret looks up, startled. The post office was empty a minute ago. And for the last half hour. Email. UPS. FEDEX. Now people go elsewhere. She's working for a dying institution. Everything in her life is vanishing. These late October days are so short. Then there's her dormant back garden. By now, she's usually planted the winter vegetables.

"Sorry, I didn't hear you come in." Margaret studies the young woman's shaved head, bulky sweater and jeans. She'd be lovely if she let her hair grow. The blond fuzz accentuates those azure eyes. Reflexively, she fluffs out her own red bangs. She understands how to treat diverse clientele. This is California for heaven's sake. And she's had sensitivity training although an open-minded person doesn't need such falderal. Margaret is preternaturally polite. "How may I help you?"

"Priority, please," she repeats, handing Margaret a package, light as a feather.

"Would you like tracking?"

"Not necessary."

"Insurance?"

"Got it covered."

Margaret recalls another training session. Terrorists come in all guises. Like flaxen-haired Jihad Jane in Pennsylvania. Yes, there is something quite peculiar about this new customer.

The woman is grinning.

Margaret nods and asks, "Do you mind if I ask the contents? Normal security procedure these days." She smiles.

"Great smile." The woman nods.

Cyrus liked her smile, said that's why he fell in love with her. Lately she hasn't smiled much. Seems like yesterday when she traipsed upstairs to scold him for his long Sunday nap. She found him lying still as sleep, but deeper. She leaned over to kiss him and found the lips, the cheeks, so cold. Impossible. How could her vivacious husband be dead, a week after his fiftieth birthday?

Margaret pulls herself together. "Contents?" she persists politely.

"Broken feather. Sending it in for repair."

Margaret nods. An unlikely militant. Definitely a weirdo, though. She'll have the package scanned just in case. "That will be five dollars and twenty-five cents, please."

The customer pulls out several foreign coins before finding a quarter. "Thanks, Margaret. You should smile more."

Margaret does grin at the girl's fancy tooled red cowgirl boots clicking musically as she sashays through the double glass door. She supposes the footgear is sensible enough for changeable Pacific Coast weather.

Mrs. Maxwell is next, returning another item to Sears. "Was that a girl or a boy?" She stage-whispers.

"A nice young woman." Margaret smiles, for some reason. Then, "Wrong size pants again, Mrs. Maxwell?"

~

December already. How Margaret hates these murky morning commutes, peering through her windshield at the cold, dense fog settling over the highway. She hates the dark mornings after a bad night. She hasn't slept properly since Cy's death. Awful dreams about test tubes and hammers. Probably from that stupid Agatha Christie show. She should have gone to dinner with Pam. But inertia prevails on weekends; she just wants to burrow. Read. Listen to Cy's music. Put up soup for next week's dinners.

"It would do you good to get out more," Pam phoned to say, once again.

Impatient to leave the conscious world and gallivant with Miss Marple, Margaret thanked her long-suffering friend and rang off.

She's heard all the advice about moving on, reconnecting. The grief counselor advised her to go to films, take a class, expand her life. If she does that, Cy will get smaller and smaller.

Powerless over his mortal death, she can keep him alive in her imagination. Her dear sister, less diplomatic than Pam, says Margaret is "playing house with a ghost." Thank god Rose's gallery is way off in Dallas.

Margaret slips in Cy's favorite CD. "...feels like years since it's been here." He owned "Abbey Road" in vinyl and audio cassette too. Forcing herself to be alert in the dank dimness, she sings along, "Here comes the...." Cy would get a kick out of her warbling. She should have sung along when he was alive instead of teasing him for his retro tastes.

The highway is gloomier than most in winter because of the thick redwood canopy. A lovely ride on July afternoons, but ominous, almost threatening now. In fog this thick, she feels as if she's driving on sheer faith.

"Faith," Pam persisted gently. "That's what gets me through tough times, like when my youngest overdosed." Margaret's other friends have stopped phoning and dropping by. Day after day for a month they kindly left elaborate, inedible casseroles on the front porch. Their charity piled up in her kitchen until the stench grew something awful. Pam washed the pans and returned them. You can only rebuff people so many times. Still, Pam's generosity seems endless. She stops by once a week with invitations to a movie or the mall.

"Oh, no!" Margaret shouts, swerving to avoid the flagman in an iridescent orange parka. Catching her breath, she turns to wave and notices the slim hooded figure is wearing fancy red boots. Margaret shakes her head. Shock, she tells herself. Short term delusion. Last week she dreamt about the pretty lesbian customer, about her mailing another feather.

Get a grip, she blinks to wake herself. Odd to see Caltrans guards in winter unless there's been a rock slide or fallen branches. Sometimes Margaret prays a tree will crash down on her. She doesn't want anyone else hurt, just a quick end for herself. Although she doesn't believe she'd be reunited with Cy, at least she won't be living without him anymore.

Suddenly, she sees it—a five car pile-up at the next bend. If she hadn't slowed down, she'd be number six.

A highway patrolman sirens up beside her, then slows. "Good driving, ma'am," he calls.

"Thank god for the traffic guard back there," Margaret shakes her head.

"Traffic guard?" he observes her warily and drives on.

~

As winter fades, the hills assume a tender green, and the light stretches into early evening. After work, Margaret trudges along cold, damp Main Street carrying Cy's briefcase. Taxes are terrifying, but she can't procrastinate any longer. She'll lose her job, get arrested, be sent to penitentiary. Margaret shivers. Bloody fog has rolled in.

Although the taxes paralyze her, Margaret knows she's bright enough. Cy urged her to finish her pataphysics degree. But when he got transferred up the coast, she couldn't bear commuting 100 miles down to the city, cutting him out of her days like that.

Waves crash against the jagged rocks. She could jump in, tied to the weighty briefcase, and sink, sink. Really, what was the point of going on? Of paying damn taxes? Working at the P.O.? Getting up in the morning. She dreams of living under the sea.

Turning a corner, Margaret sees a simple blue and white shingle: "Angela Minion, CPA."

Margaret rings the bell.

"Come in." A woman's voice. "I'll be right with you."

The office is a warm hideaway on this misty grey coast. Bright green curtains, light blue walls, pillowy furniture. Margaret expected the CPA office to be packed so close to the IRS deadline. But she's alone in the peaceful room. Exhausted, she sinks into the couch, rests her head, closes her eyes, humming blue and green notes as she floats in an underwater garden.

"Ah, there you are, Margaret! You must have needed a nap."

Margaret wakens, thinks she wakened, to the face of the bald woman in the swanky red boots. She tries to speak. Nothing comes out.

"Would you like tea? Or perhaps Ovaltine? It's such a chilly afternoon for late March."

"Cy always liked Ovaltine in cold weather."

The woman nods as if she understands. Or maybe she thinks Margaret is a nutcase. Probably a lot of nut cases need help with their taxes.

The post office scanner revealed a broken white feather. "Thin fracture through the upper quadrant," the tech guy reported deadpan.

Her appointment flies by. Within an hour, all is resolved.

Margaret is incredulous and chastened. Ashamed of her suspicions about Angela, she declares gratefully, "These papers were chaos itself. Immobilizing. Oh, I'm so relieved."

"You won't be going to the penitentiary," Angela laughs kindly.

"How did you know?" Margaret blanches.

"A common fear. Especially among the innocents."

"Thank you. What can I say? You're a miracle worker."

Angela beams. "Just a minion."

Minion, her last name. It takes a second for the penny to drop. Margaret grins widely.

Angela escorts Margaret to the door, her boots clicking softly on the oak floor.

~

Spring on California's north coast. Margaret dreads the vernal schizophrenia: sun and plum blossoms one day; torrents of water and pale petals scattered in mud the next day. She's always hated in-between times like this. And ever since Cy's death, she's been living in a waiting room.

She's also gained 20 pounds. Now it's hard to tie her shoes, almost impossible to squat down to the low shelves for canned goods. Pam urges her to join a gym, has even given her a free trial coupon. But she's tired all the time. Belligerently, she presses the snooze alarm until guilt drags her from the bed. Each day, work is a struggle.

On her April evaluation, Edison reports she's received four complaints for rude or curt behavior.

Really, Margaret wants to ask, how many times can Mrs. Maxwell return items to Sears? Last week it was gumboots. Of course she doesn't talk back to Edison. She needs the job in order to live. The real question is, why does she need to live?

~

One night she dreams of a turquoise world, warm below the storm, near a cave. Where she can dance and sing with Cy. A lovely spot to swim about or to rest her head.

The next morning dawns bright and sunny. She has no idea what gets into her, but she calls in sick to work. She finds Pam's coupon and calls the Coastal Range Health Club for a fitness assessment.

The gym parking lot is packed with SUVs, station wagons, Priuses and small Hondas.

Who knew so many people exercised? She's going to be late.

Breathless, Margaret thrusts her coupon at a pierced young receptionist. To her amazement, he buzzes her in without question.

"Hey, welcome to the club!" a pretty desk clerk offers her towels.

She looks surprised.

"In case you shower after your workout. Maybe visit the sauna or steam room."

Margaret accepts the towels, dazed, as if she's entered a space station. Sauna. Steam room. Who has the time? Then she remembers she has the whole day.

"Margaret, how's it going?"

"Sorry, I'm la…." She is staring at that woman. The one who made her smile at the post office, who warned her on the slick highway, who solved her tax problems. This settles it. She doesn't need a grief counselor or a fitness trainer; she needs a psychiatrist.

"Angela," she reminds Margaret.

"The minion." As if she could forget. "What are you doing here?"

"I have a couple of jobs, like a lot of coast people. After tax season I teach step aerobics, take a couple of fitness clients."

"I see." Margaret is flustered. "To be candid, I'm on a tight budget, myself. I came with a coupon and hoped to get a *diagnosis*, and then work on things myself."

"That's one approach." Angela looks amused.

"I'm sure you're very competent as an exercise coach. Lord knows you're a whiz at taxes, but the club membership is expensive, and they're talking furloughs at the post office.

"I understand. Let's just see how it goes today."

By the time the buckeye trees flower pink and gracious throughout the valley, Margaret has lost 15 pounds and is doing yoga twice a week. A magic feeling.

Edison commends her improved attitude.

Mr. Darling asks if she'd like to go out to dinner.

Pam can't believe her eyes.

Margaret feels too shy to explain about the fitness scholarship and her inspiring young trainer. Imagine, pecs, quads, abs and gluts, at her age.

Aside from the gym and work, she sticks close to home, sometimes puttering in her fertile garden when the sky is blue. Not much to the patch, just lettuces, two tomato vines, carrots, onions, peppers, peas, zucchini, and a pot of zinnias. She loves sitting in the shade on hot nights watching ice slowly melting in her lemonade.

~

One evening, she glances up to find an apparition. Angela, the Caltrans CPA fitness coach, is tootling up to her bungalow on a lavender Vespa.

"Evening, Margaret."

She's wearing Birkenstocks. Yes, it's too hot for boots, but shouldn't she have a helmet? Is it safe to motorcycle in sandals?

"Hello, Angela. Would you like some lemonade?" Margaret is oddly unruffled by the surprise visit. She must have gotten the address from the gym.

"Sure, thanks."

Angela dismounts, perches on a lawn chair, drinks the lemonade in one gulp and regards Margaret with an uncharacteristic frown.

Margaret remembers her mother's ubiquitous remedy for social awkwardness. "Have you eaten? There's still some fresh pea soup and arugula salad—all from the garden. Easy to warm up. The soup, I mean, not the salad." How stupid can she sound?

"Thanks, I'm fine. Just came to say good-bye."

Margaret stops breathing. She shakes herself. What's wrong with her? She hardly knows Angela, yet feels unaccountably attached.

The young woman takes Margaret's hands, holding tightly.

"Where are you going?" She reaches for good cheer, "On a vacation?"

"Indonesia, I've got a new assignment." Her aspect lightens with the confession.

Margaret pulls over another plastic chair, invites Angela to sit in the shade.

"Lovely warm evening." Margaret practices yoga breathing to mask her disappointment.

"Divine." Angela nods.

"Why Indonesia?" She doesn't think she's ever processed a letter from that long nation of far-flung islands.

"Rickshaw driver in Surabaya."

"Rickshaw? You repair rickshaws, too?"

"You still don't understand, do you, Margaret?"

"Guess not." She closes her eyes, savoring the fragrances of early summer.

"Little darlin', I don't usually need to come out to people after so long."

"Oh, it's fine, I mean I've always figured you were a lesbian or bi or one of those new identities."

"Thanks," Angela grins. "I mean come out as your *Guardian Angel*."

Flummoxed, she blinks, then rushes ahead. "I'm a nonbeliever, myself."

"Cool. I'm not into conversion."

"What about propagating the faith?"

"No, no, no. I'm not one of those angels. Just your average agnostic kind. I get assignments all over—atheists, Jews, Sufis."

"*Average* angel?"

"Sure," Angela laughs, as one practiced at explanation. "There are arcane seraphs, cherubs, putties. And the New Age High Vibration spirit guides. I'm not in either camp."

Margaret pictures Cy's fine brandy in the little teak cabinet. "Would you like a cognac?"

"No thanks, but go ahead. You look like you could use one."

In the kitchen, Margaret splashes cold water on her face.

Shakily she fills a wine goblet with cognac, then wonders if this is too much. The fumes have a pleasant effect.

Back in the sunny garden, she raises a glass to Angela. "Cheers!" The hot, smoky liquid sears her throat; it's all she can do to keep from coughing. "Now where were we? Oh, yes. So you have angels from both sides of the aisle, sort of thing?"

"Aisle? You churching me again? No need for aisles. Lots of space up there."

"Up there? Do you mean...Heaven?" Four, Five, Six, Seven...she hears Cy's baritone, "*All good children go to....*"

"Call it whatever."

"I don't want to call it anything," she bristles. "I don't want you to go. It's unfair, being abandoned again. I never asked you to hang around."

"You're my assignment."

"Who sent you? Rose or Valerie? They're Catholic."

"Believe me, they don't have that kind of mojo. I do know their G.A.s."

"G.A.?"

"Think, friend. You work at the P.O. and I'm a G.A."

"Oh, right. Does Pam have a G.A.?" Margaret takes another sip and realizes she's losing it. Carefully, she aims the amber liquid at a patch of weeds.

"Good move," Angela salutes her. "Everyone has a G.A. The man who sleeps in the park, the nightclub singer, the Queen of England."

"Even Dick Cheney?"

"That's snarky."

"You didn't answer my question." Maybe she should drink more often. Margaret is enjoying this new boldness.

"Yes, a few people do have rotating angels. The tough cases. Think how he wields that silver hammer."

"Hmmn, you're making sense in your own wacky way." Yes, she thinks, I believe her now.

"I promise to keep a close eye on you from Surabaya, but Abdul needs urgent attention from his *malaikat pelindung.*"

Margaret thinks back to the priority mail feather. The highway accident, the taxes, the fitness training. "*I have a couple of jobs, like a lot of coast people.*" You'd think honesty would be a requirement for an angel.

"Anyhow Margaret, now you're flying on your own."

She closes her eyes, sleepy from the cognac, enjoying the warmth, remembering how she and Cy used to sit out here after dinner, listening to the birds and naming the summer scents. He's still with her; she feels this. They've been through a rough patch together, but she's doing pretty well now.

The phone rings from inside the house, stirring Margaret. But the caller hangs up before she fully wakens.

She looks around, still sleepy, puzzled by the wine goblet and two empty lemonade glasses.

She should go in soon, but these days she tries to squeeze in every second of light. Summer always puts her in a good mood. The Bridge Group is fun. And the Spanish classes, something she should have done years ago. The girls are coming to dinner on Saturday. Pam wants them to take a cruise. At first she wasn't interested, but thinks, Indonesia, now there's a place she'd like to go.

Suddenly she looks up. Ah yes, the rewards of dusk. An *Elanus leucurus,* a lovely white tailed kite, hovering electrically at the far end of the garden, as light and quiet as the moon.

Iconoclast

"There went in two and two unto Noah into the ark,
the male and the female, as God had commanded Noah."
Genesis 7:9. King James Bible

Uçhisar, Cappadocia. A crisp March morning. Our twentieth anniversary. We really are here.

I slide gently from bed as sun begins to pink the sky. At the window I watch the rosy horizon relinquishing to a pale spring blue. Then. Balloons! Striped and polka dotted. Red, fuchsia, chartreuse and golden hot air balloons. Shimmering plump jewels ascending and floating over the Gaudi-like formations of porous rock.

Heaven is what I'd call this place. Gratitude is all I feel: for Layla; for twenty years of love; for finally spending our honeymoon in this mythical land we used to call Asia Minor. Home to Noah's family and his ark of creatures. Lapped by the Bosporus Straight, the Mediterranean, Aegean, Marmara and Black Seas. Birthplace of Layla's Kurdish grandparents who met in a Detroit Laundromat.

She's always dreamed of ancestral voices and people with familiar faces walking down the street. Light brown eyes; dark, wavy hair; long, elegant noses.

For my part, I dreamt of Noah and eggplant—or aubergine as they call it on the English menus here. Ah, this is the land of a thousand aubergine dishes.

"Hey, hey, where'd you go?" Layla sits up sleepily, the white sheet over one shoulder exposing a sweet brown breast.

"Stunning morning," I say. "Balloons!"

She pats the bed. "It's what? Dawn?" She's groggy. "And we're supposed to be on vacation. Please Beth, come back to bed."

I kiss her forehead, and tempted as I am by her dark, alert aureole and the warmth between those sheets, I decline. "Sorry, sweetheart. I'm wide awake. Think I'll stroll into town, get coffee and meet you back here—when—eight o'clock—for breakfast?"

"Deserted on my honeymoon," she moans, already halfway back to sleep. "Better make it nine."

I slip on my down jacket, perfect for spring at this high altitude.

Then, as if from a coma, her voice rises, "Be careful! Remember that kidnapped American photographer."

"Yes, sure," I answer softly, hoping she'll drift off to sleep. I don't remind her that the American was taken way out east of Gaziantep, hundreds of miles from here. "Your grandmother told you too many stories, darling. Sweet dreams."

The air is crisp, and I'm glad I brought a shawl, silk and cashmere according to the hobbled old merchant in Istanbul's Grand Bazar. Who knows? Whatever the fabric, it's warm and deep purple. A lush, aubergine shade.

The scruffy little coffee shop is surprisingly crowded.

Of course I'm the only woman. Bald men leaning on small tables, chatting softly in Turkish. In the background: an intricate Persian oud piece. I sniff the coffee in my miniature cup. Yes, enough to propel me right into the day. The first sip is sublime. Thick, black, Turkish sludge. Edges of the room suddenly sharpen. I smell musky tobacco, sweet honey and fresh yogurt. Heaven.

"Pardon, you look like a visitor here." He's tall, thin, red-haired. Midwestern accent. Wisconsin or Minnesota. His tweed jacket and horn-rimmed glasses are the perfect costume.

I do not want to chat. I want to continue sipping *kahve* and marveling that I am in Turkey. Fertile womb of civilizations. Ancient land of the Hittites, Assyrians, Jews, Romans, Byzantines, Kurds, Alevis, Sunnis, Shias, Orthodox Greeks, Armenians. Home to Holy Mary and the Apostle John.

"Parlez-vous français?"

Yep, his accent is quintessential Milwaukee.

He smiles earnestly, waiting.

No point in being petulant. "Yes, I'm visiting for a few weeks."

"American, hey," he sighs, "Great. Do you know the way to Göreme?"

I look through the intruder, willing him to disappear.

He tries again. "The UNESCO World Heritage Open Air Museum?"

He says this slowly as if recalling a page straight from *The Lonely Planet*. And I do mean straight.

Thing is, my entire life is about caring for people— the kids I counsel, their parents and lots of burned-out teachers in Philadelphia. Here I'm on vacation.

"They say walk through Pigeon Valley," I allow, "but...."

"Hmm." He frowns. His eyes look watery—watery sad or watery sick, I can't tell—and his hand trembles as he lifts the tiny cup. "I tried by that way yesterday and got lost. This is my first trip to Cappadocia, a world apart from the rest of Turkey. From the rest of the cosmos."

"You can walk along the road. Not as picturesque, but direct. That's what Layla and I are going to do."

"Ah," he says, expectantly.

It takes all my willpower not to invite him. The hazardous helping reflex. I swallow the rest of the coffee too fast and grab my purse. So much for savoring village color.

He nods good-bye. "Nice to meet you."

~

Our hotel serves breakfast in a charming brick room with a roaring fire, evoking the famous local underground caves. Eight tables are discreetly set apart in the windowless, lamp lit chamber.

The first to arrive, we take the corner spot.

Layla selects a fragrant lemon poppy seed muffin from the inviting basket. "Glad you made it back alive." She winks.

"Good sleep?"

"Delicious. Just missing one thing. The warm body next to me." She takes my hand.

I squeeze her long fingers. "This isn't Philly," I whisper. "You have to tamp down the PDA."

A waiter pads up and places two steaming omelets on our little table. "*Teşekkür ederim*," I say in my best Turkish. My only Turkish so far.

"You're welcome." He grins.

~

We've fantasized about visiting Turkey since we met. Layla ached to see her grandparents' land. She adores the rugs. Yes, I was hooked on the food, but I also felt a childhood tug from my church days, to see where Noah landed. Although access to Eastern Turkey—where our dreams reside—is prohibited, Cappadocia strangely feels close enough.

Both of us shed religion in college. Mine was evangelical Christianity. Layla was Kurdish Muslim on Mom's side and Nation of Islam on her dad's. Her brother Mika is still in the Nation. We both, in our separate ways, always felt we belonged here.

~

Mr. Lonely Planet ambles into the dining room, laden with maps, two newspapers, a paperback guide and a library book.

I concentrate on the delicious omelet. "Perfect," I coo to Layla, "golden on the outside and gooey on the inside."

"Like someone I know."

I blush. "Really now, cut that out. Save it for home— or for our fall trip to San Francisco."

"Hello again," calls the ginger-haired tourist. "I didn't know you were staying here."

Layla looks him over with practiced journalist eyes.

"Oh," he explains uneasily to her. "We met this morning in the coffee shop; we didn't introduce ourselves." He extends his hand, dropping books and papers. "My name is Richard Maxwell." He's distracted by Layla's beautiful face. A lot of people stare; some ask what ethnic mix created this woman with cherry wood skin, haunting pale eyes and softly curling hair.

I don't draw much curiosity since my blond locks and blue eyes bespeak a pretty common English-German partnership.

In spite of myself, I reach down and hand him his copy of *For Whom the Bell Tolls*.

Layla continues studying him. All she has to do is look and people yield, not knowing to what. "Where're you from?"

"Wisconsin. I teach history at Beloit."

"Beth Langley from Philadelphia. And this is my partner, Layla Waters."

He pulls up a chair, then places his books and papers on the floor. "Mind if I join you?"

Layla is quick. "Plenty of tables, Rick, if you want to spread out your library—over there or there." She points to the farthest tables.

"Richard, actually. And I wouldn't mind company. My wife stayed behind in Istanbul—for the museums. And, of course, the shopping. I could hardly pry her away from that damn covered bazaar."

Layla smiles thinly, unwilling to admit her fellow feeling.

Our waiter appears with an extra place setting and more muffins.

"So you must be on spring break." Cordiality is my professional reflex and liability. "When do you go back?" I'm hoping he'll say tomorrow.

"In fact, I'm on sabbatical, so I have all the time in the world, until late August."

Layla asks, "How do you like the novel?" Somehow, this seems a more polite question.

"Hemingway, one great writer. A classic. I've read everything he's written."

Layla digs into her eggs, handing the conversation back to me. I can just imagine what she'll say on the walk to Göreme.

~

I learned to read her expressions in college. Douglass completely transformed our lives. As a hyper Christian freshman, I was phobic about near occasions of sin. I graduated as a lesbian socialist with a full fellowship to grad school and a most unlikely lover.

President of the Black Caucus and two years older than I, stunning, brilliant Layla was thoroughly intimidating. Like everyone else, I admired her from afar. Late one evening we found ourselves walking in tandem back from the library. In the chilly darkness my shyness lifted. The following week we went out for pizza. Then a couple of movies. One threeday weekend, we checked in at the Starry Night budget hotel, and we've been together ever since. I chose a graduate program in Philadelphia because Layla had been recruited by *The Inquirer*. A fast, and as I would have said in the past, a "blessed" two decades.

~

Naturally, Richard tags along on our walk to the museum.

"Terrible sense of direction," he explains.

"I bet," Layla says archly.

"Hope you don't mind the company," he's speeding, looking better after a big breakfast and four cups of *kahve*. "I always find it more interesting to *share* an expedition."

"Especially on one's honeymoon," Layla mutters not quite under her breath.

"Oh, my, congratulations," he declares. "When did you get married? Can you do that in Pennsylvania? I know you can in Iowa and Massachusetts."

Layla pretends to clean a spot from her sunglasses.

"We've been together twenty years." I don't bother to express our queer disdain for bourgeois matrimony.

Eventually, Layla quit *The Inquirer* to do investigative work. For the last two years she's commuted to DC as the goto freelancer on the DIA, DHS, NSA, CIA. I'm still learning about the Bureau of Counter Terrorism and the National Reconnaissance Office and—hundreds—thousands—of other intelligence programs. Her articles are weighty, edgy and a little scary. I'm a worrier, so she spares me some background. Anyway, we both love our jobs and do pretty useful work. Nights and weekends, we enjoy our comfortable condo and wacky dog.

Each December, I send a donation to Douglass and a Christmas card to the Starry Night Hotel.

"Ah," he fills the silence. "Aren't we lucky with the weather?"

Neither of us responds.

"I mean, because it's an open air museum."

"Unh hunh," Layla allows.

Her resistance winds him up. "They have the best Byzantine art in Cappadocia. Frescoes and paintings dating from the 10th century."

"You've done your homework. Or do you teach *Turkish* art history?" I ask in spite of myself.

"The art, it's all part of studying a culture."

"Perhaps you can show us a thing or two," says Layla, making the most of our abduction.

"I'll try. Hey, thanks for letting me join you."

"It's nothing." Layla shrugs, then glares at me.

Our trek takes us through a greening valley. It's longer than we expected—four miles—and we arrive at the same time as four coaches.

"Let's start at the end," Richard says. "That way, we'll avoid crowding into those little churches with the organized tours."

"Good idea." Layla nods, almost warming up.

Richard, of course, knows all about the Byzantine bishops and saints and icons. He's full of information, but not pedantic. Probably a good teacher.

He promises Dark Church is stunning. "It's worth waiting for." He snaps his fingers nervously.

Richard is right. Under protective dim candle light, the ceiling murals are astonishing, yet nothing compared to the almost living scene of the crucifixion above the altar. The iconoclasts missed this church in their rampage, beheading and defacing Christian images.

Four hours pass, and we're starving.

Our companion knows a café in the Cave Hotel and greets the owner Mehmet by name.

"Richard, you are back! And with beautiful women. Come, come to my best table, here against the wall."

Richard ushers us in as if he's the local pasha. "What would you like to eat?"

"I don't care as long as it's aubergine," I proclaim.

Layla cracks, "I'll have a bacon cheeseburger." Registering Mehmet's troubled eyes, she quickly adds. "Joke. I like all the food in this country. What do you recommend?"

Two hours later we are sated.

Throughout the lavish lunch, something nags at me. "Richard, this morning you said you didn't know the way to Göreme."

He takes a sip of the dark purple wine. "Yes."

"But you've been to this restaurant." I'm getting nervous. "You know Mehmet."

The men exchange cursory glances.

Richard starts laughing.

Mehmet blanches, retreats to the kitchen.

"You know my terrible sense of direction," Richard falters, staring absently at Mehmet's empty chair. "Yesterday I got off the bus here, I mean, uh, outside Göreme, instead of in Uçhisar at our hotel."

"That's right," Mehmet confirms, carrying a tray of coffee and sweets. "At lunchtime. So Richard ate. And since it was early in the season and he was my only customer, I drove him to Uçhisar."

I cock my head waiting for Layla's response. She's blissed out by the dessert.

"Rose petals, sugar, almonds. Perfect," she purrs deliriously.

"You know?" Mehmet throws up his hands in surprise. "You know this dish?"

"My grandmother made this for birthdays."

"A Kurdish dessert," observes Richard.

"Yes," she grins.

"Of course. Layla is a Kurdish name," Mehmet muses.

She smiles, takes another bite. "My grandparents were born east of here."

"Really," remarks Richard. Then adds for some reason, "I have a lot of Kurdish friends."

Why does he make me so anxious? He's just an awkward nerdy guy, right?

By late afternoon, we manage a successful escape. Richard does not follow us into the hammam.

Quiet. Yet another place where we are the only customers. Layla was right about traveling off season.

First: the facials. A small young woman wearing a turquoise hijab paints our foreheads, noses, cheeks and chins in a grainy substance with a rude odor. Then she leads us to the sauna. It's pretty much like our YWCA sauna except for the presence of a majestically large woman in a black bra and lace-trimmed black panties.

Layla raises her killer eyebrows.

The woman ignores us. She exits every five minutes to shower and returns quickly with wet hair. Finally, she leaves for good.

We hear a rap on the sauna door.

It's our midnight negligee lady. She takes my hand and whispers, "*Seni seviyorum.*"

I smile, completely lost, but this is just a bath house, nothing to worry about.

She tightens her grip on my fingers. "That means, 'I love you,' in Turkish."

"*Teşekkür ederim,*" I murmur.

"My name is Aydan, meaning 'moonlight.'"

"Nice to meet you." I don't reveal the meaning of my name— house of figs—to her or anyone else. "I'm Beth."

"This I know."

She scrubs me as if I were a muddy five year old— between my toes, behind my ears—then orders me to lie on the marble slab. Across the room, Layla is getting similar treatment. All of a sudden, I'm pummeled by a huge plastic bag of sudsy water. Again. And again. And again.

Aydan sits me on another marble surface, pours clean water over my head and torso as I watch the soap gurgle down a large drain in the stone floor.

Layla is already stretched out on the massage table on the other side of a latticed room divider.

"You OK?" she asks.

"Clean," I say, "and apparently well-loved."

"What?"

Our masseuses swish in. Kushi from Krgyzstan diagnoses my back as "a catastrophe." After twenty minutes she says, "I think you need another half hour."

I admit, Derinkuyu is my idea. I've always loved hidden things, and this ancient city is ten stories underground.

We've rented a car for the expedition: as we drive through the emerald countryside we find snow clustered around tree trunks and in crevasses in this season between winter and spring. A few purple and blue wildflowers grow low to the ground.

"OK." Layla looks at me pointedly from the driver's seat; I want her to focus on the twisting road. "I'll visit this ancient town for you because you agreed to have dinner at the Museum Hotel for me, but I'm not looking forward to it."

Although I fret about prices at the posh hotel restaurant, I've agreed. You learn compromise during twenty years.

"At least we have privacy today." She shakes her head. "I really thought Richard was going to trail us into the hammam."

I laugh at the image of him pummeled with soapsuds by those sturdy women. "He's just a lonely guy." I'm following Khushi's advice to lighten up.

"I don't know." Her eyes grow serious. There's something weird about him."

Along with the entrance ticket, we each accept a plastic-wrapped hand sanitizer wipe. I've collected five of these wipes at different tourist sights. Are they meant to protect us or the museums? We pass through a metal detector and enter the cool, dark cave where the last vestiges of a traditional museum disappear.

"Can't see a fucking thing," groans Layla.

"*Voila!*" I switch on a halogen flashlight.

"I've always said my girl was brilliant."

"And practical," declares a man behind us.

My stomach flips.

"Professor Maxwell, I presume?" Layla doesn't bother to turn around.

"From your voices, I'd guess Bethany Langley and Layla Waters."

Lightheaded, I wonder how he knows my birth name. Everyone assumes it's Elizabeth, and I never reveal my tribe of raging born-again sibs: Constance, Beulah, Caleb, Gideon and Zachariah.

"Clever to bring a flashlight." He fills the silence. "If you don't mind sharing your illumination, I'll share some of mine about this astonishing site."

"You're an expert on underground cities?" Layla assesses him.

He's wearing a striped sweater over his checked shirt, and I'm grateful I can't make out the colors in the dim light. He seems even taller and wraith-like in this spooky atmosphere.

"I've read up on the place, but I'm no expert."

Resigned, Layla concedes, "Lead on."

"The site goes back to 2,000 BC. The Hittites built here first, digging into the porous rock to make winter shelter for themselves and their animals. They settled the top two floors."

One by one, we slither down narrow, low-ceilinged passages toward the floors and civilizations below.

"One long chamber," he explains, "was a classroom. Early Christians hid down on this level from the Romans."

Throughout the rooms and passageways, we find air holes reaching to the sky, to admit light, to release smoke.

He takes our photo in front of the baptismal font. He says he wants to send it to his wife, to show her what she's missing.

So much in this country happens *underground*. The hammam yesterday. Derinkuyu today. Although the mysteries of Turkey always attracted me, the hiding, the secrecy is a bit unnerving.

"They have everything: bedrooms, kitchens, wine presses, animal stalls," He says. "The Byzantine Christians were the ones who dug the very bottom floor, hiding from the Muslims, who—depending on your politics—were conquerors or invaders."

"And yours would be?" Why am I so testy?

"Pardon?" He snaps his fingers nervously.

"Your politics?"

He steps back. "I'm a registered independent, but actually I'm a wishy-washy liberal like most of us."

Us. I wonder.

Layla is moaning.

I rush over. I've been so preoccupied with Richard that I just now notice she's sweaty and trembling.

"Oh, god." She slips to the floor.

"Are you OK?" He bends down to take her hand.

"It's just," she wheezes, "that I'm having trouble breath… breathing."

"Are you claustrophobic?" He's acting like Dr. *Médecin sans Frontières*.

"No!" she snaps as if he inquired about an STD.

"Some people react."

She takes a long breath. "This place is kind of freaky. Imagine 20,000 people burrowed together down here."

"Take my arm," he says, all bedside manner. "We'll walk slowly. You'll be in the fresh air before you know it."

Outside, the late morning light is blinding.

"Breathe deeply," he instructs, "slowly."

Color returns to her cheeks and focus to her eyes.

"Gee, thanks," Layla rubs her temples. "I knew I didn't like heights but this is my first—and last— underground city." She continues hectically, "I guess I'm a basically functional person; there isn't much call to climb ten stories down into the earth."

I wonder how deep missile silos are.

"This happens to many people." His hand is still on her shoulder, the red curly hairs creeping from the cuff of his green-checked shirt down to his manicured nails.

We stand silent and awkward for a moment.

"Thanks Richard," Layla says with renewed confidence. "Nice to see you. We're off to Soğanlı for lunch and some above ground churches. Enjoy your adventures."

As I open the door to our rental car, he calls to us.

"If I'm not intruding…."

I get in the car, pretending not to hear.

"Yes, Richard, what is it?" Suddenly, she's solicitous.

"I have an old bus schedule, and it turns out I'll be waiting another two hours. I was going to those churches— some of my favorites—9th to 13th century—too." He looks pointedly at the empty back seat.

"Hop in," she says, as if he were an old friend.

He buckles the seat belt and leans forward. "I know a café where we can get great lentil soup and *Patlicanli Pilav* oozing with onion and eggplant."

"I bet you do," I say, almost *sotto voce*.

Despite my big attitude, I enjoy lunch.

He's as curious as ever, asking about life in Philadelphia. Our work. Again, he knows just the right wine to order, and Layla, still ascending from Derinkuyu, enjoys several glasses.

"I admire good reporting." He's leaning a little too close to her. "It's like being an historian, only in real time. I guess you always have to be 'on;' anyone could be a source."

"Not really. Here, for instance, Beth and I are just on holiday."

"Oh." He's momentarily disconcerted. Then: "Tell me more about your family. Where in Turkey were they from?"

"Grandfather was born in Hani. Grandmother left the Dersim region in the 1930s."

"Ah, the famous Dersim Rebellion. Was your grandmother a hero for the cause?"

I fiddle with the pepper mill, untwisting the bottom to look for a hidden microphone.

"No, but she was proud of her father's involvement. Quite a fiery guy, apparently."

I've never heard of this relative, her great-grandfather, let alone the famous rebellion. The wine—and the relief of escaping Derkinkuyu— are having strange effects on Layla, who is cryptic at best with strange men.

"Those were hard times in Turkey." Richard nods. "But now the country is so open."

Naturally Richard knows all about the churches. He explains which frescoes were defaced by Muslim iconoclasts and which by more recent vandals. Still much of the ancient paint—deep blues as well as the bloody reds—survive.

At a higher elevation now, we're bundled in coats and scarves. The photos Richard takes make us look like Siberian refugees. I doubt his wife will feel she's missed much.

Driving back to Uçhisar, past snow-covered fields, I gaze at the late sun blazing in the golden grasses.

"Thanks for letting me tag along."

"No problem," says Layla. "Our luck to find a whiz in Turkish history."

"Hardly a whiz."

"But you're a professor at Beloit," I declare. I feel prickly, perhaps it's the red wine headache. "Speaking of the college, doesn't Nick Adams teach literature there? He'd be an old man now. But it's a small campus, right?"

"Now that you mention it, I think I met him at a reception." He drums his fingers on the door handle. "So many of these social functions, you know."

Layla is grinning, looking like her old self. "Richard, as thanks for guiding us around, not to mention for rescuing me from Derinkuyu, let us take you out to dinner tonight."

"Why I'd love…."

I interrupt. "Layla, don't you remember we got the last reservation at the Museum Hotel?"

She stares at me. "We could go somewhere else."

"You promised the Museum Hotel. Don't you remember, for my birthday?" I'm frightened now by all the coincidences and inconsistencies. And determined to dodge Richard—or whatever his real name is—from now on.

"Riiight," she says finally tuning into my urgency. "How did I forget? Sorry, Richard, but thanks for everything."

"My pleasure," he says in that forlorn Mr. Lonely Planet voice.

~

This last evening, I try to concentrate on the beautiful village. I listen to the percussion of our heels on the cobblestones as we walk from dinner to our room. A sliver of moon shines along with Jupiter and Venus, and I recall the logo of the Starry Night Hotel.

Layla is softly humming "If I Ain't Got You."

I can't help myself, and soon Layla and I are arguing about Richard again.

"I'm usually the suspicious one with my journalistic trigger." Layla shakes her head. "He seems harmless. So there are a few discrepancies. You think he's what—CIA? MIA? MIT?" She laughs.

"A *few* discrepancies?"

"He was pretty useful in that goddamn cave."

I keep my voice low. "He's a helpless stranger on Monday morning and then gives us a complete tour of Göreme. He stalks us to Derinkuyu."

"*Stalks*? Come on. It's a small place. You run into people."

"How about 'Bethany?' No one's ever guessed my given name. You wouldn't even *believe* it at first."

"Maybe his family is fundamentalist, too."

"The guy who's read all of Hemingway cops to maybe meeting one of his fictional characters at a *Beloit Faculty Reception*?"

"Adams is a common name."

"Wake up, Layla. He was super curious about your NSA articles, Mika's work for the Nation, your Kurdish grandparents."

She takes my hand. "Darling, you were interested in those things when we met."

"Any of them could get you arrested here."

She laughs, "Calm down, Beth. Remember Khushi's hard work on your back? Besides, Turkey is a democracy, a NATO member, an American ally."

"He's probably wondering if our Layla is an American ally."

"Enough," she tickles my palm. "This is our last night. We'll be in Philly tomorrow. Let's enjoy these beautiful mountains under the stars."

I gaze at the bright sky and remember the first Cappadocian dawn of dazzling balloons. I try to be grateful that we truly are here, in the land of our dreams.

~

Damn. The flight from Kayseri lands late, so we have to sprint across the Istanbul airport. Sprint as fast as you can, lugging big suitcases stuffed with rugs, woven pillow cases and ceramics.

Check-in goes smoothly.

The security line isn't long.

"We'll make it easily," Layla says. "Time for a latte and one more baklava."

"Maybe." I'm sweating despite the aggressive air conditioning. Pulling out the hand sanitizer from Derinkuyu, I wipe my forehead. "You still have your passport? Your boarding pass?"

"Of course! What's going on with you, Beth? We're taking a simple, non-stop flight to New York. We've got good seats at the front of economy. We'll be fine."

Obviously, she's right. Security is a breeze. Now we have seventy minutes before the flight, plenty of time for coffee and browsing the duty free chocolate for our dog-sitter.

"Sorry, don't know what got into me."

"You've stopped fantasizing about J. Edgar Jr?"

"Yeah, yeah." I rub my tired eyes.

"Coffee?" she offers.

"No, I'll watch the carry-ons. I don't want to get too wired before the flight."

As she walks away, I hear a child giggling. I turn to find a woman waving a yellow balloon animal at her toddler.

A sports team—young boys in green uniforms—are laughing and jiving outside the electronics store.

Beyond them, in a corner, I notice a uniformed man listening closely to a tall, thin guy in a baseball cap with his back to me. I try not to stare. Try not to watch the skinny guy snapping his fingers.

Suddenly, the world turns red and silent.

The men are both running toward the coffee bar.

Layla looks up, startled.

The click of handcuffs echoes across the Duty Free zone. Some travelers stare. Others turn away quickly.

I run toward them, dragging the briefcases and backpacks, shouting, "No, no, no!"

Out of the blue, a round woman uncannily resembling Aydan from the hammam takes my elbow. "Relax. They will just ask her a few questions. But your friend may miss the flight." She checks the baggage tags and hands Layla's carry-ons to another woman. "I will escort you to the gate." There's a compact black pistol at her waist.

"Layla, Layla," I scream.

She turns, tugging away from the man in uniform. Richard has disappeared. "Call Uncle Daras," she shouts. "As soon as you land. And Mika."

I pull away, but the guard's grip is too tight. "Yes, yes." Tears stream down my cheeks. I can't leave her. But Aydan's sister gives me no choice. "Oh, Layla, Layla."

"Come!" the woman demands, yanking me toward the gate.

I stand firm, turning back, but Layla is nowhere in sight.

La Fourmi Faim

It's a sunny April day at Le Marché d'Apt, the oldest continuous market in Europe, held *chaque samedi* for over 900 years, a market that has seen many young people grow into old people. Today it's crowded with local shoppers, as well as with villagers from nearby towns and perhaps a score of foreign visitors.

Ah, yes, there he is—Thierry.

Thierry has driven over from Ménerbes, out of habit, even though Mireille has been gone nine months. He begins shopping, as *she* always did, at the Arab stalls, because the excellent produce is better priced and because so many French people spurn these women in *hijabs* and men in *djellabas*. He already has most of what he needs for the week, but it's never a genuine Saturday if he doesn't chat with Fazad at his *Halal poulet* stall. He also looks forward to the weekly lecture from Hortense about her olives. Since the *fromage* stand is adjacent to Hortense's, who can blame him for selecting some *tome de montagne* and his favorite, sinful *epoises*, for Sunday lunch? Just as he advises patients to go lightly on the *fromage*, he requests modest portions.

A doctor in a small Luberon village for forty years, generous and attentive, Thierry is cherished by his patients. Work is fulfilling. But *les Week-Ends* are hard. Empty after Mireille's death, as would be expected. Thierry enjoys the exchanges with the garrulous vendors as well as with the occasional neighbor.

Nearby two young women, Jessica and Hailey, are grinning, elated to arrive at the height of morning commerce and conviviality. Hailey insists that they also visit the *vielle ville*, nestled behind the walled buildings. She wants to see the 11th century Cathedral, 18th century *Bouquerie* and 16th century *Tour de l'Horloge*. She is hungry for the legendary *fruits confits* but is worried about her bulging suitcase. Jessica, grateful for her friend's travel acumen, follows any itinerary as long as Hailey agrees to stop at least twice a day for *café et croissants ou pains et confitures*.

It's right here, by the cheeses, that they notice one another. Or don't, depending on your point of view, your degree of candor.

Jessica, tired of Hailey's dithering over the *fruits confits*, glances at the attractive silver-haired man in the tweed jacket and red muffler, pricked by recognition, no, rather by a vague intuition. Shouldn't someone his age wear a hat in chilly weather? Monsieur is studying the cheeses intently. Before he looks up, Jessica turns back to Hailey and advises against the candied fruits.

American voices carry, and her accent startles him. This lovely young Asian woman reminds him of a long ago friend. There's something familiar about *both* these *jeunes femmes*, both wearing jeans and sneakers; the short haired one in the pink parka and the other with long red locks shimmering over the shiny pillows of her black down jacket. He observes their closeness, the teasing and laughter, sensing he's known them longer than they've known each other. He has to restrain himself from welcoming them to France. Ridiculous. Always a reserved man, he's startled by this oddly sociable impulse and immediately turns down toward the linen stall. He promised his daughter in Sydney an embroidered table cloth.

"Of course you're right," sighs Hailey. "But aren't the glittery colors—those brilliant reds, oranges, yellows— tantalizing?"

Jessica nods, distracted as the old man threads his way through the crowd. "Maybe they'll sell them at Duty Free when we leave in May. Fresher that way."

Hailey points to the next stall—"Yum, look at that soap—which we also won't buy today—lavender, rose, lemon verbena. Oh, *smell* them!"

Thierry carries his shopping bag into the new café recommended by Fazad. *La Fourmi Faim.* so many places are named for La Cigale, he feels an odd, underdoggish sympathy for the small bistro. He chooses a place at the back corner of the patio, ideal for watching the Saturday crowds.

"*Regardez!*" Jessica exclaims. "*La Fourmi Faim.* Remember La

Fontaine's fable?" Grandma read her one fable a night in English, all of them before kindergarten. Sometimes she thinks this is why she studies folklore.

Hailey reviews the agenda: the Tower, cathedral, shops. She checks her watch.

Jessica frowns. "You promised—*a croissant et du café*—at the market." She takes Hailey's hand then notices the old man chatting to a waiter. "Come," she says and tugs her friend. "This table looks perfect."

Thierry, recognizing the voice, looks up and can't help smiling.

"*Bonjour!*" Jessica tries to sing the greeting the way French women do, fluting the last syllable.

"*Bonjour à vous!*" He pauses, about to say *Mesdemoiselles*, then remembers his daughter's lectures about *sexisme*. "*Bonjour, Mesdames.*"

As the waiter takes their orders, Thierry regrets his lost solitude. But these two do take him back.

Nordic Lena—oh, those stunning blonde de fraise locks, served him in a tavern on Hennepin Avenue in Minneapolis. Lena loved his "exotic accent." She explained that the street was named after that 17th century Père Hennepin. A few years older than Thierry, Lena had her own apartment and quite modern ideas about free love.

The girl in Seattle had a delightful name. "Ping." Ideal for her petit frame and bright almond eyes.

She explained, "In Chinese, 'Ping' means 'peaceful' or 'fair' or 'apple' depending on which of my aunts you consult." She spoke fluent French as well as Mandarin and English. Ping showed him the Pike Street Market, Green Lake, the Space Needle. He often suggested stopping for a chat over tea or coffee.

Ping promised something more enticing than free love: a rendezvous in Paris the next year when she would study abroad. It was a long twelve months of letters; hers in his language and his in hers. Thierry's English improved immeasurably as did his optimism about the future.

His reverie is broken by a voice, "*Pardonnez moi, mais nous avons besoins de direction à la gare routière convenable.*"

He can't help himself. He knows it's rude, that he should allow her to continue in French, but he feels the strain in her voice. And it's been two or three years since he's had a proper conversation in English.

"I'd be happy to direct you. By the way, my name is Thierry Boucher."

"Jessica Miyasaki," she says.

Miyasaki, he knows, is a Japanese name, and he wonders why this girl brought back Ping so palpably. He covers his disappointment with a gallant, "*Enchanté.*"

"I'm Hailey Gulbrandsen. We're grad school roommates in Minneapolis, but Jessica is from Seattle."

Jessica grins. "I've trained her to say that. Seattleites are super-chauvinistic."

"Ah, Seattle—Mount Rainier. And Minneapolis—*Père Hennepin.*"

"Oh, my," Jessica laughs. "He was a Franciscan Recollect there. How did you know?"

"As a student, I was inspired by the strikes in Paris then headed to your country to explore *la contre-culture.* I took a Greyhound from New York to Chicago just in time for the crazy Democratic Convention. Then to Madison. Minneapolis. Missoula. Finally Seattle. Everywhere people were so hospitable."

"The reverse of our trip," Hailey declares.

"Yes, forty-five years ago." He looks wistful.

Forty-five years, thinks Jessica. He doesn't look that elderly.

Soon, somehow, they are at the same table, ordering *plus de croissants* and chatting about international travel.

Thierry, wary of being intrusive, distances himself with the safe, intergenerational question, "What do you study at university?"

"I'm in the social work program," says Hailey. "Jessica's doing her Ph.D. in literature."

Thierry nods, then smiles at their bright, open faces. "Poetry or novels?"

"*Je ne sais pas.*" Jessica feels tongue-tied. Explaining "folklorist" to people is complicated.

The waiter brings fragrant croissants with fresh coffees.

"Who are your favorite writers?" He persists gallantly.

"I love Seamus Heaney, Toni Morrison, Haruki Murakami."

Struggling to come up with a French writer, she remembers slogging through *La Peste*. "And naturally, Albert Camus."

"Camus! Excellent taste." He's delighted. "Did you know Camus lived not far from here in the village of Lourmarin?"

"Really," Jessica blushes at her fib.

Hailey watches, braiding the tassels of her shawl. She remembers Jessica's tormented week reading *La Peste*.

"If you'd care to see Lourmarin and make *un petit tour du Luberon*," Thierry can't believe he is saying this, "I would be happy to drive you about and bring you back to the Apt station."

Hailey drops the end of her shawl. "Thanks so much, but we can't intrude on your day." She tries to catch Jessica's eye. "I'm sure you have better things to do—with your family or your work."

"I'm a doctor and no longer schedule Saturday hours. My children are continents away, and my lovely wife died nine months ago."

"So sorry for your loss," Hailey murmurs.

"Yes," Jessica adds. How very hard. I can't imagine."

Of course she can't imagine. The early years struggling to be accepted in Ménerbes, the joy and terror of raising two children, the sadness when they left for university and opposite ends of the earth. The relief of having the house to themselves. Decades of mostly happy days, of passionate and cozy nights. Dreams of the trips they would take in retirement. Dreams. He still sees her at night, feels she's holding tight, then he wakes.

He realizes they expect a reply. "Thank you" is all he can manage, holding back surprising tears. Grief assails him at such odd moments.

"A doctor," Jessica nods to Hailey, as if to reassure them both that he is a safe, responsible man. "What is your specialty?"

"Family practice, as you say. Not the most lucrative but for me the most interesting."

"William Carlos Williams, an American poet and fiction writer, had a family practice." Hailey reports neutrally, kicking Jessica under the table.

Jessica ignores her.

"Thanks so much for the invitation, but we do need to get back to the hostel this afternoon."

Jessica studies her friend. "We'll be *fine*, Hailey. We have our cell phones. I'll call the hostel and tell them we'll be a little later that we thought. This tour sounds awesome. Please let's join *le docteur* for a couple of hours."

Thierry is troubled. "Discord between friends! What calamity have I caused? Perhaps you would like to discuss this privately? I must collect something at the shop. Why don't I do that and return for your decision?"

"Sure," Jessica says. "And why don't you leave your groceries here. No sense in lugging them around."

Mireille always told him he was an innocent. Of course Hailey might be worried for her safety. To them he's a complete stranger, despite the curious affinity he feels.

They watch him thread through the market crowd, waving to vendors and shoppers.

Jessica pleads, "He's a harmless old man. A doctor. Someone who reads literature!"

"Hitler had a huge library."

"Oh, come on," Jessica sips the last of her café, craving another cup.

Hailey sighs heavily. "I don't mean to be unfriendly, but I was looking forward to exploring with you today. The Tour, the Cathedral. I love talking about our discoveries over dinner, and now you want to add a stranger. I don't know. Aren't I enough?"

Jessica winks and squeezes Hailey's hand, "You *know* you're my BFF."

Hailey pretends to search her wallet for something.

Jessica feathers her blue-black bangs. "He's lonely. His wife just died. His kids are far away."

"But Jess, he looks at you in this intense, I don't know, weirdly *intimate* way."

"I'm sure he's fine. Besides we have the kazoos."

The kazoos were Hailey's inspiration. Whenever they hitched with a driver who tried to make a move in the front seat, the girl in the back would pull out her kazoo and start to play. The sound was so ridiculously irritating that driver recovered their manners. On the downside, they were usually dumped at the next exit.

"OK," Hailey relents. "Let's be careful, though. One of us should be following along with GPS."

"You are so careful, Hailey."

Of course I'm careful with the love of my life, she wants to say, doesn't say, may never say. It's enough that they have this month together, that they're returning to their sweet apartment in Uptown. Enough for now, anyway.

Strolling back from the hat shop, Thierry shakes his head at his forwardness. What's got into him? An exquisite young woman in Seattle almost half-a-century ago. What are sentimental memories compared to his fortunate, loving, long marriage with Mireille?

At home, he aches with grief in their empty bedroom, kitchen and garden. How can he live the rest of his life without her? These sorrowful days, he cringes at condoling nostrums he has offered patients over the years: grief groups, travel, time.

Time! Most painful of all. The first weeks and even months were numbness. Now each day he feels as if his flayed skin is exposed to caustic rains. Sleep is almost impossible. And waking is a bitterness—especially after those nights when Mireille visits him: they are sharing breakfast or walking on a Sunday or shopping in Apt. When he awakens, he drops into a deep cold well. No matter how hard he tries, he cannot materialize her sweet self. So lately, he bounds from bed at dawn, goes to the café, and arrives at the *cabinet* an hour early, much to the distress of his nurse, who has begun offering motherly self-care advice.

Thierry runs his fingers over the fine reweaving in his grey Harris Tweed cap, a gift from Mireille for his twenty-fifth birthday.

"Oh, no, I will look like an old man," he burst out laughing, then watched her face fall. From then on, he wore it every day—autumn, winter and spring—even as he became, if not an old man, an older one.

He shall be convincing when he lies to the young ladies, saying he's absentmindedly forgotten an afternoon engagement.

Jessica waves as he approaches the café.

He tips his hat.

Before he can beg their pardon with his fabricated commitment, Jessica is chattering, "We absolutely insist on contributing to the gas."

Momentarily baffled, he finally declares, "Ah, *l'essence. Mais non. Lourmarin, ce n'est pas loin d'ici.*"

"Still, we insist," Jessica continues.

"It's what friends do at home when they travel together." Hailey resolutely supports Jessica. Possessiveness can kill a relationship.

Friends, he's nonplussed. Until now the girls have been more like apparitions.

Soon the three are ambling along the cobbled streets of Lourmarin. The golden buildings gleam after yesterday's storm. In every direction, they enjoy views of greening hills and manicured farms.

The sun is full; they shed their jackets.

Thierry wishes he had worn a newer shirt, the blue one Mireille gave him for his last birthday.

Hailey thinks Jessica looks super in her purple turtleneck.

Thierry points across the valley, in the direction of rival villages, recounting long ago battles between the Catholics of Bonnieux and the Protestants of Lacoste.

"Like the North of Ireland," Hailey frowns. "Crazy. When did hostilities end?"

He admires the passionate curiosity of both girls. So wise and secure, just as he was on that Greyhound.

Ping boarded the bus on the last leg of his All-American Tour.

He willed her to sit next to him, and she did. Of course she loved his French accent. And when she responded in his own language, he was just mildly surprised. Such is the entitlement of the young.

"Tell us more about your American odyssey," Jessica asks. "What were your favorite places?"

Not missing a beat, he declares, "Minneapolis and Seattle."

"The Norwegian Corridor," giggles Hailey.

He looks confused.

"You picked our cities to please us," scolds Jessica.

"*Mais non.*" He blushes, remembering warm, sweet kisses from Lena and Ping. "Not at all."

"But you had a girl in each port, eh?" Hailey jokes.

"Would you care for a coffee?" he stalls.

Once the steaming cappuccinos arrive, he realizes he hasn't talked this much in ages.

"What about your romantic conquests?" Jessica teases.

Thierry blinks. Why not tell them? Mireille understood he'd been with others before her. Maybe she didn't know his deep and guilty ache for Ping, but she understood his early flings; they'd both enjoyed *aventures* in their youths.

"Lena in Minneapolis," he smiles, suddenly recalling her generous breasts.

"Lena?!" Hailey exclaims. "Are you sure that was her real name? Minnesota is rife with jokes about Lena—with Sven and Ole, our archetype bumpkins."

He shrugs. "Ping in Seattle. We were to meet in Paris the next year, but she got engaged. I stopped writing out of what I imagine to be chivalry but now know to be pride."

"How sad," Jessica murmurs, finishing her *café*.

"That was a long time ago. Another world. I had a fortunate life with Mireille and our daughters and my practice and…" he pauses, sweeping his hand across the pastures flecked with pinking fruit trees, and beyond to the dramatic mountain ridges, "the beautiful Luberon."

By the time they are driving to Ménerbes, Hailey has relinquished her suspicions. This kind, lonely man seems genuinely interested in each of them. He clearly loves sharing his stunning countryside.

First a stroll around the top of the village to admire the dramatic spectacle of still snowcapped Mont Ventoux, the graceful vineyards with their bare, dark gnarled wood. And, of course, the grand estates peeking from behind wrought iron gates as well as bizarre houses built into the old caves of Beaumettres.

They wind up sitting *al fresco* at La Veranda. 6pm, still light and warm.

Thierry stretches his arms wide around the early evening. Time for an aperitif, he thinks. But the girls are young. How young, he's lost the ability to tell, especially with foreigners. He orders a chamomile. Hailey does the same. Jessica asks for a *farigoule*.

"Yum, I taste thyme, orange, lemon and something, something else?"

"*Anise*," says Thierry, regretting more than a little that he did not take his favorite drink, a pleasure he has forgone since Mireille's death. Still, he must remain sober to drive them to Apt. Surprisingly, he is no longer tired. He could go on and on, as if he were a young man.

The guest room, indeed the whole house, has been creaking forlornly these months. They might enjoy a few nights in a real home. He wants to invite them but knows better.

Hailey is delighted with the charming town. "Jess, we should have stayed here instead of the other side of Apt. Ménerbes is the prettiest village we've seen."

"Ménerbes doesn't have a hostel, remember?"

Thierry leans back, listening. Perhaps they are *waiting* for an invitation. What harm in asking? He's spent his life being too cautious. He could have flown to Seattle and proposed to Ping. He finishes the tea in one gulp, as if it will sustain him, and ventures, "Mireille and I have/had a comfortable guest room. You're welcome to share it for a few nights...if you like."

"Oh, no, we couldn't." Hailey's flushed face belies her protest.

Jessica looks pensive.

A beat later, Hailey turns to her best friend. "Hey, why not? If Thierry is sure we're not imposing."

He shakes his head graciously, astonished by how fast his heart is beating. "No imposition at all. You are free to come and go as you please," he declares, completely refreshed. How wonderful to have the house occupied by more than memories. He hasn't felt this lighthearted in a year.

Hailey grins. "What a treat. To stay in a real French home." She wonders if their room will have a double bed.

Jessica clears her throat.

His spirits plummet.

She ignores Hailey's disappointed sigh. "Thank you, Thierry, but our bags are at the hostel. It's OK to return late in the day, but to miss a night would be taking beds from people who want them. *Merci encore, vous êtes très gentil.*"

"Oh, Jess, come on. We'll pay them for the night. We can get our bags tomorrow and…."

He has stopped listening. Studying the dusky sky he sees that suddenly the day is gone. "Jessica is right. I am being impractical. Of course you have your plans."

Sensing her companions' disappointment, Jessica adds. "Maybe next year? Hailey and I are coming back. We never got to see the *Bouquerie* and the *Tour de L'Horloge*. Do you have the internet? Do you have email?"

Certainly, he has email. Does she think he's a *dinosaure*? Unreasonably, he feels annoyed, abandoned. Yawning, he manages, "As you like."

So it's definite, Hailey's heart lifts. Next summer again. And who knows what will happen in the seasons in between.

Thierry notices that the blond girl is glowing, despite her disappointment.

Traveling back to Apt, through the shadowy evening, the three chat in *Français* and English and Franglish about the next stops on the young women's journey—Montpellier, Barcelona, Madrid.

Although he yearns for more of their company, Thierry feels invigorated, having shared the lively afternoon.

In Apt, from the train platform, they wave exuberantly—Lena and Ping—across forty-five years.

Thierry sits in his study bent over two creased black and white photos from the 60s. He switches to the bright faces on his cell phone. The young are getting younger. And he? He's slipped into the wrong story. How can he be this age? He's the same as always, with some small improvements. Of course, for his new friends the idea of mortality is even less credible than aging. Everything is possible, and the future is a long road ahead.

Beep. He's startled by an email alert. Then another. Facebook "friend requests" from Hailey and Jessica. How absurd! How sweet.

How interesting. He rarely consulted this joint account Mireille set up for them to stay in touch with their far flung daughters.

He pours another *farigoule*. Bad to indulge but it's been an eventful day.

Pressing a few more buttons, he sees the Facebook page emerges—a blue and white site busy with pictures and words and cartoons. A search function emerges.

Tentatively he spells out her name.

But she is not any of the Ping Lees or Lee Pings in Seattle. Perhaps she's too old for Facebook, too sophisticated. He doesn't dwell on other possibilities.

Instead he opens the Greyhound ad—even though he knows this is called clickbait. Does he use the internet, indeed!

Apparently the American coach now is a luxurious vehicle—with Wifi, individual electrical sockets and contoured seats. They've removed a row to provide extra leg room. That's something an old man can appreciate. His eye is caught by a photo of Bison grazing in a lush green field. Wyoming. A stunning, exotic world with gigantic mountains and wild rivers and antelope. He's never seen an antelope.

Hollow

"Hey, Shana."

She pretends to ignore the caller because she's just started a new canvas, and there's only an hour of good light left. But the strained cheer in her sister-in-law's voice is chilling.

"This is Belle, Shan. Pick up, OK?"

Who else with that peppy Georgia accent and her "Hey!"? Shana adores the kids and Belle, which is good because she's increasingly dubious about her brother Doug who, for some reason, Belle married fifteen years ago. The rest of the Morrisseys are gone. Unlucky genes, Doug says. A little too frequently.

Attention flitting between the phone and the canvas, Shana shivers.

"Quick call, promise," Belle tries again. "You're likely working."

Shana's grateful for Belle's understanding that making art is *work*. Doug keeps asking, *why don't you get a real job?* Actually, since the bank laid him off, he's stopped pestering. He's always been Mr. Financially Responsible, resolute to avoid Dad's spectacular bankruptcies. Now, like lots of people in this economy he's out of work.

Sighing, she lifts the receiver. "Hi, Belle, how's it going?"

"Fine, hon. The kids are great. But Doug's kind of down. It's the back pain. Last week the new doc said he was lucky to survive the accident. Anyway, damn meds make him depressed, irritable, so I'm calling for a favor."

Please god, not a visit. She's just finished her landscaping work on the Watson compound and cleared a whole week before she has to mow or prune again.

"It would be a blessing if we could come to the island *just for a night,* maybe on a weekend." Belle's talking fast and thick as she always does when she's nervous. "We could stay at that little cabin where the

Watsons stow their distant cousins or dog walkers. We wouldn't get in your hair. I'd take the kids away during the day—to the beach, into town for pizza—and I'd cook a bang-up dinner."

Belle, the Cordon Bleu chef, has had no problem finding work in Seattle's vast culinary wonderland after Doug's layoff. Weekends are usually her busiest times, Shana knows, so they must be desperate. Still, she hesitates.

This is your only family, she hears her mother say.

"The kids adored the ghost stories you told them last time," Belle rushes ahead. "They're always talking about Aunt Shana's haunted woods."

Why, exactly, did she invite them in January?

"It would be a tonic for all of us."

Shana gives in. "I'd love to see you and the kids, but I just began a series of small canvases. How about two weeks from now?"

"Anything." Belle starts to cry, then recovers. "We'll stop at the Farmer's Market to get some of those Early Girl tomatoes you love. What other treats can we bring?"

"Just yourselves."

Shana has learned with Belle; if you ask for a little parmesan, she brings a chunk the size of a doorstop. If you say, maybe a bottle of red, she presents six bottles of fancy Bordeaux.

"Hon, you know we'll arrive with goodies. Oh, and I have sort of news about Doug."

"Sort of?"

"He found a job. Four afternoons a week."

"At another bank?"

"No," she speeds up. "Sales."

"Sales?" Who would buy anything from her jittery brother?

Belle accelerates further. "At Northwest Rifle and Gun Exchange."

"Guns?"

"He's held the job two months. I waited to make sure it was permanent before telling you."

Shana can't let it go. "How do you feel about guns?"

"The paycheck restores his self-esteem and...." She seems to be floundering, "that Army training is paying off."

Shana and her mother had pleaded with him not to enlist. He lucked out with the Germany posting. Maybe they could tell this hot-headed, but sweet, guy wasn't combat material. And the Army did pay his way through business school.

"He's steadier. Says he feels like head of the house again."

Shana always admired his fiscal focus. She and Doug hated those middle-of-the-night family bunks to the next sleazy apartment when Dad's rent money ran out. Guns, she shakes her head. Yes, she does suffer from the oldest-siblingsyndrome: knowing what's best for everyone.

"Before you protest," Belle says, "I told him no guns on the island."

"You mean he has guns *at home*? With two kids around?"

"I hate it. He insists he needs a couple to be credible with management. He locks them in a safe on a high shelf in the bedroom closet."

Shana is speechless.

"Oh, hon, if you could see how the job restores his confidence. He's the good, responsible man I married again."

Except for the addiction to prescription meds and that volatile temper. She takes a sip of tepid green tea, then manages. "I'm glad he's less depressed."

Shana's heart goes out to Belle. Belle, who supervised the funeral arrangements for her burned beyond recognition parents-in-law after Dad ran off the highway on a route he'd driven for fifty years. Belle, who helped Shana nurse their younger sister Sally through the final stages of liver cancer. Yes, she'll host them for a weekend, for Belle and the kids. And for Doug, who in spite of everything, she loves and worries about.

Too restless for the canvas, she walks out to the deck finishing the tea. Sun gleams on spider webs laced through the lower limbs of copper beeches. She relishes the fresh, tart smells of this wild place, which has become a sanctuary from Seattle traffic and, usually, from family worries. Here at Fern Hill, she has discovered solitude and safety. Here she can paint. Here she is her own person, Shana Morrissey, artist and occasional groundskeeper.

Gratitude. Fresh air. Lustrous spider silk. Long, slow breaths. Shana rolls out her yoga mat and does six sun salutations, followed by a long stretchy pigeon pose and tells herself the demons have gone.

~

Of course she'll give them the main cabin. Coleen Watson always says, "Make yourself at home. Bring friends. I love sharing our beautiful place. Makes me feel better about leaving it for weeks at a time."

Shana spends all day Friday fiddling with the big house, making the beds, airing out rooms, picking flowers. She stocks the kitchen with coffee and tea; the bathroom with toilet paper and fresh towels. About four o'clock, she realizes two things: she hasn't eaten all day and she's looking forward to the visit. Maybe she's spent too long alone in the woods.

~

Late Saturday morning, deep into a new canvas, she's interrupted by a high pitched little voice.

Then another.

"Wheee! Wheee!"

"Wheee!"

A door slams shut.

"Come now, collect yourselves." Belle clutches Fanny and Charles. "Aunt Shana must be working. We don't want her to think we're a lunatic circus."

Still unnoticed, Shana watches from a side window on the second floor.

"Grrrr," laughs Charles. "I'll be the lion leaping flames."

"Squeak, squeak," Fanny yips at the top of her lungs. "I'm the mouse acrobat."

Doug slowly extricates himself from the car, as if leveraging a hefty package; those meds have put fifty pounds on Shana's sprinter brother. He grasps the door to steady his legs. "OK. OK." He shouts louder than all of them. "Simmer down. You heard your mother. Don't disturb Aunt Shana!"

"Welcome everyone," she calls, running into the yard.

Belle embraces her tightly. Then noticing her intensity, she laughs and draws back. "Great to see you, Shana. So good to be out of that car."

"Yeah, yeah, Aunt Shana," towheaded Charles grabs both her hands. "We thought the trip was *never* going to end." He's an eight-year-old version of his movie star mother.

"Hi, Aunt Shana." Fanny bear hugs her. Shana notices for the first time how much she resembles Doug when he was a boy. Thin and dark, with bright blue eyes. She's much taller than Shana was at eleven. A little stunner.

Doug is still clenching the car door. Shana knows he's steadying himself for his walk to the cottage. For the Morrissey weekend ahead. Sometimes Shana thinks Doug is better suited to a monastery than to complicated family life. If only he believed in a god or Buddha or something.

To lighten the mood, she announces, "I've set you up at the big cottage, right where you're parked."

"The mansion, Mommy!" Charles exclaims, then growls. "Lion is staying at the mansion."

Shana walks over, hugs her brother and offers a hand.

He nods, waves her away.

"Hi, Doug, great to see you." She tries again.

"You, too," he manages.

Belle frowns. "Are you sure, Shan? I mean this is where Mr. and Mrs. Watson live."

Coleen and Carter Watson are local aristocrats to Belle. Unpretentious friends to Shana. Famous in Seattle as progressive activists and philanthropists, you see their photos in *The Seattle Times*.

She shrugs at Belle's protest. "Colleen says to make my friends feel at home. The beds are made. The kitchen is supplied. Windows are open, just adjust them to your comfort."

"Thanks, Shana," Doug says in a thickened voice, hand heavily on her shoulder now.

She remembers the long ago loyal brother and tries not to recoil at his sour breath. She's filled with sadness and rage at these damn meds.

"OK," she snaps out of it. "Why don't you get settled? Unpack. Shower if you like. There are plenty of towels. And when you're ready, I have soup, salad, some cheeses."

"Pea soup?" asks Fanny, trying to look indifferent.

"What else but my favorite niece's favorite soup?"

Fanny hugs her aunt with Belle's intensity. After a month alone in these peaceful woods, Shana feels shy.

Charles pipes up. "She's your *only* niece, and *I'm* your only nephew."

"Quite right," Shana says, "and my favorite nephew who will be eating his favorite Swiss cheese. Now go explore the *mansion*, and I'll serve lunch in my cottage around noon."

"Holey cheese, Mom, did you hear?"

"Yes, Charles, don't get over-excited. You know Daddy needs calm."

Fanny clears the table after lunch. Charles runs into the living room and pulls out his iPod.

"Thanks, Shan, that really hits the spot," Doug slurs several words. "Now, if you don't mind, I may lie down for a bit."

She takes a deep breath to hide her sadness. "Please, make yourself at home. That was a long drive. You must be exhausted."

Belle insists on helping with the dishes. "Thanks for the invitation. You don't know what a treat this is. The kids have bubbled all week, and Doug has a good color to his face."

Shana doesn't comment on her brother's pallor. "This must be really hard on you, Belle—the accident, his slow recovery, the pain meds—you've been so solid. How's your job? The Chateau got a nice review last week."

"That was last month, dear Shana. Perhaps you and the elves have been in these woods too long. But seriously, I confess, I *love* the work. Doug wouldn't hear of me taking a job before...well, before what happened. Now I truly believe we have a more balanced marriage.

He's a super loving father and gets to spend time alone with the kids those nights I'm at the restaurant. That's a plus for everyone."

She knows Belle is a smart woman; sometimes, though, her optimism makes Shana think she drank the Kool-Aid.

"Enough about us. We'll leave you to your painting. I've got the afternoon planned. A walk on the beach. A visit to town. And remember, I'm cooking dinner tonight."

"You don't have to, Belle, we...."

"Hush, I can only imagine what this invasion feels like. My Uncle Harry was fierce about protecting his writing schedule. We'll pick up the last supper ingredients at that nice natural foods shop in the village. Dinner should be ready around seven. OK?"

"You're one organized dynamo, sister." She does like the word sister but says it softly.

"Takes one to know one."

Shana hears them crunching over the gravel toward the car and races to the deck to wave good-bye. She observes warily. Charles is insulated with his earbuds. Fanny's frilly dress is suitable for a school dance. "Squeak, squeak," she says to Charles' "Grr." Good thing she didn't have children. All that personality. Belle looks fit in her jag jeans and a light green pull-over. Doug, as always these days, appears a little odd. The red sweatshirt hangs over his butt, and there's a tumorous bulge in front. How has he put on so much weight?

~

Belle's feast surpasses gourmet. Fresh salmon perfectly poached and presented on a bed of tomatoes. Farro with shiitake mushrooms. Crisp green beans. A kaleidoscopic salad. Gelato for dessert.

After dinner, they play charades with the kids. Belle and Shana that is. One adult and one child on each team. Doug is more interested in finishing the gelato. First player is Fanny, who does "The Lion King." Charles hams up "Finding Nemo."

Then Cinderella sweeps the hearth. Belle rolls up her sleeves, then blushes, quickly tugging them down, to cover several bruises.

Fanny flinches, watching closely.

Belle tries on an imaginary slipper.

Shana and the kids giggle.

Next, they're all laughing hysterically at Charles' Little Mermaid.

Shana turns to Doug. His eyes have shut. The ice cream dish is tilting as chocolate and vanilla pool at his feet.

"Oh, Doug, Dougie," Belle rushes over and takes his bowl.

"What the hell?" he mumbles.

She places the bowl on a table and wipes the floor tiles with paper towels.

"Hey, I wasn't finished with that!" He grabs her wrist tightly.

"Daddy, it was dripping all over," Charles explains, standing between his parents. "You were falling asleep again."

"Don't talk to your father that way." Doug reddens. "Show some respect. I followed the game. Just now, Fanny was a great Lion King."

Charles sets his jaw.

"Doug dear," Belle pulls her hand free, "maybe we should go to bed."

"No, I'm fine. Sorry I closed my eyes a second. It was a long schlep here, all right?"

~

The next morning Belle has laid out a banquet for brunch.

The kids, after running around the woods for an hour, are starving. Even Doug looks eager to dig in, much more alert and lively than last night. Perhaps Shana exaggerates his unsteadiness.

Belle's centerpiece is a stunning array of sweet peas, wild greens, white and red berries from bushes up the hill. She must have been up for hours preparing the perfect meal.

Charles appears with the iPod.

"Unplug, little man," Doug chides. "You don't want Aunt Shana to think you're a space cadet."

"But Dad, I'm just getting to the good part...." He regards his father warily.

"You heard what I said!" Doug shouts, then reaches over as if to swat his son.

Fanny's eyes fill, and she helps herself to more wild rice.

Doug smiles thinly as Charles stows the iPod.

Belle sighs. "That's good, dear, now we can see your handsome ears. It's so much nicer when we're all *completely* present."

Doug, Shana wonders, is Doug completely present?

To her surprise, morning conversation is brisk and lively. Belle insists that they each tell a joke. The kids start laughing before they finish the first "Knock, knock."

Belle's pièce de résistance is a blackberry apple galette.

Doug reaches over, helping himself to a quarter of the pastry.

Shana starts to object, then realizes he has little enough pleasure.

Belle's brewed the coffee with chicory—now where did she find that?—and they're so engaged in tales of her famous patrons at Fern Hill that Shana doesn't notice Doug has nodded off until he starts snoring.

Charles pops in his earbuds.

Fanny makes an origami bird with her paper napkin.

Belle's face falls momentarily. Then she bounces back. "I think we'll leave a little early today—to beat the ferry line and the traffic. Sundays can be a bear."

"But Dad, he's asleep," Fanny winces.

"It's OK. I'll drive."

"He'll be mad," the girl trembles.

"Come help me clear the table," Belle calls.

Shana collects a couple of plates.

"No, no dishes, Shana. You've done enough. Thanks so very much for the lovely respite. It's meant a lot to us. All of us."

"Squeak, squeak, the mouse can help," giggles Fanny.

Alone with him now, Shana leans forward on the table studying her brother, wanting him to wake, to talk, to be her partner in sanity, the other Morrissey with lucky genes. They've fallen out of touch since their parents' death. Her fault, she knows because she can't shake a weird, irrational aversion she feels to him. His head is bent toward his chest, and the snoring takes on a high whistle. "Wake up, let's talk," she whispers, too quietly for him to hear above his wheezes and snuffles. Still, she waits.

~

After they leave, Shana tosses linens in the washing machine and hikes to the summit of the property. It's a mile and a half up a steep path, and her head is almost clear by the time she finds the spot Colleen calls Paradise Meadow. The Watsons have placed a handsomely carved wooden bench there. Shana sits, rewarded by the sight of Mount Rainier rising from the clouds. Below, Puget Sound is still and blue. Relax, she reminds herself. You've shared the sanctuary. Now enjoy your seclusion.

She's on a roll with these mini landscapes, already imagining how Anton might hang them at the opening and doesn't get around to a thorough cleaning of the main house for several days. She sees Belle has swept assiduously and wiped every surface to a shine.

Upstairs, the bedrooms are orderly, each window is cracked for air but not enough to admit mercurial Washington showers.

Likewise, the bathroom is spotless. She finds a cold pack compress tossed in the trash.

Maybe for one of Doug's headaches.

Making sure everything is perfect for the Watsons' return next week, she checks the TP supply under the sink. Four rolls. And behind them, something wrapped in a red sweatshirt.

The bundle might belong to the Watsons, but she doesn't remember noticing it when she stored her family supplies. She reaches in and withdraws something heavy. Suddenly she's enveloped by a familiar musky odor.

Sun streams through the stained glass skylight as she stands in the turquoise tiled master bathroom inhaling her brother's distinct sweat. Also lingering in the air are faint scents of Ginger Root oil and French vanilla candle wax. She's glad Belle treated herself to a bath. Gradually, she disentangles something from what she now recognizes as Doug's shirt.

She's staring at several magazines of bullets. In spite of herself, she studies them closely. She's seen these on TV. Three magazines of hollow nosed bullets. Shana shivers. They're just bullets, nothing harmful in themselves. She shakes away the senseless dread.

A deep breath. She dials their number.

Belle answers after one ring.

"Oh, Shana, lovely to hear your voice. I hope you got my thank you card. Such a refreshing weekend."

"Yes," she answers slowly, wishing she'd prepared what to say.

"Is something wrong, hon?"

"I did get the card. Thanks. Also…I found something."

A pause. Then, "Oh, no, that was my worst fear. He left them there."

"You knew?"

"Ohhh." She sounds exhausted. "Only when we got home. He promised not to bring a gun. Back here, he started to complain and swear about his missing bullets. I was stunned and demanded 'what the hell were you doing with a gun at Fern Hill?'"

Shana waits.

" 'Wild animals out there,' he told me. 'I'm looking after you guys.' "

Shana's head is spinning. She tells herself to focus, but she is the sane survivor in her family.

"I'm so sorry." Belle's voice is a whisper.

"What do I do with the bullets? I thought of taking them to the sheriff, but he might ask where I got them." She can't believe how shaky she feels. "I can't put them in recycling. I keep telling myself they're just bullets…."

Belle's tone is brisk, businesslike. "Listen, you're coming back to the city next week. Let's meet at Toaster's. I'll cash them in at the Exchange. We can use the money, to tell you the truth. I couldn't cover our gas bill last month."

Doug's worst nightmare, turning into his insolvent father.

"But won't he keep looking for the bullets?" Shana's voice quavers.

"I bet he's forgotten already. The tantrums only last a couple of days. He's on to some new battle now."

Shana's heart sinks deeper. What's going on with her lost brother? With the whole family?

"I'm so sorry to involve you, Shan."

"Oh, Belle, I didn't know money was still a problem with you both working."

"Those meds aren't cheap."

"Oh, god, how are you faring?" She's completely unmoored. "Are you getting any support? Seeing a therapist?"

"We don't have money for counseling," she snaps as if Shana has suggested flying off to a Norwegian shaman.

Shana feels terrible about how much Belle spent on that fancy salmon dinner and elaborate brunch. "Is there anything I can do?"

"Every morning and evening I pray," she says. "I know it's not your thing."

"I'm glad it helps you." Shana knows Belle isn't telling the whole story. Of course she'll meet her at Toaster's next week, and maybe she'll learn more.

For three nights, sleep is hard to find. She keeps reminding herself that Belle is one of the smartest, strongest people she knows. And none of Shana's attempts to save her family have helped before.

Somehow, on the fourth day, with only half-a-week to go before departure, the peace of Fern Hill returns. She finishes the small canvases and, to her surprise, starts on a large abstract.

Before locking up the Watson compound, she triple checks the master cottage against final surprises, peering under every bed and bureau.

Shana leaves Colleen and Carter a bouquet of freshly cut dahlias and a welcome home note.

The ferry line is impossible. It will take two hours to board. Still, she should make it in time to meet Belle at Toaster's Café on the Wharf, which they call their conference room. She's stuck the bullets, still wrapped in Doug's stinky sweatshirt in the trunk, at the bottom of a shopping bag, underneath cans of tuna and refried beans she didn't get around to eating.

Once on the highway, she drives cautiously, alert for cops, monitoring her speed, vigilant about turn signals and energized by Yo

Yo Ma's cello suites. Traffic is horrendous. Friday, dammit, she should have planned better.

Almost out of gas, Shana stops at a Valero station, fills up and dials Belle's mobile. No answer. Odd, her prompt sister should be at Toaster's by now. Maybe she's also caught in Friday road madness.

Toaster's is packed with people chatting, checking email and Facebook, zoning out on their java and the postcard view of the water. Normally she's cheered by the aromas of coffee, sweet rolls and the café's signature grilled cheese sandwiches, but today she feels nauseated.

Shana strolls through the restaurant, peering at each table, as if Belle might have arrived in masquerade. Most people look away. A few stare suspiciously. Finally, she sits down and sips a latte. Still no answer on the cell.

She's too jittery to eat. It's the shock of urban reentry. The café is so loud with music and laughter and clacking computer keys. Cars whiz to the drive-up window and zip away. She aches for Fern Hill and those placid weeks before the family visit.

Doug and Belle's Subaru is parked in their driveway. No lights in the house, but it's still light out here. Maybe they're all eating pizza and watching a movie in the den? Maybe they've gone for a walk. Get a grip, she tells herself, Doug never took neighborhood strolls even when he was mobile. Once he gave up sprinting, he became a hop-in-the-car-and-drive-two-blocks kind of guy. They could be playing checkers or Monopoly or reading. She's shy about showing up unannounced, so she dials Belle again. The phone rings and rings. Ditto their land line.

A cool breeze catches the back of her neck. Seven p.m., an hour to sunset. Funny how a hot August day chills to autumn by evening. She remembers the first week of junior year when Doug beat up Fredrick Rink for goosing her after assembly.

Shana grabs her purse and leaves the bullets in the trunk for now. She feels faint, displaced—maybe it's the hunger—why didn't she eat at Toaster's? She floats in slow motion up Belle's pretty pastel pebbled path to the front door.

Suddenly panicked, she spins around to make sure she's locked the car. Seriously, what could happen in a neighborhood like this?

She rings the bell. Waits.

No response.

Two squirrels screech chasing a third up a red alder. A motorcyclist sputters into the neighbor's driveway.

She knocks loudly on the front window, imagining Belle shaking her head tomorrow as she wipes away the careless prints.

Two minutes pass; she tries the door knob. Locked. She's trembling, clearly going over the edge. There must be some simple explanation. A friend picked them up for an outing. They're eating dinner at a neighbor's home.

The nearby houses begin to light up; she can see men and women talking in their kitchens. Kids watching TV. Occasionally, when she gazes at houses like this, she fantasizes about having a family in a big place with a garage and a yard. Always, she imagines herself as a little girl, finally in the right home.

The back screen door is hinged from inside. "Hello, hello, anyone home?" she calls. "It's me, Shana. Belle? Are you there?" She rattles the door. "Doug? Charles? Fanny?"

From somewhere inside she hears—or imagine—a faint noise.

She checks all the ground floor windows. Then she remembers her Swiss Army Knife.

Lifting the sliced screen carefully, she reaches through and unhooks the door.

Inside their house, the stillness is eerie. She uses her voice for company. "Belle? Did you forget our coffee date?" She sounds ridiculous.

"Doug, where are you? How are you doing?"

"OK, favorite niece and nephew, time to come out of hiding."

Heavy…still…silence.

The house is impeccably neat. Even the kids' rooms are tidy and clean.

Only the door to the master bedroom is closed. She hesitates. Surely she's imagining things. Any minute, they'll come in the front door. Or through the back, freaked out by the hacked screen. Then it's Aunt Shana off to the asylum.

A sound. From behind.

"Squeak."

"Fanny!" she swivels.

The thin child is quaking, sobbing in the corner.

She kneels, clasps her niece's hands and peers into red, wet eyes. "Fanny, are you OK?" "Squeak," she says again.

"Oh, right, my little monkey. I remember."

Fanny grabs Shana by the waist, holds on stiffly, as her small body erupts in wails.

"It's OK, Fanny. Everything will be OK."

The kid draws back and studies Shana with those gorgeous, blue saucer eyes of Doug's.

She shakes her head.

"Tell me, Fanny love, what's going on?"

She grips Shana's hand and leads her to the closed bedroom door.

Shana touches the handle, then turns to Fanny for permission.

The girl nods.

Shana gasps and Fanny whimpers as they stare at Belle, holding onto Charles, both of them slumped to the floor against the blood-spattered wall.

Lying in bed, his eyes wide in surprise, is Doug, a red gash through his abdomen.

"Daddy shot them," the little voice gets stronger, angry. "He yelled and drank and hit them like always, and...."

Shaking and crying, Shana wants to vomit. She must take care of her niece.

"He opened another bottle and.... I ran away."

Shana hugs her tight.

Fanny pulls back.

"He came looking for me. 'Oh, Fanny! My canny Fanny,' he called and called. But I knew where to hide."

"Good," Shana manages, steadying herself against the horrible smell and the macabre diorama. "Good that you're safe and sound."

She wants to rock the girl, protect her, but Fanny stands upright, testifying.

"He always falls asleep when he drinks in the afternoon," she speaks in an eerily adult voice. "When he couldn't find me, he went back to the bedroom. I waited until I heard his snores. The gun was right there and...."

Shaking with horror and grief, Shana can't take it all in. She squeezes the girl's hand. "Oh, Fanny, Fanny. You're OK now."

Fanny slides to the floor, looking dizzy and pale.

"When? I mean...." Shana sits beside her.

"Yesterday, I think." She puts three fingers in her mouth, but not before Shana can see the bruises and burns.

Shana flashes back to Cinderella covering her discolored arms.

Fanny moans.

"Sweetheart, have you eaten anything?"

"No." She's barely audible.

Shana helps Fanny to her feet, hugs her again.

"Will they execute me?" the girl cries. "In the electric chair?"

Shana ushers her out of the bedroom. "No, Fanny, they most certainly won't do that. You are a child. You were protecting yourself."

Fanny closes her eyes.

Of course she should call 911, but Shana's still in shock. A lawyer, first. Yes, she'll call Alistair.

"Will they send me to prison for the rest of my life?" Tears stream down her red cheeks.

To steady herself and Fanny, she says, "Don't worry, dear. I'm here to take care of you. There's a lot to do. But first you're going to eat."

Fanny stares at her aunt.

Shana caresses her little fingers—how did the child find the strength to pull that trigger?—and leads her into the kitchen.

Fanny absently reaches into the cupboard for the can of pea soup. She's her mother's gracious daughter and her father's canny Fanny.

Shana feels strange, intrusive in Belle's domain.

Next door, the neighbor sputters his motorcycle down the driveway.

Shana starts the soup and pops two slices of whole wheat in the toaster. After dinner, she'll call Alistair and ask him to defend them, to bring the police.

Stirring the split peas, Shana recalls Paradise Meadow. Hears Belle's laughter at the knock-knock jokes. Thinks about the hollow-nosed bullets in her car and the back screen she's hacked open. She sees handsome young Doug breaking through the finish line tape with his hands in the air.

Fanny sets the table: two green placemats, blue napkins, water glasses, knives, forks and soup spoons.

Moving In

Faces obscured by thick, shaded branches and scraggly beards of Spanish moss, they whisper. The ancient oaks stand guard outside Maureen's, rather, Susan's house. I pull myself together. This early evening air is pleasantly warm.

Susan waves from the redwood deck, looking vital, even athletic, in her shorts and Arts Council T-shirt. Her black hair drapes over one shoulder in a heavy braid. Of the three of us, she's always appeared the healthiest, the most likely inheritor of long life.

I wave back, noticing how natural, how 'at home' Susan appears at the cottage door. Our trio is a duo now that dear sweet and sour Maureen has died. She did want Susan to have the house, declared this several times in the last, almost breathless weeks. So my visit is no betrayal. I'm glad Susan lives closer to me now and hope she likes the housewarming candlesticks. I linger among the fragrant, glistening oaks and dark sequoias: June evenings are splendid here in the country.

We embrace a little stiffly.

"Dear Audrey. Guess I'm kind of nervous," she speaks for both of us. "This is the first dinner party I've had in my 'new house'."

"A dinner party for two?" I laugh at the formality.

Three, I hear Maureen's familiar raspy voice.

Susan shrugs, "OK, supper with an old friend—that's a better way to say it."

"A housewarming gift." I hold out the candlesticks.

Susan smiles, ushering me in.

As she makes her way through the wrapping (It takes a while. I've inherited my mother's belief that every package should be secured as if being sent to a nation under siege), I notice the table is set with

Maureen's Oaxacan plates and that at the center are my favorite of her blue ceramic candlesticks. I take a deep breath. Ridiculous to feel hurt.

Yes, you were supposed to get them, Maureen sighs. *Janie lost several pages of the will.*

I remind myself that I inherited so many pretty things from Maureen. She was scrupulous about selecting the right pieces for each friend. And her poor niece was a little young to handle all the details. Truth is, I don't want the candlesticks. I want Maureen.

"Candlesticks!" exclaims Susan. "Pewter candlesticks! Now who's being ceremonial and formal?"

I blush, so overwhelmed with grief that I simply want to go home and crawl under the covers, one of them a heavy woolen blanket that the three of us found in Merida. I will dream that we're all together again.

"What a lovely gift, Audrey." She is still talking, mercifully unaware of my temporary exit.

"Come." She offers me a glass of Sauvignon Blanc and tugs my other hand. "Let me show you what I'm doing to the house."

I follow her to the cantina where she has blocked out the view of our golden valley with bookcases. Only two of Maureen's beveled glass windows remain.

"What do you think? This room will be a perfect study, with space for books, plus the grand vistas. I might throw some rugs on the floor to warm it up for winter."

My cantina. Can you believe it? Where I would sit and drink in the garden aromas, maybe take a nap on an August afternoon? And she wants to hide these splendid tiles I selected one-by-one in Mexico!

"It will make a fine study." I nod. "It's your home now."

"Let me show you what I'm doing to the bedroom."

Apprehensively, I follow her up the familiar stairs. I see she has already torn out part of the second floor.

"Ah, do you like that?" Susan asks. "See how much light I get?"

Upstairs I see, too clearly, what is missing—Maureen's meditation space. Her embroidered floor pillow. The bells.

Light! Light! Is this woman going mad? She blocks the downstairs windows and fancies light up here. In the bedroom. What about inner light? What about stillness?

Susan's room does look cozy—the double bed covered with her grandmother's quilt. A mock Tiffany lamp on the table. Nepalese rugs on the floor. Elegant. Just like Susan. She deserves a precious refuge after years of raising a difficult son alone.

"And over here, where Maureen hung her clothes from a freestanding rack, I'm going to install that antique wardrobe I've been coveting. I can hoist it upstairs now that I've removed the spare flooring."

She could move in a couple of circus elephants, too, if she pleased. Maureen's Boston accent adds an extra edge to her sarcasm.

Susan follows me down the polished stairs. "When does your summer vacation start?"

"Next week." I sigh, pleasurably, recalling I had just shifted from junior high to high school teaching when we all met at the book club. "Is it possible that twenty years have passed? That we're all, well, both of us, are in our mid-forties now?"

"I don't know what I would have done without you and Maureen when I first moved up to Sonoma," she declares. "I wanted to get out of the City, but I didn't know a Manzanita from a Madrone, a wrench from a screwdriver."

"We all helped each other." I smile. "You guided the not-always-methodical Maureen through fellowship applications. Maureen taught me to cook."

"Save room for dessert." She grins. "I've made something in the *façon de la maison.*"

Susan has placed a framed photo of Maureen on the mantle. A nice shot. Her auburn hair streaming over the shoulders of her best pottery show dress. She always looked beguiling in green.

Suddenly the familiar face winks at me.

"Hey, Susan." I distract myself from the picture. "May I have a splash more wine?"

She fills our glasses, and we step down into Maureen's pottery studio which Susan has transformed with two beds. A vase of dried lavender stands where the kiln used to be.

"For visitors," she says with satisfaction. "Isn't this the perfect little guest room, looking out on the neighbor's orchard?"

"Lovely," I whisper, remembering how fiercely Maureen protected her artistic solitude against guests. I believe Janie, her niece, did stay overnight once—during a storm when the access road was blocked.

"And I found this pot!" She holds up an oblong container glazed blue-green that I don't recognize. "I'm going to get a wooden base for it to remind people this was Maureen's studio. I want my friends to know about her work."

I wondered where that damn piece had gone. Used it as a piss pot those nights I was too lazy to climb downstairs. "Know about her work,"—that piece is one of my thunderous blunders. Doesn't this person run the Arts Council?

"The yard needs a lot of grooming." Susan shakes her head. "I've wanted to invite you for ages. I guess I just hoped to settle in first, to make this *my* house."

I see how exhausting—emotionally and physically— this move has been.

She opens the back door. "I just don't know where to start with the yard."

Garden. How often did I tell her this was a garden?

I follow nervously, remembering what good friends they had been when Maureen was alive. Maybe things will settle down in a month or two.

"Fruit trees." She frowns. "I don't know fruit trees."

Sun nears the horizon. Clouds enfold the western mountains. But it's still warm and dry here amid the golden grasses.

She looks around, overwhelmed. "I remember Maureen's scrumptious cobblers. What are these? Plums? Peaches? Nectarines?"

"Peaches," I murmur, hoping, ludicrously, that Maureen is out of earshot. "And those are apricots. See here's the nub of fruit."

"Cool," she grins shyly.

It's great to see Susan happy. She's had a rough year with her son. Later, when it feels right, I'll ask if Craig is out of rehab.

"What about Maureen's blackberries?" My mouth waters at the memory of those late summer dinner parties she concluded with bowls of blackberries and vanilla ice cream. I always skipped the ice cream. Her berries were that sweet.

"Oh, they were such a tangle that I pulled them out. I never had the patience for berry picking."

You could say that again. Maybe if she meditated a bit.

"Meditation isn't for everyone," I slip, then bury my nose in the clean sharpness of a eucalyptus branch to compose myself.

"Meditation, Audrey? Pardon?"

"Nothing. I was just thinking that cultivating berries is a meditative exercise."

I inhale the scents of sage and roses and pennyroyal. Maureen settled her garden in a sunny spot, down from the windmill. I've always loved her eclectic mix of flowers, vegetables and fruit.

"But the oddest thing." Susan moves to the far end of the garden near the apple trees.

Evening sun gilds worn patches of oak limbs and sets fire to the yellow grasses.

"I know these trees were full. A few apples were ripe, but I didn't feel right picking them until Janie and I officially signed the realty papers. And when I returned in November —you remember, it took a month to move because of the renovations—well, I brought two shopping bags. But the apples had disappeared. Nada. I mean they hadn't even dropped to the ground. I don't understand what happened."

Knowing better, I suggest, "Maybe the builders helped themselves, thinking otherwise they'd go to waste."

I wasn't going to let them rot. I had watered and pruned those trees for fifteen years.

"Apple pie." I move the conversation forward. "I remember it's one of your favs, Susan."

She shrugs. "I hadn't thought of the builders. Like in Agnes Varda's film, *The Gleaners and I.* Yes, that makes sense."

Among the three of us, sense was my specialty. Organization was Susan's. Maureen was the creative one. The generous one.

Sun beams on the shoulders of those mountains as we walk back into the kitchen.

Mars is warm and ready in the mid-June sky. The purple sage at the deck's edge is busy with the electrical buzz of native black bees. A chartreuse humming bird soars up and down. I look closely and spy the ruby throat. Calliope it's called.

The dinner table faces west. We eat and talk and watch the transfiguring sky. I'm glad to hear that Craig has stayed sober for 40 days now. Delighted to learn Susan's plans for the Hill Country Opera. Susan is creative in a different way from Maureen.

As sun vanishes, the sky explodes in streaks of gold and coral. Lavender shadows hover. Long after it dips behind the mountains, a ball is reflected in the clouds above. I've never seen these particular fireworks before. Outside, bats swoop away from the eaves. Mauve weaves a longer and longer drape and eventually the world turns pink and grey.

"You've saved room for dessert?" Susan asks hopefully.

"A little." I pull a face. "I did eat more than my share of that terrific pasta."

"Relax and digest while I fiddle in the kitchen a while."

How often the three of us sat at this table savoring Maureen's gourmet meals, hashing out daily problems. Grumbling. Laughing. Planning trips. Three to Mexico. Two to London. Reviewing travel photos, then planning again.

I stare into the blackness. Maureen's cancer was diagnosed in July when we were supposed to return to Cuernevaca, and summer vacation metamorphosed into doctor visits for second and third opinions. Then we took Maureen to traditional healers. Blended organic fruits and vegetables. Susan and I alternated nights on the sofa. Only for five weeks. They say you go fast with lung cancer, and Maureen did. Out like the sunset.

"Ready?" Susan calls from the kitchen.

No, I want to say. Let's rewind. I'm not ready. I didn't even get to say good-bye properly.

The room is dark now except for two white candles burning low in Maureen's gorgeous cerulean candlesticks.

I can't tell what's on the plates until she sets them on the table. Then I marvel at the gleaming golden flan.

"The recipe is from Maureen's cooking notebook."

She turns to a shelf of books with worn jackets. "She left me all her cookbooks."

Left them! Did she think I could take them with me?

I shrug.

"Something wrong, Audrey?" worries Susan.

"Nothing at all. This looks delicious."

"Brother, I had no idea how hard it is to make a simple flan."

"I never get them right myself."

"I tried recipes from three books and wound up with inedibles ranging from liquid to gelatinous. Then I found Maureen's handwritten notes and this fourth one turned out. You be the judge."

I take a spoonful. "Perfect."

Silently, we devour the flan. I'm overcome with exhaustion. One more week of school.

"You could spend the night in one of the beds in Maureen's studio."

"I thought it was your new *guest room*." I feel like a ventriloquists' dummy.

"Guest room," she laughs. "Vsitors will always know it's *her studio*." Susan smiles pensively.

"Thanks for the invitation, but I have school tomorrow."

"I *am* sorry. I was hoping the three of us could have breakfast in the morning." She nods at the photo. "She's still here you know."

"What do you mean?" I glance at the picture then look away before Maureen can grin or bark or clap her hands.

"I feel her presence and—do you think this is crazy? —I hear her thoughts or her voice or something. I know it's her, always with and edge and a wink. Really, do you think that's crazy?"

"No." I smile. "Not at all."

As Susan wraps the flan for me, I wonder why I thought I was the only one who knew the cranky potter would stick around.

I hug Susan good-bye. "Thanks for a splendid evening."

Walking out to the car, I hear the bees still mumbling in the sage. White clouds zip across the blue black sky. Below us the valley is feathered in fog.

Susan waves from the door. I blow kisses to both of them.

Under Stars

Bombay. Mumbai. Maharasthtra. Konkan Coastline. Arabian Sea. Indian Ocean. Char writes in her journal to make this visit more real. Palm trees. Hot, sweaty air. The astonishingly successful choreography as crowds throng from one side of the street to another. Ocean breezes. Hot spices. *Namaste*. Friendly faces.

"Mario," Char whispers to her old friend. "I've a feeling we're not in Manhattan any more."

Across the rattan table, gobbling a samosa and sipping a fresh lime soda, Mario is as focused as any starving man.

She can't help it, these lines from Oz. "People come and go so quickly here!"

"You do a decent Garland." Mario offers a crooked grin. "SNL material but I bet you'll channel one of your own past lives here. I'm sure you were a Mumbaikar in some century. White girls just can't make stunning paintings of Indian motifs like you do."

His boyfriend, John, is, as usual, busy with his BlackBerry. Since landing in India yesterday, Mario has delighted in the food and John in his excellent internet connection. "What time did you say your friend would pick us up?" he murmurs.

Mario finishes the samosa, mournfully regarding his empty plate. "They taste better in Goa. Much better. Wait until you eat my mother's *chamuças*."

"Sweets," John says. "I know I'm a little obsessive about time, but *when* is he coming?"

"OK, Johnny Fusspot. Nanshar said he'd arrive about four."

John pecks Mario's cheek.

"Maybe I should let you two guys go to the party by yourselves and have a romantic New Year's Eve." Char wipes the sweat from her neck. "I hate being a third wheel."

Mario fans her with his menu. "Darling Char, without you, Johnny and I would be the lone queers at the gala. Nanshar's wife has invited a bunch of neighbors and couples from her university. Nice people, but s-t-r-a-i-g-h-t. Actually, she especially wanted one of the guests to meet you, Radha, an art historian, theorist—something—who studies Indian motifs in Western art."

John pockets his BlackBerry and stares at her with mock sternness. "Babe, this could be your Warhol. The door to discovery by a billion people."

"Besides, it'll be fun," Mario cajoles. "Better to boogie with us under the stars than mope around the West End Hotel brooding about your ex. Better than wondering what wretched Wendy and that vampy witch from MOMA are doing in Chelsea tonight."

Char shrugs. She's been a consummate mope since her partner split.

She returns to the present. Ah!—back in India, her first trip back here since that grad school fellowship. What a wonderful gift from John and Mario. She has longed to return, but Wendy was always more interested in Europe or Mexico. And the flight was so expensive. Perhaps in some way she's feared India would change too much and her connection would be broken.

John teases, "And with that hot new coiffure, you'll break the heart of at least one Bombay lady."

Char fingers her blonde bangs; her hair feels too short and prickly. Wendy loved her long, dark curls. Untwisting the strap of her sun dress, she thinks back to when she met Wendy in painting class at Berkeley thirty years before. "I better go upstairs to dress. Listen—" she reaches for and squeezes their warm hands. "I want to repeat how grateful I am to you guys for bringing me here—John for treating me to this trip and Mario for introducing me to your friends and family."

"Wait till you *meet* my family; maybe you're a hostage! Besides, John has zillions of airline miles. He could have brought the whole apartment building."

"No, no, you're both so generous. True friends."

"I'll cop to that." Mario kisses her hand.

~

At 4:15, Nanshar pulls up in a battered black Toyota.

Mario calls out, "Hey, man, a miracle of punctuality in this wild traffic. How did you manage?"

Char hears Mario's Goan lilt return, watches his face fill with joy.

"Brother, you've been away too long," Nanshar shouts. Fit and handsome in his grey t-shirt and black jeans, he jumps out of the car and embraces Mario.

"It's so nice of you to let us crash your party." John shakes his hand. "Are you sure you want us to stay the night? I mean, we could take a taxi back to the hotel."

"From Bandra to Coloba? On New Year's Eve? No way, man. You'd be lucky to arrive back tomorrow afternoon."

"More likely midnight." Mario laughs.

Char shrugs. "I always bow to local authority."

"Besides," Nanshar says and grins. "You'll be the hit of the whole party—three famous Americans, two big time artists and a New York District Attorney!"

As they ride along sunny Marine Drive lined with palms, Nanshar shows them Nariman Point, Babulnath and Malabar Hill.

"Wow, look at those art deco buildings," gasps Char. "House after house."

"This is a largely Parsi neighborhood," Nanshar explains, studying her excited face in the rearview mirror.

Mario pivots to John and Char in the back seat. "At night this drive is called the Queen's Necklace because the streetlights gleam like pearls."

John whispers, "Yeah, I know my own queen looks adorable in pearls."

Char closes her eyes. She thinks about the Arabian Sea. About being so blessedly far from the Hudson. About being back in here after dreaming and drawing and painting the motifs of Indian textiles for decades.

~

Sadika waves from a second floor balcony. The gorgeous, graceful woman appears the proper chatelaine of this chic white stucco house with its bright red tiled roof and tasteful garden.

As Char takes in the freshly mown lawn and pots of golden flowers, she's tugged by nostalgia for her childhood California. And for the sense of possibility and ever-after that she shared with Wendy at Berkeley.

Before Nanshar has parked the car, Sadika floats out the front door in a gossamer green and purple salwar kameez.

Char feels like a uniformed New Yorker in her black silk slacks and blouse. She thinks back to her college roommate Minissha, whose gorgeous saris and shawls first kindled her infatuation with Indian textiles. She wishes she and Mini hadn't lost touch in the whirlwind of life between Berkeley and New York. Char sometimes imagines Minissha will show up at one of her openings. But the last word was that Mini had settled down with a Cuban she met on a Venceremos Brigade. Gradually she's learned to be more conscientious in her friendships, all her relationships. Wendy used to say, "Forgive yourself for being young." Perhaps it's the fate of her generation to find home elsewhere.

"Welcome everyone," Sadika says and hugs Mario. "You've stayed away too long, my dear. But you've made up for it by bringing your friends." She extends a manicured hand. "John, we've heard so much about you."

John shakes hands, then fingers the BlackBerry in his pocket.

Char notices dark rings under his eyes. Clearly the pressures of the DA's office are nothing to being vetted by Mario's friends and family. She resolves to be more sensitive to her intense friend.

"Clara?" She shakes her guest's hand firmly.

"Welcome to you as well."

"Char," Mario whispers. Then louder, "For *Charlene*, a diminutive of Charles. You know how these Euro names are so male dominated."

Sadika wags her finger at Mario.

"Come in," Sadika says. "Let's have a drink. We get three hours to ourselves before the guests arrive."

After shedding sandals in the vestibule, they pad over the cool tiles into the living room and relax on overstuffed white couches. Giant red and green pillows are scattered on the vivid rugs. A fresh breeze parts the upper curtains. Below are picture window views of the sea.

Nanshar fills their drink orders.

"What a stunning house," Char says. "And so comfortable." She misses California's benign weather, coastal vistas, swaying palms. But it's been twenty-five years since she followed Wendy to their dingy small apartment in New York where they prospered—a hip queer couple— gifted painter and edgy critic.

"Look at the space." John can't contain his amazement. "Tell me again, Mario, why are we crammed into that flat on West 19th?"

Mario grins, taking in his two worlds. "The location is good, and perhaps it has something to do with the fact that I'm a starving artist, and Nanshar runs a big investment firm. You nabbed the wrong husband, I guess."

John demurs. "You're a fabulous painter. You and Char are my entrée to the best parties. You have pieces in top galleries—"

"Yes, yes," Mario interrupts. "No advertising necessary here."

"Now he's brought you to the best party in Bombay," Sadika trills and takes John's hand. "We'll have a light dinner on the veranda. But first, let me show you the house."

~

The other guests start to appear around 9pm.

Anita.

A water rights activist.

Ashok and Brinda.

Psychiatrist and dancer.

Dhruv.

Filmmaker.

Anjolie and Irfan.

Physicist and...Char is losing track. Maybe it's the jet lag.

Nanita.

Gopol.

Urvashi and Kanwahar.

Smita.

Nice smile, that Smita.

How will she remember their names and jobs and interests? Relax, she reminds herself; she's on holiday, not running for office. "All is good," as the porter at the West End Hotel had reminded her when she mispronounced "Thank you." "'*Dhanyavad*,'" he had corrected gently. "Everything is forgiven. You are a foreigner."

John takes a step back from Gopol who is avidly quizzing him on *Law and Order*. "I do miss Jack McCoy. And your own impression? Truly I value your opinion, for I've never met a genuine New York DA before. What luck."

"Wonderful show." John inches away.

Char admires his tact, recalling evenings they'd watched the series, laughing as John kept a tally of inaccuracies.

"Honestly," Gopal persists, "do you think Mike Cutter hits the bench mark?"

"Great cast all around." John reaches for a beer.

Gopol slaps his forehead. "I should have foreseen— professional discretion."

Mario tugs Char's hand. He introduces Radha, the art historian-curator, and her husband Sanjay, a dour mathematician.

"Char does dazzling work. She has such an eye for textiles; you want to reach out and touch the saris, dupattas, salwar kameezes, kurtas in her paintings."

Radha smiles. "Do you have a website?"

Mario pulls one of Char's cards from his eel skin wallet. He leans toward Char. "Shh, this is what friends *do*."

Char smiles shyly at Radha. What's happened to her Manhattan mojo?

"Sadika tells me you're in Bombay another week. Perhaps we can meet for tea?"

Sanjay wriggles toward the drinks table.

"Yes, thanks. That would be great."

A tap on her shoulder.

John rocks back and forth, clapping his hands. "'Cain't get no… satisfaction. I cain't get no. Oh, no, no, no.' Come on Char. This is *our* song."

Radha laughs. "Do dance. We'll make our date later."

They join the swirling saris and gyrating jeans and cotton shirts and khaki pants dancing on the rooftop patio this balmy night. Their hosts have strung blue and white lights around the potted palms.

The Rolling Stones have parched her. The drinks— orange squash, mineral water, Bombay Pale Ale, Johnny Walker Black, Bushmills, Absolut, Bacardi, Nasik wine—are arranged on a brilliant yellow table cloth. She runs her hand over the thick, tightly woven cotton. The menu is equally generous—*aloo Chat, aloo tikki*, bread, *pakora*, cheesy pizza, *masala dosa, dholey bature.* Brie. Camembert, crusty baguettes, *namkeen.* Char inhales the aromas of coriander and turmeric, feeling grateful she didn't stay at the West End Hotel tonight staring out at their bleak view of the Bombay Hospital and remembering her own grimy windows in Chelsea.

Sanjay is pouring a neat Bushmills. He proffers the bottle.

"No, thanks. I'll try one of these ales."

"Our pale ales are tasty, but nothing compares with a cold Corona and lime."

"Do they sell Corona here?"

"Not much. No, I drank it as a student at Berkeley."

He starts to walk away.

"I went to Berkeley, too."

Sanjay studies her closely, then frowns. "Big school," he sighs, then wanders off.

How did this churlish guy win over vibrant Radha? Still knackered from dancing and jet lag, she drops into a comfortable net chair at the edge of the party. She's always been a corner booth kind of girl. Tonight's waxing moon invites an array of stars. Taking a deep breath, she inhales the sweet mustiness of some tropical flower.

Mario puts his arm around her shoulder. "How's it going, little Charles?"

"Divine," she murmurs, "as close to Heaven as I'll ever get."

John appears. "I've got a bizarre cultural question."

"Local authority at your service," Mario grins.

"This music—Stones, Pink Floyd, Bob Marley, Elvis, the Beatles. I know Indians are hospitable, but are your friends playing this for us?"

Mario laughs so hard his rum and coke splashes onto the shiny blue patio tiles.

Char steadies his glass. "I don't think so. I mean, we're all the same generation. Look around."

"Yeah." Mario is still laughing. "We all listened to the same music."

"Right," John nods.

"Naturally." She fiddles with her wispy fringe.

Sanjay saunters past, turns to Char. "Kips?"

"Pardon?" Char blinks.

"Do you remember Kips?" He repeats impatiently. "I used to drink Corona and lime at Kips."

"Oh. Right. I think I remember the juke boxes."

"Precisely. Such a strange contrast to the Peoples' Park crowd."

"Yes," she says. "So many different worlds in Berkeley then."

He looks at her long and seriously.

A little unnerved, she asks, "What kind of math do you do?"

"I detect a polite question." He purses his lips and pushes back thick, dark-rimmed glasses. "It's complicated— and perhaps boring for you—probability statistics of—"

He steps away before finishing the sentence.

"What's with Mr. Peepers in the Stone Age glasses? Creepy guy." Mario rolls his eyes. "Watch out, girl."

Char pats her friend's hand. "At first I found him arrogant. Maybe dismissive of self-indulgent artist types. Now, I think he's just, well, awkward."

"You're a good person, Char Fraser."

"So are you, Charlie Brown. Wanna dance?"

The Mashed Potato. The Pony. The Locomotion. The Pogo. The Hully Gully. The Swim. Even the Twist.

"Rest stop!" Char pants.

"No, not already!" Mario shakes his head, sweat dripping from rings of black hair.

"I'm six months older than you, remember?" she manages to say breathlessly. "I think you should check on your boyfriend to make sure he hasn't found some comely lad with a cozy Bandra condo."

"First class paranoid thought!" Mario high fives her.

She finds her half-finished bottle and takes a draught of the pleasantly bitter brew, grateful for the chair, the warm night, the amiable people.

The evening unspools agreeably. She dances with John, by herself, with Nanshar and Sadika. She chats with Anjolie and Dhruv and Brinda, making mental notes of films to see, books to read. She's excited, content. In Manhattan, she's wounded when people at a party don't recognize her. But tonight she feels happily anonymous. Just a friend of a friend under the twinkling canopy.

By 11:15, she's famished. Flying always does this to her appetite. She puts a fragrant samosa on her plate and looks for a place to sit.

More stars now, shining, winking in and out of the black sky. Who needs Wendy? The grief is turning. Morphing into anger and the tiniest bit of indifference. Before she takes a second bite, she hears a voice.

"What dorm did you live in?" asks Sanjay.

"This is really nostalgia night," she says softly. "Please." She gestures to the adjacent chair. "Join me if you like." She senses something familiar about him. Maybe not— how many dorky, shy boys grown into men has she known in her life?

He repeats, "Which was your dorm?"

"Freeborn. Then an apartment. I spent senior year in I House."

Startled, he sits straighter.

She looks around, feeling vaguely trapped. "Did you enjoy Berkeley?"

"Absolutely." He seems distracted, as if by something she's wearing. He stops staring. "Best years of my life."

"The place, the time, transformed me." She finishes the samosa, still hungry. The recent tranquility has evaporated; she's anxious, irritable. Jet lag, she tells herself again and continues to be cordial. "Berkeley changed everything. I was the first person in my family to finish high school. They thought college was a miracle. To them Berkeley was intergalactic. To me, too, for a while."

"Intergalactic." He blinks up at the sky. "I remember watching the planets and stars on spring nights from Heller Patio."

"You know International House?"

"I lived there four years."

Radha appears and places her hands lightly on Sanjay's shoulders.

Char stands. "Sanjay and I were talking about our college days in Berkeley. It seems we overlapped."

Radha smiles tightly. "I wondered what was engrossing you both so much. Sanjay, you mustn't monopolize Char's time. Everyone will want to meet the American artist. Besides, it's been years since we danced together to the Beatles. Come. Do come."

Char pours another ale. Maybe if she uses a mug, she'll drink more slowly. Truth is, she'd only been to Kips once. The kids were loud, and the place reeked of pissy Budweiser and Coors. (Did they even sell Corona at Kips?) She spent most of college in the library, at the studio or on her work-study job. In her down time, she preferred the Caffé Mediteraneum to beer joints, lingering pensively over a latte on the second floor balcony. How odd to come to Bombay and find herself wistful for California.

An eruption of shouting. Clapping. Hooting. Red, green lights streaking across the sky.

Char almost misses it.

"*Bonne Année!*" "*Naye Varsha Ki Shubhkamanyen!*" "*Naya Saal Mubbarak Ho!*" "Happy New Year!"

She raises a sweating mug to the kissing couples and hugging friends. Wendy and her MOMA witch won't be celebrating for another nine hours. John and Mario lift their glasses to her from the far side of the veranda.

Sadika walks over with Smita, a psychologist planning to visit New

York in April. Oh, yes, the woman with the million rupee smile. Sadika slips away briefly, returning with a manila file. "I downloaded these yesterday from the website Mario sent me." She pages through five sheets of color prints with Smita.

Char watches, amazed at Sadika's attentiveness in the midst of her big party. This would never happen in Manhattan where people are too harassed being their own PR agents to promote anyone else's work. Oh, she still loves New York, another place, like Berkeley, where she has been able to grow beyond her imagination.

"Aren't they stunning?" declares Sadika. "I love the purples and violets."

Char wants to protest that the true colors are only visible on the original paintings, that even the size of the jpegs limits one's experience of the work, but she's modest enough to remain silent and feel grateful for Sadika's generous spirit.

Smita's patients are mostly coupled young adults, trying to balance their liberated lives with duty to extended family. "I have local patients but also a number who phone or Skype from Boston, London, Dallas. It's hard to grow up being told you are a citizen of the world and then to be beset with family responsibilities that are totally incompatible with that."

"I would think so." Char nods, feeling a complicated relief that she lost her parents twenty years ago.

Across the patio, Brinda is waving good-bye to everyone.

"She has an early morning flight to Sydney," Smita explains, then checks her watch. "Look at the time. It's been lovely talking with you, Char."

"Do call me when you come to that New York conference." Char hears herself being expansive. She usually discourages visitors.

They're playing slow songs now. Elvis imploring, *love me tender*. Bob Marley crooning, *is this love?*

Char perches contently in her corner chair, marveling at the warm night/morning air, intense conversations, joyful dancing. Wendy would have loved this. Before she embarks on that resentful road, Paul McCartney begins *Yesterday*, the recent Concert in New York version, so much more nuanced and resonant than the original. Age does bear some gifts.

Sanjay materializes, regarding her quizzically.

Maybe Mario's right about Mr. Peepers being a little off. Surely he's not going to ask her to dance. Why would he do that? Three hours ago he found her question too boring to answer.

"Do you ever visit I House?" he asks awkwardly.

"I live in New York."

"Of course." He takes off his glasses and wipes them with a party napkin. "Silly question." They fall silent.

Keith Richards' guitar. Jagger's sandpaper voice. She tries to recall the title.

"*Wild Horses!*" Sanjay declares. "Brilliant, brilliant song."

He's grinning for the first time all evening, she thinks.

Two more couples make their farewells to Sadika and Nanshar. Char watches them, looking forward to lying down after everyone has left and they've washed the dishes, but that won't be for a couple of hours.

"Wild horses," he's singing, and not badly. "…we'll ride them some day." His dark eyes glisten. "I have fond memories of I House, you know. In those years everything was promising. I felt I was living in a mansion. The dining room with its big windows, Middle Eastern rugs on the walls; long refectory tables. I guess a college boy concentrates a lot on food."

She's trying to keep up. "I loved the auditorium's ornate ceiling and those glass chandeliers."

"Do you remember the wide front steps? How many evenings I would come home from the math building and feel at home as soon as I started climbing those steps."

"Yes." She warms to the subject. "Studying late at the Coffee Shop."

"I had a crush on an American girl who studied in the corner booth."

Time stops. Her mind admits a vague memory. "Did you ever… tell her?" Somehow all the nerdy guys were drawn to her. There was an Italian, a guy from Des Moines, and, yes, an Indian. None of them spoke much, and she supposed now that they all might have misinterpreted her polite cheerfulness for something else. Wendy kept an eagle eye on these lads; she'd remember Sanjay, if it were Sanjay, but Wendy is probably savoring a romantic brunch at the Chelsea Market right now. Her anger is simmering down toward irritation.

"I tried to. One night we were sitting under stars on Heller Patio."

"You mentioned those stars." She considers his face. He could be the same guy. She didn't know any of them well. Besides, who can predict how a person wears thirty years? Her own long dark locks have turned a spiky gold.

He looks up at the Indian sky.

She imagines a nervous boy enduring a crush, a middle aged woman suffering betrayal; and feels her heart open, wide enough to say, "You know, maybe that girl liked you, but as a friend. Maybe— maybe she wasn't into men."

His eyes brighten. She thinks how handsome he would be without those ancient spectacles.

He smiles. "You mean maybe she *played for the other team?*"

Their eyes catch, and they both burst out laughing.

"Here you are." Radha allows a long sigh to run through her body. "Come, Sanjay, we must let Sadika and Nanshar clear up. Their overnight guests look worn-out. Aren't you jet-lagged, Clara?"

"A little. Kind of you to ask." Then Char turns to Sanjay. "Thanks for the good memories. It's been really fun talking to you."

"My pleasure," he says and nods solemnly, adding in a softer voice, "once again."

~

She draws a long breath and can almost smell the sea. With her eyes shut, she sees the moon and stars lighting the night of this entire world.

Then and now.

Long Distance

"It's probably nothing. I shouldn't bother you." On the tinny answering machine, Loretta's voice sounds more frenzied than usual. "What time is it in Boston, anyway?"

I'm not a fan of telephones and I always monitor, rarely answering unless it's a return call. Otherwise it's my nutty brother-in-law. Or a campaign plea. Or fundraisers from St. Cecilia's School; god knows how they found me.

Sometimes it's startling news. If people live far away—distant realms like Emporia, Kansas, for instance—they call with good or bad news. Really bad news. Loretta's never phoned before.

"Your father," the metallic voice persists, "he's in the hospital with viral pneumonia."

Last night I dreamt he was dying. I cried bitterly because we never had the chance to really talk, for any kind of honest intimacy. Never in my childhood and never since. Anyway, in the dream he suddenly recovered. Had I resurrected him? Well, it was an improvement on my girlhood terrors of driving him away, so Loretta's words this morning make me feel weirdly psychic. As an urban ecologist, I transit in scientific evidence, practical strategies, political tactics. Rationality—not intuition—is my strength.

"Hello, Loretta," I say breathlessly. Am I gasping out of fear or because I have bronchitis or because I'm worried she'll hang up too quickly? Long distance calls are expensive on their budget phone plan, so she would never call spontaneously. Dad is always complaining about the tiny pension. This is the worst part of family; they confound your reaction to the smallest thing, like a ringing telephone.

"Hello, Janet? Is that you? In person?"

"I'm right here. How is he?"

"I didn't know I was getting through. We don't have an answering machine. I guess by now most people do. What a relief, talking to you *for real*. Sorry, I'm such a hick."

"Don't worry, Loretta." I smile, as if Loretta can see my reassurance from Emporia. I'm sure she's smiling too. After years of shunning my runaway father, I'm taking care of his wife—who even the world's kindest person would label a ditz of the first order. She calls herself my step-mother.

I call her Loretta. I don't need a step-mother. My own mother is very much alive despite what she still describes as the devastation of Dad's desertion. And how could anyone as relentlessly cheerful as Loretta be my mother?

Damn telephone. Family always reduces me two feet and thirty years. Who would believe I'm a whiz at my job; I have a fabulous partner; I've worked in Tanzania and Brazil and Mississippi. I have lots of loving friends. Tony and I climbed Mount Rainier last summer. My shrink says my family is crazier than some and not as bad as others. He says I'm a survivor. Right now with the hacking bronchial cough, I feel like a limp survivor.

~

The sanest way to think about my parents now is as stage actors. My charming, outrageous, inconstant father. My loving, serious, ironic, steadfast mother. The only trouble is they're performing in different plays at the same time. My father stars in something by Martin McDonagh or J.M. Synge. Mom is cast in Strindberg or Ibsen. Possibly a servant in Chekov. While I was growing up, I willed us all to be like the families on *Happy Days* or *The Brady Bunch* even if Dad was the prototype for Archie Bunker.

Not only would Mom and Dad never appear on the same stage, I have a hard time remembering them in the same room. To recall them together—eating dinner, presenting Christmas gifts, taking long drives up the Coast— would be to summon absence—my mother's silent longing and my father's contrary, stifled discontent. The only times I remember them truly happy were when friends came for cocktails.

They made jokes, laughed, sipped from pretty glasses with pastel umbrella toothpicks stuck into soused onions and olives. After a little tippling, they were the old carefree Bob and Dot who larked around New York in the late fifties, the couple in the photo which is still on Mom's dresser.

~

I unravel the long cord and move the phone from my desk over to the couch where I can stretch out and sip my eucalyptus-echinacea tea.

"I'm very glad you phoned." It's taken me years to be civil to Loretta—after she stole Dad—and I'm sure it will take the rest of my life to understand her. Why would she want this fat, broken-down drunk who squandered his considerable beauty before they met? I try to comprehend with an earnestness inherited from Mom's side of the family. "Tell me how Dad is doing."

Deep down, a small voice demands, "*Is he coming or going?*"—the question which has hovered since childhood.

"Today he's OK. He had terrible bronchitis for a week then insisted on getting out of bed and working in the garden. You know how he dotes on those roses. We've been having an awful wind lately. One thing led to another and phhht, just like that, he couldn't breathe."

I close my eyes, holding back my cough. I inherited Dad's lungs, and my sister Sarah has his temperament. This is a trade I'd make anytime.

Tony ordered me to stay in bed all day. But rest isn't a big part of my repertoire, so I've got the laptop here on the couch and the files scattered all over the coffee table. The plan is to clear it up before she gets back from the office. I'll tuck myself back in the bed, and my beloved will be content.

~

I often wondered why Dad married Mom, who was pleasant looking, but no stunner and seven years older than he. I want to think he liked her nerve, quick wit and rock solid character. I imagine he was also looking for a mother. But she was never enough. Never able to compensate for the indignities he suffered in the merchant marine. For his grievances about missed promotions. He did savor her cooking as, increasingly, food and drink became the sources of his lust and solace.

What did *Mom* want? Most likely something simpler. She probably expected a loving partnership in guiding children toward happy, moral lives. She had those quaint ideas about the roles of husband, wife and parent. Although she was a meticulous bookkeeper, she let him do the finances, and the family went into bankruptcy. He was the man of the house even when we had to move to a small apartment. And, of course, he kept leaving her—all of us—behind. Up another gangplank and off to Pakistan or Argentina or Japan. The handsome man she married was no homebody. He was always coming and going.

It's hard to remember with forgiveness and impossible to look back steadily without it.

~

"I called Dr. Cohen, and they took him to the hospital right away. They say his weight didn't help any. He's up to 250 now."

The precise details anchor Loretta. Perhaps she's trying to calm me, too. I can see her sitting in that pretty window seat looking out at Dad's garden. On my last visit, Dad showed me four types of tomatoes, but he was proudest of the heirloom roses, the Albas, Damasks and the Centifolias. Loretta had her own roses all over the house on her rather good canvases. So odd to think of a sailor settling down inland to potter in a garden. My dad, retired King Odysseus.

"He's feeling better than when he went to the hospital?" I can't just ask: what about it? Is he coming or going?

I wait, sipping the tepid medicinal tea, distracted by swarms of emails jamming my in-box.

"Oh, yes, and he's out of the oxygen tent. The priest came to do the Anointing of the Sick."

Prayers for the Dying, we were taught at St. Cecilia's. *Extreme* Unction, the last sacrament. Is Loretta mollifying me, or is she, as a convert, confused? Maybe they renovated the ritual when they added peace kisses to Mass and fast track annulments. Being ex-Catholic is like having a life-long hangover. You can't quite remember or forget.

Her words tumble out: all I can hear is the Kansas twang. Twenty years ago she brought Dad home to Emporia as if he were a trophy.

"What's his condition now?" I persist gently, trying to locate a common language. *Serious? Critical? Fair? Good?* Surely these are standard categories.

"Better and better," she says. "I don't know why I'm calling except he said you'd want to know, and of course it's nice to hear your voice."

"Do I need to fly out?" Of course I *will*. My bronchitis has to be better soon, and if not, I can take double doses of the Mucinex. I could probably meet the consortium deadline if I work flat out on the plane. Tony will be so disappointed if I cancel our trip to the White Mountains. I also have a tutoring session at the Escuela with Belen on Thursday. Not to mention the big party for Yogi Anna's birthday.

But, jeez, he might be dying. I'll fly out in a second because that's what one does. Because I love him.

"Heaven's no, don't come. To tell you the truth, that might scare the wits out of him."

"Have you talked with Sarah?" I say, wondering if Loretta called my older sister.

"He just said to call Janet." Her voice is tense, and I wonder if it's because of the expense of the call.

"When can I talk with him?" I rush ahead. "Do you think Dr. Cohen will accept my call?"

"After tomorrow your dad can take calls himself, and I'm sure the doctor will speak to any relative."

I'm not just any relative, I want to say. I've known him 17 years longer than you. I'm his daughter. His *Pink and Pretty*. Instead, I ask for numbers and promise to call early tomorrow. "Now tell me, Loretta, how are *you* holding up under all this?"

"Just fine, hon, thanks for asking." Her voice is high and winding. She reminds me of Mom on valium after Dad left. The woman must be asking our proverbial family question, *Is he coming or going?*

~

Come and go, that's what he did. On colossal merchant ships, old victory vessels then container liners. I'm not sure which I recall more clearly—his absence or his presence. When he was gone, it was as if he'd always been away. We passed each week waiting for his return. Letters arrived from Caracas. Birthday calls from Yokohama. Mom kept promising he'd be home soon. Always soon.

Then suddenly, there he was at the front door, carrying wooden shoes from Rotterdam or Chrysanthemum tea from Korea. He was always bringing home *deals* like a bolt of Javan batik silk or a crate of Noritake china. He bought a knock-off Webster's Dictionary somewhere in Japan for $5.00, the size the libraries kept in reference rooms, he told us. He was proud of that dictionary, made a table to display it in the living room, but never opened the book.

Often I'd come home from school to find Mom on the couch reading the giant volume. "It's fascinating, she often said. "One word leads to another."

~

At six, Tony's car sputters to a halt outside. Quickly, I clear off the coffee table and jump into bed with a book.

"I'm glad to see you're obeying instructions, Janet." Tony kisses me on the forehead. "Hmm, your fever seems to have gone down."

"I'm getting better by the minute," I murmur.

"What's the matter? You sound blue." She sits on the bed and takes my hand.

"Loretta called."

She raises her eyebrows. "Your dad's floozie?"

I laugh, then cough.

"What's up?" She frowns. "Is your dad OK?"

"I'm not sure; he has pneumonia. Loretta seems to think he's getting better, but—"

"I'm sorry." Tony squeezes my hand.

"I'm going to call Dad and the doctor tomorrow. I should know more then."

"Good," she says. "I'll put together some supper."

"I'm not all that hungry."

"That's not the point." She shakes her curly head. "I'll be back in half an hour. Meanwhile, would you like some more tea?"

"How about a double shot of whiskey?"

"You don't drink."

"Could start."

"I'll take that as a yes about the tea."

Twenty minutes later, she appears with a tray, puts my cup on the side table, then raises hers. "Salud!"

The tea is refreshing going down, and the dinner smells terrific.

"Will you fly out?" she says.

"I think so. It's so hard to know, but I think, yes, I will."

~

In addition to all the souvenirs, Dad brought home a list of complaints. About working two weeks straight without a break. About a seventy-five pound rope dropping from an impossible height onto his back. Damn understaffed company. Each trip was murder. He earned his leave.

I think he found solace in that big red mock leather recliner. He stretched before the Magnavox, drank beer from his Bavarian tankard and called us in to change TV channels.

Did Mom want to talk with him? To catch up? Consult on finances? Go into the bedroom together and close the door? I remember she washed her hair more frequently when he was home, and she baked deep dish apple pies and devil's food cakes with fudge frosting.

Dad did love to eat. He would lie back on his red throne gobbling multi-layered sandwiches watching the Giants' games. Willie Mays was his man.

Twenty-five years afterward, my girlhood friend Anita asked me if I remembered my father in the recliner wearing a t-shirt and boxer shorts. Of course. I still feel mortified by the dark hairs and the blackish red penis slipping out of his fly. He wasn't an exhibitionist. His body wasn't the kind you exhibited. He simply wanted to be comfortable. As he got fatter, clothes were constricting. This was his home. He paid for everything. He didn't care if I brought my friends over, but he was going to live the way he wanted in the palace he built, or at least re-paneled.

He seemed content on leave. Mom, I know, tried to be content. She counted her blessings and told us to do the same.

Dad did take time out from TV for fatherly tasks. He constructed a dolls' house out from midget logs. He built a miniature speedway in the basement. Sarah and I took turns being the red car and the green car. After we went to bed, he spent hours down there. I could hear the whoosh, whoosh as I lay beneath the sheets. I could *almost* hear my mother turning the pages of her novel when she read alone in their bedroom next to mine.

As abruptly as he arrived, he disappeared. Although I knew something was missing, some crucial part of what constituted a family, I was surprised at how a certain weight lifted with his departures. The house grew quieter and filled with fresh air. It was easier to sleep at night. My friends visited more often.

~

"Dinner is served," Tony calls from the kitchen. "I'll be right in with your tray."

How did I get so lucky?

"I think it would be good for me to get out of this damn bed and sit at the table." I pull on a robe and head to the dining room table.

"Salmon, asparagus, farro, salad. Just what the doctor ordered."

I wonder if I should have called Dr. Cohen this afternoon, but I felt I needed some time to absorb the news, to plan my questions.

"You're being very kind to the invalid."

"Is this the same invalid who spent all day at the computer?"

I blink.

She laughs. "You don't have to be Sherlock to figure it out. The dirty lunch plate on the coffee table. The computer switched to email, and I got your Facebook post."

"Ooops—I *was* a little restless, but I promise I tanked up on herbal tea."

"I've been thinking about your dad. I'd want to come with you, especially if he's—"

"Going," I murmur. "No, you should drive to the White Mountains with Kenny and Naomi as we planned. No sense ruining your holiday, and it could be a false alarm."

"I've already looked into tickets. We can get a good deal if we book by tomorrow."

I don't know what to say, and even if I did, the tears flowing down my cheeks have rendered me mute.

~

Despite Dad's temper and attire and drinking, I missed him. Mom and I made plans for his return. At thirteen, five years older than me, Sarah had a life of her own: clubs, cheerleading, boys who vied to dance with her.

I decided to write Dad a letter of my own. I described my First Communion, dotted Swiss ivory dress, white patent leather shoes, lace veil. I told him about my pretty swimming teacher, Miss O'Brien, and my favorite class—geography. I told him that our dog Woody missed him.

One month later, an envelope arrived addressed to me in his beautiful penmanship. A lefty, he wrote with his right hand in perfect Palmer cursive because the Christian Brother teachers had tied his left hand behind his back. Years later, Dr. Sarah, now an eminent psychology professor, declared that the tethered hand foreshadowed a lifelong struggle against authority. Unaware of such complications, I simply treasured the script and his short reply.

Eventually I had everything—the dream of a father, a tranquil home, my very own letters. I knew this was as good as it would get, but I tried to look forward to his return as much as Mom did.

~

The hospital number is ringing, and I'm still debating about alerting Sarah. She hasn't talked to him since he "went off with that vamp from Podunk, Kansas, for gods' sake." Still, this could be an emergency—

crucial enough to endure my sister's second-hand wrath at Dad which was matched only by his own rage at the many assholes who'd done him wrong over the decades.

The operator says the doctor will be on in a moment. She knows I'm calling long distance. Do I mind waiting?

Emporia, Kansas is a perfectly OK place; people are very, very friendly, and the town has thirteen sites on the National Register of Historic Places. When I visited Dad last year—much to Sarah's disdain—he drove me around to see the Old Emporia Library, Finney House, The Granada Theatre, Keebler-Stone House, the Kress Building, Soden's Grove Bridge.

The first evening Loretta made a mac and cheese dinner, something our health conscious mother would deplore. I ate as much as I could. They both noticed.

"Yeah, well," said Dad, "Loretta isn't the queen of fresh vegetables, but this sure is tasty, isn't it?"

The next night she served a layered salad in which the major ingredient was mayonnaise. I did my best to follow her commentary about morning soap operas but didn't have much to add to the conversation.

On the third morning she decided to visit her sister in Wichita for a few days "to give you a little time to yourselves." I was relieved by her graciousness, and I could tell Dad was too.

~

"Hello, Dr. Cohen speaking." The voice is brisk, New Yorkish.

I wince recalling Dad's florid anti-Semitism and hoping it doesn't slip out when he's sedated.

"Hello, I'm Janet Morse. Bob Morse's daughter and I called—"

"He's doing better now. It was touch and go for a while there. Your dear father isn't the world's easiest patient."

"Yes," I laugh, recalling how hard it was to keep him in bed after he totaled our car and broke his arms. That was the year before he went off with Loretta. We did our best to help him heal, but we all had the feeling he wouldn't be sticking around for long.

"You know, I find it difficult to treat your dad because he's a good friend."

Are we talking about the same person? My father? The doctor is a friend of Dad's? Of my incurious father who keeps one book in his house—the local telephone directory. (He left Mom the dictionary). A Jew friendly with the man who always spat out his contempt for "arrogant kikes, yids and hymies." I don't understand, but Dad was never a simple puzzle, and he does have a certain Gaelic charm. It's what Mom has been mourning for two decades. It's why I'm on the telephone when I should be resting. Or at least meeting three important deadlines.

"I see" is all I can muster.

"Your mother will tell you he's had a hard time of it lately."

He thinks Loretta is my mother. At first I'm offended. Then pissed at my father for colluding in the charade.

"I expect him to pull through." He sounds genuinely concerned.

"Do I need to fly in?"

"It's not that serious any more. I mean, don't you have things to do?"

"Of course," I answer a little defensively. "A lot of pressures at work. Yesterday's deadline."

"Right. He tells me you're a university professor."

"That's my sister Sarah."

"You're the other daughter."

"Yes." I shrug it off. Of course he would brag about Professor Sarah. Even I do, sometimes. He's never understood my research, wonders how consulting can be real work.

"I wouldn't worry. He'll be fine but stay in touch. You never know about this sort of thing as much as I'd like for all of us to be one hundred percent sure."

Even the damn doctor doesn't know if he's coming or going.

~

My school friends always asked when the renovations would be finished. Dad loved to work with wood. He'd start paneling a room and then get called back to sea. Sarah's bedroom was almost finished in knotty pine when he left for Toyko. I carefully selected a light ash, and he had paneled one of my walls before sailing to Sydney. At least the gap in the dark walnut at the base of the dining room was concealed by the hulking serving table. It never bothered him to leave things unfinished; he liked new projects.

Mom explained to visitors he was completing the job, but even she lost hope after a while. It was like living in one of those model renovation homes where the walls exhibited samples of *before* and *after*.

I can picture him high on the ladder, calling Sarah to fetch a level or hammer. "God damn it, girl, can't you move any faster than that?"

Mom would call from the kitchen. "Bob, dear, watch your language, please."

"Get some earplugs," he yelled. "The girl's slower than turtles in the tropics."

Of course if he asked me, he'd have his tools in a flash. But he asked Sarah, maybe because she was older.

"Hush, hush," Mom called out, although neither of her daughters was speaking. "He doesn't mean it; he just has a fiery temper," she explained as she chopped garlic, onion and tomatoes for her famous cioppino.

The fish soup was my favorite. I had an appetite, took after Dad that way.

"He's an excitable man," Mom continued, mostly to herself. "Never gets enough rest between voyages." Her mantra always ended, "Everything will be different when he gets a shore job."

~

At dinner I tell Tony that I got the airline ticket. "It cost the earth."

"What about the deal I found?"

"I checked, and all the discount tickets were snapped up. Who would imagine so many people traveled to Kansas? But I don't mind the cost. By the time I take the bus or the train, he could be gone."

Tony waits a beat. "Or he could be back at the house watering his damn roses."

Tony has gradually lost patience with my devotion to Dad over the years. "Let me come. I don't think this is something you should do alone. Besides, you're not all that well yourself. You need someone to look after you. You live too much in your head."

"No, no, you go on that hike. You've all been looking forward to it so much. I'll be fine."

"But you wanted to go to the mountains. It was your bloody idea!"

I start to tear up. "I have to do this. I have to say good-bye."

"Oh, honey, I understand. All the more reason to let me be with you."

~

The miraculous shore job never appeared. So we waited, never taking summer vacations because he might call or come home unexpectedly. Mom did long to see Aunt Teddy in Wyoming and Uncle Richard in Idaho. She grew up in a close family, and each of her siblings visited us once a year while Dad was away. Still Mom kept the home fires burning, the dutiful wife long after Penelope went out of fashion.

Dad was proud he made it home for Christmas every year. We'd always get a giant blue spruce and hung delicate glass ornaments from Mom's Czech grandparents. After midnight mass, we'd drive home through the snowy streets admiring the holiday lights. He brought exotic presents for his *ladies*. One year we all got kimonos. Another year, brilliant shawls from Argentina. Mom gave him things he'd circled in the *Sears' Catalogue*: a band saw; a double ratchet screwdriver.

Usually he was called away in January. Our bedrooms never did get the floor molding before the finances went south and we moved to the apartment.

~

"Hello, Dad? It's Janet."

"Yeah." He sounds low, tired.

Maybe they're wrong. Maybe Loretta and the doctor are stringing me along. His voice is creaky.

I've tanked up on pills to keep me from coughing.

"How are you doing?

"Fine. I'm on oxygen now, you know. I lost ten pounds in the last couple of days. It's tough to breathe. I've had a fever, clammy skin, headaches, stiff joints." He recites the symptoms as if they're portentous accomplishments.

"Are they taking care of you all right?"

"Sure. They're filling me full of fluids. They've installed a room humidifier. I've got a great doc, a nice Jew Boy from Brooklyn."

"Please don't talk like that, Dad."

"Like what?"

"Jew Boy. It's offensive."

"No way," he declares in that voice of comic affront he often adopts when he knows he's got my goat. "That's what he is. I don't mind if he calls me an Irish Harpy."

"Let's change the topic," I suggest, grateful for an option not apparent in childhood.

"Yeah. Of course I'm getting better. Looks like your old man is coming back."

I thought he would have the answer.

~

We were driving north of Boston, Dad and I, to check on a ship. He'd had the longed for shore job four years now. I sensed something strange. I didn't yet know her name was Loretta.

"How's school going?" he asked.

Those days he understood me better than Mom.

"I really want to go out for basketball," I whined. "Mom hates the idea. Says I'll get muscular. I explained it would be good for my legs. She told me to take up dancing."

Dad puffed on his Lucky Strike and peered out the window. He smiled in a way that seemed to betray my mother. I liked it anyhow; he was on my side.

"Girls' sports." He coughed, then took another drag. "About time you females got your cut of the pie. Sounds fine to me."

"Then you'll talk to her?"

"Sure, hon. You two just don't get each other. Lots of women have trouble communicating."

Women. The color rose in my cheeks.

"What she's afraid of just ain't possible with you. You're my Pink and Pretty, remember when I used to call you that?"

I looked out at the grey trees, grey sky. "Yes." I nodded. "When I was a little girl, you brought me back a pink satin comforter."

"From Singapore."

"Hong Kong," I corrected, without thinking.

"Good memory. Like your Dad's. I always said you took after me."

It was so smoky; I cracked the window for air.

"Hey, whatchit, hon, that's sleet out there. God damn Massachusetts winters. Someday we're going to get a house in Florida with a swimming pool."

~

"And you," he rasps. "How are you doing?"

I blink. "Actually, it's been a rough month here."

Silence on the other end. Is he sailing off again?

I persist. "I've been pretty sick, bronchial stuff. I've been down for two weeks. I guess respiratory problems run in the family. I mean I'm not as ill as you, but I feel rotten and—"

"You gotta take care," he allows. Then: "Out here, we've had hard times. Even the dog, Fiona, the girl, you know, she pulled two ligaments in her leg. Cost $180. Tell me, how does a dog pull a ligament? At least you kids were smart. Really took care of yourselves. I never had to worry. But Fiona, I tell you, she needs a Papal blessing or something."

I cough in spite of myself. Turn away from the phone to muffle the sound. He told me the story about Fiona last month. I'm tongue tied. "Sorry, you've always loved those dogs."

"Your mother and I might have stayed together if we had a dog."

What?

"Loretta, to tell you the truth, doesn't cook as well as your mother, and she may not be the brightest bulb, but we get along on the

134

important things, like the dogs. And for some reason she loves your old man. That's important, someone loving you."

"Yes, it is."

I feel he's opening up. He must know I love him. I wait.

He's silent.

"I miss you, Dad. I got a great deal on a ticket to Kansas. I'll be there by noon on Friday."

"Don't bother yourself. I'm fine. Didn't Cohen tell you? Save your money. I'll be around for a while, don't you worry."

I turn away from the phone, coughing.

"Hey, I don't want to burn up your wire." He sounds tired now. Bored maybe.

"I love you, Dad."

"Me too, hon. Oh, and when you talk with your big sister, Sarah, fill her in on the news about the old man, OK?"

He coughs and laughs and coughs, and the line goes dead.

I start to redial, to say good-bye.

Suddenly the room feels stuffy and over-heated. Instead of calling back, I set the message machine and go for a walk. The air is brisk with a tinge of autumn. Two yellow leaves shimmy before me, dropping to the sidewalk.

He's not the father I'd choose—a cranky, bankrupt, racist philanderer. But he's the only one I'll get. I try to tell Sarah, "...*love the one you're with.*"

I'll call him tomorrow and hope to change his mind about the visit.

I do love him, with spunk and warts and everything.

I miss him. I'll always miss him.

Incident on the Tracks

Rachel paces the blindingly hot Caltrain platform, recalibrating her hectic afternoon. She's missed the usual train and this next one is already ten minutes late, so she'll have to drive straight to soccer practice for David and Sara. She planned to festoon the dining room with blue and lavender crepe paper. But she can send Sara to Auntie Esther's shop for milk, then call Auntie to delay Sara while she and David decorate and put candles on the cake. It'll be a rush, but that's life now.

Fifteen minutes late to the station, today of all days. Damn. She never thought she'd give the kids a phone, but now it's an urban survival tool. No point calling until she's on the train with a clear ETA. Damn sun, you'd think Caltrain or Redwood City or someone could put up shelters or awnings or something. Haven't they heard of skin cancer? *They*. So many incompetent *theys* in her life.

She leans against a wall and closes her eyes. It will all sort out. Relax. Think how well work went today. In fact, it's been better ever since Dr. Goodman took over the ER and started referring families. Hospital social work is meaningful. A good job, especially for someone with a new graduate degree. Even Dan is impressed with the pay and benefits, no small concession after all his griping about her return to school.

Twenty minutes late. Really, this weather is too hot for spring. Yet nothing compared to Dan sweltering in Iraq. His own fault, of course. Joining the Navy in middle age—leaving his medical practice, two kids and a wife. Why do they need the Navy in a land war? Why the hell are we fighting in the first place? God (Yahweh, Allah, Zeus—whoever's up there) keep him safe.

Let him return home before her selfish resentment locks the door.

Knowing that heat always puts her on edge, she reminds herself that Dan is doing this out of patriotism, not selfishness. Gratitude, she thinks, practice gratitude for all that you have.

The red and silver leviathan roars into the station. She clenches her teeth and looks down, hasn't been able to fully watch an arrival for five months now. The doors suck open, and people crowd on board. Usually she's at the front of the line. Usually she gets her choice of the back seats on the top deck, but she didn't get much sleep and has no energy to push today. This tardy, packed-to-the-gills choo choo is even less hospitable to hermits than her regular train.

Shit, not one window seat facing forward.

Well, she's seen people stand all the way to San Francisco, so she's relieved to find a place on the aisle. She hates these booth-like configurations with twin seats on either side of a shelf that looks more like an ironing board than a table. Only two other spots in this quartet are occupied—at the aisle across from her, a young guy is busy with his laptop. Next to her, by the window, an older woman is reading student papers. They don't seem to know each other, so conversation is unlikely. Yup, tally those small blessings.

Piercing screams fill the car.

Rachel grips the armrest.

A ragtag stream of miniature people pours in, holding hands, shrieking and laughing as they surge through the next car. Three brave or sedated teachers—one at the front of the procession, one in the middle and one at the end—usher kids through the next carriage, shushing to minimize disturbance.

Across the aisle, an old man smiles indulgently.

The little boy sitting on his mother's lap waves and laughs.

A sullen guy in a Stanford t-shirt ups the volume, and music seeps from his earbuds.

Doors whoosh open, and the shrill parade disappears.

Rachel likes children. Her day is filled with kids at the hospital, and her nights are occupied with her precious daughter and son. So she looks forward to the train as an inbetween respite, to read for her book group or shut her eyes and zone out. Sometimes she practices meditation or rather practices practicing meditation. Yesterday she was disappointed to reach her stop. Now she glances at her companions.

The guy is typing rapidly. She notices one of those small airports on the side of his computer. Technology moves so fast. Wasn't it yesterday that Mom took her to work and showed her how the white paper scrolled into her fancy IBM Selectric? Now you're supposed to save trees with email, PDF and word attachments, jpegs, Excel spreadsheets. Leah sent her farewell note on email. Imagine. No, she tells herself, don't go there.

The woman next to her is shaking her head and marking papers with a pencil, occasionally erasing and starting over. Committed teacher, Rachel can see. She's really distressed at the errors. Rachel admires the woman's hair and hopes her own turns silvery straight like that one day. Meanwhile, she's pretty happy with this chestnut color she got after Leah's funeral. Small, silly decision, dying her hair, but it was one of a thousand things that gradually helped her turn a page. One page.

"Tickets. Passes." A pretty woman wearing cornrows projects a faintly Southern voice down the center aisle. "Please have your tickets and passes ready." Proficiently she threads her way through the crowded train, alert to feet, briefcases and purses in her path.

"Thank you."

"Got that."

"Good to see ya."

"Yup, thanks."

~

Loy likes the conductor's spicy perfume. Normally you only smell perfume or cologne or aftershave on the morning train. Maybe she just started her shift. Maybe for her, it's the morning.

He notices each of his tablemates has a Clipper card. He does prefer to sit with other members of the tribe. Passholders are skilled travelers fortified with books or computers or ear buds. Or school papers like this teacher. They don't expect conversation and leave you alone, taking up minimal space, understanding that none of you are really here. Everyone is just riding between realities. Work and home. Remembering; looking forward.

Loy has almost developed an immunity to train distraction. He has it worked out. Since most passengers like to face forward, he always sits with his back to the destination. Today, as usual, he's cadged an empty seat next to him for a backpack and shopping bags. Even on crowded trains, he scores space. He's very good at figuring things out. At work, he gets paid to figure things out.

At first, he dreaded the commute, forty minutes each way between Menlo Park and the City. He simply couldn't live on the Peninsula, which held so many memories of high school and college. And rehab. In the City, he's anonymous, free. He loves walking among strangers. When he does run into someone he knows, it's fun, not a punch in the solar plexus the way it was at home. To his City friends and acquaintances, he is that hip programmer or the buff guy from the gym or the fantastic tenor in the Nouveau Castro Choir. He isn't Mrs. Chang's awkward nerdy son who discovered his sexuality, duh, years after everyone else knew. In Sunnyvale, shame droops like Spanish moss. His San Francisco studio is two blocks from Badlands on 18th Street. Transformation. Complete transformation.

The City is promise. Especially tonight. After a quick workout and sauna, he'll wash his hair, shave and put on the slacks and shirt he ironed last night, slip into the amazing Tommy Bahama Vallarta Driving Moccasins. He'll listen to Rubén Blades while steering his Mini Cooper to the Zuni Café to meet Jorge for dinner before the salsa flick. He downloaded some dope music today in case Jorge cares to come to his apartment for some after teatro cha cha cha.

Five weeks now, he's been scoping out Jorge. He couldn't believe it Monday night when he walked into Badlands and found the very object of his fantasies perched at the bar. Sitting on a stool, winking at him. The relationship —with all their mutual interests in books and music—has some actual potential. Of course, it isn't a relationship yet, but it feels good. How many people do you meet at cool bars who also drink mineral water and love jazz and Iris Murdoch? You can't tell Loy their stars aren't aligned.

A spray of bitter smelling beer arches across the aisle, spattering their table.

The new woman pretends to ignore it, tightens her jaw and continues reading her hardback.

The teacher, shaking her head at a student paper, appears not to notice.

Loy raises his perfect eyebrows, pulls out a Kleenex and wipes the table.

"Excuse my friend here," calls the red-haired woman from across the aisle, talking so quickly she's almost incoherent. "Joey's super-hyped about the game tonight. Giants against the Dodgers. Want another tissue?"

"Thanks, I've got it, Ma'am," he answers with cool finality.

"Ma'am! You get that Joey? He called me *ma'am*. The name's Tammy." She grins at Loy. "And yours? Who do I have the pleasure of meeting?"

He sighs. *Loy* requires conversation. Long ago he learned to respond, "Bill, nice to meet you" to people it isn't nice to meet and whom he hopes will be raptured away.

"Great to meet you, too, Bill."

Laughter erupts from the boyfriend and the other couple. She joins in. They're all wearing black and orange caps.

"Excuse me, bud," the boyfriend leans over.

"Bill," Tammy explains.

"Right, Bill. Have a cold brewski? Might mellow you out."

Tammy cracks up.

~

Elena loses her concentration and glowers at the baseball fan. She didn't intend to glower. She guesses it's a reflex now, after thirty-five years of wrangling goof-off students in the back row.

For the first time she notices the seat mates who joined the train several stops after San Jose. One good thing about boarding at an early station is that you have a choice of seats. Elena prefers the window, even if she rarely looks through the filthy glass. How can the state afford to wash train windows when they can't even buy textbooks? Elena feels safer by the window, away from the hurried, jostling people.

She's determined to finish marking these papers on the train. They're only exercises. She doesn't need to devote a lifetime to them, as Alicia would say. As her oldest sister will say if she brings school work on the casino bus tonight.

Elena pictures them now—she and her sisters in the last two rows of the posh bus to Reno. Their spring trip. She's looked forward to it for weeks. The four of them staying in two rooms of their favorite casino hotel. They come so often —three times a year—and they are a memorable bunch, so the manager calls their suite "Música Chavez." Elena believes the cute Guatemalan guy has a crush on Dacia. But her younger sister shrugs it off. A beautiful woman, Dacia shrugs a lot.

They plan carefully because it's tricky for all four of them to get the same three day weekends. After Juan's death, she rediscovered her sisters. There they were, with open arms, as if they had been waiting for her. Marta will pick her up at the train, swing by the apartment for her suitcase and the tamales, then collect Dacia and Alicia and drive to the bus. "A fine tuned plan," Marta chuckled last night on the phone. Elena wanted to say "finely tuned" but has learned to censor the grammar police.

~

"Hello, Mason?"

"Yeah, it's me, Brittany? Let me tell you about last night?"

"On the train? Where are you?"

"Excuse me."

"Oh, hang on. There's a lady. I think she wants the place next to me."

Brittany stows her backpack under the seat and pulls in her legs to let the woman pass.

Rachel remains standing in the aisle. Hovering.

"Would you mind lowering your voice a bit?" Rachel is surprised to find herself glaring at the cherub. The kid's loud inanity has simply propelled her down the aisle.

Brittany pops her gum, scowls, as if thinking this wrinkled lady could really use a good haircut and makeover, not to mention a gym membership.

"I'm sitting way down at the far end of the car and I can hear your every word," Rachel tries to sound reasonable.

"Oh, right," Brittany replies slowly, then returns to the phone. "Call you later Mason? Some dinosaur hasn't heard of the First Amendment. Or maybe she's allergic to cell phones."

Wordlessly, Rachel swivels and returns to her seat. Tonight she'll review telephone etiquette with Sara and David.

Seated again, she closes her eyes, exhaling the irritation. Just a kid, she tells herself, an excited, hormonal teenager. When she opens her eyes, the Asian man across the table is smiling at her.

"Thanks," Loy says. "She was driving me nuts, too."

"Yes," Elena touches her arm. "Thank you."

Rachel releases a long breath. Maybe she's not a crank. Maybe it's normal to want to concentrate on your book, to nap, to burrow among the hundreds of strangers as the train barrels up the peninsula.

Inadvertently, she glances down the aisle and finds Brittany staring back. For the moment, at least, she slips into *Middlemarch*, savoring the names Dorothea Brooke, Tertius Lydgate, Humphrey Cadwaller, Camden Farebrother, Nicholas Bulstrode.

Loy has returned to his iPod and computer. He's getting close with this new project. Really close. Ingram will be pissed off, and DuBrow will be way impressed. This is what they call a breakthrough. Totally original. Nothing else comes close. He's sure to get bumped up. A promotion and a new boyfriend and the light lasting longer every day. Who was that pathetic, sullen addict looking for jobs and lovers in all the wrong places? Dr. Green warns him not to get cocky, to track his moods, make sure not to get too angry or too tired. But he's nowhere near either of those places and only a few stops from evening in Paradise.

Elena is the first to sense something. Sirens, she hears sirens. Eerily insistent whining over the loud rattle of their train. She peers out the window; the landscape is slowing down.

As they rock to a stop, Rachel looks up.

Loy is so into Baby Daddy's guitar and his own brilliant breakthrough that it's not until Brittany's shriek that he notices anything.

"Ambulance and four police cars." Brittany is hyperventilating into her cell. "Oh my god, oh, my god."

"Let's hope it's not another suicide," Elena whispers, shaking her head.

Rachel nods, stiffens.

"What?" Loy unplugs. "Pardon?"

"Ladies and Gentlemen, this is your conductor speaking. Our train is being detained between stations for a short time. We will inform you when we get a green light. Thank you for your patience."

"Oh, wow, I," Loy sputters realizing he's talking.

The women wait attentively.

"I have *plans*…a lot to do when I get off the train."

"It's my daughter's birthday." Rachel's eyes widen; she's incredulous at this new piece of bad luck. "I have to collect the kids from soccer and decorate the dining room and—"

"Last time this happened," Loy pauses, slows down and continues cautiously, "we waited two hours for the ambulance and the police and the—"

"And the people who clean the track," Elena says sadly.

He feels sweat pooling under his arms and down his back. Damn, he knew he should have saved his new Francomb shirt for evenings. But he hasn't had a panic attack in six months.

"My colleague lost four of his sophomores this way." Elena knows she's talking too much. Still, sometimes like this you need to communicate, even with strangers. "One of those *clusters*, they call them."

"But we don't *know*." Rachel struggles to hang on. She cannot dissolve on Sara's birthday. "This could be anything. An engine malfunction. A piece of wood in the tracks."

They each regard her sympathetically.

Pulling back her shoulders, she sits taller and stronger. Who do they think she is—a protected housewife—not that there are many of those any more—a Martian? She blurts, "I know about suicides. This year, my sister took her life." Did she really say this? To strangers? "I was only—"

"I'm so sorry." Elena leans in.

"Yes," Loy stares at the table. "My condolences." They had to practice condolences at the recovery center. Yes, he had learned about grief, the guilt and anger bequeathed by acts like his.

Rachel sniffs back the tears. "It was five months ago." She's held it together all week. She will not break down in front of outsiders. For some reason she adds, "Leah had been battered. It had been going on for years, and I had no clue. My own sister."

Elena wants to take this woman's hand but can tell the gesture would embarrass her. She thinks about Marta, Dacia and Alicia—each of them beautiful and whole and alive. She would know if one of them were having problems at home. Of course she would know at once. They are all so close. She hopes she would know. "How very sad."

"We were really tight," Rachel is blathering. What the hell, she needs to talk about it. And she'll never see these people again. "I should have seen the signs."

"That's not always easy." Loy sounds older, more authoritative.

Both women are startled.

"I survived," he says tenderly, looking into her eyes.

Rachel returns his concerned gaze. "You've lost someone, too?"

"No." That's all he can manage. It's so hot on the god damned train. Air conditioner always shuts down during a delay.

Elena catches his wandering eyes and holds them.

"I'm very glad you didn't succeed." Rachel bobs, recovering from the blow.

"So am I." Loy brightens. "But believe me," he says urgently to Rachel, "no one in my family knew. No one could have stopped—" He hasn't talked about it outside home and therapy. He does have to find a way tell Jorge. This is harder than he imagined. But the woman should not feel responsible about her sister.

"How are you now?" asks Elena.

"Fine. Just fine. My job is awesome. I have a hot date tonight. I love living in the city. Life is great."

"Good. Very good." Elena smiles. "I'm so happy to hear that." She wishes he were talking to her sweet sophomores, wishes she could roll the whole sad semester back, wonders if Loy would actually consider visiting her class; it would be so helpful to have a young person speak from experience. But no, she stops herself, he's clearly still mending.

"I'm so relieved to hear it, too," agrees Rachel, feeling wrung out, tired, but also, strangely comforted.

"Ladies and gentlemen. Your conductor again."

The car falls silent.

"I'm sorry to report that we may be detained for another forty-five minutes."

A collective groan.

"Forty-five fucking minutes, Mason!" Brittany is shouting into her phone.

"We will keep you posted as soon as we hear anything."

Across the aisle four beer cans snap. "If you can't beat 'em; join 'em," proclaims Mr. Spray.

"What's that supposed to mean?" giggles Tammy.

"Don't know," Joey grins. "Sounded good enough."

"Hey, Bill." Tammy leans over. "And you ladies. Care to join us? We've got plenty." They all shake their heads.

"Thanks anyway." Loy somehow feels like the spokesman.

Another forty-five minutes late, she'll never make the Reno bus, Elena thinks. She'll have to call Marta to say go ahead without her.

"God, my kids are going to be alone at the soccer field." Rachel sighs as she pulls out her phone. "Sorry, I have to reach the coach."

Elena calls Marta. Facing the grimy window, she explains in a low voice, "No, you go without me. Maybe I can catch the casino bus tomorrow. No use ruining everyone's weekend." Through the window, she makes out the insipid lights of a strip mall and way behind that, the green rise of the coastal range.

Loy recalculates his time. If he skips the gym and sauna, just showers at home, he can make it to the Zuni Café. He'll be fine. A little wiped, but fine.

"I got them," Rachel sounds relieved. "Coach Malouf is taking them to our apartment. They'll be OK. I mean, they're eleven and twelve. They should be just fine, right? I was babysitting when I was twelve. They'll be fine." She curses herself for missing the regular train. On her daughter's birthday. She just can't handle everything, every bloody thing, by herself. Damn Dan. Damn Iraq.

The car grows eerily quiet after the initial flurry of exclamations and complaints and phone calls.

Light drains from the sky, and evening fog seeps into the train.

Rachel pulls out a sweater.

Brittany is sobbing.

Elena knows she should get up and comfort the girl. But she's suddenly exhausted, having lost the adrenaline for/ from her Nevada journey. The exercises lie, unfinished, on her lap.

"Ladies and Gentlemen," the conductor begins.

He's like a carnival barker, Rachel thinks, gradually losing credibility.

Loy tugs out his ear buds.

"We have an update for you."

"What? What was that?" Joey wakes up.

"It is estimated that we should be able to leave in thirty minutes."

"But it's already been over an hour!" Rachel protests, then registers the sheer panic in her voice. She breathes deeply, reminding herself she's talked with the kids twice. They've double-locked the door. They're fine. They'll be fine.

"We regret the delay. But there has been an incident on the tracks."

Elena knew this, of course. They all did when they saw the ambulance. An incident. Oh, she cannot bear to think of Jason, Courtney, Whit and Charley.

"My name is Elena." She bows from her shoulders toward her two seatmates.

"Nice to *meet* you," he laughs, feeling like a kid for some reason. "I'm—Loy is my name."

"I'm Rachel." She smiles wanly. "So what are you working on there, Loy?"

Five minutes later he is still explaining the program. The women's eyes meet in bewildered amusement.

He catches himself. "Sorry. I can get lost in this stuff. I try to hang out with non-nerds to sharpen my social skills."

"A sense of humor about yourself is the best skill." Elena laughs.

"Where, I mean, what do you teach?" he asks. She looks a little like Mrs. Garcia from the fourth grade. He's always intended to go back and thank Mrs. Garcia for introducing him to IT.

Soon they are all laughing.

About what?

One of Elena's helicopter parents, perhaps.

Or the three weeks Rachel spent shopping for the perfect eleventh birthday lavender and blue bathrobe.

Or the night Loy fell on his ass in salsa class.

Speaking of salsa. Of course it's now too late to catch the film. Excusing himself, he takes the phone out to the corridor. "No, go on to the premier without me," he insists. Then pausing, telling himself he'll be OK no matter what the answer, he asks, "Any chance you're free for dinner on Sunday?"

A long silence at the other end.

Loy counts his breaths.

"Sure. Zuni Café again?" His eyes fill and he reaches for a casual voice. "Sweet. Let's say 7:30?"

~

Elena is telling Rachel about Música Chavez. "Reno is a beautiful city. Oh, the mountains! And so much to do. It's a real bargain, the coach and the hotel, especially if you don't gamble."

"You don't gamble?" asks Loy, happy to be back in conversation with these two people who an hour ago had been members of his serious, silent tribe.

Rachel notices that the baseball fans are sound asleep. Many people have their eyes closed, listening to music. Brittany's Lady Gaga is so loud Rachel can almost make out the words. But she's shed her irritation, wants to walk back and reassure the kid.

"Ladies and gentlemen." A crackling noise on the loudspeaker like an early rumble of thunder or a heavy truck creeping up a gravel road. "Ladies and gentlemen. Yes, that's a better connection. I am pleased to report that we can move on our way. The incident has abated. Many of you have expressed concern, so I will tell you that the worst thing that has transpired today is your delay. We apologize for the inconvenience."

A loud clang; then a jolt; then the train moves slowly and gradually picks up speed.

"That means the jumper was saved from the tracks," Loy explains. "They have to speak in euphemisms."

"Naturally." Rachel feels her shoulders relaxing.

"How wonderful," Elena declares. She's spent, as if maintaining her optimism might have saved the jumper. "Just three more stops."

"Me, too," Rachel says.

"I guess we all get off at 22nd Street," Loy grins.

Rachel, eager as she is to get home, feels oddly sad as they begin their good-byes.

"Hey, Elena, can I give you a lift?" Loy feels awkward calling someone his mother's age by her first name. "I mean since your sister isn't picking you up any more?"

"No, no thank you. I don't want to disrupt your evening. I can take the bus."

"What evening?" He laughs. "The train ate my evening. No way I could make my date. I'd be delighted to drop you off."

"Ate my evening." Rachel shakes her head. "My poor kids must be starving. So much for Sara's favorite chicken cacciatore. I'll have to pull out the frozen pizza." She hopes she gets to catch some of Dan's birthday call from Iraq.

"Do your kids like tamales?" Elena asks.

"How about salsa music?" Loy offers.

Rachel laughs happily. "A surprise party. Wouldn't that be fun?" She should be more spontaneous; take more risks.

"Oh, good." Elena feels curiously elated.

"YOLO!" declares Loy, raising his hand in a high five to Elena.

Rachel's heart sinks. She can't do this, bring two strangers to her daughter's birthday. It's Sara's evening. They've planned it for weeks. Even persuaded David to watch *The Princess Bride*, once again as a gift to his sister.

Elena catches Rachel's expression. "Maybe this isn't the best for your children? Yes?"

"I'm so sorry," Rachel rushes on. "It's very kind of you, but yes, Elena's right. Sara has been looking forward to her dad's call and her special film and I just think—"

"Hey, it's cool," says Loy, hiding his disappointment.

"Wish Sara a happy birthday for me."

"And for me, too," says Elena. "She's lucky to have such a loving mother."

"Thanks, but, I'm so—oh, we're pulling in."

Quickly, each of them gathers their things, seasoned travelers who never miss a stop.

On the platform, Rachel pauses to phone the kids. First, she waves good-bye to Loy and Elena.

"Farewell," calls Loy, "See you on the train!"

Rachel nods, waves again.

As they walk up the steep stairs, Loy takes Elena's briefcase for her.

Rachel watches from the cool, dark platform until they vanish down the street.

Far Enough

They were like the Summer Triangle, an asterism, not quite a constellation, yet radiant to discerning eyes. Sparkling in the way of average people with excellent hearts. Over the years, they would change positions. Vega becoming Deneb. Deneb merging into Altair. Altair into Vega. More than the sum of their parts.

Liz, Jeanne and Marney had been in and out of each other's houses since they were eight. They knew each other's dreams and vanities. Each other's parents and siblings. They harbored secrets. Confided about their first periods. Traded 45s, then albums, cassettes and cds. Talked too long on the telephone. Whispered about crushes. And disappointments.

Promised to remain in each other's lives. Forever.

Then a boy died. A sweet, nervous boy grabbed a live wire after a surprise rain storm. No one was there to warn him, to see the sparks, to hear the scream. The death made his sister an only child, caused her parents to move the family out of town. Not far, just into the next county, but far enough.

Although it was hard to leave Jeanne and Marney, Liz wanted to grow up as quickly as she could, to create her own life, in a safe place. The friendship continued, the asterism shimmered, in the middle distance, over many years.

THE LONGEST DAY

Liz sits in her dusty green Subaru contemplating the sign *Gateway to Wyoming* at the Casper/Natrona County International Airport. She's listening to Glenn Gould's 1955 recording of *The Goldberg Variations* as she always does when she wants to calm down.

What the hell is she doing here? She has a life. Great job. Beautiful home. Far enough from crazy family and sad history. Is she really waiting for a flight from California carrying her two *best friends* from the third grade? OK, they do get together every few years. But, really, *what* does she have in common with them anymore?

Liz checks her Blackberry. Still due at 2pm, an hour late. Well, she's enjoying humming along with Glenn who, she imagines, was something like her brother Chuck would have turned out to be. Smart, quirky, talented, uneasy.

Their first stop will be Maude's High Plains Spa, where Liz has found a pre-season deal. Tomorrow it's on to the ranch. God knows what they'll make of her place. How she'll fare as a hostess. She's not exactly a recluse, but she left that girlie stuff behind years ago.

Liz checks her watch. Five minutes have passed. Shaking her nervousness, she reviews directions to the spa. Makes a list of groceries to pick up before they head out to the ranch tomorrow.

Suddenly she's filled with panic. Her scrupulous plans have gone awry before.

~

The three eighth grade cheerleaders make up in spirit what they lack in coordination. They weren't elected cheerleaders; rather they saw a need and filled it. The popular girls were already preoccupied with steady varsity boyfriends and skiing trips to Tahoe. Liz, Marney and Jeanne decided they would take the whole basketball team as boyfriends.

Liz suggested they make up chants, yells and cheers. Jeanne, always the boss, was the head cheerleader; no question. They modeled their routines on songs from her cousin's high school. And on high-camp reconstructions of the Mickey Mouse Club Show.

"Bis-hop E-a-g-a-n.

Bishop Eagan.

Forever let us hold our banner high ....

High, high ...."

At first the other students snorted, hooted at them. Some joined in.

By the second stanza, most kids were singing along, clapping. This was, after all, a suburban Catholic junior high school in the 1960s, where kids felt both ironic about and nostalgic for a show about the dopey Musketeers, about their fast fleeting youth.

"Liz! Hey, Izzie!"

Izzie, she's managed to keep that name out of the state of Wyoming for twenty years. Only her two old friends call her Izzie.

Old. As in former. As in aging. As in the most important people in her life.

It is good to see them. Not much has changed in five years. Five years since Mom's funeral. Does she, herself, look different? She shakes her head in wonder, pleasure, and hops out of the car.

Marney's beaming through new horn–rimmed glasses. "Don't worry. The pilot made up time—winds or something—and here we are. Yes, here we are all together. As we should be." She hugs her old friend tightly.

Jeanne embraces Liz. "Nice to see you, Cowgirl."

Liz catches her breath, enjoying the strength in Jeanne's long arms and the fresh lavender scent of her hair.

"Great to see both of you!" Liz is taken aback how much she means it. "Let's load those cases in the back. Do you need anything—water? coffee?—before we set off? It'll take an hour to the spa and—"

"We're *fine*," Jeanne reassures her. "I'm just so thrilled to be here. I can't believe we're in Wyoming. Finally on your turf."

Liz nods. It's not a reproof. Jeanne would never scold her.

Truth is, since college, Liz has always been happy to set the visits, once a year when her parents were living one county away from her old friends. Drinks and dinner. Now less often. Letters float back and forth from and to Marney. The occasional email from the more reserved Jeanne. Enough contact. Right now, their appearance is part terrifying and part seductive. Calm down, she tells herself, it's just a week and you've known them over thirty years.

After the boy died, everything changed. His accident, wept Liz's limp, grief-broken mother. His suicide declared her angry, sad father. What did it matter? thought Liz, who insisted she didn't care how he died, just that he died. Her side-kick. The annoying pip-squeak. Her impish brother. They were a family of three now. With more to argue about. In a home that was suddenly too large. Of course they had to leave the rambling house.

When Liz complained that this move was the end of her life, Dad took her out for an ice-cream soda and talked about the momentum of change and adventure. The change would be exciting, he assured her, would be good for her character. Mom made more sense. You never really lose good friends, she explained, you simply add new ones.

High school was the first chapter of the trio's separation. During that year, they saw each other every weekend. But life grew complicated with dances and drama club and college prep classes. Who knew how much more time it took to be a teenager? Her dad had been right about momentum; change, what an elixir.

~

Maude's High Plains' Spa is a hit. Marney and Liz immediately sign up for mud baths and herbal wraps and massages.

A swim and a firm massage is enough for Jeanne. She hopes the masseur can do something with her left shoulder. Harlan warned her she was crazy to put up that fencing alone.

At seven they rendezvous in Maude's dining room— five oak tables covered with a blue cloth and green napkins. This early in the season they're the only customers.

Maude, herself, appears with a single sheet of Xeroxed menus. "You girls look properly buffed and polished," says the tall, lean, fortyish woman, country elegant in jeans and an embroidered white blouse. "How do you like the facilities?"

"Divine." Marney smiles. "Just what I needed. It's been a long year. What a relief to *let go*."

"Yes, wonderful." Jeanne allows a long sigh to run through her body.

"Where are you all from?

"California, the Bay Area," Marney explains.

Maude looks doubtfully at Liz.

"I've lived in Wyoming for twenty years," she clarifies.

"Somehow you don't look quite the same."

An almost imperceptible smile creases Liz's lips. She distracts herself, running her fingers over the embroidered table cloth.

"We've known each other since the third grade," Marney persists, vaguely affronted by Maude's elusive distinction. "Forty-two years."

"That right?" Maude lights the votive candle on their table. "I hope you find the food to your liking. Everything fresh, organic. I'll come back for your order."

The fragrance of the burning wick reminds Liz of church, of when they joined the Soldality of the Blessed Virgin Mary.

~

They all made a try at college, the first in their families to do so.

Marney went to Mills, became a librarian and married a guy named Frederick. Her husband has been perfecting a genius (but thus far profitless) computer program while she has supported him and the four boys for twenty years. She wears the time well; she's as wiry and lively as always.

Jeanne started out at San Francisco State, then quit because her mother died and someone needed to take care of the family. She and Rob, a virtuoso auto mechanic, had one daughter. These days, Jeanne's a tall, blondish clerk in a public records office. A little blonder than when she was in school, but the brightness suits her.

Liz went east, as they say, and got a degree in English. She published two books of poetry which weren't as successful as she hoped. If she couldn't be on top, she wasn't going to waste her time. For two decades now, she's been running Arts Ranch in Wyoming, where she sponsors jazz concerts, literary festivals, painting exhibits. Over the years, the romances—three men and two women—have come and gone. She's content with her two Australian sheep dogs and their handsome house by the creek. She is—as ever—medium height and weight with medium brown hair. Unremarkable, she likes to say, appreciating the advantages of nondescript appearance.

So that's how time passed—in the normal procession of degrees and partnerships and babies and mortgages and the occasional trip to far, far away. Of course progress isn't always steady or in one direction. Parents grew ill. Several died. Children excelled, then failed, then found even ground. Friends, well, more acquaintances, but contemporaries, were killed in Vietnam. Others just disappeared to another state or country or identity. Liz's first lover left her for a rich woman. Then came the really hard, inexplicable changes. Rob's Leukemia diagnosis, followed by twenty-two months of hospitals, bone marrow transplants and other tortures. Finally, he died in January, leaving Jeanne the memory of his courage and a vast portfolio of medical bills.

This is why they're in Wyoming. The visit is a respite for Jeanne after a tough three years. Marney suggested the trip, offered to pay Jeanne's plane fare. Liz, of course, agreed to her part; she'd put them up and show them the glories of Wyoming. That's what you do for old friends, isn't it? She hadn't thought twice about it. Until she said yes.

~

Uneasy silence sucks air from the room. Liz traces the embroidery again, looking down to see an elaborate figure of a cowgirl roping a horse. Maude doesn't look like a fabric artist, but people in Wyoming surprise you.

"Oh, god, did I embarrass anyone with the third grade reference?" Marney flushes. "I mean fifty is young these days. We have almost half our lives head of us, our generation."

"Some of us," Liz steers to another topic. "I'm sure Maude—or whatever her pre-organic name was—found it charming."

"Almost half our lives *if we're lucky*," Jeanne says quietly.

"Jesus," Marney takes her friend's hand. "I'm such an asshole. With Rob gone six months. Of course you're right. I'm sorry. So sorry."

"Don't worry." Jeanne pats Marney's shoulder. "I was just making a point. Since he died I take nothing for granted."

Silence steals back.

Jeanne raises her eyebrows. "I'll have the rib-eye." Her voice is strangely loud.

"That looks good," declares Marney, relieved to move the conversation along. "But I'll order duck. Unless our host has recommendations. Izzie?"

"No, no." Liz tries to suppress the word *host*. She doesn't know how to ask Marney to stop calling her Izzie. Why is she feeling so ornery with her old friend? "Tonight is my first meal in this fine establishment. I'll go for the trout. I bet it's local."

"Don't tell me you're an aquatarian," Marney hoots.

Jeanne stares.

"I don't eat meat, if that's what you mean."

Healthier diet for sure. Two of my boys, Charlie and Al, are aquatarians. They think Frederick and I are *barbarians*. Frederick plays it to the hilt. Picks up the drumstick and acts all Henry the Eighth."

Liz has always preferred Jeanne's husband. A quiet guy with a wry sense of humor. She's never known either man well because their reunion dinners have always been a threesome. She thinks it's odd—maybe not—how they've all retained the same personalities since third grade; Marney, the earnest, good girl; Jeanne, the understated boss with her native authority; and she, Liz, the wild card.

~

After dinner they loll in the sultry hot tub, gazing at the stars.

"It's too early for our Summer Triangle," Marney muses.

"Actually, you can see those three stars all year long," Jeanne says. "They're just not as bright in other seasons."

"Now how did we work this out?" Marney peers into the sky. "Oh, yes, Jeanne is Altair in her realms of higher intuition. And Izzie is Deneb, the emotionally complex, and I'm that boring Vega—tamed, earthy nature."

"No, no," laughs Jeanne. "I'm Vega, you're Deneb and Liz is Altair."

Liz, who has no opinion except that the conversation makes her nervous, turns on the water jets. The heat is beginning to loosen those muscles around her neck. She may even be able to turn it tomorrow. Should make for a safer drive. Her shoulder feels looser too.

"Wonderful to have this whole place to ourselves," sighs Jeanne. "I feel like a queen."

Liz guesses Jeanne can't afford hot tubs and massages back home. It was generous of Marney to plan the trip. They're doing a good thing for their friend. Yes, she's beginning to enjoy the visit. It's a just short time, after all.

Marney starts in, quietly humming.

Jeanne harmonizes, "*Bis-hop E-a-g-a-n.*"

Liz is grateful they're the only guests at Maude's tonight. Of course it's hours to Arts Ranch, but news travels in Wyoming.

"*Forever let us hold our banner high!*" Marney warbles into the steamy night.

They all collapse in giggles, bob up and down in the bubbling cauldron.

Who is the first to stick up her feet?

Soon there are six feet hovering above the water, each of them pressing a sole to that of a friend. Cozy despite the bracing night air.

"Water ballet at fifty!" Marney declares.

Sweet moment, thinks Liz, then takes a deep breath, abashed by her sentimentality

DAY TWO

The next morning is cloudy, which irritates Liz because she wants Wyoming hills to gleam for her friends. Spring thunderstorms arrive unpredictably, and she hopes they won't have pyrotechnics for the next few days. Ridiculous to take responsibility for the weather. Liz reminds herself that they'll be gone by Thursday and she'll regain her solitude—the creek, Sandhill Cranes, frog song.

"Is that an antelope?" cries Marney from the back seat.

Liz squints. "Looks like a deer."

"Frederick wants photos of every antelope."

"We will see antelope," Liz promises. "I'll point them out. And bobcat, fox, coyote. Maybe I can take you to a prairie dog town. " She decides not to mention cougar; she hasn't seen one in six months. And it's still too cool for rattlers.

"Gorgeous landscape," Marney declares. "Now I see why you live way out here."

Liz hasn't thought of it as "way out here" for 18 or 19 years. These high plains are now *her* place, where she belongs.

"Don't you get lonely?" Marney asks.

Sometimes Liz worries about the isolation. Still, she cherishes her evenings watching the sun set, the stars come out, then relaxing by the living room fire with music or a good novel.

"I see people at the Institute every day," she tries. "We have a program manager, a book keeper, a tech person. A secretarial temp. That's usually Millie, who also substitutes at the local grade school. Sometimes we eat lunch together."

She hears their silence. It is a rich, full life, they'll see.

Or maybe they won't.

"I can't wait to meet your friends," Marney declares.

Friends? The Institute staff aren't exactly her *friends*. She hasn't thought of taking them to the office. She's on a four day leave, except for the evening program.

"There," Jeanne points to the left. "There! Those gold animals with black stripes. Antelope, right?"

"Yeah, a good herd." Liz is relieved to be talking about something normal again.

"Look at those large, protruding eyes," Marney says.

"Well spotted as my Aunt Bronwyn would say." Liz smiles to the friends and the antelope. "See the upper body and outside legs are tan to brown. The cheeks, lower jaw, chest, belly, inner legs and rump are usually white. The male has a broad black band down the snout to a black nose. Black horns."

"You could narrate for PBS nature shows!" Marney teases. "Our local expert on Wyoming fauna."

"Some of my best friends are antelope," Liz says, her eyes on the road. PBS. God, she must be droning on.

"Life here; it's like another country," says Jeanne. "A new language; a different way of being."

"In a way." Liz is pleased, but she doesn't want to make it out as exotic. "How about some music? I have a CD of these great fiddlers who come to the Institute every fall."

"Sounds good," Jeanne nods.

Liz pops in the disc and takes a deep breath, returning home. The willows are that delicate spring shade of gold. Impatient for everything to bloom, she rests her eyes on the striations of yellow and olive and brown in the ragged hills, which are so distinct from the sensuous rounded contours of California memory.

"I feel we've traveled *west*, you know what I mean?" Marney taps Jeanne on the shoulder. "Doesn't this feel more *western* than California?"

"Not really. Have you been to Shingletown? Or Marysville, where Rob's mother lives? That's pretty deep Western."

Liz understands Jeanne's defensiveness, and she also agrees with Marney. To her the West has always implied some kind of brink. Wyoming is edgy; the place provokes her, energizes her.

As they approach Widner, she wants to tell them it's just twenty minutes to the ranch.

Right now, they're quiet, listening to Charlie's fiddle.

If you blink, you miss Widner, with its general store, compact Methodist Church and—barely visible from the highway—Cheerie's Quilting Paradise. Cheerie advertises two thousand brightly patterned bolts of cotton. Liz hears women drive a hundred miles to Cheerie's when new stock arrives. She'll tell them about Cheerie's later—an amusing frontier oddity—but hopes they won't want to visit.

The sun is fully out, and the warmth feels good on her shoulder. Wind slices into the fat clouds. Even from the highway, you see buds on trees, bushes. Brilliant late morning light on the hills brings the rock extrusions into great relief. A stately heron flies across the road before gliding over the greening field. Above a corrugated metal firehouse, a hawk sails and soars. Myra's stunning horses graze. Two red ones and the third, which seems oddly green in the direct sun.

Closer to the ranch now, she spots Mindy's clapboard house with the banged up station wagon outside. Have massage table, will travel. She's just one of dozens of intrepid people who found home on this plateau and manage to earn their livelihoods here. Liz is suddenly wistful for the place where she lives.

Harlan waves broadly from his pick-up. He makes a "T" sign with his hands for *town*. He's seventy-eight and always driving to Widner to get the last nail or screw or window for his ever-unfinished cabin. What would he do if he ever completed the place? It's been his job, vocation, his spiritual practice.

She waves back, then notices the creek. Higher than when she left yesterday. Good runoff from the mountain so far. Maybe less of a drought this year because of the storms. Thunder always resurrects Chuck. She wonders whether they'll talk about her quiet little brother, wonders how much her friends recall. Of course they remember her loss, but what do they recall about Chuck? His shy little voice? His curly hair? Is she the only one who carries him on?

"I'm around the next bend," Liz explains, startled by her own flat, strong voice above the reedy string melody.

"You live way out *here*?" Marney's eyes widen.

"Why not?" Liz is puzzled.

"I mean there are no other houses, *no neighbors*."

"We passed several places a mile back."

"What if you get stuck?" She's wiping her glasses with the edge of her sleeve.

"Stuck?"

"I don't know. You lock your keys in the house?"

"No one out here locks doors."

"Right." Marney absorbs this. "Makes sense. Yeah, it's not a city."

"We do lock the Institute." She doesn't want Marney to feel silly. "Because of the computers and the copy machine. All the files. Insurance rules."

As they approach the final curve, Liz is startled by how widely her heart opens. She flips on her blinker, a city habit, although there isn't a car in sight. Here's the peeling green wooden gate. Home.

"This is it. Can you unlatch the gate?"

"Sure," Marney offers. "I'll jump out."

Liz shuts off the music. Time to re-enter. Make herself available.

Marney raises the chain, tugs hard, lifts another part. She won't give up, but she hasn't a clue.

"I better go," Liz opens her door.

"No, I've got it." Jeanne puts out her hand. "Rob's mom has a latch like this."

Still the take-charge girl, but more easygoing in her prime.

As they pull up to the long, wooden house, Trix and Soba scoot through the dog door, then race to the dirt road. Barking, jumping on each other, peering expectantly.

"My blended family," she grins. "You both said you were OK with dogs, right?"

"They're gorgeous," coos Marney.

"They look so much like you," Jeanne cracks.

"I was hoping you would notice."

Once Liz opens the door, the dogs are all over her.

"Ok, ok. Now you have to meet my old friends, Marney and Jeanne."

Marney throws her arms around Trix's neck, nuzzling her forehead. Jeanne rubs Soba behind the ears.

While her friends get to know the dogs, Liz drags suitcases from the trunk. She's got them halfway to her house before Marney and Jeanne can intercept.

"This is some place!" Jeanne grabs her bag. "How many acres do you have? It seems to go on forever."

"Look at that!" Marney points to a cluster of cottonwoods on the far ridge. "Is this all *your* land?"

"Ten acres." Liz gestures to the west with a wide palm. "That's the property line. The rest belongs to the Institute—all given as conservation easements to prevent development."

"I bet that's a relief," Marney nods.

"Yes." She grins at her friend, who minutes before had worried about neighbors being too far away. Marney's getting it. And Liz knows that she, herself, can be a patronizing bitch. She ushers them both into the house.

"Mmm, smell the pine," sighs Jeanne. "Ah! All this natural wood. The gorgeous ceiling beams."

"Yes, beautiful," muses Marney. "I love the wood burning stove—oh, a cast iron Waterford. They don't make these any more. And look, Jeanne, the great comfortable couch. And the snug dog beds."

"So let's get you settled." Liz is gratified and a little embarrassed by their enthusiasm. She knows they worry about her, that they've worried since Chuck's death. Every couple of years, Marney inquires if she's gone into therapy yet. She explains that her brother died (accident, suicide; it still doesn't matter) a long time ago and that she's her own person now. "We should eat lunch." Her voice is too loud, a little imperative. "Ok with you? Then maybe have a walk around the place?"

"Oh, yes." Marney stretches widely and circles her stiff neck. "I could use the exercise. I spent last week in info tech seminars. Airless rooms with headless people."

Jeanne laughs. "Info tech?"

"I became a librarian because I love books. Now everything's online. We used to be asked questions about religion or philosophy or literature. Now we're supposed to be experts on information retrieval systems. I've joined the cast of *Max Headroom*."

Liz grins, then opens a door.

"Here's the guest room. It's really my study, so pardon the plastic file tubs in the corner. I've slept on each of these futons myself, and they are pretty comfortable."

"Looks perfect," Jeanne nods.

"But if you prefer separate quarters," she knows she's sounding like her mother now, but she can't seem to stop, "one of you could sleep on the couch. I want you to be comfortable."

"We're fine." Marney shakes her head. "Relax. We're your old pals. Not visiting royalty. This is lovely."

"Get settled and I'll unpack the groceries we picked up. I made some lentil soup on Sunday. Does that appeal?"

"Delish," says Marney. "I'll pitch in and make a salad."

Liz doesn't want a salad.

But Marney needs to help. She pulls out lettuce, cucumber, pepper and carrots while the soup heats.

Only two-and-a-half days to go, she thinks, a little guiltily.

"We could visit the county fair," she says.

"I love fairs. Oh, yes, please," Marney assents. "The farm animals and all those jams and pies."

The kitchen steams with the fragrance of garlic, bay leaves, onions, tomato and French lentils.

Liz peers out the window for that hawk with the dappled head. For some reason, she's fifteen and back in California. *You'll get over your friendship with those girls, her mother tells her. They're sweet, but not really your caliber. You'll find this new school more challenging, and you have a big future ahead of you. People will be your cheerleaders.* Her big future—the one thing on which her parents could agree. They never criticized her life in Wyoming. By that time Dad was in AA and most of the shouting, most of the demands were over. Still she knew they felt they lost two children.

Her friends look more relaxed now, in jeans and sweatshirts. Almost Wyoming.

"Yum, soup and salad." Marney washes the lettuce thoroughly. "So healthy. This little vacation is the perfect thing. I confess I've been depressed. Your gorgeous place is just *the* pick-me-up."

Jeanne stiffens, then focuses on folding napkins.

Liz knows that Marney's been anxious about her husband, about money. "Frederick?"

Marney nods.

Jeanne finishes setting the table. "All ready."

Marney takes a sip, then releases a long sigh. "He was an idealist when I married him: I knew that, but what's quixotic in a twenty-five year old is delusional for a guy in his fifties. I mean he's earned two Ph.D.s and has been working on this cryosurgery computer model— important stuff— forever. Almost there, he keeps saying."

Jeanne is picking at her salad.

Marney grows agitated. "One day soon, he keeps saying. One day soon this software will transform medicine.

He's contacted seventy, eighty surgeons here and in Malaysia, Japan, god knows where, and so far no one appreciates his vision." She stretches her arms wide, leaning back in the chair. "Move over Bill Gates."

What can Liz say? She wishes Marney had left him years ago. But it's her friend's life and clearly she's suffering.

During the soliloquy, Jeanne remains silent.

Liz considers Jeanne's own paralyzing loss. It doesn't diminish Marney's troubles; still she can feel the sting in Jeanne's reserve.

"If he would only compromise a little." Marney is tearing up. "His perfectionism has hardened into a kind of arrogance."

Liz thinks about Chuck and wonders for the thousandth time which parts of her were closed off forever by his death.

"I love his optimism. Truly."

You can't compare suffering, but in some way she worries more about Marney. There's nothing like the loneliness of a splintering relationship.

Marney gets a second wind. "Now, more and more I'm beginning to see it all as a pipe dream."

She's almost finished talking about Frederick and the boys and ebooks as they empty their bowls.

Liz loves the salad; a great, crisp addition to the hearty soup. She should have thought of it herself.

"Fresh air?" the host offers. "We can get those dishes later. Might as well walk while the sun is shining and the weather's calm."

"Storm coming?" Jeanne frowns.

"Here, you never know." Liz fills three water bottles. "Weather races across the plains without much notice."

They head out toward Spider Creek. Ducks make a mad flutter and then flap clumsily into the air. Geese honk. The wind ebbs and blows and ebbs.

Marney is holding the brim of a sunhat down against her cheeks. "Wow, these gusts. How do people keep the skin of their faces?"

"This wind is like a presence." Jeanne sips her water.

"The unholy ghost or something."

"Never thought about it like that," Liz muses. "It is a force. And a kind of…company."

"I imagine one could feel a bit lonely out here," Marney says sympathetically.

"I guess," Liz answers quickly. "Myself, I like the solitude. Think I was made for it."

Marney and Jeanne exchange glances.

They follow the creek to a dirt road and then walk uphill to the teepee circles. By now the sky is blue; heat rises from the ground. One by one, the women shed jackets.

"See how the rock pattern reveals where they put their tents? I don't know who these people were. Wyoming had a lot of Dahcotah, Arapaho, Crow, Shoshone." "And of course, Cheyenne," Jeanne says.

"Give that girl the geography medal!" laughs Marney admiringly. "Wow, these views! It's like I've climbed to Vogelsang, getting the reward of all this beauty without the steep, dusty hike."

"Do you still go to the High Sierra every summer?" Jeanne asks.

"Not for ages. Can't afford it, with the boys' college and all. My therapy bills don't help. It's been ten years since we've gone hiking. That's why this," she fans out her arms, "is such a tonic."

Hardly any clouds now. Buds about to explode. Above, a hawk drifts.

"Is that a fox?" Marney whispers. "That reddish brown flash?"

"Yes, yes," Liz says, aware that she sometimes just stops noticing.

"And catch that magnificent magpie," says Jeanne.

"Let's walk to Miner's Road. There's this old yurt." She bathes in the bright spring light, so full of promise.

"What do they mine?" Jeanne maintains an easy stride. "Silver? Gold?"

"They dig for coal, bentonite, trona and uranium." She's come a long way from Elizabethan sonnets to Wyoming earth sciences. Just another kind of beauty.

Marney's pace is slowing. The half mile takes twenty minutes. Finally they arrive at the abandoned yurt, edged with overgrown grass. A Canadian Cherry is starting to flower.

"Who lived here?" Jeanne runs her hands curiously over the wood-lattice frame which sticks out through the disintegrating felt. "How did they earn a living?"

"Something to do with crystals," Liz shrugs.

"Hippies, way out here?" Marney asks breathlessly as she catches up to them.

"A lot of people come to Wyoming to do their thing, to be their thing. The place isn't big on labels," she says more sharply than she intended. Why is she getting on Marney's case so much? It's her sadness. Compounded by Jeanne's sadness. And her own. Marney is just an easy target. It's simpler to snipe at her than to hold her sorrow.

Liz notices her friend's red face. It's not sunburn.

Just then, Marney appears to crumble, slumping against the edge of a large boulder.

Liz wonders about rattlers but reminds herself it's too early, too cool, for them.

Marney's weeping, trying to hold it back, gagging. "I'm sorry. I didn't mean. I guess I'm so depressed."

Jeanne takes a deep breath and turns toward the creek.

"You look pretty tuckered," Liz says. "It's about a mile and a quarter back to the house, but if you two like, I can leave you here. Or over there—that shady place under the tree. And I can swing back with the car."

"That would be good," Marney says deliberately, pulling herself together. "I didn't realize how out of shape I am."

"I'll walk back with you," Jeanne offers. "If you're OK on your own, Marn?"

"Sure. I brought my phone and water. You'll be back in an hour, right?"

"Twenty-five minutes tops," Liz reassures her. "You're completely safe. This is all Institute land."

They walk, enjoying the silence between them.

"How are you doing?" Liz asks. "Must have been a tough six months."

"Feels like ten years. Ten minutes. I'll be somewhere —today, here, for instance, and I'll want to call Rob and tell him all about this place." She shakes her head. "At night, I startle awake wondering where he is. The other side of the bed is cold. It's like an amputation."

"You guys had a good marriage."

"We had our ups and downs, but hell, yes, we were lucky. We loved raising Marie. We all hiked a lot. Took fun vacations every summer, two weeks—usually to Marysville, that's why I'm the expert on latches. We'd stop at a state park on the way there and back. We all enjoyed fishing, the campfire at night.

Liz recalls Jeanne's admiration for the pine beams and the wood stove. She's working hard to keep up with Jeanne's pace and her legs feel good.

"Am I walking too fast?"

"No, boss. Good exercise. You were always the leader growing up."

Jeanne shrugs. "Hope it wasn't too obnoxious. Comes from being the oldest of seven kids."

"I remember how you quit school when your mom died—"

"People make too much of that. No heroics. I probably wasn't college material anyhow."

They're almost at the cabin. Liz is aware how much she wished she had said on the walk, wonders if they'll have another chance to talk privately. Of course there are two whole more days.

The dogs bound out to greet them. Startled pheasants scoot away primly, heads erect, dazzling feathers unruffled.

The house is pleasingly cool. Liz grabs the car keys.

"I'll just hang out here, if you don't mind going back alone?" Jeanne ventures.

"No. Fine."

"I could use a little rest from—a little down time."

Liz nods. She should have thought about this herself. Now she muses that it would have been a calmer visit with just Jeanne. But Jeanne wouldn't be in her life without Marney. Marney introduced them, continues to keep them all in touch. The triangle works. And since her parents died, really since Chuck died, they've been her real, if distant, family. Perhaps she's taken them for granted at times, but they know she loves them. She hopes they do.

"Hey, why don't you relax on the back deck with a cup of tea or something? I need to run to town, and I'll take Marney. This'll give you over an hour."

Jeanne smiles sheepishly. "That would be nice."

~

After four or five games, Marney proposed uniforms. Nothing elaborate —simple skirts and sweaters in gold and blue. B and E in felt on the back. Marney excelled in the domestic arts. You knew she would grow up and have a well-dressed family. Liz spent a happy weekend in the Clancy living room sewing with her friends, away from her loud and angry parents. She felt guilty telling Chuck he couldn't come, even though he would have been bored to tears.

As the worst seamstress, Liz was put in charge of pompons.

The following Friday night, they were a sensation. Bishop Eagan beat St. Kate's by a large margin.

"And the score goes up another notch. Boom, boom.

Clank, clank. Ding dong."

Team and cheerleaders were fêted in Saturday's Miles Record.

The cool girls who usually made the Saturday paper with their parties and skiing trips just laughed at such juvenile school spirit. Honestly, who cared?

The mothers of the cool girls were not amused.

Sister Rose announced competitive cheerleading trials.

Marney and Jeanne complained they'd spent two months allowance on the uniforms. Liz, however, thought the competition was fair enough. With a little strategy, they'd win easily.

All week the trio practiced three routines. "Lean to the Left, Lean to the Right," "Back into the Woods." And "Bis-hop E-a-g-a-n."

"Here's the plan," Liz declared. "We'll save the best for the last. We'll leave them with an unforgettable "Lean to the Left; Lean to the Right."

"Stand up," Marney and Jeanne laughed and sang. "Sit down. Fight. Fight. Fight!"

ALMOST OVER

"I'm psyched." Marney leans on the dinner table, sipping the last of her wine. "Like we're all going to a prom or something."

They're decked out for the Institute's Spring Performance, and Liz is a little nervous, unsure whether she's more concerned about what Marney and Jeanne think of her neighbors or vice versa.

Liz is happy Marney has cheered up. She teases, "If I look like I'm headed to the prom, I'm slipping right back into those jeans and sneakers."

"It's OK to be a little girlie now and then." Jeanne winks. "I know how you're feeling, Marn. It's a *do*. It's fun to dress up and have an evening out."

Yes, they're all mellower after a few days together. Liz feels a twinge about taking them back to the airport. Then she thinks how good it will be to retrieve her tranquil life. She gets up to clear the table, but Marney protests.

"You and Jeanne finish your wine. I'll take care of the dishes."

"Really, it's easier for me——"

"No, no, Liz. I promise to stack them in the sink. I know you have your own methods. Just try to *relax* for a few moments."

"Rob loved jazz." Jeanne talks about him more easily than three days ago. "He had all the CDs, the Modern Jazz Quartet, Acoustic Jazz Quartet, Cold Spring Jazz Quartet."

"I'm not sure we're in that league, but this Chicago group is supposed to be pretty good. We've had raves about their workshop for the high school kids."

"Way out here, that's some nice opportunity for students." Marney is almost finished clearing. Stacking the last plates, she says, "The performance is a great idea, too. Otherwise, how would local people hear this kind of live music?"

"We do get regulars driving in from the bigger towns. Some come from as far away as Rapid City. But most drive from nearby places. We do the same thing with the painters —a workshop and an exhibit." Liz hears the satisfaction in her voice.

Driving a mile to the Institute in the evening light, Liz notices late sun striating the green/gold hills. The pale moon is almost full.

"Look," cries Jeanne, pointing to a blue heron gliding over the roadway.

Sun glints along the wire of a long fence. White, purple, grey clouds reflect from Tinler's pond. Bucks sprint across the grass, so vibrantly alive in comparison to the stolid green tors receding in the twilight.

"Oh, god, the Institute is filling!" She knew they shouldn't have talked so long over dinner. What's happening to her?

At the door, Grace collects tickets and chats with new arrivals. She beams at Jeanne and Marney. "Welcome, boss. These your famous visitors?

Marney extends her hand. "I'm Marney, and this is Jeanne. We're Liz's best friends since the third grade."

Grace blinks.

"Now you *did* know I got as far as the third grade, right, Grace?"

"Never had a doubt," she grins. "Welcome to the Institute, Marney and Jeanne."

Liz can hear the jokes about her tardiness in the office next week.

"What a handsome hall," Jeanne marvels. "Beautiful craftsmanship with those beams."

"It's gigantic," Marney looks around. "How many seats?"

"We get five hundred at a concert." Liz is taken aback by the pride in her voice.

Grace has reserved the perfect seats, and Liz gives Jeanne the best view of the piano.

Yes! The music is stunning. The guy on the sax shifts to the xylophone in the second set. The woman guitarist moves to the bass. Two fellows playing drums and piano stick with their instruments, but the music changes completely in set two.

Afterward, she briefly makes the rounds. When she glances back toward her friends, she sees that Grace is introducing them to the musicians. Jeanne beams.

~

Now standing before the assembly, the fans, as Liz has come to regard them—not her fans, but the team's fans—she felt renewed confidence. Momentarily she sensed her strength with frightening certainty. Surveying the crowd, she observed Sister Rose's trembling bonne amie. And her little brother Chuck's wild eyes. Always so fearful, sometimes he made her feel scared of…anything. Everything. She had to be the strong one, standing up for both of them to their inconstant parents. Nodding to her, he shaped his fingers into an "OK" sign. She nodded back, swallowed hard, turned to her sisters on the stage.

To her friends, her future.

Jeanne stepped forward to announce the routine.

At least half the auditorium sang along, "Bis-hop E-a-g-a-n."

Yes! They'd triumph even further with the next routine.

Leave them gasping with the last.

"Come along

And sing a song

And join the jamboree…."

Vega, Deneb and Altair tossed their pompons toward the ceiling to riotous applause.

Rearranging themselves for the second routine, no one noticed Sister Rose approaching the microphone impatiently.

"Let's have another hand for Marney, Jeanne and Liz before we introduce the next group."

As the clapping died down, Jeanne whispered, "But Sister, we've only just begun. We have two more routines."

Sister smiled thinly, tented her palms, then vigilantly directed them to the wings.

Liz persisted. "Sister, we've saved the best for the last."

One hand on her shiny black serge hip, Sister Rose whispered sternly, "Thank you, girls. That will be all. We must learn to share the stage."

Liz stifled the tears until she escaped through the clumsy double door. She ran to the lavatory for solitude. The damp green room smelled of apple blossom cologne, a recent diarrhea and old banana peels. Sitting on the toilet, silently weeping, she could hear Lena, Ruth and Connie singing, bounding, flinging their extra fluffy pompons to one another.

Liz washed her hands, then heard the roaring applause. She opened the taps full blast in all three sinks—satisfied by the deafening surge of water—and closed the door.

As she approached the thrumming auditorium, where classmates were gossiping, falling in love with each other, planning their evening TV schedules, whispering about cliques, she knew she couldn't open those heavy assembly doors. She decided to leave school early. Chuck could walk home alone.

That afternoon, Liz learned that there are no second chances, that small acts of rebellion are cathartic and that nobody was going to— ever—tie her down.

~

"What a fantastic night." Marney drops into Jeanne's easy chair and kicks off her pumps. "Ohh, new shoes, just a wee bit too tight for a whole evening."

"Thanks for joining me." Liz burrows into a cabinet for single malt, then dusts off the bottle. "Night cap?"

Jeanne is humming. She stares into her glass for a minute. "Rob would have loved it. I loved it. I felt he was with us tonight."

Marney's eyes fill. "Thanks, Izzie, for sharing your extraordinary life."

THE END SO SOON

The last evening, after a lavish vegetarian feast prepared by Marney and Jeanne, they loll on the back deck finishing a bottle of zinfandel and watching the fat, full moon rise. A fresh, bright evening. The air is still. You notice that in windy Wyoming. Comforting heat rises from the ground. The long winter has finally turned over.

"We've brought a little care package from California." Jeanne proffers a gold and blue gift bag.

"You shouldn't have."

"A few small things, that's all." Marney grins.

Liz pulls out a jar of blood orange marmalade. A packet of dried apricots, so fragrant, she smells the sweetness through the cellophane. Two bars of eucalyptus—oh, how she misses those pungent, rangy trees—soap. And a bubblewrapped bottle of Mendocino Pinot Noir. "What bounty!"

"Now you'll have something to remind you of the visit," Marney says.

Liz is speechless.

"Aren't you forgetting something?" Jeanne asks.

"Yes, well, I hope you like this. Frederick made the picture frame."

"Frederick," Jeanne repeats.

Liz takes a long breath, holding out the restored and blown-up photo for all to see. Three beaming adolescent girls —not the prettiest or the bounciest but very appealing— waving gold and blue pompons.

Jeanne sighs. "Remember, '*We'll have a strategy. We'll leave them with an unforgettable 'Lean to the Left/Lean to the Right.' We'll save the best for the last.*"

"Do you still hold that against me?" Liz's heart sinks.

"No, it was a great adventure," Marney exclaims. "A great friendship."

"Was?" Liz is uneasy.

"Is." Marney corrects herself.

"Is!" Jeanne declares.

"Let's get together again next year." Is Liz really saying this? Just as she's reclaiming her house, her schedule, her precious quiet?

Marney raises a glass in agreement.

"I could fly to California. Or you could come back here. I mean there's so much you haven't seen." Maybe they could talk more about their parents, their sisters and brothers next year. She would restore Chuck's picture to the living room bookcase.

"Here. Let's come back here," exclaims Marney.

"Sounds perfect," Jeanne agrees. "Just let me work out the finances."

Liz grows still, listening to two owls in the twisted cottonwood. The moon shines brightly above and below in the gleaming creek. She sips the last of her wine and wonders what on earth she's just got herself into.

~

Rain cascades as they set off for the airport. Liz hopes the storm doesn't delay traffic. People here are used to owning the road. Everyone drives fast and too certain on slick highways.

They're lost in thought for the first five minutes.

"Mind if I put on some music?" Liz asks.

"Fine," they say in unison.

Glenn Gould begins the first variation again. Why does it sound different every time?

"I feel we've been here four seasons." Marney sighs in the front passenger seat.

Liz looks through the rearview mirror at Jeanne. Her friend is pensive, rested.

"What was your favorite part, Jeanne?" Marney asks.

"Sitting on the deck looking at the hills and animals."

"I think my favorite part was that I didn't step on a rattlesnake." Marney laughs.

"Oh, yeah?" Liz is curious what she knows about rattlers.

"Of course Frederick researched the perils of visiting Wyoming and lectured me every night last week."

"What a champ!" Jeanne grins.

"His way of saying he'd miss me. Actually, I'm looking forward to seeing him. But things are going to be different."

Liz lowers the CD volume.

"How different?" Jeanne asks tentatively.

"Witnessing Liz's independent life, I get it that I have to speak up more. We'll see how I do."

Liz swallows, keeps her eyes on the road, tries to concentrate on the fourth variation.

"Back to the question," Marney says earnestly. "I liked the fairgrounds best. I'll never forget that girl grooming her goat and at the same time chatting away on her pink cell phone."

Jeanne nods.

"What about you, Izzie, what was your favorite part?" Marney persists.

Marney has always persisted. The triangle would have cracked long ago without Marney.

The question surprises her.

The trip was for *Jeanne*, to comfort her.

And to cheer up Marney.

Her favorite part? She imagined this drive would be her favorite part: taking them back to the airport, finally.

"Well?" Marney said.

When they exclaimed at the antelope and really listened to the birds and delighted in the shadows on the evening hills, they made her grateful. Happy to be alive in a way she hadn't been since…

She wants to reply but can't concentrate on an answer because it's pouring and the traffic is crazy and they need to get to the airport safely if they're going to come back again. Next year, Liz thinks, she'll take them deeper into the mountains.

Coming Through

As the plane finally settles at the gate, you pull on your simple black coat with its zip in/zip out lining. Zipped back in now that you're returning to the tundra. You edge toward the exit, bracing for that blast of winter air between plane and gangway. Three tortuous hours squeezed between a bickering couple while the child behind kicks your seat to the rhythm of *The Lion King* seeping from his earbuds. You offer to let the couple sit together. "No way!" they answer in unison. You address the child and then his father about the foot percussion. Each stares back silently as if you are hallucinating. The flight attendant swears he has no empty seats.

Finally, you're leaving them all behind. Relief is shortlived. Inside the clangorous terminal, you remember your *four-hour* layover. If all goes well, you'll get to frigid Minneapolis at midnight. Then snatch five or six hours sleep before appearing at the office.

OK, you're a seasoned veteran of Greyhound Airlines; you can handle this. Keep busy. There's plenty of unfinished work. So you laboriously roll your heavy bag, fiddling with the brief shoulder strap to forestall another rhomboid injury. Then, voila! An abandoned luggage cart. You unload and glide along, searching for a restaurant where you can read your charts on the laptop.

~

Just last night, in Orange Blossom Land: this reunion with your oldest friend in her favorite South Beach Café is the reward for that boring conference. A sweet, swanky night.

After her second glass of wine, Janice leans over, smiling mischievously. "Tamar love, where did you find that dreary coat?"

"It's a classic black coat. Versatile, mid-calf, slimming," you say, taking in Janice's mauve mohair jacket over her emerald green shift. Muy tropical. All the Midwest is purged from your girlfriend, or at least camouflaged.

"Tamar, really, you look like a nun."

"Come on," you argue. "It's practical, chic like a basic black dress. See how the red scarf brightens it up?"

"OK, a post-Vatican Two nun," she laughs.

"Honestly, Tam, it reminds me of the coats our moms wore to synagogue for Aunt Dina's funeral. Next time I'm in the Cities, we're going shopping, and I'll introduce you to the twenty-first century."

"I'd like that." You grin. Sometimes you envy her Florida adventure. But your parents are frail and you can't leave St. Paul. Janice, whose parents are cruising the Mediterranean, calls your filial attentiveness saintly, but as the only child, it's just your job.

~

The new terminal, they say, will be state of the art. Right now, it's a chaotic construction site with culinary choices ranging from dismal to forget it. You opt for sushi. Sushi at a Midwest airport: maybe not the brightest idea. Well, you feel like a light meal and a large Sapporo and they allow you to wheel in the luggage cart.

Focus, Tamar. Opening your laptop, you ignore tomorrow's charts and feel called to scrub your inbox. A perfect task for the interstices of life. You do a search for Jonathan and resolve to delete all his messages as he deleted you from his life last month. Pathetic to hang on to these emails. With a sense of triumph, you press delete and watch them disappear. You boldly click again, emptying the trash. Would it be so easy to erase loss or longing?

Now onto work—answering client questions, negotiating with the engineer on your new office design. Too soon the sushi and, more disappointingly, the Sapporo, are finished. There's a lot more email, but weary travelers hover nearby, hungrily eyeing your table. You pack up, bus your plate and start strolling. Still 4,000 more steps to walk today.

Bargain ticket. Why did George get you the cheapest seat on earth? A lousy middle spot all the way from Miami. You've only been pleasant to George, offering lifts when his jalopy breaks down, soliciting his thoughts on designs. Your partners would never consult the office manager, but George has fresh, candid ideas. Maybe you're too considerate, and he takes you for granted? He manages great bookings for Dan and Angus and Lloyd. Half the time they're bumped up to first class and get passes to those sleek airline lounges. Meanwhile, your flights are always botched—crummy seats and long layovers. It's not some sort of sexist thing on George's part. Of course it is.

Just buck up. At least you have a job. And a free luggage trolley. Exercise will clear your head. You push the cart from one terminal to the next, past shops selling accessories, briefcases, cell phones, expensive men's clothing. Walking briskly, it feels good to stretch your legs after three days of panels and papers and board meetings. The airport is packed with stranded winter holiday families: tired children and even more exhausted adults. So many passengers are dressed in pastels, perhaps an ancient pagan reflex to appease the gods of winter darkness. Still you can't imagine wearing pastel to an airport.

"Excuse me, Miss." An old man steps close, grabbing your arm anxiously.

You're startled, a little annoyed, then you sense his panic. "Are you OK?"

"You work for the airlines, right?" He's breathless, flushed. "Or the airport?"

"No." You're sorry to disappoint him. "I'm just a passenger."

"I thought with the black uniform and all."

You will *never* tell Janice this story.

"Sorry." He's trembling now. "Sorry to bother." He turns away.

"Hold on." You reach for his boney shoulder. "Is something wrong?"

"Well." He draws nearer, whispering hoarsely, "I lost my wife."

You take his hand.

"Misplaced!" he adds quickly. "She's not dead or anything." His voice winds higher and fainter. "I told her to let the children visit us for Christmas."

"I bet she's fine. Let's look for Travelers' Aid." You walk him over to the airport map.

177

"See that desk there?" You guide him closer. "They'll help you. They can call her name over the loudspeaker. I'm sure you'll find her soon."

Drained but resolute, the old man pivots toward the desk. He walks away without saying good-bye.

You stride for another thirty minutes, 3,000 steps and decide to look for a seat where you can review Monday's meeting agenda. Bingo! An empty gate. Your concentration lasts exactly forty minutes.

One-hundred-ten minutes to take-off. Yawning and stretching your arms wide, you remember those isometric exercises but are too shy to do them in public. Instead you consider another Sapporo.

Nope, resume walking. Why did you leave your ear buds at home? A little music would muffle all this clanking, buzzing, sneezing, coughing and clattering. The overhead TVs blare alarm about a snow storm in New England. A man in a shiny green gabardine suit leans against a pillar shouting into his cell phone. You imagine he's a giant frog and wonder if you're losing your mind. At the next gate, a baby wails as a pasty-faced woman listlessly rocks her stroller back and forth, back and forth. People more sensible than you—Black, Asian, Latino, White, young, old, the whole world—are sequestered behind headphones or engrossed by paperbacks, deep in survival mode.

Abruptly, a boarding pass is thrust in your face, grazing your cheek.

You halt, feel temper rise at the intrusion. Then you look at the woman, perhaps twenty-five, perhaps North African or Middle Eastern, wearing a black hijab, long navy dress and holding a hefty toddler. You recall Janice's crack about the nun. A hand of Fatima dangles from a gold chain around the woman's neck.

Poor thing is terrified, worn out, lugging her son and a battered houndstooth satchel, the kind you only find at yard sales any more.

"Flight," she demands. "Where?"

Immediately you understand you may be her last resort. When you read the ticket and discover the flight leaves in twenty minutes, you're sure of it. "Let me check the terminal."

"Must hurry," she stresses, frowning and on the verge of tears. "Late. Very late."

"Yes." You nod. "But you'll be fine." You say this with your eyes as well because you're not sure of her English.

Doubtful, exhausted, she shifts the boy higher with her right arm, and he squeezes her thin shoulders. The knuckles on her left hand are white from gripping the valise.

"Here." You adjust your luggage and hold out your hand. "We can put your bag in front of mine."

She regards you suspiciously. But you are, after all, some kind of airline agent, so she accepts the offer, relief flooding her face.

"Your son." You point to the upper rack then touch his foot lightly. "He can sit here."

Her eyes widen. Shaking her head vehemently, clasping her son with the one arm, she reaches for the valise with the other.

"OK, OK," you say softly, holding up your palms. "Just the bag."

She nods, as if she's given you something.

"Gate B-23," you say then whistle. "That's pretty far."

She stares at you almost angrily, anxiously.

"Cleveland." More upbeat now, you speak slower. "Going to Cleveland?"

"Cleveland, Ohio," she answers solemnly.

"OK, Cleveland!" You point to the Terminal B sign. "Cleveland here we come."

Every gate is crowded. The damn airport grows ever more hectic. Hundreds of vacation refugees have been dumped between delayed flights. In a corner, a group of ten or twelve South Asian women lie on the floor, sound asleep. All around them other passengers talk and eat and laugh.

"Coming through," you call. Then louder. "Boarding flight." Where did you get this language? This authority?

The human sea parts for you, the young mother and her squirming son.

Several people approach with questions, but you wave them away politely. "Emergency Boarding flight." A loud, controlled, professional tone.

Two wheelchair caddies eye you skeptically, then shrug to each other.

You don't care. "Coming through!"

The Food Court presents special obstacles as dazed passengers stand, immobilized by bright lights at Cinnabon, TCBY Yogurt and Starbucks. The air is ripe with salt, sugar, liquor and cooking oil. Good thing you didn't have that second Sapporo; you're high enough.

"Coming through." You suddenly slow down for the woman to catch up.

She puts one hand on the cart, as if she's still worried you'll make off with her houndstooth bag. The boy is sniffling now, on the verge of a meltdown, you can tell.

Threading past McDonalds and Chilis and Curry Express, you spot B Terminal and show your companion.

She nods, blinks.

A man waves eagerly.

Really, you can only handle one passenger at a time.

The old guy, clasping his wife's hand, raises it in salute.

"Merry Christmas!" he shouts.

"Happy New Year!" you cry back, glad for their reunion.

"Coming through," you call again.

You haven't had this much fun in ages.

B23 is one of those tricky gates, around the corner from the desk. But you spot stragglers boarding.

"Final call for Flight 78 to Cleveland," a broken voice crackles over the loudspeaker. You can barely make out the words. How would this young woman understand?

You roll the cart up to the queue. "Cleveland!" You smile at her.

"Cleveland," the young woman says and sighs.

You hand her the bag. "Have a safe—"

Before you finish, she's checking in, then rushing down the gangway, balancing bag and baby. No wave. No thank you.

Why should there be? It's all in a night's work.

Sixty more minutes until the Minneapolis flight.

You brush off your coat, turn the cart around and wait.

The Women at Coral Villas

"The letter was astonishing, but so were the whole four days," Lorna writes to her friend Tracy in London. *"We were the most unlikely traveling companions, three mismatched, but oddly complimentary women."* She wants to explain the surprises and frustrations and hilarity and trauma and delight of their time at Coral Villas. But how to begin?

Lorna rocks on the deck of her compact *demi-villa* sipping a pleasantly bitter, cold Bintang beer. She makes out two mountains across the Lombok Strait in Bali. Are they volcanic like so much of this shape-shifting country? The call to prayer is slowly whirling to conclusion. Now, from a neighboring garden: peeping birdsong and lowing water buffalo.

"Paradise." She said to her friend and laughed. "What the hell are you supposed to do in Paradise?"

Tracy said, "Find a lover. Climb a mountain. Be adventurous. For godsake, take a break from your bloody books."

Lorna's other friends agreed.

"You work too hard!"

"Take a rest."

"Unwind and explore."

So after three weeks in the archives and lecture halls of Java, she's flown to Lombok, a sultry island where she can see Bali, but where the local beach has fewer sunburned tourist bellies. Lorna's grandparents came from Madagascar. Her own field—some would say her expertise—is the ancient trade routes and migrations between Indonesia and the Malagasy world. She loves the yellowing records, the musty, fabric thick covers of ships' logs, the curious stains on the paper of antique diaries. She's most at home in the *there* and the *then* in currents of long ago.

Friendship is important to the good life, her grandmother used to tell her. But Lorna's passion is work. Lovers have come and gone; no one wanted to share her with the archives. Now at forty-five, Lorna has given up on an enduring lover.

She inhales, noticing the fragrances of saltwater, tropical flowers and some garlicky dish from the café below. *"The café, Tracy, it all began at the café."*

~

MONDAY

The beachside restaurant is empty except for a handsome older white woman sitting erectly at the adjacent table. Lorna nods.

The woman smiles wanly.

Lorna scans the menu, glances at the beach where French and German tourists recline on red striped chaise lounges. Lombok men entice tourists with snorkeling flyers. One woman offers massages. Another sells gaudy towels. Finding few takers, the vendors wander down toward the cheaper hotels.

She sips a glass of the outrageously priced wine and waits for her meal.

The white woman is also waiting.

Lorna admires the stranger's taupe linen sundress, the pale green cardigan shrugged over her shoulders. Her own loose cotton shirt and pants make her feel slapdash. Suddenly, she hears herself inquiring, "Is this your first visit to Lombok?"

"My fifth." A tart Australian accent. "I used to come with my husband. He died last year."

"I'm sorry."

She nods, then brightens slightly. "It's as beautiful as ever."

"I'm dining alone tonight," Lorna says by way of invitation.

"Me too. I usually sit at your table. Somehow they lost my reservation."

Lorna realizes she's feeling a little lonely and tries a final time. "Would you care to join me? You'd have a better view from here."

"That might be nice. Thank you." She slides over on the bench.

"Lorna." She extends her hand.

"Celeste." The woman tents her palms in *Namaste*, bowing.

Lorna blinks, wonders if she gargled today. No, no. It's the woman's acute physical reserve. Lorna feels positively easy-going in comparison.

Celeste likes to talk. She comes from Melbourne, fourth generation of Irish prisoner stock, quite fashionable now, she laughs. Her husband Roland was a merchant banker. After the boys grew up, she and Roland took early retirement to enjoy his hard-earned money.

"You're from here, then?" asks Celeste?

Even locals assume she's from Indonesia. A prodigal daughter with an English accent. Such welcoming people, they also call Barak Obama Indonesian. Actually, she has the same coloring as the American president, a complexion that blends in easily here. As a scholar, she's learned Grandpa's stories about Indonesians settling his part of Madagascar are true. As a kid she paid little attention. Back home in multiculti London, she's clearly of color but few people ask specifics.

"I'm English."

"Yes, the accent," Celeste's Australian twang broadens. "But—" she reddens.

"My four grandparents emigrated from Madagascar to Kenya with their vanilla plants. Mum and Dad immigrated to London under the right of abode provision." She's told the story to puzzled colleagues all over Indonesia, most of whom nod comprehendingly because they know about the trade routes. Celeste, however, looks more baffled than ever.

As Neela serves their meals, fish stew for Celeste and calamari for her, Lorna studies her companion's face. Late sixties at most, she guesses, only about twenty years older than herself. Yet chic women with such bearing seem from a bygone era.

Her ruminations are interrupted by a broad, American voice.

"Mind if I perch here a sec?" The Asian woman with the sunny blond hair asks breathlessly. "I'm Rosie."

Celeste glances curiously, almost clinically, as if awaiting an explanation.

Rosie accommodates. "See that massive German over there. He's been shadowing me all afternoon. *Does Fräulein wish to walk on the beach? Welcome to my room for a drink. Please join me for dinner?* Sheesh. My colleagues swore the Villas were cool for single women. She grips the table's edge, trembling. "He's starting to freak me out."

"Welcome." Lorna smiles at the pretty young woman—Japanese American?—with the intelligent eyes, diamond nose stud and flamboyantly spiked yellow hair. Her trim figure is disclosed to excellent effect in a skimpy pink halter top and tight shorts. This is a beach resort, Lorna reminds herself. Now, across from Rosie, she's transformed from the young frump into the prim auntie.

"Do join us," Celeste says kindly. "We're each dining alone."

Clearly puzzled by the comment, Rosie doesn't question her temporary refuge. "I'm Rosie Hongo, just here a few days. Or not. If Lothario persists, I'll escape back to Jakarta."

"You live in Jakarta?" asks Lorna.

"I work for the U.S. Embassy. Minor, minor post. I put in for Indonesia because I wanted to see Kalimantan, Papua, the Flores Islands, but I've been stuck in the Jakarta office all year. Weird place. Poverty everywhere, yet the city center is crammed with five star hotels and malls splashed with Max Mara, Harvey Nicks, Dona Karan. Nutso traffic. L.A. without the good flicks."

"I'm Lorna, and this is Celeste."

"In every city, say Delhi, one just needs to know where to look." Celeste finishes her wine and signals Neela for another glass.

Neela takes Rosie's dinner order.

In Celeste's pretentiousness Lorna recognizes something of her own discomfort, an inadvertent haughtiness born of vulnerability.

"My last posting was Delhi." Rose sounds nostalgic. "I'd give anything to be back. When were you there?"

"My husband died in India this past October." Celeste looks out toward the bright lamps the bobbing fishing boats.

Lorna follows her gaze. These deck lamps are tiny stars blinking in the black sea.

Celeste composes herself and continues, "Roland was cremated in Udaipur."

Rosie blinks.

"That must have been so hard," Lorna murmurs.

"Hardest for my sons, who…." She loses her train of thought.

Lorna's still taking in Celeste's loss.

"Both Douglas and Arthur were pallbearers. Douglas, as elder, lit the pyre."

"Heartbreaking." Rose nods.

"Yes." Lorna reaches out, but the woman withdraws her hand before they touch.

Rosie's voice softens. "Sometimes I work with bereaved families. And you did the right thing. Cremation is the least painful way to take a loved one home."

"Oh, Roland didn't go home. He was a traveler at heart. I am carrying on for both of us. The boys and I scattered his ashes in Pushkar Lake. So many good people there—Gandhi, Nehru. Roland would have wanted that."

Good people, Lorna muses: major figures in Indian history. Celeste doesn't mean to be pretentious. They're all flustered in this new place. She craves a glass of the overpriced wine.

Catching Lorna's bewildered expression, Rosie says, "So we each wound up in this Eden alone." She turns to her subdued companion. "What brought you here, Lorna?"

"Archives and a few lectures on early trade routes from Indonesia to Africa and India."

"Yeah," Rosie blushes. "Isn't it cool—this entire world of culture and commerce existed before the Euros got on their boats. And they think they brought us civilization."

Celeste gets something in her eye and pulls out a mother of pearl mirror.

"So what are you?" Rosie persists. "A geographer? Historian?"

Americans are so direct, something she admires, yet finds faintly abrupt. Most people outside the academy don't get past her one sentence potted research description. "Interdisciplinary post-colonial studies."

"Dope." Rosie grins.

"Students earn degrees in that?" Celeste's eyebrows lift.

"It's a graduate focus."

Neela serves Rosie's Very Veggie Napoleon.

Glancing into the darkening night, Lorna notices the sunbathers have disappeared. Some have metamorphosed as diners in the now crowded restaurant.

Celeste turns to Rosie. "What drew you to the Foreign Service?"

She shrugs. "I longed to see the world and didn't want to join the marines."

Lorna laughs.

"To be honest, I used to have grand ideas about bringing peoples together."

"But now?" Celeste tilts her head.

"I don't know. It's easy to get discouraged, even cynical. Everybody wants something. Visas, work permits, green cards, scholarships. In and out of the office. Oh, I do have some great Indonesian buddies. Super people. It's a lucky life, but the day to day job...."

Lorna likes Rosie. Imagines they might be friends if she lived in London.

"Since you're familiar with Lombok," Lorna asks Celeste, "can you tell me what to see? I heard about a weaving village and a fishing beach at Ampenan."

Celeste smiles. "Both excellent. You can hire a car at the front desk."

"Hey," Rosie says, "Lorna, want to do that tomorrow? Together?"

"I'd love to."

"Good, we'll make a great duo." Rosie beams.

Celeste signals for another glass of Sancerre.

They fall silent, waiting for Neela.

"I wonder if I might join the expedition?" asks Celeste. "It's been ages since Roland and I visited those little villages."

"Of course," agrees Lorna before she sees Rosie lower her eyes.

"Fine," Celeste addresses Lorna. "We'll ask for Amin."

"Amin it is." Rosie brightens. "Thanks for the sanctuary from Hans. I'll skip dessert because I'm kind of wiped." She folds rupiahs and tucks them under her plate.

Back at the demi-villa, Lorna slips into a nightgown and surveys her posh room. Accustomed to rudimentary university guest houses, she can't believe the opulence of this four star resort. Even though Tracy found her a deal online. For the first time in years, she feels like a foreigner in Indonesia.

She pulls a Bintang from the mini-fridge. It's refreshing, alcoholic and five times cheaper than the wine.

Her sheet is turned down—what a bizarre custom—and the room reeks of fresh pesticide. Better than malaria. She's grateful for the ceiling fan cutting through the evening's thick humidity. Finally, she slides into bed with her novel, an endless Richard Russo that Tracy said was funny.

This holiday is like a train journey, Lorna tells herself. She's heard great stories traveling across England, India, Malaysia. Meeting people, opening up, then disappearing forever.

The Bintang is empty, and she hasn't turned a page of the book.

~

TUESDAY

Rosie is waiting at the front desk when Lorna arrives.

"Sorry about last night; I got the feeling that you're not keen on Celeste joining us."

Rosie smiles ruefully. "It was the polite move—to invite her. Very English."

Lorna shrugs.

"It'll be fine. It's just that I deal with rich expats all the time. They *know how to do* India or Korea or wherever. Guess I thought the two of us together would have more fun."

Fun, yes, Lorna considers; she's right.

Celeste and Amin appear from different directions.

The short, alert man in his thirties greets Celeste with a small bow. "Ibu, welcome back."

Celeste sits in the taxi's front seat, clearly her place. Rosie and Lorna climb in the back.

Just past the hotels, touristy cafés and batik shops, they're deep in countryside. Blue sky, blue sea, green, green farmland, and a shore trimmed with palms, high grass, tropical plants. Lorna can't name half the flowers. She's realizing, day by day, that despite years of studying the archipelago's history, despite her close Indonesian colleagues, she doesn't know much about daily life here today.

"We're lucky to arrive after the rains," Celeste explains. "By high season, this thirsty land drains to brown. Now we have the best of both worlds, dry *and* green."

Lorna recalls last week's lecture in Malang, her voice straining against the shrill thunder.

Soon they're overtaking horse carts crammed with people holding unwieldy bundles. Amin deftly weaves around bicycles. Now: an invasion of motorcycles. Vroom. Vroom. Sooty exhaust thickens the hot morning. Her colleague Aliv claims the motorcycle is Indonesia's national animal.

Next week, Celeste declares, she'll travel to a small village in Thailand. "The sweetest little hotel on a lagoon." Then it's on to Jaipur, Udaipur and of course Pushkar. She doesn't spend much time in Melbourne these days. "Dull as dishwater without Roland," she groans. "I'm lucky to have friends all over the world inviting me to visit."

On the roadside, people dry brown rice for mills which strip the nutritious skin and produce white rice. For years Lorna assumed this bad habit was inherited from Europeans for whom white was the optimum color then she learned that indigenous people had shucked rice for centuries. So much for her post-colonial theory.

Suddenly, Amin pulls into the village of Sukara, a collection of small houses constructed of woven grass and tiled roofs.

"Amin will find us a local guide," Celeste explains, glancing around.

A young woman walks in their direction.

"Oh, look, it's Indri, the girl we had three years ago." She lowers her voice. "Hard to believe she has three children, isn't it?" She gazes expectantly at the young woman.

Indri extends her hand. "Welcome to our village. May I show you around?"

Celeste smiles thinly, steps back and tents her palms.

Lorna remembers Celeste doesn't shake hands and wonders if she's disappointed that their host doesn't recognize her.

Rosie pumps Indri's hand. "I'm Rosie. This is Lorna and Celeste."

"Americans!" she declares in a polyglot accent.

"Nope," chuckles Rosie. "A mini United Nations here. Lorna is English. Celeste is Australian, and I'm American." Indri nods blankly then offers a few details about the village and her family. The pretty young woman—eighteen or nineteen at most, Lorna surmises—parts her glossy black hair in the middle and secures it with a plastic flower barrette. Her gold-green batik sarong is accented by a pink Garfield tshirt. She looks younger than Lorna's students—which she is—not like the mother of three kids.

They follow Indri through a gaggle of ducks. "We use them for eggs, sometimes for meat."

The sweet aroma of cow dung envelops this neighborhood of small, neat houses. An open door reveals three chairs, a simple table and straw floor mats.

Lorna wonders, if her grandparents hadn't emigrated from Madagascar, would she be living like this?

Indri stops at a home where the veranda is larger than the house. In one corner of the porch a young woman holds a baby in one arm, weaves with her other. A gleaming green and yellow cloth with the occasional strand of pink. In the far corner, a grandmother swirls newly spun thread into skeins. The weaver's mother chats with a neighbor rocking another baby.

Who's watching whom? Lorna wonders.

"*You* try now." Indri invites them to work the loom.

The women regard one another.

"I'll give it a shot," Rosie says, laughing. She slips off her sandals, steps on the porch.

The weaver's mother—a round woman in her thirties—pinches Rosie's arm, murmuring approval.

Indri translates. "Very white, she is saying."

"Whatever." Rosie looks chagrined.

She carefully steers a stick back and forth through the radiant threads. With each row, the older woman raises her right thumb in approval. Lorna and Celeste click pictures.

"*Terima Kasih.*" Rosie stands, bowing to the weaver and her family who wave as Indri leads the group back toward the village center.

Two boys are chasing puppies down the road. "*Pergi! Pergi!*"

Lorna tightens, aware of the Islamic proscription against touching dogs.

Indri looks intensely relieved as the dogs scamper into the bush.

Rosie starts to tear up.

Celeste strides ahead with Indri.

"Sorry," Rosie sniffs, "My own little mutt just died. I found Kutta in Delhi five years ago. Last month he got cancer, and...I guess he's one reason I'm here. I couldn't stand to be in the flat alone."

"I'm so sorry." Lorna puts her hand on the younger woman's shoulder. "My cat Mimi has been with me eight years."

"Thanks. People think *just a pet*, but Kutta was my pal. Made me laugh every day."

"Welcome to our showroom." Indri leads them into a small concrete building.

The village cooperative boasts shelves and shelves of folded ikat, batiks and weavings.

"Would the ladies like to try on traditional costumes?" Rosie and Lorna demur.

"Oh, come, come," Celeste chides. "It's expected. Yes, Indri, by all means, please."

Celeste reappears, gaudily draped in chartreuse and gold.

Rosie blinks.

"Would you like a photo?" Lorna asks tentatively.

"Of course," trills Celeste. Turning to Indri, she asks, "May I try this? The whole outfit and that one in purple, please."

Indri smiles for the first time that morning.

Nodding approval at his passenger's packages, Amin opens the car doors.

Lorna hopes he gets a cut.

Back on the main road, Celeste twists toward the back seat. "Sukara girls marry young and don't use birth control. Most have six or seven children. All villagers share in the store profits. In an odd way tourists help revive and foster traditional weaving."

Lorna knows this, but she's never really done the tourist thing like this. The shawl she bought for Tracy is nothing compared with Celeste's munificent purchases.

Back at Coral Villas, Celeste showers before her massage. Rosie investigates snorkeling gear, and Lorna plans to spend the afternoon swimming laps in the pool, resting, absorbing the visit to Sukara. Perhaps one thing you do in Paradise, she thinks, is pay attention.

~

WEDNESDAY

Each woman settles into her appointed seat. Amin drives them down the coast to Ampenan, a storied fishing village.

Rosie leans forward, speaking slowly and clearly. "Do you have a family, Amin?"

"Yes, my wife and I have a son and a daughter, and we all live with my mother."

"Busy home," Lorna says. Although she misses her mother, she could never live with such a fiercely opinionated person.

"I would like to build a house of our own. Yet that is very expensive."

"I imagine." She recalls yesterday's story about his route from dishwasher to waiter and, when his English improved, his coveted ascension to driver and guide.

"But soon the international airport comes and brings more work." He nods.

"A disaster!" Celeste claps her hands. "Lombok will change immeasurably. It may be good for people's pocketbooks, yes, but a catastrophe for our quiet paradise."

"*Whose paradise?*" Rosie clearly can't help herself.

"My dear, you must understand the seclusion enhances Lombok's appeal."

"But *more* tourists will come when they can fly directly from Europe, the Americas, Africa, other parts of Asia."

"Yes," Amin says to Rosie in the rear-view mirror. "More jobs, many more."

Celeste is speaking to the windshield. "Those tourists will stay in ghastly high rise hotels. A completely different class of people."

"It will bring income," Rosie says flatly.

Lorna knows her own sadness about modernization of these ancient islands is an academic indulgence.

Amin parks at a small, congested port. Blue and white boats bobble close to shore; container ships float further out to sea. Two men repair nets, talking and laughing. Nearby, a clutch of silent bare-headed women in t-shirts and sarongs squat around baskets, curing tuna.

Lorna takes a long breath of salty air. Being present in this every day island scene makes her research feel more and less real. People have fished here for millennia. They've sailed in and out of the archipelago to remote ports, recording many of the journeys in her cherished yellowing logs. Yet today the fish and the ports are different. Technology has totally transformed navigation and record keeping.

On the drive to their next site, Lorna contemplates the green rimmed coast and the calm turquoise sea. A world apart from the turbulent waters around her own chilly Albion.

Today, Lorna joins Celeste at the massage spa. If you don't get a massage in paradise, where will you get one? She hears Tracy's voice.

Muhri, a quiet, self-contained man, points Lorna to the dressing room where she finds a robe and a pair of black plastic panties. Baffled at first, she then realizes the color will show through the white sheet. A compromise between Koranic taboo and resort capitalism.

Muhri's touch is gentle and assured. Soon she's inhaling a dozen tropical perfumes from the oil he rubs into her shoulders. Half-listening to the dulcet gamelan music, she dozes. At 6pm, a ridiculously relaxed Lorna floats downstairs to the restaurant.

Tonight, Celeste sits at the view table.

Lorna considers the divergent worlds of her two acquaintances. Celeste grew up in the bush, the first person in her family to finish high school. She found unexpected success at college. Ten years later, she left an auspicious sculpture career to marry Roland and founded a charity to send at-risk youth to art school.

About Rosie, she's discovered the imp was a Rhodes Scholar and speaks twelve languages. She's torn about her State Department career, mundane now, but promising. How long can she stay if they discover she's a lesbian? Well, she's not sure of her sexuality but wishes her boss would stop asking pointedly about boyfriends.

Lorna hates the tension between the two women. Rosie distrusts Celeste's assured declamations, and Celeste is uncomfortable with Rosie's rough edges. Once again, as with her parents and then her colleagues, Lorna is right in the middle. Not the best spot for chilling out. Lorna reminds herself to think about the train. Stories remain; people vanish. She likes these very different women, feels sad and relieved that they'll soon disappear.

"So, my dear, what did you think of Muhri's massage?"

"Completely revitalizing," Lorna admits. "I haven't had a massage in years."

"Truly?" Celeste is astonished. "There are spas all over London. I recommend a superb place in Belsize Park right near you."

"Murhi took his job so seriously," Lorna says smiling, "as if it were a sacrament or something."

"But it is. It is!" cries Celeste. "Have some wine. I bought a bottle to celebrate."

"Celebrate?"

"Our little trio. You simply don't know what you've done for my spirits. Thank you for breaking through the gruff reserve that first night. I do apologize."

"Not at all," Lorna protests, embarrassed. "Is Rosie back from snorkeling?"

"Snorkeling?" Celeste is alarmed. "Alone? Where? No one told me."

Taking a long sip of the refreshing wine, Lorna answers, "Gili? Gully?"

"Oh, not the Gilis!" Celeste is shaken. "Neela." She waves to the waitress, then pivots back to Lorna. "We must ask the staff if she returned safely."

"What's wrong with the Gilis? I read they were a popular beach with families."

"The Gili Islands are vile spots off the Southwest coast. Men hang out there. Oh, god, she went by herself, didn't she?"

"Amin drove her, and he was supposed to collect her at five. I bet they're just delayed on the road." Lorna reminds herself Rosie is a taekwondo black belt.

"Yes, *Ibu*?" Neela appears.

"Dear, please ask reception if *Ibu* Rosie has returned from those dreadful Gilis?"

"Certainly."

Lorna detects a faint smile on Neela's face.

Celeste is shaking her head. "Perhaps she's upstairs showering. She's not the promptest person."

Lorna dwells on the dramatically shifting sky, on the sun setting over the nearby Bali mountains. Indonesia is so fierce and unpredictable compared to her docile English countryside. The moon fills in from the opposite side down here. The sky lights up with different constellations. Yet these are the very stars under which her grandparents slept in Madagascar. Drawn as she is to this place, she knows she couldn't live in a world lacking the simple Northern pleasures of lavender and early autumn pears.

They each sip wine in silence.

"You guys look glum!" Rosie drops into a chair. "Disastrous massages?"

Celeste claps a hand over her heart. "You had me in quite a panic."

Rosie, whose wet hair is flatter and darker than usual, seems bewildered.

Lorna thinks she looks prettier without the spikes and realizes Rosie's mother probably agrees with her. God, when did she become such a fuddy-duddy?

"Traipsing off to those remote islands alone." Celeste can't let it go.

"The Gilis are pretty close," says Rosie. "So sad about the coral getting damaged by sea level rise and local sewage."

Celeste offers wine. "But you were all alone."

"I had plenty of company. A Belgian couple and a family from Malaysia were snorkeling on the same beach." She pours a glass of wine, savors the first sip with her eyes closed. "But hey, it was nice of you to worry."

Celeste bursts out laughing. Lorna finds herself giggling. Rosie joins in. Around the café, heads turn toward the jolly women.

~

THURSDAY

"Our last morning!" Celeste laments from the front seat. "It's a shame I have foot reflexology at two because we could explore the other side of the island. Sembalun is a sweet mountain village. Next time! Roland always says, said, you have to leave something for your return. We'll save Sembalun for our next visit."

Rosie whispers to Lorna, "Does she think we've joined her Explorer Troop?"

Lorna clears her throats. She, too, is growing a little weary of Captain Celeste. Gazing out the window she watches children walking to school in pressed beige uniforms. Many girls wear what they call the *jilbab*. How do they bear the heat?

"Here we are," announces Amin. "Lingsar, ladies."

Their guide, Wayang, a thin man from Bali, points out two separate sites—one for the Islamic and Animist Sasaks and one for Hindus. "The holy eels swim at this shrine for Lord Vishnu. They can be enticed to the surface for a boiled egg."

Celeste blanches. "You two go ahead. Roland once lured them, and I reckon you'd call them fascinating creatures."

"Thanks." Rosie pops a Tic Tac. "But I don't want eels swimming in my dreams tonight."

Unfazed, Wayang guides them through the holy site, paying particular attention to the impressively large rocks pilgrims reverently lug here from Mount Rinjani.

Amin taps his foot impatiently beside the car. Holding the door for Celeste, he asks, "When is your appointment, *Ibu*? Do we still go to Narmada?"

"We must, of course." She turns toward the others, "This gem of a park lined by waterways, dotted with lakes and Cambodia trees, was designed in the 1700s—"

"Pardon," Lorna interrupts, "but Amin is right. Don't you have a 2pm appointment?"

Celeste opens her pendant watch. "I had no idea. Thanks, Lorna dear, for the reminder."

How can the woman be so sensitive to local customs one moment and so imperious to Amin the next? Remember the train journey, Lorna.

Amin makes good time until he hits the village of Sengiggi, where the road is jammed with trucks, buses and motorcycles.

"Can't you hurry?" Celeste frets.

"I must be careful, *Ibu*." His voice is gentle but authoritative.

"Do just scoot around that bus," Celeste demands.

"People on the road," he answers coolly.

"God knows how long it will stand there!"

Amin hunches over the steering wheel, steps on the gas.

"Oh, no," Rosie calls out. "There's a little dog. Amin, Amin! Watch out!"

Lorna sees a clumsy black puppy dodging traffic. "Right here," Rosie is shouting, "in the road."

Lorna hears a thud and knows they've hit the dog.

Now she sees the puppy slumped down, dark red blood seeping from its scar of a mouth.

Rosie throws open the door of the moving car, leaps out.

"Careful!" Celeste reaches for and misses Rosie's hand.

Amin screeches to a stop.

Celeste calls, "Rosie! Watch the motorcycles. Rosie!"

"Help. Help!" Rosie cries. "Amin, we need to get him to a veterinarian."

Tourists and locals gape from the sidewalk.

Lorna rushes out after Rosie, directs traffic around her friend, the dog and the stalled taxi. Oh, damn, passionate, dog-loving Rosie. She can't leave her out here amidst the swerving, squealing vehicles. She hears Celeste sobbing.

"Amin, please!" howls Rosie. "Help us! Please!"

He steps out reluctantly. I am sorry, *Ibu*. I cannot assist." He shakes his head sadly, keeping a distance. "Dogs are unclean and haram."

"Please." Tears stream down Rosie's red cheeks.

Amin looks more uncertain than resistant.

"Please!"

He stands, paralyzed.

Lorna sees Celeste has collapsed against the door, trembling, her eyes squeezed shut.

"Look, he's hemorrhaging."

His face frozen, Amin returns to the car.

As he steps on the gas, Celeste is sobbing again, her head between her hands.

Deftly, Amin weaves through the congested street.

Lorna watches until they turn the corner, out of sight.

Rosie screams, "She's going with him. For a massage! Can you believe it?"

Lorna says evenly, "We'll flag down another car." She learned this calm, this practice of *behaving as if* from her grandmother. People think she's serene; she's simply learned to postpone terror.

"It's all her fault." Rosie's voice is panicky. She sniffs back tears, stroking the dog.

Accident. Lorna thinks the word was coined for this situation, but she can't say that to Rosie. Instead, she waves to advancing vehicles. They slither by.

Anxiously, Rosie thumbs her Blackberry with one hand, texting Jakarta contacts about Lombok veterinarians, while comforting the dog with her other hand.

It starts to rain.

Hours later, Lorna is still drained and agitated. As she walks to an early dinner, she hopes to catch the sunset, maybe from a table on the lower terrace, out of sight.

Approaching the café, she notices Celeste is already at *their* table, which is set for three. Lorna considers retreating, ordering room service and eating peacefully on her deck.

Something impels her forward.

Celeste's face looks as if it's been shattered and reassembled with several pieces missing.

"I was praying you would come."

Lorna slides next to Celeste. "Rosie is still in Mataram with the veterinarian."

"She found a vet!" Celeste exclaims happily. "That resourceful sprite."

Lorna can't think how to respond.

Celeste raises the bottle toward Lorna's glass.

"I don't—" she begins, then recalls the woman sobbing next to Amin. "Thanks, I could use some wine."

Tentatively, Celeste asks, "Will the dog be all right?"

"It was doubtful when Rosie sent me home. Nothing I could do. Maybe nothing the vet can do."

"What a shame. I was looking forward to our farewell meal." Her voice is fluting again.

Lorna notes the bottle is almost empty. She waits.

Eyes red, breath short, Celeste grasps Lorna's hand. "I am so ashamed. It's all my fault, urging Amin around the bus. Then I abandoned you both. And the poor dog."

Lorna wonders unkindly if Celeste had a good reflexology session, then she softens, aware she's never seen Celeste touch anyone before.

"Today's horrible accident brought it all back. Every detail so vividly."

"Your husband?"

"Rol suddenly collapsed to the street. People, dozens, clustered around. I couldn't get anyone to call an ambulance. I stood there, waving like a berserk windmill at passing cars and rickshaws when Roland breathed his last. Waving my arms when I should have been kneeling next to Rol, holding him. When I should have—"

Lorna tears up. "It was a crisis. You did your best."

"I should have held his hand," Celeste sobs,"caressed his face."

Neela appears. "Something is wrong with *Ibu*? Can I help?"

"No, *terima kasih*, Neela," Celeste manages. "I think I'll have dinner upstairs."

"Here, I'll walk you back," Lorna offers.

Celeste nods, her eyes closed.

"Perhaps Neela, could you bring my prawns and my friend's dish upstairs? We'd like to have dinner in my room."

"How very gracious." Celeste looks like a girl rescued from the bottom of a well.

Lorna glances back dolefully as sun hits the horizon of endless water. Her last night in Paradise.

About 10 pm, Lorna is released from her novel by a knock on the door.

A ragged Rosie, hair askew, dress dusty, collapses in a chair. Half her spikes have drooped in the rain. Grateful, she accepts a Bintang and the roasted vegetarian sandwich Lorna had wrapped for her.

Lorna waits as Rosie eats and drinks, then asks hesitantly. "How is he?"

She yawns. "The vet thinks Buster will pull through. We'll know by morning."

"Buster? You found the owner? Tourists?"

"No, but I couldn't keep calling him *Dog*. I considered the Indonesian *anjing*, but people use that as an insult. *Kutta* didn't fit. He responds to Buster," she says sheepishly.

Great name!" Lorna giggles. Rosie joins her, cracking the tension.

"Will the vet try to locate the owner?"

Rosie sighs, obviously exhausted. "He says no one would claim a dog with these injuries. He'll take months to heal, if he survives."

Lorna stares out the window at the rising moon.

"But that woman!" Rosie clenches her teeth. "That wretched woman and her fucking foot reflexology. I've never met anyone so heartless."

"Maybe," Lorna begins tentatively, "maybe not heartless." Why does she need Rosie and Celeste to understand one another?

"Gutless then."

"Let me tell you about our dinner conversation."

"You ate with that woman after all—"

"Wait, Rosie. Listen."

~

FRIDAY

Lorna sits alone at the café. It's been a sleepless night, and she's up too early.

Neela welcomes her with coffee and big smile.

Lorna wonders if omnipresent Neela sleeps in the kitchen.

Inhaling the warmth and aroma of the steaming cup, she watches a predawn sky alchemize to gold as the sun rises over the sea. *Yes, she'll tell Tracy truthfully; she has learned to relax. A little each day. To savor the salty bounty of the southern waters 900 years after "her" first boat journeys. To enjoy today's sun. And in accepting the contradictions within Rosie and Celeste, she acknowledges some of her own. She still loves her work, but now she also relishes the shimmying of palm fronds and the scents of flowery perfumes. Mission accomplished, Tracy. Almost, anyway.*

"Hi, friend!"

Lorna turns to a grinning Rosie.

"Buster made it?!"

"Looks like I have a new dog." She rubs sleep from her eyes.

"You're taking him to Jakarta?"

"Vet said it was a peachy idea since it's impossible to find him a home here. Because of Muslim prohibitions. I should have been more sensitive to Amin. Attitudes change from island to island. The Balinese like barking dogs for protection. I told you my Jakarta neighbors loved Kutta. A lot of city professionals have pets. Anyway, the vet was super relieved that I could adopt Buster." Yesterday's anxious face is now alive with relief and excitement.

"You'll have one more friend in Jakarta."

"Can't have too many." She laughs. "Hey, where's the massage queen?"

Lorna frowns. "I haven't seen Celeste this morning."

Neela pours Rosie's coffee. "You ask about *Ibu*. She sailed for Bali to catch an earlier flight to Thailand. She left you ladies a letter."

Rosie accepts the ivory vellum envelope then hands it to Lorna.

Lorna removes the letter, placing it on the table between them.

Dear Friends,

Apologies for my stupid, panicky behavior yesterday. I was too full of my own heartache to respond with any dignity. I admire the nobility you both showed.

Attached is a money order which I hope Rosie will give the veterinarian to pay for treating what I imagine will be her dog.

Rosie stares at Lorna, who grins.

There is enough left over to help him develop the clinic. I'm certain more animals will be rescued by other decent folk.

I hope against hope that we meet again. All of us. My address and email are below. Farewell and thank you for four idyllic days."

With great affection,

Celeste

Rosie is shaking her head, and Lorna once again marvels that the gelled spikes don't move. "The white lady buying absolution. So damn typical."

Lorna studies her young friend's resolute eyes. "Maybe," she begins, then pauses for the right words. "Maybe it's only a matter of degree how different we are from Celeste."

Rosie shrugs, stares at the ocean.

"Even if my very ancient ancestors were Indonesian, I now travel with a London education and salary."

Rosie glowers.

"Which buy me access, comforts, which largely insulate me."

"OK, Professor," Rosie sighs. "OK, maybe she did her best."

"Maybe we each did."

"And Buster survived."

Rosie can't help herself. "*Idyllic?*"

Lorna shrugs. You're the linguist. I'm just an historian."

Neela places two elaborate breakfasts on the table: breads, fruit, eggs and potatoes.

"Sorry, I didn't order—" Rosie begins

"Compliments of *Ibu* Celeste." Neela smiles sadly.

"*Terima Kasih*," they say in unison.

Paradise, Lorna will tell Tracy, is more complicated than you might imagine.

Visitation

The three of us are nervous—in different ways—this graduation morning. Will he show up after all these years? What will he say? What will we say?

"Please pass the pepper," my partner Jackie asks our daughter Anna, who is gobbling her breakfast like a starving woman.

"Really, you should have ordered the pancakes, Jackie," Anna says not quite between bites. "Blueberry whole wheat, your fav." The bistro is packed with UW graduates and their parents. Also younger students who will graduate —or not—in coming years. Pancakes, hash browns, sausages, omelets, scones, 37 varieties of coffee.

"Hey, Mom, you're not eating," Anna complains. "Wanna try some pancake?"

The hip hop in Anna's favorite restaurant blares so loudly I can hardly hear her. But I raise my hand in genial protest. "Thanks, I'm too busy digesting the day." If Craig doesn't show, it will break Anna's heart, even though she hasn't seen her father in 13 years. Honors Student. Valedictorian. The accolades mean a lot. So does the word daughter.

"Mom, you've got to eat," Anna frets. "Long day ahead, demanding lots of emotional energy."

"Emotional energy." My laugh is dry and short. "What lingo!"

"Look, I know you're worried Dad won't show."

The coffee curdles in my stomach. I don't say, well, he did leave town forever six months after winning joint custody.

Following instructions, I nibble the cold eggs. Grease is all I can taste. "Will we recognize him? Will he be fat? Thin? Bald?"

Anna smiles tightly. "We'll know him for sure. But what about Connie? How do I introduce my father's second wife to Professor

Cleve?" She doesn't really expect an answer and races ahead. "He's the coolest teacher. I can't wait till you meet him." Then she stares at her plate. And their kids? How do you talk to a brother and sister you've never met?"

Jackie shakes her head. "Anna, you'll do fine. You're a mature, gracious woman. Your natural warmth will carry you through."

Jackie's right. Anna may well be more composed than her birth mother who is an utter wreck today. I was piqued, at first, that she wanted Craig at graduation after all those missed cards and presents and phone calls and visits. Of course she does. I want him here. I just wish I were another person—calm, accepting, forgiving, open-hearted.

Just last month, life was much simpler.

~

I love how late sun lights up the green water in Anna's small aquarium. At day's end, the fish glide slowly as if in a warm bath.

I can still picture Anna in her red checkered bandana, which barely covered her black curls, lugging that tank up the stairs, all those steps, huffing and puffing and laughing.

"Jackie," I call impatiently from the new tweedy couch. "The sun has almost set."

It's been a long day, and I've already poured our glasses of wine, left them breathing on the kitchen table.

"Be there in a sec, Hope," Jackie shouts from her study. "I just have one more score to copy."

Light lasts longer on Potrero Hill, well after shadows fall onto the East Bay and downtown. The hill houses glisten greedily in the late sun. Greed, that's what Craig accused me of during the divorce.

Anna's graduation announcement is framed on the oak mantle. BA in Music, *summa cum laude*. Does Craig have a clue about his beautiful, accomplished daughter?

I accept Craig's silence with me. But I cannot believe how he's ignored Anna.

"You can't have everything," Craig said when he finally signed the divorce papers that July. Greed was an odd word, my lawyer said, since we split the meager assets.

Visitation went OK for the first few months. Then he started forgetting to pick up her. She'd hold up in her room, crying, refusing supper.

By November, he jumped at that job in Seattle. "I need a clean break. We all do. I'll call you when I get settled. Then I'll come down and also buy Anna regular airline tickets."

He cancelled the first two trips for business emergencies. I was patient, knew he felt panicked about being alone. He made it down for Easter. And the next Christmas. One birthday card. Then he disappeared into his new family.

What kind of life does he have now—with Connie and the twins on Lopez Island? They must have a view there. Probably too close to the water to want a fish tank.

I still think Anna chose the University of Washington to reconnect with her father. Somehow. Maybe she hoped to spot him shopping in downtown Seattle. Maybe she fantasized about spending a weekend at an inn on the island and sauntering past his house. None of this happened, of course. Now that she's twenty-one, I have to let her go. I have to let go of his neglect, too.

Jackie carries the two glasses of zinfandel from the kitchen. She looks so pretty, her short blond hair coiling every which way and the green sweater bringing out the turquoise in her eyes.

"Uh-oh," she pauses, "from that glower, I detect the presence of, hmmm, could it be the Arch Demon Craig?" Carefully she sets our glasses on the coffee table. "Just a guess."

I love these large goblets, gifts from Anna on our last anniversary. "Two great Moms, what more could I want?" she wrote on the card.

How about a father, even an intermittently engaged father?

A shiver riffles down my neck. Jackie's right. It's as if he possesses me, even though I've been blissfully happy with her for 13 years.

~

"Hi, hon, how are you doing?"

"Thanks for calling, Mom. I was just thinking about you, too. Hey, you and Jackie are still coming up for graduation, right?"

I pause at her anxious voice. "Of course. We each have a new Mother of the Valedictorian dress. Jackie made a dinner res at this hot new café. You still want to go out with us old fogies after commencement?"

"Obviously, Mom. I can't wait to see you both. I have a friend, Mira, who's moving to the City this summer, and she's interested in the Chorale, so I want her to meet J."

"I imagine an audience can be arranged."

She laughs. Then a heavy sigh.

"What's wrong?"

"What do you mean?"

"You sound a little low. Have you been studying too hard?"

"I'm fine."

"You don't sound fine."

"What? You have some kind of periscope into my brain?"

"What's going on?"

"I just wish everyone could come to graduation."

I hold my breath. "Everyone?"

"You know, Dad."

Cupping my hand over the receiver, I exhale slowly.

"It's just that all my friends' parents will be there, even the ones who are divorced. Sally has three step moms coming. It's a big day."

"Oh, sweetheart, I wish things were different." I tear up. "But he made his choice all those years ago."

"You're right. You're right. I'm just being silly. And spoiled."

"Beg to differ, ma'am. I think you're feeling sad."

"Yeah, sad. I guess, sad."

~

"Here's to the day." I raise a glass toward the gilded hill.

"Here's to the night!" She grins. "See how long the evenings are lengthening? It's almost 8:30 and still—blue sky."

I inhale the bouquet of this new Bordeaux. "In a couple of weeks, we'll be celebrating with Anna, where the light lasts even longer."

"Hmm," she murmurs, "Midsummer in the Northwest. Heaven."

"Yeah," I sigh.

"You don't sound very convinced," Jackie says. "What's up?"

"Nothing."

She takes my hand, gazes into my eyes.

"I called Anna today, and she was feeling down. She wants him at graduation."

I glance at the maps of Turkey and Greece Jackie framed for my birthday—five trips to the antique land and another coming up this summer.

"Of course you *both* would miss his presence."

Shaking my head, I start to object, then recall that old fantasy of détente with my ex. Of friendship. I'll never understand how you can completely disappear from someone with whom you've had a beautiful child. Someone with whom you've shared eleven years of Sunday mornings.

"OK, I want her to have a father. Even at this late date."

"Sweets, I'm not defending him. But maybe it all got too completed for Craig. Not everyone is as resilient as you."

"Ha! Flattery will not distract me from our daughter's pain."

"So give in and tell Anna to invite him to graduation."

"What?"

"Better yet, *you invite him.* The guy can't be hard to find on the internet. He's a consultant. You're going to mope until you *do something* about this."

I stare at her.

She kisses my neck, lightly rubs my knees.

"You're joking, right?"

~

That final week of marriage was Bickerson City. After a year of arguing, he's come up with another complaint.

"We had an agreement." Craig keeps his voice low so as not to disturb Anna.

"You make our lives sound like a business deal." I'm freezing on the back deck of our little bungalow way down in the Avenues, watching the grey paint peeling, thinking I can't get out of here fast enough.

"Marriage is a contract," he whispers, "as well as a sacred bond."

His voice is chilled and hushed as the ubiquitous fog. He's deluded if he thinks the child doesn't know what's going on.

I draw my shawl tighter. "Then why wouldn't you come to a marriage counselor like I pleaded for two years?"

He ignores me, sucking on his latte to keep warm. "We chose this house together."

Craig isn't one of those people who gets cute when he's angry. Rather, his eyes narrow and his voice hardens. "You chose the furniture."

Is this the same laid-back, funny guy from UVA, the one I hiked the Blue Ridge with? The person who introduced me to the Grateful Dead? The tender lover who would cherish me always?

When—how—did he become this upright, brooding, bossy man? Friends say he's taking out work stress on me, that he feels competitive because I'm teaching and he's just been laid off his lab job. But he's smart and inventive. Surely he'll find other work.

"I let you choose the furniture," he protests. "Every marriage involves compromise."

I breathe deeply to keep from laughing. Sarcasm is one of my worst traits. "You want to stay with me because I chose the furniture?"

"You picked our daughter's name."

This is surreal. "You said you really liked Anna. You wanted another name?"

"You know I did." He sucks the coffee until the straw makes that hollow, empty sound.

"What?" I'm at a total loss. The fog is so thick; I can smell the cold.

"Eleanor."

My eyes pop. This again. "Your mother's lovely name. A beautiful 1940s name but hardly appropriate for someone growing into a 21st century woman."

"I happen to adore Eleanor."

I look around as if for help or advice. All our neighbors, even their pets, have had the good sense to hunker inside during the heavy fog blanket. "Eleanor *is a wonderful name, Craig. It's perfect for your wonderful mother. It's just not contemporary. It's...."*

"Were you going to say outdated? That's it. You think our marriage is outdated too."

He has a point, but I'm too tired, too sad, to answer. Shaking my head, I take a long breath and cough out the frigid air.

~

Over the years, Jackie has made me more aware of seasons and colors and sounds and tastes. Every day I pay attention to sunrise, noon and sunset. Of course I never actually saw the sun rise or set with Craig and Anna in the misty Avenues. Now we have a house with views of both bridges that Jackie inherited from her uncle. A tall, slender house on a hill. Perfect for our compact family.

"I smell onion." Jackie closes her eyes to savor the wine. "Mmmm garlic and onion."

"I started the veggies roasting. And the fish will take fifteen minutes?"

"Ten." She regards me skeptically, always the more precise cook.

"Got it."

"How was school, Hope?"

"I did the last grades. Phuff. Every semester I swear I won't cave to grade inflation, but these people are trying so hard. Attending school is such a sacrifice of money and time."

"They're lucky to have a kind-hearted professor."

They don't call us *professor* at my little community college across the Bay, but Jackie awards full honors.

"Or I'm a complete push-over." I shake my head. "And you, maestro, are your concert scores all set?"

"Pretty much. I wish you were still in the Chorale."

"If only I had the time."

"You work too hard. You could make time. It would be good for you."

I shrug, unwilling to lighten up. "I know I should." God, I owe so much to the Chorale. It kept me sane during the divorce, and it's where

I met Jackie. I kiss her hand gallantly, hoping she'll drop the advice, at least for this quiet moment at day's end.

"Any news from Craig?" she asks tentatively.

"Nada." I sigh. "I can't tell Anna I invited him and he never responded."

She draws close, sets her glass on the table, then mine, and kisses me. Tender, ardent, fiery, all the things I hoped would happen one day with Craig. No one ever told me it had to *start* this way.

The light is orange now. From the west window, we could watch the sunset over the Golden Gate. Anna's favorite view. When she's on school break, she follows the sun slipping into the ocean, as if making sure day has truly closed. Jackie and I prefer to watch Berkeley and the city go to sleep. Downtown office buildings blink golden light into the evening and there's Potrero Hill, still slurping up the sun.

Jackie kisses the top of my head and shifts away slightly, reaching for a box. "What do you think of this small addition to our graduation presents?" She withdraws a delicate purple scarf threaded with gold. "I saw it in that new shop on 24th and just thought...."

"Perfect. U-Dub colors. Subtle version. But," I wag my finger, "you've already bought that Finale music software. What if she decides to give up composing and become a movie star?"

"Anna's pretty focused. She got into the best grad program, and she's wanted to compose since she was ten."

"Since you started taking her to the symphony." I savor the spice in this new zinfandel. I wonder about the vegetables but am too content in this perfect moment to move. Jackie claims she likes crispy veggies. And if they were really burning, we would smell them, right?

"Is that an accusation? Where did you want me to take her—the circus?"

Glancing at the framed photo of Anna and Jackie after the last Chorale performance, I laugh. "You're the best thing that's happened to either of us."

"We're all lucky to have each other." She sips her wine.

Perhaps I *am* greedy.

~

After two weeks, the sperm donor, as I jokingly call him around Jackie, accepts the invitation. He emails that he'll meet us at the reception with Connie and the twins. Brief. Detached. Precise.

~

Graduation day *is* ideal. Cloudless, blue-blue sky. Brilliant sun. Almost as brilliant as Anna's valedictory speech was. Amazing to think she's composed of my genes. Half my genes.

Anna glows as she bites into a juicy strawberry. She has my dark hair and complexion and Craig's height. High school friends used to call her "Cher." Today she looks so nifty, with splashes of her Marimekko sheath visible under the half-zipped graduation gown.

"Got it!" Jackie snaps a photo with her android.

Anna grins. "God, Jack, you're going to out-tech me any day now."

Jackie looks so fresh in her sleeveless blue cotton dress. Much more appropriate than my jacketed shirtwaist. Seattle, I thought, rain, chill.

~

"Your leaving. It makes no sense," he protests during the final, final (god, I hope final) argument.

Anna is sleeping over with a friend so at least we are in the warm kitchen at the table drinking tea.

"If only...." I stop myself from mentioning the marriage counselor.

"We promised forever after. How can you shatter this life I've worked for—a family. San Francisco," he rambles. "It's not fair."

Increasingly the divorce sounds like an inconvenience.

He bites into a second scone.

"So I should stay because I chose the furniture and the name?"

"More or less. That's what marriage is. More or less. Less and more."

For me, it's been less and less. "Listen , Craig, you're a good man. You're smart and ambitious. You'll be a great success. Someone will be very happy to have you in her life, but this marriage is over, has been for more than a year."

"Grow up, Hope. You'll get tired of Jackie, too."

He forgets I asked for the divorce months before I met Jackie. She's become his convenient lesbian vampire.

"What's next? A tranny? Some stewardess morphed into Mr. Atlas?"

It's hard to be angry against such desperation. "The crassness is unworthy of you."

"My bleeding life is being ripped away. Everything I've built, my house, my family."

Outside fog is the color of skim milk. I shiver. "First, your daughter will always love you. And the house is yours if you buy me out."

"You fucking don't get it. Nothing will ever be the same. You just can't understand."

"Maybe not," I say gently. "So why are you fighting for a marriage with someone who doesn't understand you?"

He drops the half-eaten scone on his plate. "Because," he begins slowly. "Because it's my marriage."

"Once it was our marriage," I whisper.

"Grammar bitch."

That's it. I stand. "Time to pick up Anna." *He'll come to his senses. We're sophisticated adults. We'll be friends again in a year or two.*

~

I see him first. Or do I? Can this balding, slightly thick-set man be Craig?

Anna runs toward him.

I gulp my sparkling water.

Jackie squeezes my hand.

"Professor Cleve! I'm so happy to see you. Let me introduce my mom, Hope Prentiss, and her partner, my stepmom, Jackie Coiner."

I clear my throat to disguise my surprise, relief, disappointment.

"Your Anna is one of our stars," Cleve declares. "We're sorry to see her go, but Northwestern has a superb graduate program. I look forward to hearing her premieres at the Seattle Symphony in a few years."

Anna rolls her eyes fondly. "You can see why all the students love him."

I want to concentrate on her dazzling future, but I'm furious with Craig. The reception started thirty minutes ago. Half the strawberries and all the chocolate truffles are gone. It will break Anna's heart if he doesn't show up.

I eat a fourth strawberry, mindfully.

Anna, Jackie and Cleve are deep in conversation. My two wonderful women.

Another slow strawberry. I focus on gratitude.

Suddenly: "Anna! Hope!" a familiar gravelly baritone with a slight Virginia drawl. I spot a tall, trim man my age, with slightly greying hair. I see how I fell for him years ago.

He's a stride ahead of a pretty younger woman with two red haired children. His mother's hair.

I wonder if the girl is called Eleanor. He didn't say that—or much else—in the email. Except that he would come.

Professor Cleve makes his farewells.

Anna reddens, smiles shyly as Craig approaches.

I will not cry. I will not cry.

He extends his hand. To give him credit, he knows a handshake is all he deserves.

Anna pulls him into a tight embrace.

Tears stream down my cheeks.

Jackie hands me tissues, touches my shoulder lightly.

I feel joyful, looking at Anna's bright face. An old grief surfaces about our too imperfect family.

By the time he shakes my hand, I'm working hard on composure.

"Hello, Hope." Then he turns to Jackie. "Nice to see you again."

The younger woman strolls up on high heels.

"I'd like you to meet my wife, Connie."

I nod, smile, extend my hand and present Jackie.

Anna's eyes widen as she watches her half-sister and brother.

He introduces the twins. They wave shyly.

Anna hugs each of them; then, for some reason, they're all giggling.

Craig looks like a squarely middle-aged man, which is exactly what you'd expect for a fifty-year-old guy.

I blink twice at this mirage.

Connie declares, "That was a stunning speech, Anna."

Nice woman, I think.

"Yes, wasn't Anna splendid?" Jackie agrees. Good old friendly Jackie with her easy social graces. "I loved the instrumental metaphors."

Craig is also acting like a pleasant, ordinary person. Like the guy I married. He showed up to graduation because his daughter wanted him here. He's brought a present. He's beaming proudly.

It's a bit of a letdown, really. What did I expect? A mustachioed villain with a black velvet cape? A somber penitent on his knees?

The spell has broken.

He's a regular guy who is facing his mistakes.

We're all ordinary, decent people.

The father-daughter reunion I longed for is actually happening. And more: Anna grins as she takes a hand of each sibling and offers them strawberries.

Smiling at Craig, I gesture to our radiant, hospitable daughter.

His eyes fill.

Oh, I am full of gratitude and melancholy for the unexpected gifts of life.

After thirteen years, we start with a small repair.

Now Anna has two families.

Have her parents achieved détente? If so, what's next? Dinners at each other's houses on alternating years? No, don't be snarky. Accept this grace note.

Jackie takes my elbow in her palm. My sweet, predatory lesbian vampire.

It's five o'clock, hours until sunset, and the sky is a dazzling blue.

Bread and Salt

a novella

In gratitude for your bread and salt,
I must preserve you from all danger.
Rumi

September 30, 1207 – December 17, 1273

~

Hundreds Die In Madrid Train Bombing;
Tunisians Suspected
March 12, 2004

TUNISIA, 2004

What would have happened if she had stayed? To herself? To the
people who have disappeared in the last thirty years?

Caroline surveys the fairytale hotel room: striped satin bedspread;
cozy couch, silk skirted dressing table. She can't believe the palatial
bathroom and the flat screen satellite TV. Of course she's stayed in posh
American hotels (at conference rates). But she doesn't remember—
and never imagined—such lavish fabrics, triple fluffed towels and
handcrafted pillow chocolate—on the north coast of Africa.

Remember; imagine. Distinguish between then and now. Can she
account for the years since that last visit? Years when she not only
became an adult, but a wife, a mother, divorcée, professional renegade
and a *senior figure in her field?*

A senior figure and a distinguished museologist like yourself read the invitation. To think she almost zapped the email bearing the unlikely subject line *Your Tunisian Fan*. So much coy spam these days.

Yes. She has returned. As he said she would.

AUGUST 1975, TUNISIA

Caroline is savoring the sun, the thick Turkish coffee, writing to Wayne about her impressions of a balmy, ancient, eversurprising country. Her old friend would love this café in Sousse, Susa in Arabic, with its panoramic Mediterranean vistas and high, whining street music. He'd be delighted by the men holding hands. *Terri's jogging along the Corniche*, Caroline writes, *a beautiful path on the Sousse Coast. Don't know when she'll be back.*

Sousse is her favorite so far, not as crowded as Tunis, more urbane than Sfax. A wonderfully mysterious medina, handsome mosques, seductive fabrics and acres of olives. Terri reminds her not to get romantic. For all its vaunted secularism, Tunisia is no place for a woman. Perhaps not for a man either considering the reports of underground cops, the whole police state and Bourguiba, the current *President for Life.*

She continues writing. *Terri calls me a slacker. But if I don't take time for letters, the memories will evaporate.*

"Corresponding with your lonesome fiancé?" says a mischievous, lightly accented voice.

She glances at a tall man with a trim moustache even darker than his curly black hair.

He tilts his head in curiosity, as if he has every right to know who she is and what she's doing.

Ignoring him, she reviews the letter, tries to slow her breath.

The handsome, muscular guy leans forward in his purple Santana t-shirt and faded jeans. Self-assured, sexy. Something appealing about his confidence, expressing more ease than cockiness.

Pretty cute, she thinks.

Secret police is her second thought. Terri says the place is crawling with security, ever since Bourguiba tried to merge Tunisia with Libya. Young westerners are carefully watched. Color drains from her face as she sips the now bitter, cold coffee, ignoring him. Pretending to.

TUNISIA, 2004

Caroline checks the messages on her cell, then plugs in the charger. She's a little impatient for Tess's call. Imagine, her daughter auditioning for an off-Broadway play. She flops back on the bed, looking outside at the hopeful colors of this early spring. Salwa will be calling too. The curious, extravagantly cordial woman who has invited her to consult at the Kairouan museum. Quite an honor for an American. And a boon. Salwa has rescued her from the frigid Boston weather.

If only intrepid Terri, her best girlfriend, could be here. Caroline thinks about the framed snapshot of them on her desk at home. She imagines a dozen empty picture frames that should have held photos of them aging together, a little heavier, a little saggier, but the same close buddies. Instead she remembers that photo on the corniche that Anouar took.

The pictures of Anouar fill a big leather bound book, moldering somewhere in the basement.

Terri. Anouar. Vanished. What happens when the people who were the very bones of your life disappear? How much of you, yourself, becomes a mirage?

TUNISIA, 1975

"I'm Anouar," he declares, pulling up a wooden chair. "And your good name?" He extends a slender hand with raised black hairs.

Automatically she answers, "Caroline. Je suis hereuse de faire votre connaissance."

"*Le sentiment est mutuel.*" A hearty, corvid laugh. "But you don't seem *Française* or *Québécoise*. And I can speak American."

"So I hear. Where did you—" she begins.

"Master's in Chemical Engineering from the University of Minnesota." He grins. "I survived three years in the tundra. Actually, I came to enjoy the cold. I loved how the full moon gleaming on the snowy garden. I was a whiz at cross-country skiing."

"Yes," she laughs. "I'm from Boston. Not as cold as the Upper Midwest. But lots of snow."

"I *knew* you were a Yank."

"Ah," she's intrigued now, flattered by his attentiveness. "I don't seem French?"

"French women are too neat, so *precise* in appearance, especially when composing a casual look. They're always on display. Americans are more unself-conscious. They regard *everyone else* as part of the show."

"So you're accusing me of being a voyeur?"

TUNISIA, 2004

The hotel buffet is bountiful. Suddenly ravenous, she fills her plate with couscous, *tajine*, baked lamb, *brik*. She finishes with *tisane de menthe*. Alas, no room for that Date Charlotte. Terri would have nimbly slipped the dessert into a plastic bag and secured it in her purse for the next day. Terri was the real traveler, the one with ideas, antennae for adventure and a natural sense of direction. Caroline was the side-kick. Why, then, was it Caroline who fell in love with this place? Because, Terri explained, a traveler's spirit is meant for moving on. Caroline was more of a barnacle, a detached barnacle.

Still reminiscing about Terri's exploits, Caroline sticks her key into the lock. Immediately she hears her cell beeping with a text. Damn. She's missed Tess. Her clumsy fingers play nervously over the impossibly tiny buttons.

No. A message from Salwa: Welcome 2 Tunisia. Hope u had a good trip. Limo will pick you up @ 8:30 am 2morro. 1st meeting w/ Museum Dir. Boring but… Then we chat! Can't wait. <3 Salwa.

Caroline breathes deeply. She hopes she won't disappoint Salwa or the boring boss.

TUNISIA, 1975

Everything is possible. Terri and Caroline are in their mid-twenties in the 1970s, the fortunate daughters of immigrant workers. Grad school is on the horizon. First travels to Patagonia and the Serengeti and...

Why not, she says to audacious Terri, when her friend adds Mongolia to their list.

And Tunisia.

Zip. They're scrunched on the red-eye to Paris. Then a short connection to Tunis. Local buses on rutted roads through the mountains, along the coast. To Carthage.

They've been warned by the guide book, by the tourists. The police are omnipresent. Then there are the intelligence agents—who could be *any*where. Yet everyone is friendly to the two vagabonds, gracious about their wobbly French.

Carthage! They listen for echoes of Aeneas and Dido, study relics of the Punic War, drink in the storied landscape. Caroline adores the Roman and Muslim mosaics in the famous Bardo Museum. She wants to move permanently to the nearby village of Sidi Bou Said. But which house? Which one of the charming white buildings with the pretty blue doors?

On the ride south to Kairouan they float through fields golden with wildflowers. Dusty green olive trees prosper. The ancient, holy city seems a bit dour after Tunis, so they don't linger, and, at the first opportunity, head south.

Toward the Sahara. The journey to Tozer is a hot, desert trudge; they remark on the sheep and goats.

"Watch For Camels Crossing."

Does the sign really say that?

Further south, in Douz, it gets truly hot. The dense sand blowing across the road reminds Caroline of winter fog fingering across a highway. When Terri buys a carpet in the open air market, the shopkeeper beats off the yellow granules. Shaking his head, he shrugs. "*Le désert!*"

They collect so many shawls and earrings and little ceramic plates that the buckles crack on their Army Surplus backpacks, and they have to secure them with rope.

Glistening deserts. Seductive beaches. Magnificent peaks. Exquisite silver work. Delicious food.

And the men. Black hair. Deep brown eyes. Glittering smiles.

One man. In a place called Sousse.

Anouar.

TUNISIA, 2004

Yawning, she's suddenly exhausted from her twenty-four hour travel marathon. Should she call Tess? No, better let the girl phone in her own time. Caroline isn't sure she has the energy to put on pajamas, let alone make a transatlantic call to her exuberant, talented, beautiful daughter. Over-the-top or not, the gigantic bed with its lush pillows is irresistible.

A man's voice. She wakes with a start. Turning in the empty bed, she realizes it's a call to prayer blaring from the loudspeaker of a nearby minaret. *Allahu Akbar, Allahu Akbar/La Ilaha Ill Allah.* Even half asleep, she recites, "Allah is great, Allah is great/ There is no divinity but Allah."

Anouar was most beautiful when he laughed. "My father used to say it is better to pray than to sleep. I say it is better to sleep. Especially with you."

When the muezzin next wakes her, the bed feels cavernous and cold.

After the second *adhan,* she surrenders and fishes out an Ambien. One pill can't do much damage. She'll be alert enough for the meeting.

TUNISIA, 1975

Anouar orders a croissant and *café.* "Another cup?"

"No, thanks. I need to meet my girlfriend." Caroline pushes back her chair, annoyed with herself for allowing the distraction. She'd been content writing to Wayne about her reactions, her voyeurisms. "I shouldn't be late."

"You don't want to be unfriendly to a local, do you?"

Who could resist the wry smile beneath his flirty little moustache?

"*Je suis si triste.*"

"Not as sad as I." He winks.

He does seem safe. Besides, she's going home next week. Terri's always telling her to loosen up, have a fling. Caroline knows that someday she'll marry a sweet pale man. Not for a few years yet. There's plenty of time for that comfortable house with three blond children. She and Terri have the world before them—Patagonia, the Serengeti, Mongolia.

Relaxing back in her chair, she laughs. "What's your last name, Anouar?"

"Hasan," he breathes heavily on the *h*.

"Anouar Hasan. A nice ring."

"A very common name." He raises his thick eyebrows. "Like John Smith in America." He seems both eager and shy. "And your good name?"

"Kendrick. Caroline Kendrick. Not so common." She feels awkward.

"As befits a rare lady."

She blushes. The guy has been reading too much Jane Austen.

He laughs at himself. "I'm not usually so forward. Of my five brothers, I am the quietest."

Later, Caroline will discover, he is more reserved than most guys back home.

Later, he confides he was immediately infatuated.

She could tell.

Infatuated is new to Caroline. Blonde, buoyant Terri arouses infatuation. Down-to-earth Caroline inspires solid friendship. Terri admires her chestnut hair, but Caroline thinks it's a mousey brown. Yet here is the charming, worldly—he's lived in Paris and Cairo as well as the States—gorgeous guy who lights up simply looking at her.

Always a good sport, Terri agrees they can have dinner that night with Anouar and his friend Samir at *Les Poissons Délicieux*.

At nine o'clock, the women find themselves escorted through the dusky, hushed medina past shuttered souks. The tiny ornaments on Terri's new belt jingle softly against the rough cotton of her long blue skirt. Caroline wears an ankle length green dress and a new cream wool shawl.

Out of the dark night steps an old man wearing a beige burnoose. His lined face is warmed by the red fez. Following an ancient path through the market, he limps several paces in front of them, holding a candle. Two cats tag at his heels. The four diners follow the cats.

Terri elbows Caroline and rolls he eyes—comically? Anxiously?

Caroline takes a long breath. It is all a little strange. Spooky.

Ridiculous to worry, she tells herself. Anouar is *not* a cop. Not a kidnapper. Simply a nice guy. Just one evening of fun.

"*Voici.*" Their guide veers left and halts at a wooden entrance. He turns a large, circular brass handle, opening the heavy door to a candle-lit dining room where the walls are lined with elaborate carvings and tiles. The restaurant rings with conversation and laughter. Caroline feels like a hippie. The women here are so chic, so, well, French-looking. The waiter disregards their rustic appearance and graciously escorts them to a quiet table. In the far corner, four men play drums, an oud, a tambourine and a zither.

Caroline can't stop smiling.

Terri is more composed, watchful.

"What is this glorious music?" Caroline asks.

"Like it?" Anouar grins.

"It makes me think of Spain."

"It's a riff on an Andalusian classical suite, *moussiqua al-âla*, music that came here in maybe the 12th century, but that really took off after the *Reconquista*." His voice acquires an edge. Later, he will often speak about the Inquisition, about his long ago ancestors and their good lives in Cordoba.

The evening passes in intense exchanges between Caroline and Anouar, polite listening and a few interjections from Samir and Terri.

Caroline keeps telling herself to broaden the conversation, to remember Terri is her best pal. That she is a feminist. This evening is simply a lark. The carriage turns into a pumpkin at midnight.

Anouar genially reels her in.

She drinks too much delicious wine: oh, seductive Magon.

That night in their pension, Caroline declares, "Enough!" and slips under the covers. She still feels the wine and the beat of the music. "He was one evening's adventure. *C'est tout. Fini.*"

Terri settles into the other twin bed and switches off the light between them. "You think so?"

Caroline falls asleep before she can reply.

TUNISIA, 2004

"Madame Salwa has asked me to take you on the scenic route, to Hammamet, if you like, down past Susa, then over to Kairouan."

"Thank you, Abdul, that would be lovely." Her heart catches at the mention of Susa, but they won't be visiting. Salwa expects them in Kairouan by midday.

This landscape reminds her of California. More accurately, California reminds her of Tunisia because she visited these golden hills first, these olive trees, this rugged coast and moody sea. She's held them in her memory for almost thirty years. Decades of surprise, loss, achievement. Lingering questions. Flashbacks to a mysterious handsome man. Echoes of his intense, familiar voice.

She watches a man steering his rickety donkey cart. Fifty yards ahead is a farmhouse roof covered in solar panels. The classic Tunisian riddle: 19th or 21st century? French, Arab, African?

Now Caroline wonders again, what Salwa will be like? She imagines a tall, greying, dynamic woman. She looks forward to making a new friend. And to having another story of Tunisia.

The next day, Terri declines a second date with Samir.

Caroline swallows hard. "I'll tell Anouar I'm not free." She's known Terri since high school; she'll know her forever. Anouar is a wink in her life.

"Go on out with him tonight," Terri urges. "No sweat. There's a dance performance I want to catch. Have fun. Make it a really good time. We only have a couple more nights in Sousse before we go to the *ancient isle of Djerba*, remember, with the oldest synagogue outside Jerusalem. El Ghriba dates back to 687 BC, and Aunt Dvora is counting on the photos."

Caroline is torn. "You'll be OK on your own?"

Terri sniffs, laughs. "I'm twenty-six. In certain cultures, I could be a grandmother by now."

Caroline knows she's giving in too easily. "OK, Granny."

"Listen, I'll be fine. Back in the room reading Doris Lessing by 9pm. Do not worry."

As she draws near the outdoor bistro, Caroline reproves herself. She's a bad friend. Flighty, selfish. She can hear voices from her CR group declaring we have to stop putting men before women. Anyway, what is it about this guy? She'll never see him again. So if he's just a dalliance, why is she neglecting her best friend?

Anouar is sitting at a table with a bottle of red wine and two glasses. Cool. Assured.

When she waves, his face lights up and all her doubts about his cockiness evaporate. Such a wide, genuine smile.

He holds a chair for her, then pours them each a generous glass of Magon. There's a tenderness to the way he holds the globe of his glass with both hands when he toasts.

She swirls the elixir, enjoying the depth of red, shaded with purple. A subtle, fruity taste. Focus on the food, the laughter. A simple date. Stay in the present.

"You're a serious person," he raises his glass again, watching her closely. "To my serious new friend."

She pulls into herself. Is he mocking her? She clinks his glass. "To my wisecracking friend."

"You misinterpret." He sounds bewildered, and she watches his eyes darken. "I, too, am a serious person. I had cushy job offers from Chicago, Memphis and Raleigh. Still I returned to the village to design a filtration system. I am, as you Americans say, committed. *Tiens*, I sound like I'm applying for a job."

She laughs. Filtration, she thinks, *flirtation*.

"Naturally, I also read voraciously, go to the theatre—up in Tunis— and concerts."

Here it is again. All over Tunisia people say to her *You must understand, we are a cultivated people*. She's never thought otherwise. The defensiveness makes her uncomfortable, sad.

Their waiter appears with hummus and some other unidentifiable spread heady with garlic.

All evening they laugh. She surveys the café, full of young, merry people speaking Arabic and French, some English. She hears German from the corner table. A jolly scene. So easy to forget the dictatorship, the repression. For her anyway.

They drink and eat and laugh and drink. The world is spinning a little fast.

He leans over his *café*.

She smells his deep, smoky breath.

"Now we are doubly bound," he whispers, "because we have twice shared bread and salt."

"Pardon?"

"In my country sharing bread and salt is a rite of friendship. This sharing quells all possible antagonism. It creates an eternal mutual obligation of protection."

"That's quite poetic."

"We are a lyrical people."

TUNISIA, 2004

"*Madame* Salwa says you have visited Tunisia before."

"A long time ago." Caroline hopes Abdul will leave it at that.

"Does *Madame* mind if I turn on the radio for some pleasant music?"

"Please do."

Andalusian classical guitar. Of course. What are the odds?

Before leaving the States, she continually tried to locate Anouar, but every internet search failed. Even techno-whiz Wayne drew a blank. Anouar Hasan is, indeed, a common name. She's not sure how much more searching she'll do. Really, it's just a sentimental effort. What would they have to say to each other after decades? What if he didn't remember her? What if she embarrassed him? He probably had a wife or two. And fourteen children.

TUNISIA, 1975

Over a very late breakfast, Terri grins. "I heard you crash at 7 am. My only question: was it fabulous?"

"Oh, Terri, I, I…."

"Damn, you *are* smitten," she pretends to scold. "Remember our pact. Home to Boston together. No joining the Foreign Legion. No Naked Lunches. No Lingering Lotharios."

"He did ask me to stay," Caroline whispers, still amazed by the entreaty and her feelings about it.

"Obviously." Now she's irked. "But look, he's got an American degree. If it's true love, he can visit you in the U.S. Maybe move there. Wayne has several colleagues from Tunisia and Morocco. Visas are easy these days for scientists and engineers."

Caroline closes her eyes. They've gone through all this. He says he belongs to Tunisia. She imagines her identity is more mutable, daughter of immigrants from Italy and Northern England. She wonders what it means to be American after all. It's harder to answer what it would mean for her to be Tunisian. How can she be asking herself this question? She's only known him a few days. What madness.

"We do have reservations in Djerba." Terri's voice tightens. "El Ghriba and Aunt Dvora are expecting us."

"I know." She hugs her friend. "Don't worry."

Terri looks dubious.

"Really, I get it—Anouar is, was, a delicious daydream. Really."

~

The following week, Caroline and Terri spend their final Mediterranean night making plans over dinner at an outdoor Tunis café. Basking in the warm evening, overlooking the very French boulevard, they recall adventures —such dazzling mosaics, luscious food and mellow weather. Then the intrigue and secrets and shadows.

Other diners stare at the gold braid shimmering down Terri's back. This always happens. Caroline savors the memory of Anouar's pleasure in her own dark curls. Will he write as he fervently promised? Will she?

They raise a glass to their future in Boston—to finding an apartment together, decorating it with the rugs, fabrics and ceramics they've collected. Caroline plans to brush up on her French. Terri talks about yoga and tai chi. Friends for life, they clink glasses and order dinner.

Definitely they'll return to Tunisia. There's so much more to see.

In ten years, Terri would be dead. But at this bright moment in eternity, the friends beam as they plan next June in Dido's seductive dominion.

The trip is postponed.

Life intervenes. Money. One year. Terri's sister gets cancer. Another year. School.

"Graduate work in *Museology*? What on earth is that?"

Caroline's mother implores.

Hooked on North Africa, Caroline wants to look closely at the work of the Aghlabides, the Fatimides, the Hafsides, and naturally, the dazzling ceramics influenced by Andalus. She doesn't mention these musical names to her mother; rather patiently explains that the degree will mean a secure profession, a real career.

"A steady job," answers the widow who raised

Caroline alone on a bookkeeper's salary. "I vote for that." Caroline also doesn't mention Anouar. Who knows if he will wait for her? Still, the stunning bear of a man writes to her every week.

Yet she has to be practical. She has been dating Richard, a pre-med student, for the past few months. The disappointing man is completely focused on making money.

Terri lobbies for Michael, an architect, but he, too, seems driven. His goals are commissions and prizes. When she asks about designing affordable housing, he explains patiently that he'll do some pro-bono work once he's established.

Terri says Caroline's too picky. And judgmental. Michael is a progressive guy, anti-war, tutors in Roxbury on Saturday afternoons. He's sexy as hell.

Caroline knows Anouar is a world away—until she receives his next letter. Then they are as close as ever. He promises to visit. Good, it's his turn, she reminds him. But week after week, month after month, he appears only in the mail.

TUNISIA, 2004

"Would *Madame* like to stop in Susa? *Madame* Salwa thought you might like to take a coffee or to refresh yourself."

She inhales sharply. Silly, this swelling fear.

"I'm fine, thank you, Abdul." For some reason, she adds, "I do hope to visit Susa later during my visit to Tunisia."

"Very good *Madame*. It is a beautiful city. Especially along the Corniche."

She drinks in the pretty coastline, savoring its salty aroma. Whitewashed buildings; blue grey sea. Always that sea. Splendid enough to inspire an ocean of stories. She recalls the striking Tiepolo painting of Mercury telling an anguished Aeneas to leave Carthage.

As they make the turn inland toward Kairouan, Caroline thinks about the ancient settlement which she dismissed as too dour as a young traveler. Since then, she's learned that over millennia the historic city has nurtured Arabs, Berbers and Jews. In the ninth century, Kairouan housed a mosque that rivaled the University of Paris and has played a central role in Maghreb history.

Now Kairouan showcases the world's finest ceramics. On which *she* has been invited to consult. Caroline unfastens her briefcase and checks that she has brought an important file. There it is. She hopes Salwa hasn't made a grave mistake. She doesn't want to disappoint this woman who worked so hard to bring her here as a *senior figure in the field*.

Yes, certainly, she is that. At fifty-five, she's achieved gratifying success with her book and articles and exhibitions. Following family tradition, she's raised a lively daughter by herself. She has nursed a precious mother on her deathbed. She can count dozens of good friends. Five of them, like Wayne, have been in her life three decades. How she wishes Terri had lived to be one of them. Terri has become the other ghost in her life, Terri and Anouar. Sometimes still, she feels lost without each of them.

Fifty-five. What does it mean these days? She wants models for how to behave. Is she old now or still middleaged? What does it matter? God, she misses Terri. Is she a sexual being or a matron? She can ask Wayne these questions. Caroline, Wayne and Terri were the Three Musketeers at UMass.

Caroline and Wayne have grown closer since Terri's sudden cancer. Wayne still joins her for a month each summer at the ramshackle Maine cottage they bought with Terri in the late 70s. They enjoy long dinners overlooking the bay. And each evening in the gloaming they walk to the weathered stone bench where, twenty years ago, Aunt Dvora joined them in scattering her niece's ashes. At the ritual opening and closing of the cabin, they always set a place at the table for her. "Eliana," Wayne explains, "is the female Elijah."

Dear Wayne waves away Caroline's age anxiety. "You're gorgeous," he pronounces in his campiest way. "A real babe."

She shakes her head and threatens to pitch an overripe blackberry at his white linen shirt.

"Queer gentlemen have an eye, dear. We may not want to sleep with women, but we appreciate a babe. Look, you've got a great bod, fabulous legs, stunning cheekbones, Botticelli hair. Your new red highlights are just the thing."

"Babe," she chuckles silently. Hardly. Perhaps she does look a little hipper with this new haircut Tess gave her. Is there anything that girl can't do? Why has she been so lucky to have the perfect daughter? *Babe.* She supposes you could be a senior person in your field and a babe at the same time.

"Here we are, *Madame.*" Abdul nods to the handsome gardens and beyond those to the former presidential palace now the home of *Le Musée National d'Art Islamique.* She's seen photos but is completely unprepared for such grandeur.

He pulls up before an imposing building.

A short woman flies from the entrance. A small, dark person about thirty-five, wearing a mauve hijab and black dress. "Welcome. Welcome!" she calls and opens the limo's passenger door.

Caroline steps out, momentarily dumbfounded by the tiny woman's ebullience. She extends her hand and is pulled into a firm embrace.

Salwa kisses each of her cheeks. "*Bienvenue. Bienvenue. Enfin! Enfin!*"

Recovering her Parisian reflexes, Caroline returns the kisses. "*Merci. Merci.*" She's surprised by the hijab, then wonders why she's surprised.

Salwa gently takes her elbow. "Your bags are secure with Abdul. After the formality of meeting our staff, we shall go to your hotel. Just the two of us. Then I will sit on your bed as you unpack and you will tell me about your life." Caroline blinks, feeling absurdly shy.

M. Le Directeur's office is musty, cavernous. She notes four easy chairs, an enormous couch, a glass coffee table laden with trays of sweets and savories, bottles of juice and soda pop, glasses, napkins. The President of Tunisia presides from a gilt frame over the doorway. The director— she presumes the chubby bald man wearing a navy suit and purple tie is the director—nests behind an imposing wooden desk watching a small television.

Salwa's colleagues arrive, and she's introduced to Sana, Sonia, Nour, Ibrahim and Khaled. They each peck Caroline on both cheeks and ask about the flight, the drive from Tunis to Kairouan. Caroline tries to concentrate, but she's captivated by the director's loud TV program.

Suddenly he registers her presence and presses the mute button.

Salwa takes Caroline's hand, leading her forward. "Dr. Rhaiem, I would like to introduce our distinguished visitor, Dr. Caroline Kendrick, who has traveled all the way from Boston to work with us on the new Andalusian pieces."

Caroline smiles, relieved that he remains behind the desk, making no attempt at kissing.

"Welcome." His voice is stilted, as if reading from a script. "My esteemed colleague has spoken much about you. Indeed, I've read your fine book. It is a great privilege. Allow us to offer you some refreshment. Please join us on the couch."

"*Merci.* It is an honor to be here. A dream, actually."

Salwa tugs her hand, as if they are girls on a playground.

Together they join the others at the coffee table. *Monsieur Le Directeur* returns to his show, a kind of Tunisian *Oprah!*

The others ignore him, asking more questions, pressing sweets on her. She notices, with relief, their casual attire, slacks and open-necked shirts and blouses. Salwa and her boss are the only ones more formally dressed.

Caroline selects a *kaak warka*, savoring the buttery almond flavor of the donut, a taste she's craved for years. Thirty years.

Sana confesses that she once visited Caroline's museum but was too shy to introduce herself. "For this, we need the power of Salwa's imagination!"

"And her persuasiveness," laughs Ibrahim.

"So I'm not the only one to fall under your spell?" Caroline teases.

Glowing, Salwa changes the subject. "Khaled, Sana and Nour have studied in the U.S. Khaled at Purdue, Sana at Stanford and Nour at the University of Minneapolis."

"Close," the older woman smiles fondly, "The University of Minnesota."

Caroline sucks in her breath. Aimée's very French reflex returns involuntarily. Although the question is ridiculous, she can't help herself.

"Did you happen to know another Tunisian student at Minnesota—named Anouar Hasan?" Nour is about Anouar's age.

Does she imagine the loud silence? Nour looks puzzled. Khaled and Ibrahim exchange glances.

The sweet apple juice is cloying.

Salwa explains, "*Everyone* knows Anouar Hasan."

Caroline's heart catches.

"Anouar Hasan." Salwa shrugs. "It is a very common name."

"So I've been told." Caroline feels foolish.

"Is he a colleague or a friend?" Ibrahim asks.

"An old friend from another life. We lost track."

Ibrahim chuckles. "If he's an educated Tunisian, he'll reappear. This is a small country. Too small."

Caroline resists the hope rising in her chest. Ridiculous, really. What would they have to say to each other after all this time?

Salwa has planned excursions. They will take her shopping for rugs—the finest mergoums are made here in Kairouan. Then a ride through the countryside. Then dinner at the Corniche in Sousse—only an hour away. She has arranged everything. Each colleague has a separate hospitality assignment.

"Thank you very much. Everyone is so gracious." She refrains from checking on the director's TV program.

"But we must be overwhelming you," Salwa says merrily. "After your long journey. You haven't even unpacked. Come, let me escort me to the accommodation."

The imposing sandstone hotel is called La Kasbah. Salwa helps carry and roll her embarrassingly copious luggage through an imposing portico. The sumptuous lobby is decorated with handsome tiles. Caroline takes in the wicker chairs and beyond those the long swimming pool. She admires the high brick arches and an elaborate wooden ceiling.

"This is a Golden Yasmin, our Five Star Hotel," Salwa explains proudly. "We wanted to offer you the best. My brother-in-law's cousin works here, so we were able to arrange it."

"Merci. This is so kind," declares Caroline who would have preferred a simpler place.

On the way upstairs, Salwa points out the brown and beige tiled hamman. "Perfect refreshment after a long day." She sighs. "Nour has one in her home, you know."

"I haven't had a steam bath for ages," Caroline says longingly. "Sooo inviting." She may get used to La Kasbah after all.

In Caroline's room, pretty mergoums warm the parquet floor. A mirror gleams from its hand-carved Arabesque frame. There's even a small desk and padded stool. The obligatory satellite television. And another capacious bedroom. French doors lead to a sweet veranda with wooden chairs and a round glass table.

"Lovely!" she exclaims, realizing how easily she'll settle into this unexpected luxury.

Salwa pops on the bed and declares, "While you unpack, we'll chat. I've felt from the beginning that you and I would be friends."

Caroline grins at the human hummingbird.

"You must be ready to settle in."

Grateful for the assignment, she opens her oversized suitcase and hangs the blouses first.

"You have one daughter?"

"Yes." Has she mentioned Tess in an email? "She's just starting her acting career in New York with a very small part in an off-Broadway play." Her eye is caught by the delightful blue and white tiles on the wall behind her bed.

"Oh, I should love to go to Broadway. "The Great White Way, no? I used to attend Paris theatre all the time. Ballet. Opera. Splendid, even in the cheap student seats."

"You studied in Paris?"

"For six perfect years."

"Did you think of staying?" She hangs a pair of dark slacks, recalling that both Sana and Sonia were wearing black pants.

"Naturally!" Salwa raises her arms in surrender. "I was offered three excellent curatorial posts."

Caroline isn't surprised. She's studied up on Salwa's work. Quite formidable.

"I *dreamed* of staying in Paris."

"But you returned?" she asks cautiously. The story is familiar.

"*Bien sûr.* Family. My parents had already chosen a husband. He wouldn't wait forever. My body returned obediently, if not my entire spirit. No day passes when I don't long for Paris."

Caroline is dying to know more, but they've just met. She detours to safer ground. "Tell me about your children. You have four?" She knows the answers. Salwa reports on her kids in every email, and Caroline brought a gift for each of them. She slides the bag of presents temporarily into the bottom drawer.

"Sari and I have two fine boys, Wali and Habib. And two lovely daughters, Nadia and Hager. The blessings of my life. Sari is a good man, a doctor, so we are well provided for."

"What does he think about your work?" Caroline shakes out her cotton dress. She brought her most conservative clothing and is amused to think how—aside from the traditional Salwa and *M. Le Directeur*—her colleagues are quite hip.

"In some ways, he is a deeply progressive man. He values an intelligent, educated wife and is very supportive."

Caroline nods, waiting.

Salwa looks out the window, staring into the middle distance. "The challenges are more, well, societal. We do have reproductive rights here. Polygamy is banned. Still, women are, to a certain degree, decorative. But you asked about my family. The trick is balancing the job with all the housework, the shopping and cooking and cleaning. We observe many traditions and rituals as a Muslim family, you understand, which are time-consuming. Yet also rewarding. Allah has blessed truly my life."

Caroline knows it will take some time to unpack Salwa's response. She wonders if it's genuinely possible for the two of them to become friends given their differences in age, nationality and culture. She starts with the basics. "Did you bring pictures?"

"I shall do better than photos!" she laughs happily. "Sari and I invite you to a family dinner on Wednesday if you don't have other plans."

"Thank you!" What plans could she have? She notices a small bronze wind chime on the balcony. "Yes, I would love to come and meet them all."

~

The first week has been long, challenging, productive. Relaxing on Friday night under the bedcovers, Caroline pulls out her journal. She is both cozy and uneasy. The grandiose Kasbah now feels more comfortable, at least more familiar. The cheerful chefs know how she likes her morning eggs, and she's found that the generous breakfast takes her through most of the day. There's so much to study and evaluate; she doesn't eat lunch. She does share afternoon tea at work, where she's come to enjoy everyone except the weird, reclusive director. Each day is absorbing. So far, Caroline has identified one rare piece. She's learning a lot, especially about the Aghlabids. She'll get a couple of research papers out of the fellowship. Caroline leans back, sipping brandy slowly, growing sleepy. Her duty free bottle is lasting nicely. She savors the sharp-sweet aroma officially prohibited in this dry, orthodox city. Closing her eyes, she thinks, yes, a promising start at the museum topped off with a long phone call from the newly employed Tess. A fine week, she muses in the dim room, yet it's all underpinned with a vague disquiet. Familiar from her first visit. Small. Subtle. Nothing to fret about really, especially if you are falling asleep sitting up.

Each day, she strolls through the medina admiring the bright shawls, comfortable leather footstools and intricately woven rugs. The spice vendors are her favorite, especially the one whose henna baskets are shaded by a gay *parapluie* advertising *Veuve Clicquot* in this holy city where khamr is banned.

Every afternoon, the merchants call out, "*Madame est Française?*"

"*Madame* is Greek?"

They never guess American, which pleases her.

"*Madame* is Swede?"

She smiles.

"*Madame* is Swiss?"

Caroline nods. Given the war in Iraq, the situation in Palestine, Caroline accepts almost any nationality.

The macaroon vender inquires, "*Madame est seule?*"

She just smiles, recalling Terri's long ago retort. "*We're not alone; we're together.*"

Five Spaniards pass her, on the hunt for leather bags.

The Italians today are drawn to the woven cushion covers.

She is, indeed *seule*, in the sense that she hasn't noticed any other Westerners traveling solo.

The first time Caroline watched a Euro-tour bus rumble into the Kasbah parking lot, her heart sank. But the groups are lodged in a separate section from the long-term guests and seem to keep different hours. She's not a snob—well, maybe just a little—but she's enjoying the illusion of living in Tunisia instead of passing through.

An extended metaphor is what Terri would call her fantasy.

She does miss her old friend, keeps thinking she should be here. Caroline is often on the verge of asking, "See how different? See how much the same?" If God ever had a chance with her, Terri's death put an end to that. To pluck away such vibrance, such joy, was random cruelty.

Some friends—not Wayne, of course—politely wonder why Terri is still such a presence in her life. How to explain that Terri was her co-conspirator, her sister. Would they ask the same question if Terri had been a spouse?

By the second week, merchants begin to recognize her. "*Bonjour.*"

"*Et ça va?*"

"*Bonjour, Madame.*"

"*Bienvenue, encore.*"

"*Merci.*" She smiles, savoring her extended metaphor. She never left this enchanted country. Anouar is expecting her home any minute.

One morning Salwa collects her at the hotel, and as they get in the car, she announces a surprise. "Would you like to visit our Grand Mosque? It is very historical."

Caroline likes the way Tunisians pronounce it, *mosquay*.

"Very much but aren't there restrictions?"

"Everything will be fine, I promise. We will not barge into the men's section, OK?"

Caroline loves Salwa's mischievous laugh.

As her new friend drives the winding streets of Kairouan, Salwa picks up the thread of their last conversation. "My family has been settled here for forty generations. You know our mosque was built the year after the Prophet died. Our people settled Kairouan for security. An inland place was safer from invasion." Salwa relishes her subject. "Kairouan is the fourth holiest place in all of Islam—after Mecca, Medina and Jerusalem. This is the spot from which the whole Maghreb was converted to our faith."

Caroline listens in discreet silence. She hears so many conflicting stories about the spread of Islam in Africa, about the founding of Kairouan.

As they step from the car, a bearded old man in a washed-out grey burnoose and beige skull cap approaches them offering a broad grin.

Salwa springs forward girlishly, grabs his shaky hand. "Uncle, Uncle. I would like to introduce my dear friend and colleague from America, Dr. Caroline Kendrick."

The man smiles discerningly. "Welcome."

"Caroline, this is my favorite uncle, Uncle Jalal, my father's older brother."

"Very pleased to meet you," she says and returns his unblinking glance.

Salwa whispers to him, almost giddily.

He closes his eyes and, after a long moment, nods.

"Uncle Jalal is the muezzin here." She claps her hands. "He says I may take you to the minaret."

"That sounds fascinating," Caroline demurs, nervous about trespassing, yet anxious not to insult Salwa.

Noticing her hesitation, Salwa declares, "That is, if you can manage all the steps." She points to the tiny, distant balcony of the minaret. "Two-hundred-seventy stairs."

"Good exercise," Caroline parries. Terri would have loved this. Yes,

Salwa has her old friend's *joie de vivre*. Over the next weeks, Caroline wonders why she ever doubted this new friendship. Salwa is a brilliant historian, a feminist who balances the contradictions of her life with grace and humor. Her endless curiosity has caused Caroline to open up about her childhood, the short marriage to Garth and their divorce, her delightful daughter. She's still searching for a door to the story of Anouar.

As they reach the top of the tower, a light wind ruffles Caroline's hair and Salwa's hijab.

Her friend shows off the sights of her Holy City. They circle the top platform, ducking around microphones for the complete 360 degree view.

"Breathtaking," Caroline says. "To think your family has lived here a thousand years."

Anouar said he belonged to Tunisia, and Salwa would probably say the same thing. She'll never belong to Boston, let alone the States, in the same way.

"You know what?" Salwa's hazel eyes dart playfully.

"What?"

"We're really not supposed to be up here. And you," she laughs happily. "You, especially, are not supposed to be here."

Later, in bed, she recalls Salwa's words. She *isn't* supposed to be here. She's supposed to be in Sousse or Tunis or Paris with Anouar. She isn't supposed to be a middle-aged babe, divorcée, mother, senior figure in her field doing research in Tunisia *without him*. Without Anouar. Without the deep drum of his voice, without his oak sturdy body. After she had given up and married the thin rangy Garth, that's how she thought about herself. *Without Anouar.* The very notion was infidelity, but she never knew to whom she was being unfaithful.

PARIS, 1980

As the train slides into the Gare Du Nord, Caroline collects her luggage. Enough for a year? Too much for ten years? She inhales deeply. It's a twelve month fellowship, she reminds herself. She isn't Gertrude Stein or Josephine Baker or Ernest Hemingway. Especially not Hemingway. All the same, she has glimmers of a career, of a life, in Paris.

Anouar has promised to be waiting outside her carriage. How will he know which car?

Caroline is completely prepared for him not to appear. It's one thing to woo through the post and quite another to have a relationship in person. Does he know how she's changed in five years? Yes, there have been the weekly letters, sometimes daily letters, but they haven't been in the same country, let alone the same room, for half a decade.

She will do fine on her own. She's been practicing with French tapes for months. She has three dictionaries. If he flakes out, she can easily hail a taxi to the pension Aunt Dvora recommended. After all, she's a twenty-nine year old woman with a prestigious grant. She's here for a scholarly year in Paris.

"A whole year?" Once again Mama shook her head, but Caroline knew Mrs. Sophia Kendrick was proud of her only child. She didn't distract Mama with news of Anouar. Besides, what does she, herself, know of this man with whom she spent only three days? (Clearly, this is an insane fantasy— three days!) She recalls the verses he copied from Darwish and Rumi and Kabir. His personal news has grown more cryptic this year. Yes, yes, the hydrology studies are progressing well. He misses Tunisia, but Paris has its charms and soon will have more upon her arrival. His every letter brims with impatience for her. He promises grand adventures in the City of Light.

The poetry lingers in her mind.

"*Bienvenue, ah, Bienvenue,*" calls a bearded stranger.

Caroline peers past him into the thinning crowd, choking back tearful disappointment. (She and Terri have talked and talked about this possibility, and her friend's words steady her now. "*Whatever happens, you'll be fine. Promise you'll phone me the first night, don't forget.*") She digs into her huge impractical bag for a dictionary.

As the conductor hands down her baggage, she struggles to hail a porter. "*Services bagages, monsieur, un portier, s'il vous plaît.*"

Her pleas are unanswered, ignored, unheard. People rush past her, shouting to friends. Trains screech by. Announcers compete in tinny voices for their passengers. The fabled station smells of dirt, *Gauloises*, sweat and urine.

She tries again, "*Service Bagages?*"

Two porters hurry in the opposite direction. Is her pronunciation off?

"No, no need," the bearded man says, laughing at her.

She looks up, angrily.

He tilts his head.

She catches a breath. "Anouar?!?

He wraps solid arms around her shoulders.

Walloped by keen physical memories, the familiar aroma of his musk and cologne leaves her trembling, then weeping. "Anouar!" She pulls away and stares. "You have a beard!" She's laughing through tears.

"And *you*, you've cut your hair!" He wipes her wet cheeks with back of his hands. "Very nice. The style complements your superb bone structure."

She blushes.

He can't stop grinning.

She studies him, unable to do anything but gape at this beautiful man she's dreamed about for five years.

Again, he pulls her to him.

Her body relaxes. Home, she feels, finally home.

Dozens of passengers rush by carrying suitcases and backpacks. An old woman pokes her husband and nods toward the young couple. They both smile.

"Now aren't you going to says something equally agreeable about my rakish beard?"

"It's very, very...." All she can think is virile. He looks a little older, perhaps because of a certain fatigue around his eyes.

"Not one very but two...very what?"

A word emerges. "Robust."

"*Robuste!*" He laughs and rocks her in his arms.

"Distinguished." She steps back, hands on hips, beaming. "I didn't recognize you at first. Why didn't you tell me about it?"

A young mother picks up her screaming toddler, rocking him back and forth.

"Why didn't you write to me about chopping your lovely curls?"

"You don't like my hair?" She bites her lip. Terri and Wayne agreed the style was *très chic*.

"You're more beautiful than ever, my blue bird." She flushes at his sexy smile.

"Come, let's get you fed. I've made a reservation at *l'endroit parfait pour le déjeuner.*"

Terri *said* he'd be thrilled to see her, would never let her go. One thing at a time, she tells herself. The fellowship lasts twelve months.

It is all too cinematic—a sidewalk café shaded by a blue and white striped awning. She watches the sun light up golden buildings and silver cobblestones and the shiny spokes of children's bicycles. In a nearby alley, a flutist plays softly next to a shop marked with a drawing of a man holding stringed instruments. *Lutherie Ancienne et Moderne.*

"They repair guitars?"

"And violins and cellos. Your *français, c'est vraiment formidable.*"

He looks and sounds more relaxed now after a few sips of wine. Still, she worries he isn't taking care of himself.

"My French couldn't get much worse."

He pulls out a pack of Gitanes, offers her a cigarette.

"No thanks. You're smoking now?" Brilliant question.

"I've lived in Paris for three years," he says and gestures to the other diners and lights up. "Unlike you, I have no strength of character."

Actually, she enjoys the earthy aromas of *Gauloises et Gitanes*, so different from the acrid bitterness of American cigarettes.

Soon their small, round table is cluttered with salads and plates of *frites* and cheeses.

They are on their second glasses of an opulent merlot.

"Aren't you impressed that I ordered vegetarian?"

She lifts her brows dramatically. "I would have been more impressed if you had allowed me to order a dish as well."

"But I am your host." He is resolute.

"I can't let you *pay.*" She's startled by the panic in her voice, surprised by how much she actually would like him to take care of her.

"I remember. I remember. Dutch treat. You taught me. I, too, have become egalitarian. *Féministe, moi même.* Still, you must permit me to welcome you back to my *hemisphere.* This is one day, simply lunch. A little bread and salt."

Not a Naked Lunch, she recalls Terri's long ago admonition. Just one al fresco meal. It sounds fair enough. Safe enough.

They spend the rest of the afternoon strolling through Paris, admiring the fruits and vegetables and meats of the *épiceries,* the pastries and cakes of the *boulangeries.* One bakery sells only bread—their round and long loaves arranged seductively on pale wooden shelves. Oh, the fragrant, sweet yeast.

For the first few weeks, Caroline is constantly hungry. Her favorite shops are the *fromageries.* Anouar is content trailing after her, sampling the bitter, creamy, ashy, herbal cheeses that never look as tantalizing in any other country. If she keeps this up, she won't fit into her clothes.

But this is her first month, her *Bienvenue,* her debut. In September, she will become more sensible.

Levelheadedness requires planning and restraint. They will see each other on Tuesdays, Thursdays and weekends. Despite his passionate protests, her common sense prevails. She explains that this way they'll relish each other's company more. He calls it her Declaration of Independence.

She does wants to get acquainted with her colleagues in the program, to prepare for her classes at the *Alliance Française.* She doesn't say, doesn't even realize, that she also needs time to be alone.

They can sleep together at his room. They'd have no privacy in her pension. His garret comes with a funky green pull-out couch, a small oak table, stained ceramic sink, gas ring. It's just a *chambre.* at the top of a century-old house. The shared toilet and shower are one floor below. They both find the place tawdry, but say romantic. She imagines it as the sort of seedy dive the young, passionate Simone Signoret and Yves Montand might have shared.

"*Vous avez un fiancé? Un petit ami?*" Mme. Dupuis offers her a hazelnut macaroon.

This Monday evening she shares a pot of tea with her elderly neighbor. Most of the other pension residents are graduate students or young professionals. The two exceptions are Mme. Lanthier, the landlady, and her friend, Mme. Dupuis, both in their late seventies, smelling of stale *Rive Gauche* and the musty dander of aged skin.

"A friend, yes," Caroline dissembles, "not at all *un fiancé.*"

"*Un Parisien?*"

"No, yes, he's lived here three years. He's originally from Tunisia."

"Ahh," the old woman dips a macaroon in her *thé*. The corner breaks, and she fishes it out with her spoon, reverently lifting the wet host to her lips. "*Un Pied Noir.*"

Caroline stiffens. Mme. Dupuis can think what she likes.

Mme. Dupuis looks up expectantly.

She can't help herself. "Not a Frenchman. A Tunisian from Sousse, the beautiful coastal city."

"Ohhh. *Maintenant je comprends.*" Madame purses her lips as if the macaroon has turned sour. "Do be careful with *L'Arabe*. We have all heard stories."

Caroline surveys the yellowing lace curtains, the volumes jumbled on the crowded teak bookcases, the chipped, ancient mahogany *coffer* where Mme. Lanthier stores dusty china.

"*Faites attention!*" she tries again, distractedly fingering the cold cross at her neck.

"He's an excellent person," Caroline answers as gently as she can. Why does she care about the old bat? How did she let the conversation get this far?

"I tell you this because I like you." The woman's voice is urgent, anxious. "I was also once young and impressionable. Please understand me. *Les Arabes, ils ont mauvaise réputation.*"

She's heard versions of this at the institute, at the *Alliance*.

Caroline thought she was attending the *Alliance Français* to improve her French. But racism is on the invisible syllabus; the gulf between African and European students is huge and glaring. The two times she's gone to the café after class have been painfully enlightening. Bigotry here is different from Boston prejudice. Here, even liberals freely express fear or disgust of Arabs.

Of her new institute friends, only Aimée seems comfortable with

Anouar. Sometimes they double date with Aimée's charming Raul from Buenos Aires.

By fall, Anouar's eyes have brightened. He looks younger, healthier. Even he notices the change.

One morning in bed, he kisses her forehead and declares, "You're good for me, *mon petit chou*, with your rigorous American wholesomeness."

She waits for the kicker.

"Less drinking. Less meat and more fish. All those forced marches in the fresh air."

Caroline slowly pulls back from his embrace, feigning affront. "Our romantic strolls along the Seine? Our pleasant saunters in the gardens? So I'm not your beloved companion but your drill sergeant?!"

He snuggles closer. "I confess to *une vie plus sédentaire* before you arrived."

Pleased, embarrassed, she teases him. "I haven't had much success in the smoking department."

"Ah, I must maintain my distinctiveness, my annoying edginess. I am the scratchy wool to your sheer, supple silk."

Au contraire, he's the most tender man she's ever known.

By October, Caroline's letters to Terri are feverish with excitement about her fascinating peers and mentors, the challenging resources and about larking around the world's most romantic metropolis with her *petit ami*.

Together they watch fabulous films, *La Boum, Le Roi et L'Oiseau, Germinal*. She's doesn't need subtitles; her French is that good. *Atlantic City* is her favorite movie. The magnificent Luis Malle. She likes to tease Anouar that he's Burt Lancaster; that they will always be changing each other's lives for the better. Not on the Jersey shore but on the banks of the Seine where Caroline dreams of them growing old together.

Often, walking in the City of Light, she and Anouar trade sardonic headlines about Jacques Chirac and Giscard d'Estaing. She's certain Mitterand will win. But he contends the Socialists don't have a chance. Their arguments usually end in truce over *affogato di gelato* in a smoky café. He laughs at the pleasure she takes in small adventures—finding a new metro stop, studying modish women and scouring the flea market to make their patchwork lives a little homier.

One warm evening, after a delicious and far too late dinner with Aimée and Raul, Anouar insists on hailing a cab.

"What an extravagance," she demurs. "Aimée and Raul walked home. Your place is only a couple of miles. It's a lovely night and I don't see why—"

"First, *ma chérie*, we are tired and both have to wake at dawn. Second, this is a dicey neighborhood. My friend Aymen was accosted here. Mugged pretty badly."

"How awful." She recognizes his familiar irritation with her naïveté, his strained patience. She recalls her fruitless conversations with *Madame* Dupuis and her *Alliance* tutor.

"Arab by day is passable, but Arab by night is risky. Really. And I don't want to endanger you." He waves his arm up and down, trying to hail a car.

Several empty taxis pass them by.

She hums nervously. He is right. She's ashamed and suddenly scared.

Finally a cab stops.

The Black cabbie nods coolly to them.

Anouar opens the door for her, then slides in as he recites his address.

The tall, handsome driver watches through the rear view mirror. His eyes are wintry, scrutinizing.

She's tempted to shrug Anouar's arm off her shoulder.

The cabbie addresses Anouar in agitated Arabic, tinged with a Bambara cadence which she's heard from the Malians at the *Alliance*. Her Arabic is improving, not as fast as her French, but it's improving.

She catches the phrase white heathen.

He steps on the gas, and the taxi jolts ahead.

"Just drive," Anouar says in a monotone.

The cabbie spits the word *putain* in French so she'll understand.

Anouar, red faced and sputtering, leans across the front seat, pulling a fist to slug the driver.

Caroline grabs his hand.

"*Arrêtez s'il vous plaît,*" she demands in her clearest, calmest, loudest voice.

"You can't talk like that," Anouar shouts at the driver. His face and neck are bright red. His hand, which Caroline is still holding, shakes uncontrollably. "Apologize or I—"

"No," she touches his shoulder. "Let's just get out."

The driver screeches to a halt.

She opens her door, flings several francs in the front seat and tugs Anouar from the car into the middle of the sleepy street.

"Bloody zealot!" Anouar shouts after the squealing car.

Wherever they are, it feels safer outside the cab. She's relieved, and as she takes a breath, she smells something sweet.

Ah, they've landed in front of an *épicerie*. Caroline regards the inviting sign, "*Le Panier,*" painted with a basket of croissants and brioches.

Dommage, the refuge is closed. Still, she is reassured simply by the warm yellow lights shining inside the bakery and the sugary aromas promising morning to come.

She's right about the walk. The night air clears her head. She hopes it has the same effect on Anouar.

They plod for forty-five minutes through the magic city, neither saying a word.

She has almost stopped shaking by the time they reach his room.

He's still clenching and unclenching his left hand.

Caroline writes Terri about the cabbie, about other incidents, large and small. She fears the widening gaps in their experiences here. Her own work has grown more absorbing. Anouar talks less and less about his research. Caroline watches their mutual world shrinking.

At night she stays awake mulling over Terri's familiar solution. Everything would be different if he would come to the States. Terri writes with news of a visa program designed for engineers from North Africa and the Middle East. They could love and work in peace. He could walk down the street absorbed in the multicultural stew. Terri's own firm is recruiting from Morocco. He would have lots of different friends to fill his expansive heart.

A window table at their favorite bistro. Snug here against the November chill. A sultry cabernet. Whiffs of garlic, onion and good olive oil. She plays with his cold fingers.

"Damn Paris rain." He drops her hand. "Puddles—lakes— everywhere. When it isn't chilly, it's damp. Drivers think nothing of splattering you as they careen around corners."

Caroline thinks Paris sparkles in the mist, but he's in too much of a funk to hear this. So, instead, she tries an Ella Fitzgerald riff on her favorite Cole Porter,

"I love Paris in the summer when it sizzles.
I love Paris in the winter when it drizzles."

Ah, yes, there it is, a small smile in his brown eyes, on his lovely lips.
"I love Paris, why oh why do I love Paris
Because my love is here."

"*Oui, Oui.*" He nods, then drains the bottle of vin rouge into his glass. "My love is here too. But I often think we'd be happiest somewhere else."

Maybe Terri is right; maybe he does want to return to the States. "Where?" she murmurs under her tight breath.

"Sousse, of course. With you there, everything was perfect."

She blinks in surprise.

"You were happy?"

"Yes," she gulps. "But that was only a few days. Long ago. Before we started on professional paths, before we invested years in graduate work."

"In Tunisia, we can both pursue our passions. In the sunshine."

Obviously, it rains in Sousse. He's talking about a different kind of climate.

In truth, she could probably work at the museum there. Or teach at the university. But too soon children would be expected. Many children. She's heard enough about Anouar's proudly fertile mother to anticipate her fierce desire for grandchildren. And Anouar, himself, would come to expect certain traditions. Then again, is she trying to transform him into her own fantasies? Into an American engineer who loves cross-country skiing in the winter and summer vacations on the Cape? In the end, how different are their intentions?

They agree it's too early to plan. Meanwhile, she tells herself they can flourish here in Paris where they are both visitors. Deep down, she understands they are outsiders in very different ways.

~

The December cold is crisp, enhancing the tangy scent of fir trees in the lot. She spends an hour choosing the perfect one. "*Plus petit*," Caroline insists, watching her words form a frosty fog. She searches until she finds the ideal *arbre de Noël*. His meeting will run until late, so she has plenty of time. Since Christmas Eve is a Wednesday, he won't be expecting her tonight at all. She feels like the newly redeemed Scrooge carrying their little tree, plus ingredients for his favorite dinner, with chocolate macaroons for dessert. She's even splurged on an expensive Magon.

Upstairs in his garret, she concentrates on her merry mission, staying alert for his footsteps on the stairs.

Finally, yes. This is Anouar's tread, a very tired Anouar. She rushes to hang the last string of lights, then switches off the overhead fixture. Pine resin suffuses the attic room. From the hotplate, dinner simmers seductively.

His key in the lock, then his usual irritable jiggling of the loose door knob.

Her heart pounds as she flicks on the tree lights. She stands behind the *arbre*, peeking over the top, where an ornamental angel might wait.

"What the?" He rubs his eyes.

"*Joyeux Noël!*" she calls, then runs to him, her arms wide and expectant.

He stands wooden against her embrace.

"Are you OK?" She steps back, alarmed. "Did something happen at the Institute? Or on the street?"

"Wednesday," he mumbles distractedly, irritably. "It's Wednesday. I wasn't expecting you."

"It's Christmas Eve!" She glows. Surely he will warm up when he realizes the date. "You were telling me last week you always envied your schoolmates who had Christmas trees. How you loved the lights and ornaments."

"But *we* never had one," he says plainly.

"And now you do!"

Then she takes it all in, mortified by her yuletide cheer.

"I see that." His eyes are blank.

Her heart sinks. "You're displeased." What a blunder. She is so obtuse.

"I'm sorry. It's been a rough day." He shrugs off his purple parka and drops to the seedy sofa. "They're tightening up on student visas."

"Oh, god, you're not in danger?" Her humiliation transmutes to panic. She stands back, an intruder.

"No, no." He's impatient, preoccupied. "Adel, Kamel and Ramy were summoned. Theirs have run out."

"But how? In a prominent grad program like yours, someone must have pull with the government, how can they just send them—"

"Because we don't belong here, Caroline."

She waits.

He trudges over to the window where rain spits against the glass. Hands on his hips, he stares down at the street.

"Oh, Anouar." She embraces him from behind.

"Damn, damn," he gently pushes her away. "Damn."

In his face, she sees Mom's eyes after Dad's heart attack, the expression of finality and surrender. No, she tells herself. It's not the same, not as absolute. She must not exaggerate.

He sighs, leaning against the wall. "Sorry, I'm in a foul mood."

"It's completely understandable." She stays a few steps away, wary of crowding him. "I shouldn't have presumed about the tree."

"Yes."

"I'm sorry."

He shrugs.

Taking a breath, she gestures to the fragrant pot, the wine bottle. "Will you have a little dinner?"

"*Merci*, that would be nice." He hugs her perfunctorily. "I *am* hungry. It's freezing outside, and your *coq au vin* smells superb."

As she fills the goblets, she slips the silver-foil wrapped gifts—a woolen hat and much needed gloves—into her shopping bag. Another time, she thinks. New Year's? Some secular holiday.

TUNISIA, 2004

The ride to Sousse is late afternoon sunny. Ibrahim and Sana are amusing, wonderfully irreverent. Ten to fifteen years younger than she, Caroline guesses, yet they treat her as a contemporary with their teasing. They each make cracks about *Monsieur Le Director* and laugh uproariously. "A little boring." One of Salwa's classic understatements. Sana parks in front of a bistro as the sun hits the horizon.

Ibrahim opens the café door, and Sana ushers Caroline to a window table under a huge blue fishnet hanging from the ceiling. Colored glass balls bob overhead in the welcome breeze of air conditioning.

Caroline can hear the sea, sloshing waves, cackling gulls. She thinks guiltily of her neighbors shoveling snow in Boston.

"We hope you like our local fish," Ibrahim says.

"Everything is caught today."

"I love all fish," Caroline answers. "This place is perfect." She glances around at the bright green walls and cheerful turquoise table cloths, relieved there are no old men with lanterns or musicians playing Andalusian music. Still, she's distracted by an odd nostalgic pang about *Les Poissons Délicieux*.

"It's fun having you at the museum," Sana says excitedly.

Caroline is still in that magical restaurant with two of her ghosts.

Sana speaks a little louder. "We needed new blood. Already your questions are making me think of projects."

"Thank you." Caroline comes to. "The feeling is completely mutual. I'll be taking so much back with me to Boston."

"Boston," Ibrahim repeats dolefully. "How much longer do we have you?"

Forever, she's tempted to say. Instead, she sighs, "My ticket is for mid-March."

"Tickets can be changed." Sana raises an eyebrow.

Pleased, Caroline laughs.

"That's ages from now," Ibrahim declares. "After dinner we're stopping at the market to stock up on wine. You may want to join us?"

"Yes, please. I'm afraid I'm not abstinent enough for the Holy City."

"Holy City." Sana shakes her head. "There are some—Salwa is one—who are sincerely observant."

Caroline notices a man watching the sea from a corner table. There's something about his posture, his melancholy expression. She feels the blood drain from her face. No, it couldn't be.

Ibrahim agrees, "Salwa's genuine, but most of my friends here prefer rye to dry. Tunisia is a land of contradictions. Or hypocrisies. We enjoy free health care and virtually free education. Yet, education for what? About what? When everything is censored?"

Caroline observes that the melancholy man is heavier than Anouar. Beardless but with a distinguished small moustache.

Sana nods. "Silence is the price we pay for government bursaries."

Caroline inhales sharply. It's true his moustache would be grey like this now.

"Is something wrong?" Ibrahim asks.

"No, no. I just thought I recognized someone." She tries to sound blasé.

"That's right, Salwa told us you were here in the eighties."

"The seventies."

Their startled expressions amuse her.

"Did you visit Sousse on that trip?" asks Ibrahim.

The man in the corner is sipping red wine, holding the globe with both hands. She forces herself to sit still, to remain present. Really, she only needs to know Anouar is alive and well. She tells herself this will satisfy.

"Yes," she finally answers, "but for too short a time."

"I wonder how much it's changed." Ibrahim muses.

The stranger rises slowly, walks in their direction.

Caroline sits upright, tucks her stomach.

The waiter appears bearing an abundance of *ādūs*: hummus, olives, stuffed grape leaves.

Caroline shuts her eyes, breathing deeply. Then conscious of her peculiar behavior, she pretends she's been savoring the aromas. "Umm, I can smell the oil and garlic."

Ibrahim is passing a plate.

The stranger has slipped out of sight. Perhaps he has gone to the loo.

"You have noticed changes?"

"Sorry," Caroline blushes. "New buildings. But the people, well, I imagine there are also new people, and many of the old ones have gone." She's babbling. The old ones. Anouar. Concentrate on your colleagues, she tells herself.

Ibrahim looks at her, uncomprehending.

"How would Caroline know how Sousse has changed?" Sana scolds her friend. "She just arrived with us twenty minutes ago. See how valiantly she's trying to answer your nonsensical question?"

Caroline focuses on the food, on her hospitable companions but finds herself scanning the room. Has she really seen him? Anouar? She tries to distract herself by savoring the hummus on warm pita.

"How do you like our *vin blanc de la région*?" Ibrahim tries again.

"Crisp, dry. Perfect." She looks over to find their waiter clearing the window table. Her disappointment is tinged with relief. Let it go, she admonishes, let it *all* go. But she feels as if Ibrahim and Sana are in a movie she's barely watching.

"Good choice, Ibrahim," Sana agrees.

In spite of herself, she asks "Do you know if there is a chemical engineering department at the *Université de Sousse*?" Why didn't she think of this back in Boston when she was Googling Anouar Hasan a thousand ways? He could be right here, where they began.

"An interesting question." Sana regards her closely.

"One of my Tunisian friends was an engineer," she says uneasily. "We met in Sousse."

Ibrahim jumps in. "Oh, yes, the Anouar you mentioned the first day. My brother teaches physics there. I'll ask him. And we can easily search the department site."

Her head aches. Of course he's not here. She would have found him already. She's just unnerved by the window table man. The guy was too short for Anouar. And the nose was all wrong, isn't it?

PARIS, 1981

March 11, his birthday, a special restaurant. Caroline arrives first to secure a quiet table looking out to the busy street. Two sips of wine and she checks the foil wrapped gifts that have lingered since *Noël*. The hat and gloves would have been handy in January and February, yet there's still a nip in the air most days. He's probably right about the superior climate of Tunisia.

She looks around and sees that most of the tables full. Where is Anouar? He's rarely late. She takes another drink and breaks off a piece of fresh, hot baguette. She admires two chic women wafting by with overflowing bags from *Les Galeries Layfayette*. The waiter offers another glass.

"*Non, merci. Il est un petit tard,*" she says sipping her breath quickly, a quirk she's picked up from Aimée.

Half an hour late. So unlike him. She thinks about a scary article on skinheads in *Le Monde*. The couple at the next table are already ordering coffee.

Caroline is so much more fearful than when she arrived last summer, more conscious of people's expressions and body language when Anouar walks into a room.

"Sorry, sorry." He rushes to the table, sloughing off his coat. "I know I'm miserably late." He walks around to kiss her on each cheek and gently strokes her hair.

She's too relieved to be angry. "I was starting to worry."

"I got tied up at the embassy," he says quickly, biting into the baguette.

"The embassy?" She shivers.

Impatiently, he waves over *le garçon*, ordering a bottle of Bordeaux. She's ridiculously annoyed. The waiter has already decanted the extraordinary bottle she brought.

"But you've renewed your French visa."

The waiter brings her special carafe.

Anouar regards the wine sheepishly. "I forgot—you said you wanted to treat tonight. Sorry. It's been a hectic day. Harrowing, actually."

"Tell me." She blanches.

"The Tunisian Embassy," he says and pours them each a glass of the sanguine wine.

She concentrates on the smoky bouquet—obviously there isn't a French Embassy in Paris—trying hard to ignore her panic.

"There's no other way to say this." He looks away, coughs.

It's all she can do to listen; she refuses to think, to imagine beyond the moment.

"This is horribly sudden for you."

Her eyes widen. She knows she's unable to stop him, them, the future. She's always been unable.

He drains the glass and blurts, "I'm going home next month, and I hope you will come with me."

"What? You're what?" She can't believe he's actually made this huge decision without consulting her. She feels the blow to her solar plexus; her face reddens in anger. "Why? When did you decide this? Why didn't you tell me?" She kicks his stupid Christmas-birthday presents.

"Whoa, whoa." He pours another glass of the far too pricey wine.

Trapped between grief and fury, she wills her tears to recede.

"Please just hear what I have to say. I've been offered a post, a government job in Tunis which involves traveling to Sousse and Sfax."

Caroline sips water and tries to focus. "You only have three more months before your degree." She hates the desperation in her voice. How is this happening? Their year in Paris. Eternal City. *La Ville-Lumière*.

"They'll allow me to submit the thesis by post. It's all arranged. This means that we can—"

He surprises them both by breaking down, sobbing loudly, then hand over his mouth, more quietly. The diners at adjacent tables stiffen and regard each other uncomfortably. "Caroline," he says raising his tear-streaked face, "oh, Caroline, I just cannot take it anymore. The insults. The sneers. The unofficial apartheid. Two men spat at me this morning on the métro platform."

She gives him a tissue, and as he swipes at his cheeks, she takes his free hand. "When? Where did this happen? Did you call the police?"

"The police?!" His eyes are dry now, angry. "Likely they were themselves off-duty gendarmes, happy to be in civilian clothes so they could freely abuse *les beurs, les fuck-offs, bougnoules, boucaques*. Don't look shocked." He pulls his hand away and finishes a second glass of wine. "This happens once, twice a month at least. They hate us. They don't want us here. I'm tired of being patient, of keeping my counsel. I cannot take it anymore. Not anymore!"

She's mute. Appalled once again by how he's treated. By how, truthfully, she's tried to ignore it, tried to pretend their private world was safe. Or at least better. Guilt washes through her rage and sorrow.

"I didn't know how to tell you. I've tried to bring it up for weeks, a month at least."

She gazes at the face of a distraught child, caught between impossible demands.

"Now I've dumped on our special night."

"Your special night," she answers quietly, deliberately. Life goes on, as Mom would say. Raising a glass, she toasts, *"Bon Anniversaire!"*

He drops his head. *"Merci beaucoup.* You see how crazed I've become. I didn't even remember turning thirtyfive today. Middle age, time for a man to return home." He looks over at her hopefully, beseechingly.

She wants to protest that he is still young, that they both are. Instead she accepts what she's evaded since Christmas. Now she feels the finality and surrender in her own eyes. "You must do what you must do."

"I know it's terribly abrupt for you." His red eyes flicker with remorse. "I want you to finish your fellowship, but flights aren't that expensive. We can manage several visits before you're done in August and then—"

"When do you leave?" Her voice is somehow cool, practical.

"Three weeks," he whispers, reaching for her hand.

Automatically she draws back, breathing painfully through the heavy boulder in her chest.

"Will you at least think about visiting?" he pleads. "I could come back for a few weekends, too."

Fantasy or despair, these are her choices. He's made the decision. His decision. She can either let go entirely or... not.

"Please."

"I suppose I could use a short Mediterranean holiday." She's surprised by her calm, almost conciliatory voice. "As long as you can abide traipsing to a few museums for my research." Where does this equanimity come from?

His smile is relieved, hesitant. "In August when you are finished, we can make plans," he rushes ahead.

"Yes," she forces cheer into her voice on this allegedly festive night. "We can make plans in August."

He regards her closely, nodding, silent.

Caroline sighs. There is everything to say. There is nothing to say.

"Happy birthday, *cher* Anouar," Caroline holds out the two gifts.

He grips the battered silvery packages and peers into her unreadable eyes. "*Je t'aime.*"

~

Despite vociferous protests, Caroline insists on seeing him off at the train.

"You have the address and phone number?" he asks for the fourth time, panting under the weight of suitcases crammed with gifts for his family.

"Yes, yes." She lugs his camera and briefcase, following him wordlessly down the long platform.

He slows and turns, as if suddenly remembering her. "You're coming in four weeks?"

"Sometime in late April, early May," she agrees. "Here, let me help you shelve the bags. This is way too much for one person to handle."

She hears her own plaintive appeal from the previous summer. "*Services Bagages!, monsieur, s'il vous plaît.*"

Anouar stuffs two large bags on the overhead rack and tosses his briefcase in an aisle seat.

"Ah, Caroline, sweet Caroline, this is agonizing. My heart splits." He tugs her urgently to his chest.

She inhales, hoarding his smell for nights ahead.

"I'll see you soon." He squeezes her cold hands. "We'll write. And call. And visit. Then it will be August and the end of our painful separation!"

She nods, hates how he keeps saying *then it will be August*. He has it all planned out. Their life. Odysseus will summon Circe home.

"*Une minute,*" a tinny voices echoes back and forth over the loudspeaker, "*pour le départ.*"

He pulls Caroline to him again, kissing her long and hard. Then plants thirty small kisses on her forehead, down her cheeks, to take them through the first month.

At the second whistle, she steps down to the platform, surprised that she hasn't disappeared through the earth. She taps her foot on the solid concrete to make sure she's really here and stares at him through the impermeable window.

He holds her gaze.

She recalls another train. The passionate, welcoming embrace. How she felt her body relax and she believed she had finally returned home.

Caroline has been in Paris eight short months. Eight intense months of studying and exploring and laughing and falling deeper in love with this extraordinary man. She's discovered a passionate vocation in those magnificent ceramics descended from Andalus. She's relished the art, landscape and cuisine of this stunning city. She's made a loyal confidante in the funny and wise Aimée. And she's truly discovered the love of her life. Her worldly, tenderhearted, brilliant Anouar. Such a gift this year has been.

Anouar is right; they'll see each other soon. They're both independent people. Great loves survive time and distance. And theirs is a great love, the passion of her life.

Down the platform now, his train has almost disappeared. He's far away, on the way.

She waves until his car is out of sight. Coolly, she walks through the station, alert to a new feeling, a surprising equilibrium.

BOSTON, 1982

This mild, fragrant July morning, Caroline and Terri cycle along the Charles River. She recalls stories from the most romantic city in the world. From sixteen months ago.

So much has happened and so much hasn't happened. Anouar's departure from France. Her three visits to Tunisia. The end of her fellowship and return to finish the degree at home. Anouar's promise to visit in October. His mother's illness and the trip postponed. Another promise to come in December. A second last minute cancellation, this time due to demands at work. Every day, Caroline notices or hopes she notices, she lets go a little more.

"He vowed to come in March to celebrate his birthday."

Terri sighs. "I know it's really painful. He didn't make that trip either."

Caroline concentrates on a tricky turn then says, "I don't understand. Maybe I imagined his love, his commitment. Maybe I was a pleasant fling. A fool all along."

"Maybe he isn't as brave as you?" her friend suggests.

"What does that mean?" She tilts to the left, then rights her bike.

"You are the bravest person I know, Caroline."

She shrugs. "Hardly! Maybe the most naïve."

"No," Terri insists. "You have faced and straight on accepted the contradictions of your two worlds. Maybe he simply can't. Maybe he needs you to be the ideal you were in Paris without any of the complications or compromises of real life."

Caroline glances at her friend then back on the path. "Maybe he's more sensible. How long would such a complicated relationship last?"

Terri thinks this over. Then, "I love you Caroline."

Caroline shakes her head. "Too bad we're not lesbians," she laughs. Terri is really her rock.

Terri grins. "We're lucky to be friends, friends for life."

Caroline's heart lifts.

Thus absorbed, Caroline broadsides another bicyclist.

The tall, blond, forgiving man is named Garth.

Hence, the next chapter of her life begins.

TUNISIA, 2004

M. Le Directeur's office feels brighter today. His TV is uncharacteristically dark,and the blinds are lifted to a sunny March morning. Arranged on the coffee table is a lavish buffet which Salwa has managed to prepare despite her rigorous schedule at the museum and duties at home and the mosque. Caroline already misses the indefatigable, buoyant Salwa.

She has tried to decline a farewell party, but her colleagues are determined. Salwa is especially resolute.

"Please, Doctor Kendrick," the director gestures to the most comfortable chair. "Please join us for a light meal and a toast to your future." He extends a glass of apricot juice.

One by one, each colleague makes a toast with the golden nectar.

"Thanks for the inspiration," says Sana.

"Cheers for your excellent company," winks Ibrahim.

"*Bislama et à bientôt* to my dear friend," cries Salwa.

Monsieur Le Director steps forward, holding a package. "A token of our gratitude for your contributions." He places it in her shaking hands.

Everyone is grinning. Salwa is smiling through her tears.

"May I open it?"

"*Bien sûr.*" He claps his hands, exuding a heretofore hidden cheerfulness.

Caroline has an odd image of him as a school boy. A round, bald schoolboy.

"Yes! Yes!" exclaims Salwa, who helps her unwrap the unwieldy package.

"A *mergoum!*" Caroline knew it was a rug but couldn't have imagined such a glorious one. Somehow she will manage to pack it. No doubt Salwa already has a plan for that.

Salwa leans over, whispering, "how I wish I could sneak inside it and return to Boston with you." She takes a napkin to her wet cheeks.

Caroline hugs her friend and murmurs, "I wish the same!"

Salwa holds on tight.

Caroline looks up and sees them all waiting in silent anticipation. "Beautiful. Thank you. Thank you. The ideal colors for my living room."

Oddly, she considers how much Garth would like this rug. After all, he painted the living room ivory with crimson trim. He loved making home improvements and reading together at night and planning their yearly vacations to National Parks. Dear Garth was calm and centered, easy to please. Too easy after the explosive, brooding, joyous, opinionated Anouar. Not really *after* Anouar, for the man was still in her heart, always an invisible presence in their life. The divorce was amicable. And the marriage almost forgettable except for the gift of Tess. Her daughter sees Garth several times a year and reports that he is content living in Colorado with his second wife. So Caroline feels somehow absolved of her infidelity with the ghost.

"Just gorgeous," she says again, to bring herself back.

One by one, her colleagues' bodies relax, their smiles appear.

Salwa glows. "We knew you would like it."

"Salwa ordered it," Nour intervenes, "selected the thread and harassed the poor weaver almost daily."

Caroline hugs Salwa again. "Thank you so much for everything."

She raises her glass of juice. "I am very grateful to each of you for what I have learned, for your own stimulating work, for your invigorating company and generous hospitality."

Suddenly, she's flooded with sadness. She hates farewells. Anouar waving from the train. Terri and then Mom dwindling away in those terrifyingly impersonal hospital rooms.

"To your return." Salwa raises a glass.

Caroline is grateful for Salwa's invitation to dinner tomorrow. Otherwise, this ritual would be too final. She blinks back tears, nods and smiles.

The next morning as she's leaving breakfast, Caroline overhears clusters of people in the lobby talking about explosions. Bombs. Carnage. Commuter trains. At Madrid's Atocha Station.

She hurries to her room and switches on BBC.

One thousand people have been injured, perhaps two hundred killed. The Basque ETA is suspected by some. But the talking heads disagree. Immigrant activists? Al-Qaeda?

Caroline doubts the Basques would commit violence on this scale. Basques ride those trains, too. She watches TV longer than she should; she has so much to do before tomorrow's flight.

Does she have to leave?

For her final night, Salwa brings Caroline to dinner with her mother. Raja, a short, stout woman wearing a green dress, accented by a pink and green hijab, has Salwa's broad smile and searching brown eyes. After greeting Caroline with a kiss on each cheek, she bows her head in thanks for the gift of dark chocolate caramels. Then she laughs slyly. "All for me, yes?"

Salwa turns to Caroline. "Ummi is joking. My father adores chocolates."

Caroline nods, amused by Salwa's earnest defense of her mother.

The simple, almost stark façade of the family house contrasts with the elaborate interior. Living room walls are tiled in deep blue, turquoise and white geometric patterns. A couch and two armchairs are upholstered in a floral pink. The floor is scattered with an array of luscious rugs. All local mergoums from what Caroline can discern. So different from the posh, modern home of Salwa and her husband. One similarity is Raja's display of framed photos—Salwa's sisters and brothers with spouses and children. No photo of the divorced sister in either home.

As the women chat, Salwa's father watches a soap opera in the side room. What is it with these men and their televisions?

"Tell us about your home in Boston," Raja says.

"About your daughter, the movie star."

"Not yet a star!" Caroline laughs. "She does theatre work, and I'm very proud of her."

The TV grows louder. Their faces tighten as an announcer reports new details from Madrid.

Raja shakes her head. "So sad. What makes people this evil?"

"The Basques want recognition," Salwa whispers. "The ETA have been marching and protesting for years. I remember them from my trip to Madrid."

"Yes, yes," agrees Raja. "A terrible thing not to have your rights, but this isn't the way…." She trails off, distracted by the TV announcer.

Caroline keeps her counsel, recalling a train she took to Córdoba from that station two years before. *Córdoba*, Anouar's ancestral home, ruled by Muslims for five centuries. She had kept an eye out for him there, too, she now remembers. The majestic Caliphate of *Córdoba*, center of libraries, medical schools and universities.

After dinner, Raja offers a tour of the modest house. In a corner of her shadowed, stuffy bedroom, she presses a gift on Caroline, who fumbles a thank you.

Out in the brightly lit hallway, Caroline is startled to discover an engraved Hand of Fatima linked to an elegant silver chain.

"I couldn't accept this, thank you so much, but no; it's too precious."

"Yes, dear, please. I got it years ago when I traveled to Hajj. I brought it back from Mecca."

"Then I certainly can't accept something so cherished." "Please."

Caroline sees where Salwa gets her determination.

"Yes." Raja says softly, taking Caroline's hands between her warm palms. "We are friends now, and friends may bestow such gifts We have shared bread and salt."

On the last morning, Caroline listens anxiously to the radio for new details about the bombing. Why is she so preoccupied by this? She's almost disappointed when the packing is finished, and she switches off the radio.

She wants to know what happened. Who did this? Why? It's as simple as that. Or maybe not.

Time for the last stroll with Salwa.

Salwa takes her to a quiet residential neighborhood where the only noises are the high pitched voices of children and the peeping chirps of quail and kestrel. The trees are in full bloom. Kairouan smells of spring, the air even warmer than she experienced on her arrival in sunny Tunis.

"*Le Printemps*, I always think of the Luxembourg Gardens in early spring." Salwa reminisces wistfully.

"Perhaps when the kids are older?" Caroline suggests.

"You can take a leave and go back to Paris? For a few months?"

"It is possible," answers Salwa neutrally. "But yearning is the destiny of Tunisians who have lived in France. We no longer quite fit here. Our expectations, our world views, shifted abroad. Yet if we go back, we don't belong in Paris. It's hard to explain."

I understand more than you can know, Caroline wants to say. She longs to tell Salwa about Anouar. Last month she imagined Salwa would be uncomfortable with the story of their love affair. Now she realizes she's missed a rare opportunity with her new friend who could understand Anouar better than most people in her life. So much for the bravery Terri assigned to her.

Strolling back to the hotel, they promise to write. Real letters as well as email.

Salwa has submitted a grant proposal to insure Caroline's return.

Again, Caroline invites her to Boston. And to the cottage, although she can't really picture Salwa's decorous husband roughing it in rural Maine. What would he make of Wayne and his campy friends?

Abdul's familiar car pulls up.

"*Bislama et à bientôt*," Caroline whispers to Salwa.

As Abdul loads the luggage, the women embrace, and Salwa holds the door open for Caroline.

She doesn't want to leave. Caroline rolls down the window, gazing at her friend, taking a long breath of desert air.

Salwa cries, "Send me an email the minute you get home!" She waves and blows kisses.

"Yes, yes." Caroline is laughing and crying, feeling so full of Salwa and Terri and Anouar.

Abdul starts the car.

Salwa waves with both hands now.

As they drive out of Kairouan toward the Tunis airport, she notices a sudden relief, tinged with betrayal, about leaving this fraught world where so many people ache to be somewhere else.

BOSTON, 2004

Ah, winter is still on the ground here. And another big snow predicted. She should take a nap to prepare for the transition. That's what Terri is telling her. But she's too wired, so she rolls suitcases into the bedroom and begins to unpack. Beneath a layer of books, she finds a huge chunk of her favorite, sinful nougat securely wrapped in plastic. Salwa!

She wonders if it's all been a dream, as she returns from the African desert to the frozen American north, going backward from spring to winter. No, she still feels the warmth of Tunisia in her blood; kind, generous people; a rich, ancient culture; spectacular landscapes; delicious food. And those exquisite enamels recounting tales of exile and conflict and endurance.

Promises. Contradictions. Mysteries. Ghosts.

As she unpacks, she listens to the latest news from Madrid. She no longer wonders at her preoccupation. Some moments in life are simply colored by gigantic, if far away events—volcanoes, earthquakes, tsunamis, cyclones—which rend individual lives while reinforcing a common vulnerability and humanity.

She switches on the bedside radio. The American reporters are hyper, and she misses the measured delivery of BBC broadcasters. Over 1800 people injured and 191 dead. The man explains that a Tunisian, Serhane ben Abdelmajid Fakhet, is the alleged mastermind of the attack, was killed in the blasts. At large and under suspicion are several Moroccans.

And another Tunisian. Anouar Hasan, or Hussein.

She sits on the bed staring at the radio. No. It can't be him.

A small voice tells her this is why she couldn't trace him on the internet.

But no, that's ridiculous. Anouar was, is, a man of amity and benevolence. He loved a lively political argument, but always denounced violence.

Still that conversation from his birthday dinner echoes. "This happens once, twice a month at least. They hate us. They don't want us here. I'm tired of being patient, of keeping my counsel. No, I cannot take it anymore. Not anymore!"

Impossible. Caroline turns her mind to practical things. After showering and changing clothes, she sets off on errands, avoiding news for the rest of the day. She collects her mail at the post office and withdraws money from the ATM. The uniform green currency looks so drab after Tunisia's colorful banknotes. At the grocery, she's saddened by the winter-withered vegetables. At home, she pays a few bills, listlessly sifts through the plastic bin of catalogues and old magazines. She makes pasta for supper, still avoiding the radio and TV.

Antsy, she tries Wayne's phone for the fifth time. Damn. He's off on the Cape with his new beau and isn't answering the cell. On the positive side, Tess has texted twice, promising to call tomorrow.

Pouring herself a large glass of white wine, she heads off to bed with a book by Gisèle Halimi that Ibrahim gave her.

Impulsively, she stops to check email.

The first message, of course, is from Salwa. A formal invitation to return next year. She has secured the funds and asks if Caroline would like to stay at La Kasbah again. That woman!

"How was your flight?" she writes. "Does it feel good to be home? I want news although I did appreciate the short email from your phone saying you arrived safely. Tell me, really, how do you feel? Is your house OK? Are you warm enough? Do you miss us?"

Grinning, Caroline starts to respond, but sees those people who did not arrive safely, hundreds of commuters, barely awake, carrying newspapers and thermoses of coffee and tea. Hundreds of vacationers.

Spanish, Romanian, Ecuadorian, Polish, Bulgarian, Peruvian, Dominican, Columbian, Moroccan and people from half a dozen other countries. All those injured and dead. All those missing children and parents and siblings and friends.

The next message is from an unfamiliar sender: ahtun@hotmail.com.

Chère Caroline,

I just today discovered you were in the country! I receive the museum newsletter here in Sfax where I have been teaching for some years.

You have been and gone. Quel dommage.

I am so disappointed to have missed you. At train stations, I often see you waving, until my car is out of sight.

I would like to know how you are living your life. Fruitfully, intelligently, lovingly, I know this. But what of your home and friends?

This is what I imagine: you are married and have one child. Yes, I believe you would have stopped there, satisfied with perfection. I, myself, am a widower, with two wonderfully imperfect sons as well as three precocious granddaughters who keep me alert. And humble.

What do his beautiful eyes look like on the girls? Tears stream down her face. Do the boys have his deep voice?

There is great distress here over the shocking Madrid bombings. As I told you, Anouar Hasan is a common name. Alas. Who would do such a thing?

She is relieved. Ashamed that she doubted him. Appalled. Yet until this email, his possible involvement was the only shimmer of life she could detect. How she wishes she could talk to Terri. Of course she talks to Terri all the time, but now she needs a response. Consolation. Celebration.

When do you return to Tunisia? When can we meet for a glass of wine in Sousse and stroll along the Corniche together? Dare I hope for a response? A hand of friendship after all my broken promises?

Yours, as always,

Anouar.

She presses "reply" to report Salwa's invitation to return.

A blue striped awning. Silver cobblestones. Sweet yeasty aromas from *épiceries*. Chocolate macarons. Rich bloody Magon. Sexy Gitane smoke rings after dinner.

Splatterings of saliva and phlegm.

"*Les beurs, les fuck-offs, bougnoules, boucaques.*"

"*Then it will be August.*"

She recalls their idyllic days in Paris. The painful ones. The decades during which she imagined him crossing a street or stepping on a bus. She smells lavender, *coq au vin*, the salty musk of his night body, the rainy pavement outside his rooming house.

But she is grown up now, no longer the neophyte beguiled by cheeky young men. She has learned to resist impulse; to let it sit a day or two.

Caroline clicks the computer shut.

Tomorrow is time enough.

If there is enough time.

She drifts into the living room with her half glass of wine, too wired for bed. The mergoum is beautiful, a complex weave of strong colors. From the couch she watches snow scrimming across a soft yellow puddle cast by the corner streetlamp.

Acknowledgments

I am grateful to many people and institutions that over the years have helped provoke and support my work on *Bread and Salt*.

I was fortunate to have productive and stimulating writing residencies at Fondazione Bogliasco, La Maison Dora Maar (a Brown Foundation fellowship), Fundación Valparaiso, Hawthornden Castle, Hedgebrook, MacDowell, Brush Creek, Ucross, and the University of Turku. The staff at each of these places welcomed me to comfortable workplaces, peaceful surroundings and invigorating company. I am especially grateful to The Virginia Center for the Arts, a frequent haven, which feels like a second home

The settings of some stories—India, Indonesia, Tunisia—emerged from my experiences on three separate Fulbright grants. Other stories arose from travel related to lectures or writing in Turkey, France, Italy, Wyoming, the Pacific Northwest, Boston. Particular thanks to Sheila Gulley Pleasants, Nadia Boudidah, Philip Breeden, Sharon Dynak, Vito Zingarelli, Anne Grimes, Gülayşe Somel Koçak, Anne Kovalainen, Seppo Poutanen, Gwen Strauss and others who made those journeys possible.

A number of generous friends have read drafts of the stories. Thanks to Aimee Phan, Camille Dungy, Kathryn Ma, Faith Adiele, Thaisa Frank, Kate Brady, Nat Smookler, Paul Skenazy, Tanya Hartman, Helen Longino, Toni Mirosevich, Tess Taylor, Bonnie Auslander, Sandell Morse.

Several people read drafts of the entire book as it evolved and I learned a lot from the comments of Jana Harris, Rich Chiaponne, Patricia Powell and Marianne Villanueva.

I have benefitted from the excellent work of research assistants at Stanford University: Yanichka Ariunbold, Eleanor Frost, Courtney Suhyun Noh, and Julia Sommer.

The stories have profited from the work of editors at the following journals: "Il Piccolo Tesoro," *Ploughshares*, Winter, 2017-18; "The Women at Coral Villas," *Ascent*, November, 2019; "La Fourmi Faim," *The Coachella Review*, June, 2018; "Iconoclast," *Consequence, 10th Anniversary Issue*, Spring, 2018; "Incident on the Tracks," *Belmont Story Review*, Summer 2018; "Under Stars," *The Michigan Quarterly Review*, Fall, 2014; "Escape Artist," *Solstice*, Winter, 2014 and *Solstice Selects: Two Years of Diverse Voices*, edited by Lee Hope, Solstice Publishing, 2017; "Quiet as the Moon" (under a different title), *Delmarva Review*, Fall, 2014; "Far Enough," *Five Points*, Spring, 2014; "Long Distance," *Grey Sparrow*, Spring, 2014; "The Whole Story, *Southwest Review*, Fall, 2011; "Moving In," *Southwest Review*, Summer, 2010.

I thank Lisa De Niscia for her enthusiasm and her fine work in producing the book.

And as always, I thank my partner Helen Longino for her love, support, provocative insights and excellent company on our long journey together.

About the Author

Valerie Miner is the author of fifteen books. Two of her story collections, *Trespassing* and *Abundant Light*, were finalists for the Lambda Literary Award. Winner of a Distinguished Teaching Award, Ms. Miner has taught for over forty-five years and is now a professor and artist-in-residence at Stanford University. She and her partner live in San Francisco and Mendocino County, California.